Top Cow Productions Presents

~A~
MAN AMONG YE

Created by
Stephanie Phillips
& Craig Cermak

Published by Top Cow Productions, Inc.
Los Angeles

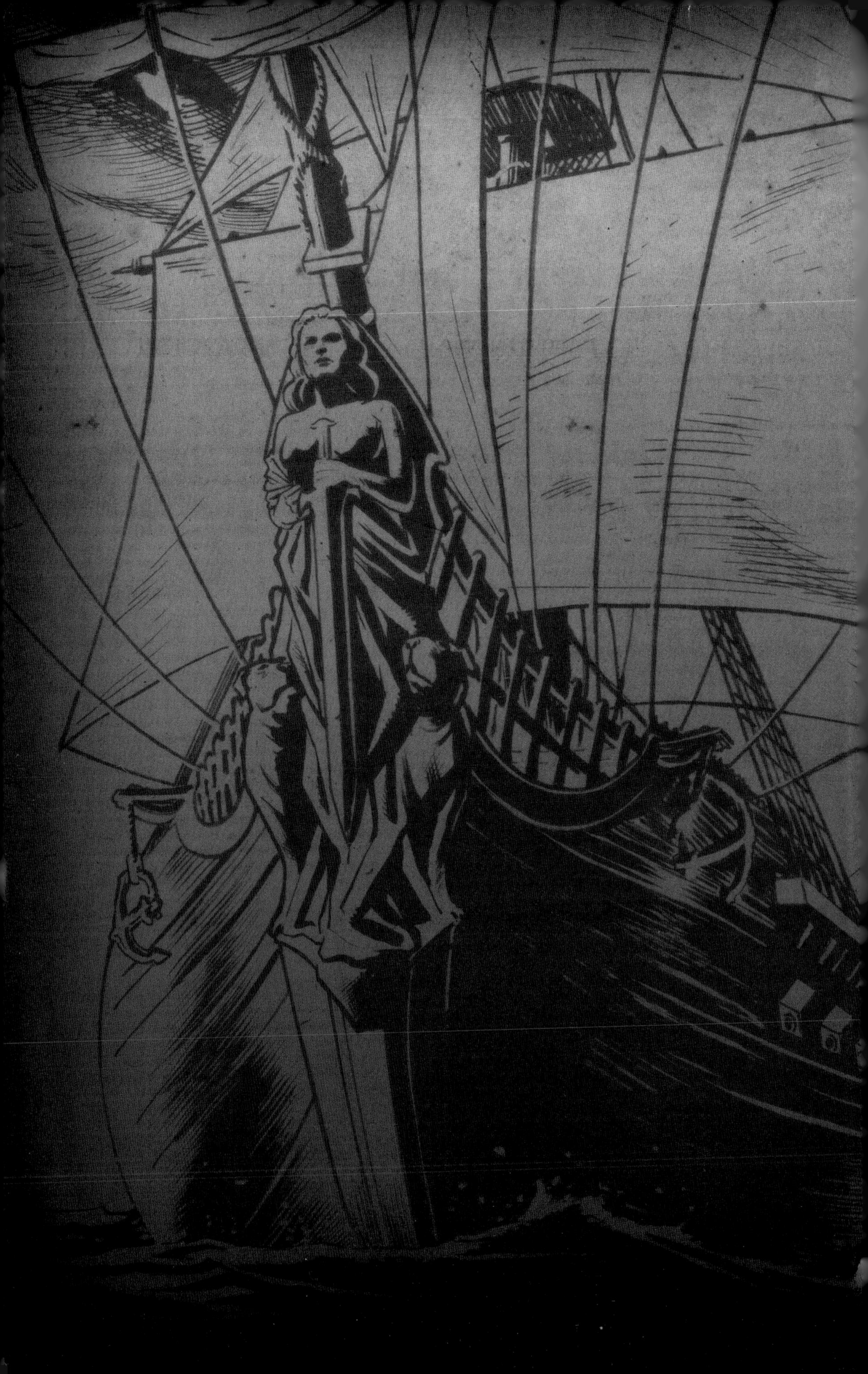

~A~ MAN AMONG YE

Written By
Stephanie Phillips

Art By
Craig Cermak

Colors By
John Kalisz (Issues 2-4)
Brittany Pezzillo (Issue 1)

Letters By
Troy Peteri

Edited by
Elena Salcedo

Logo by
Meghan Hetrick

Cover by
Craig Cermak

For Top Cow Productions, Inc.
Marc Silvestri - CEO
Matt Hawkins - President & COO
Elena Salcedo - Vice President of Operations
Vincent Valentine - Lead Production Artist
Henry Barajas - Director of Operations

IMAGE COMICS, INC. • **Todd McFarlane**: President • **Jim Valentino**: Vice-President • **Marc Silvestri**: Chief Executive Officer • **Erik Larsen**: Chief Financial Officer • **Robert Kirkman**: Chief Operating Officer • **Eric Stephenson**: Publisher / Chief Creative Officer • **Shanna Matuszak**: Editorial Coordinator • **Marla Eizik**: Talent Liaison • **Nicole Lapalme**: Controller • **Leanna Caunter**: Accounting Analyst • **Sue Korpela**: Accounting & HR Manager • **Jeff Boison**: Director of Sales & Publishing Planning • **Dirk Wood**: Director of International Sales & Licensing • **Alex Cox**: Director of Direct Market & Specialty Sales • **Chloe Ramos–Peterson**: Book Market & Library Sales Manager • **Emilio Bautista**: Digital Sales Coordinator • **Kat Salazar**: Director of PR & Marketing • **Drew Fitzgerald**: Marketing Content Associate • **Heather Doornink**: Production Director • **Drew Gill**: Art Director • **Hilary DiLoreto**: Print Manager • **Tricia Ramos**: Traffic Manager • **Erika Schnatz**: Senior Production Artist • **Ryan Brewer**: Production Artist • **Deanna Phelps**: Production Artist **IMAGE COMICS, INC.**

To find the comic shop
nearest you, call:
1-888-COMICBOOK

Want more info? Check out:
www.topcow.com
for news & exclusive Top Cow merchandise!

Chapter 1

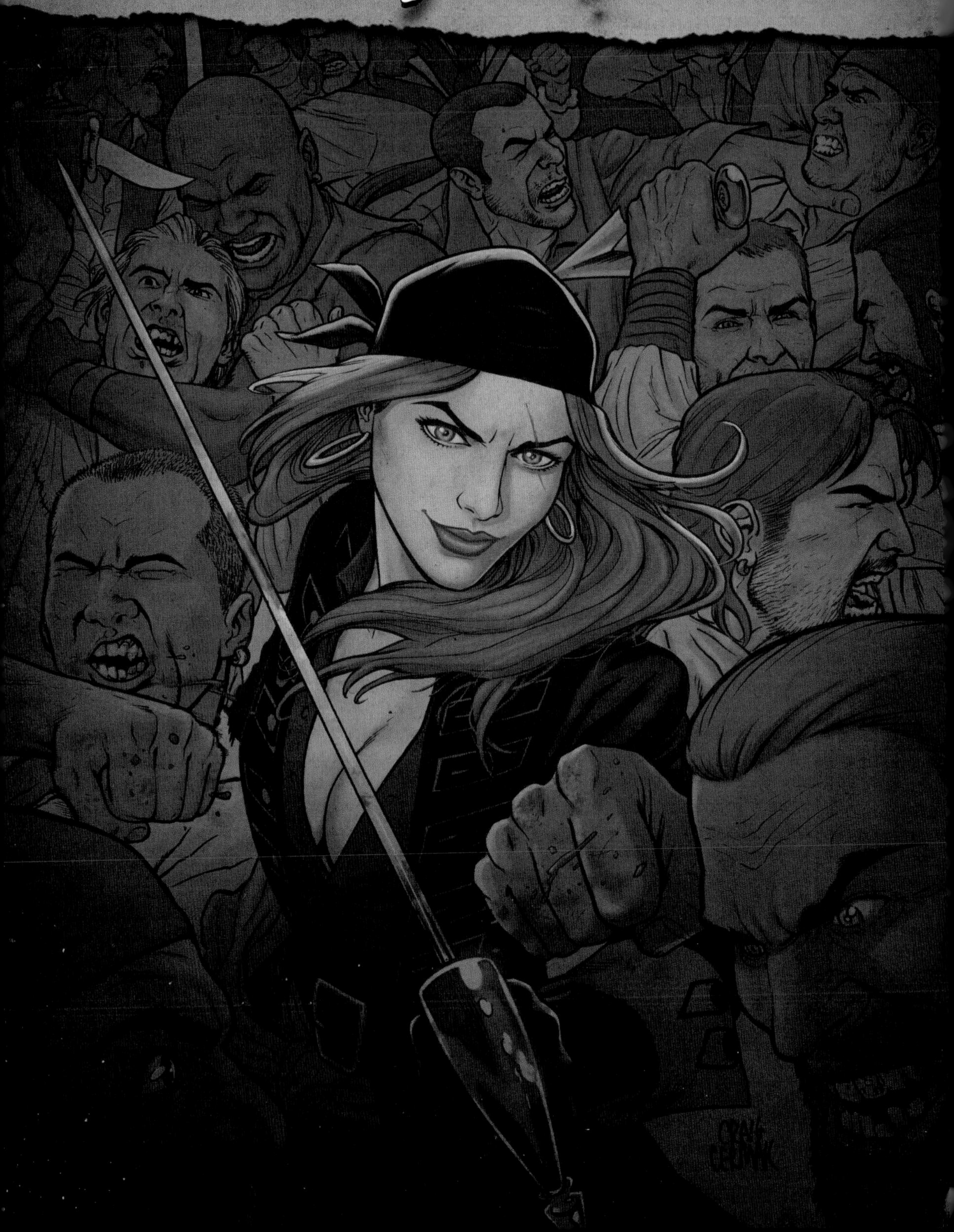

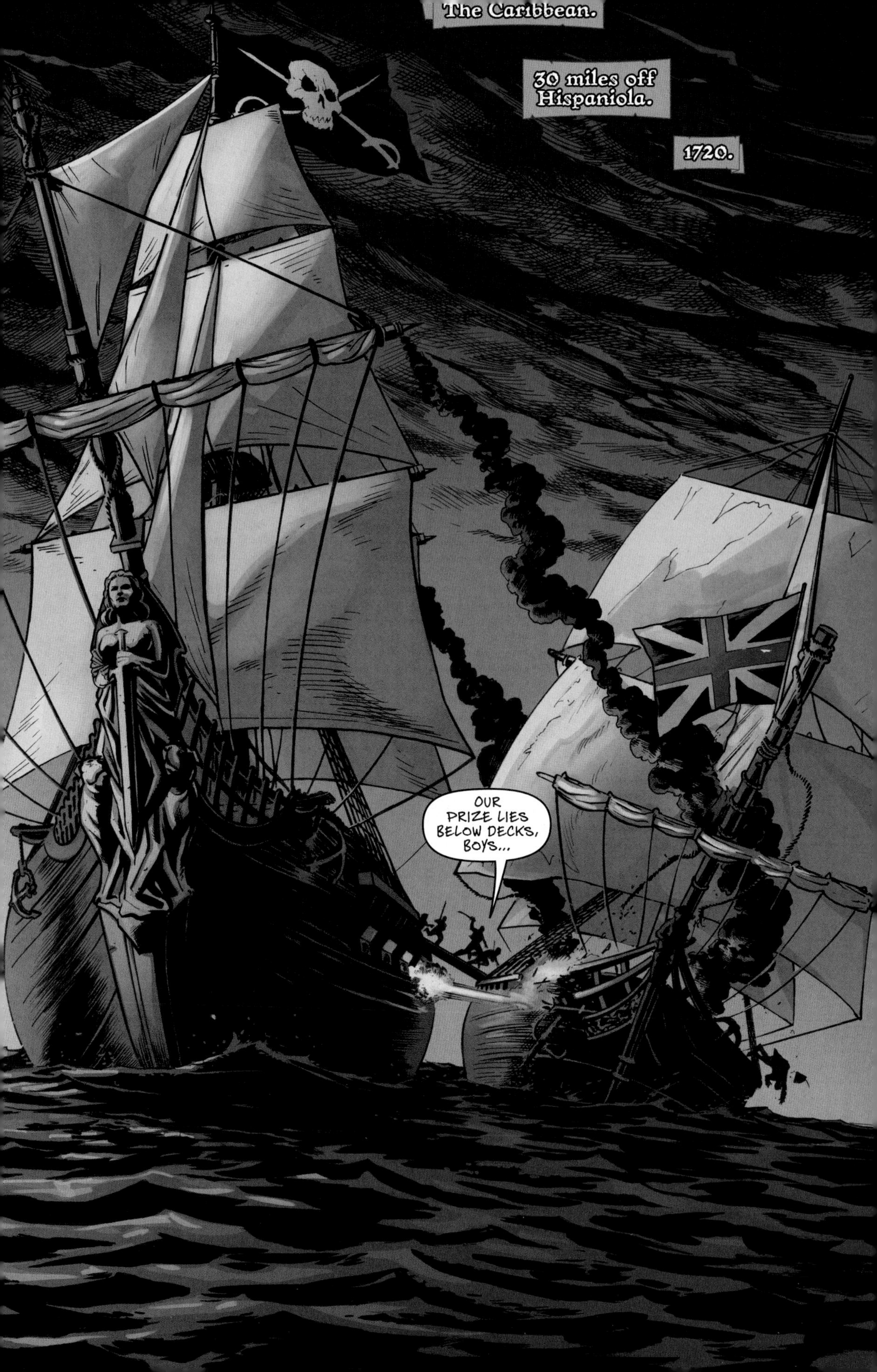
The Caribbean.
30 miles off Hispaniola.
1720.
OUR PRIZE LIES BELOW DECKS, BOYS...

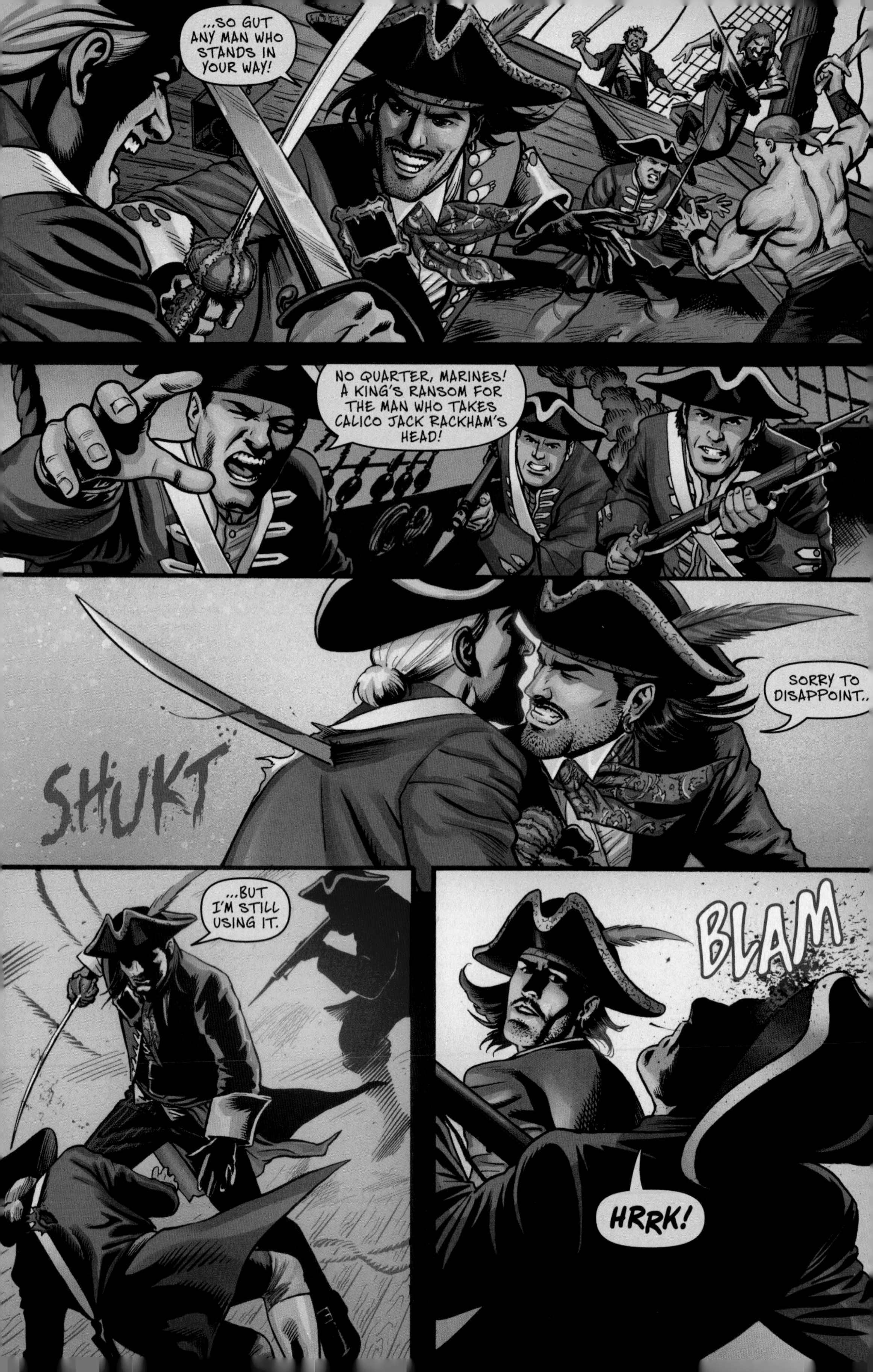
...SO GUT ANY MAN WHO STANDS IN YOUR WAY!
NO QUARTER, MARINES! A KING'S RANSOM FOR THE MAN WHO TAKES CALICO JACK RACKHAM'S HEAD!
SHUKT
SORRY TO DISAPPOINT...
...BUT I'M STILL USING IT.
BLAM
HRRK!

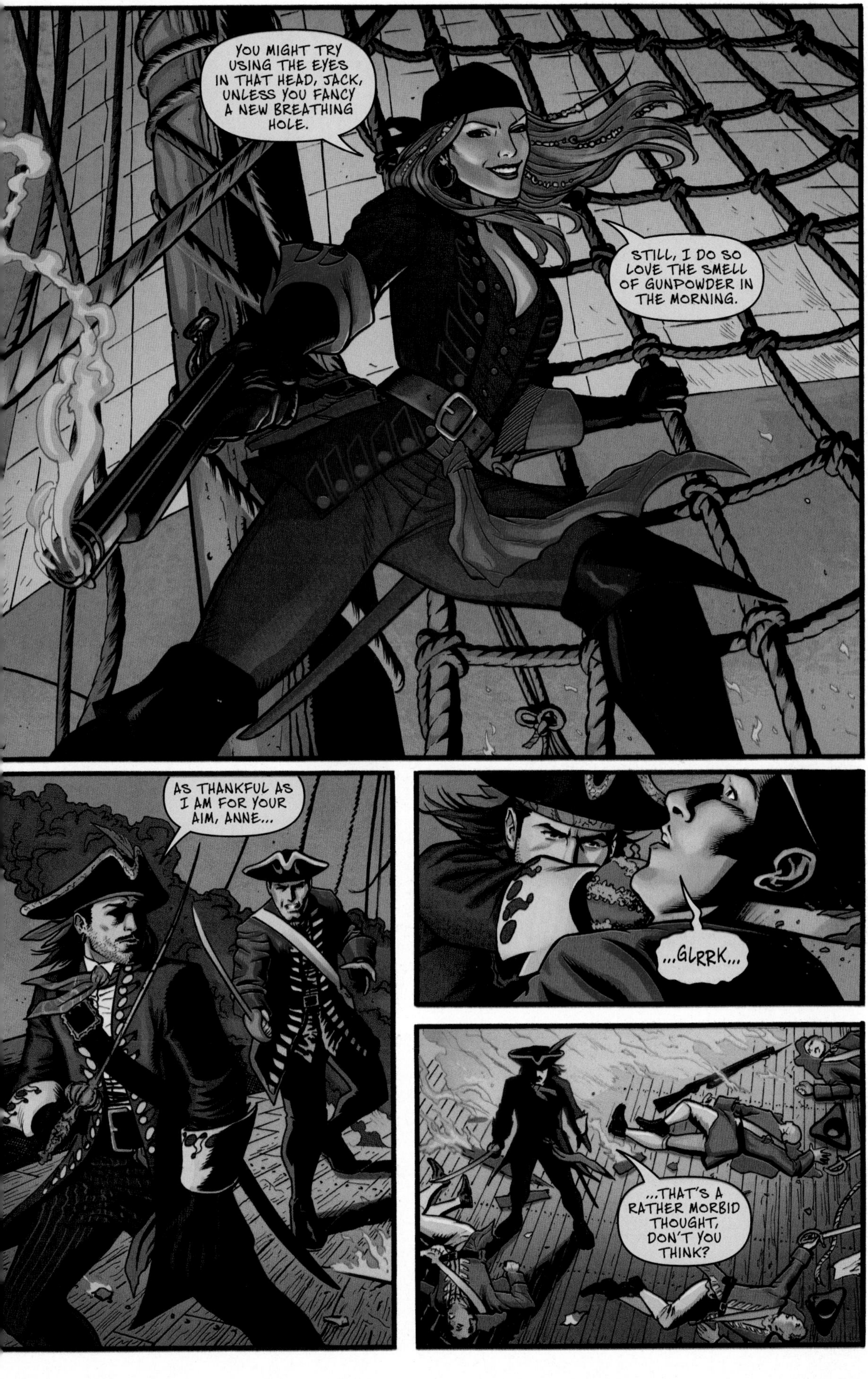
YOU MIGHT TRY USING THE EYES IN THAT HEAD, JACK, UNLESS YOU FANCY A NEW BREATHING HOLE.
STILL, I DO SO LOVE THE SMELL OF GUNPOWDER IN THE MORNING.
AS THANKFUL AS I AM FOR YOUR AIM, ANNE...
...GLRRK...
...THAT'S A RATHER MORBID THOUGHT, DON'T YOU THINK?

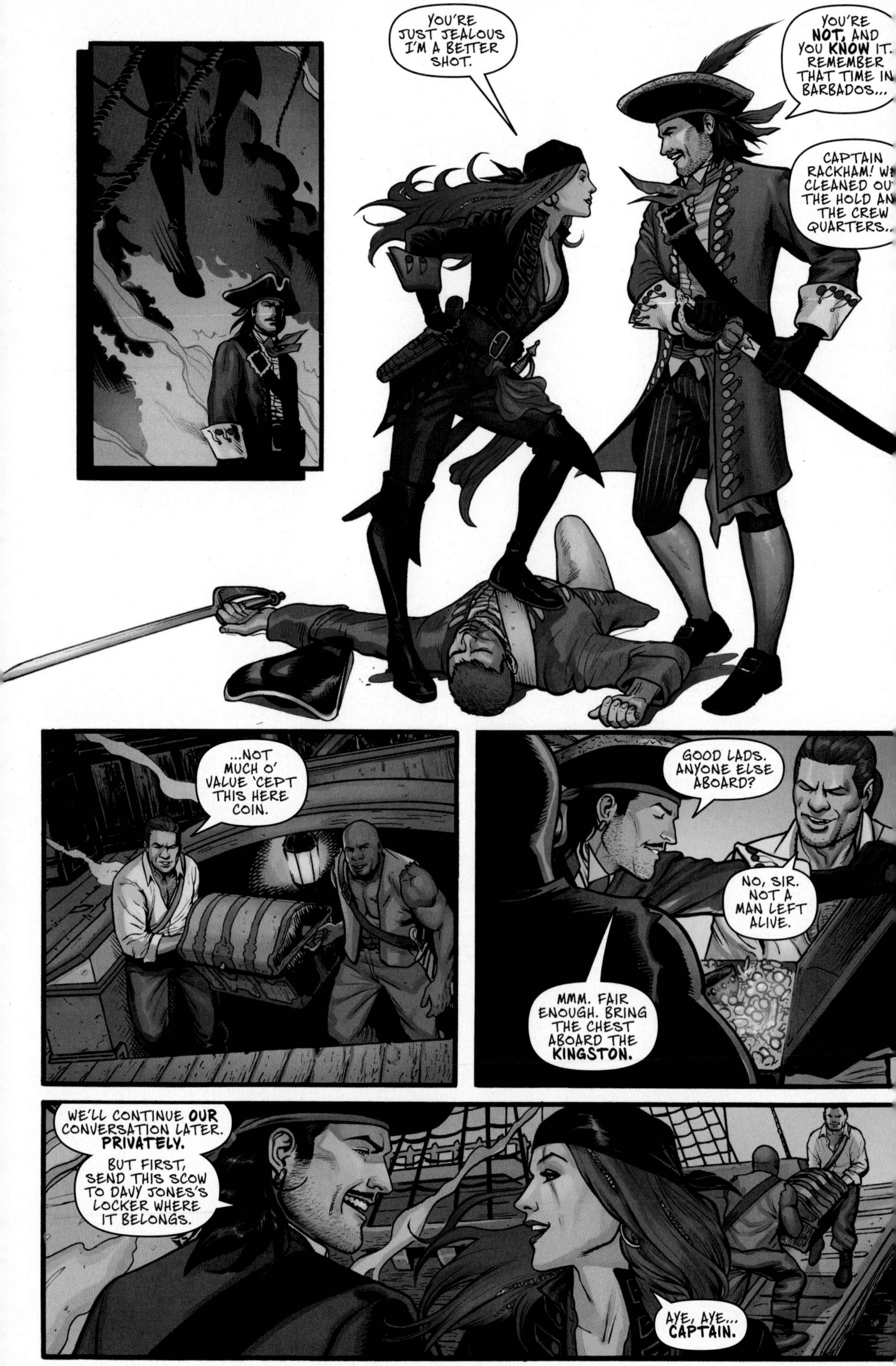
YOU'RE JUST JEALOUS I'M A BETTER SHOT.
YOU'RE NOT, AND YOU KNOW IT. REMEMBER THAT TIME IN BARBADOS...
CAPTAIN RACKHAM! WE CLEANED OUT THE HOLD AN' THE CREW QUARTERS...
...NOT MUCH O' VALUE 'CEPT THIS HERE COIN.
GOOD LADS. ANYONE ELSE ABOARD?
NO, SIR. NOT A MAN LEFT ALIVE.
MMM. FAIR ENOUGH. BRING THE CHEST ABOARD THE KINGSTON.
WE'LL CONTINUE OUR CONVERSATION LATER. PRIVATELY.
BUT FIRST, SEND THIS SCOW TO DAVY JONES'S LOCKER WHERE IT BELONGS.
AYE, AYE... CAPTAIN.

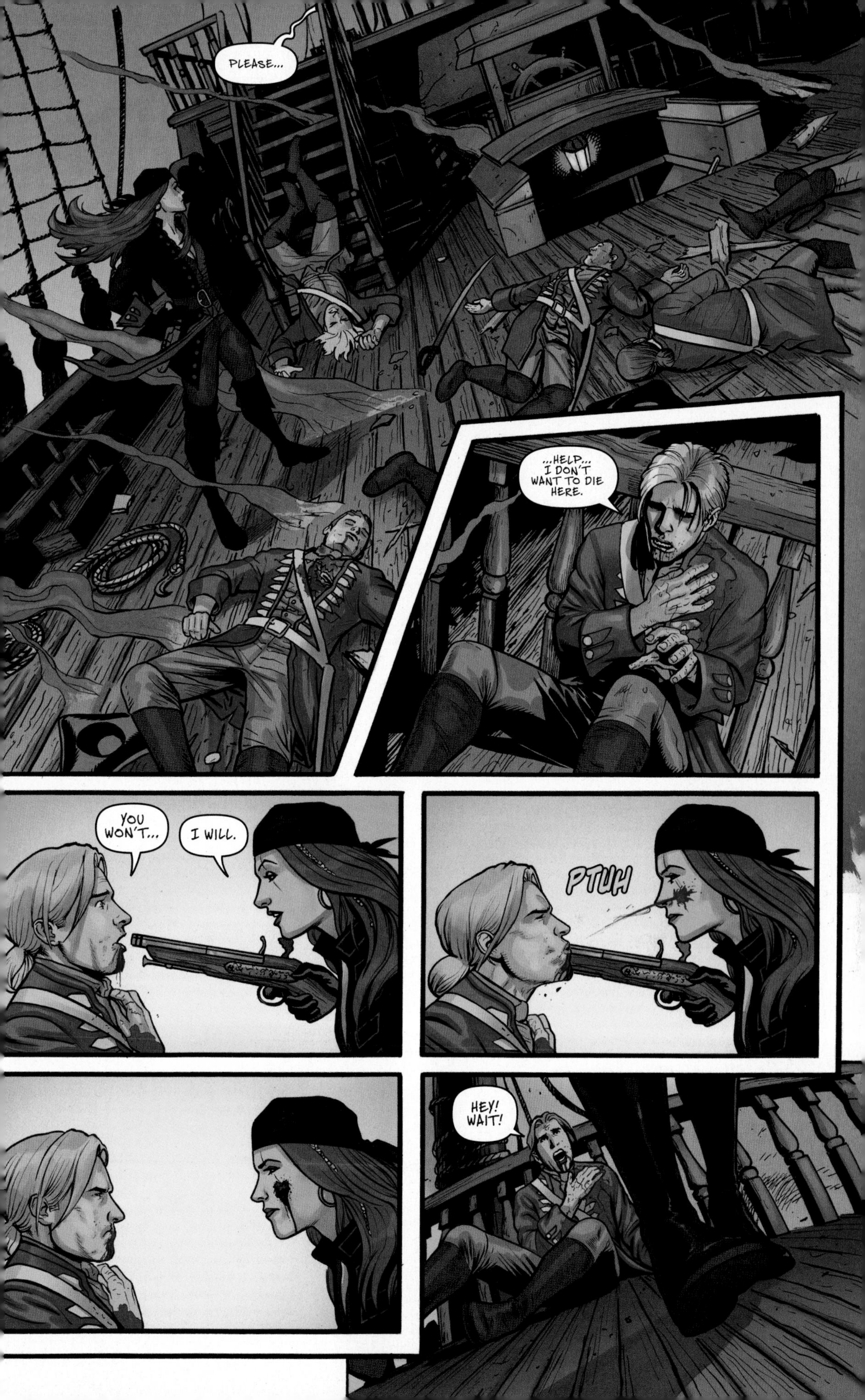
PLEASE...
...HELP... I DON'T WANT TO DIE HERE.
YOU WON'T...
I WILL.
PTUH
HEY! WAIT!

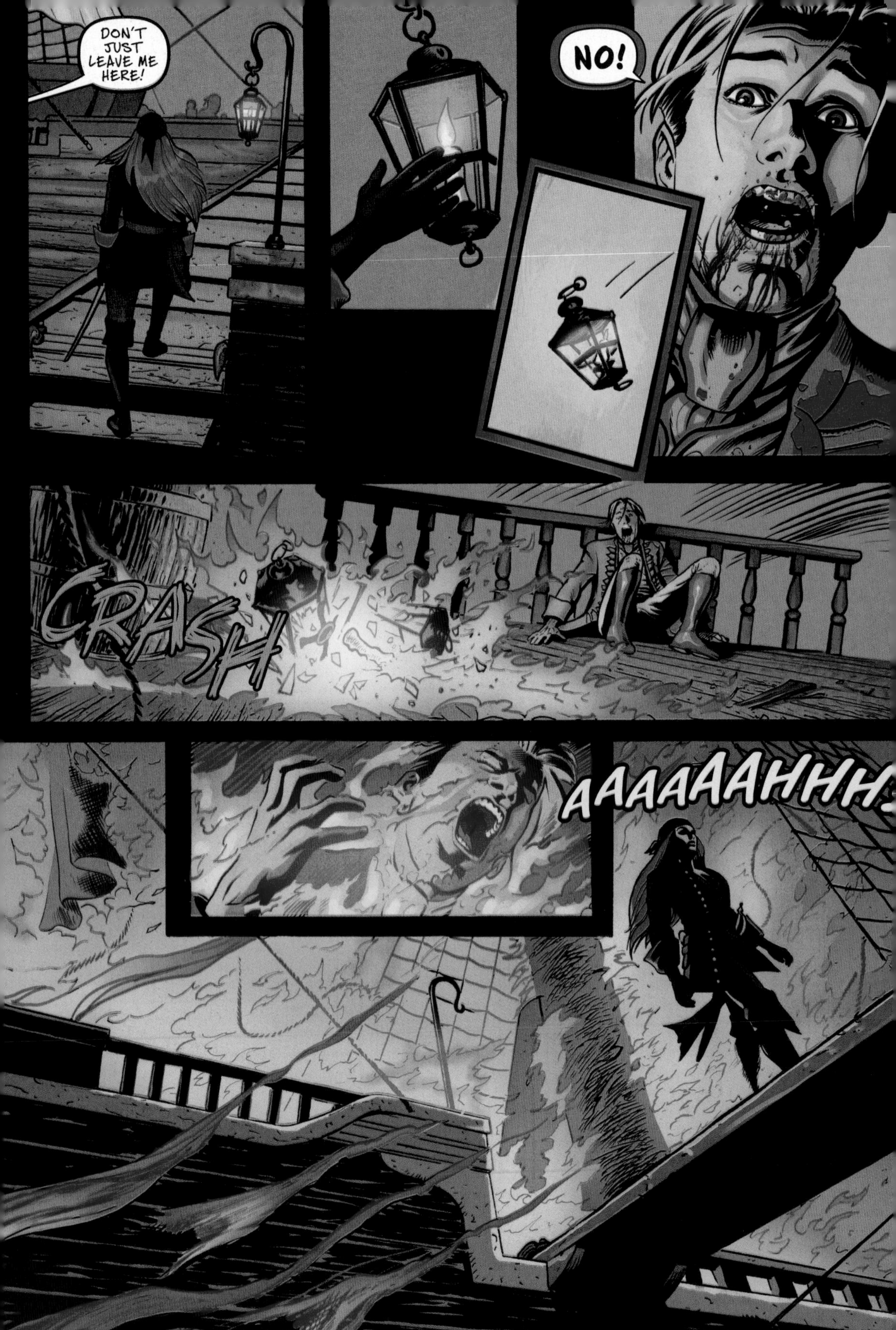
DON'T JUST LEAVE ME HERE!
NO!
CRASH
AAAAAAHHH

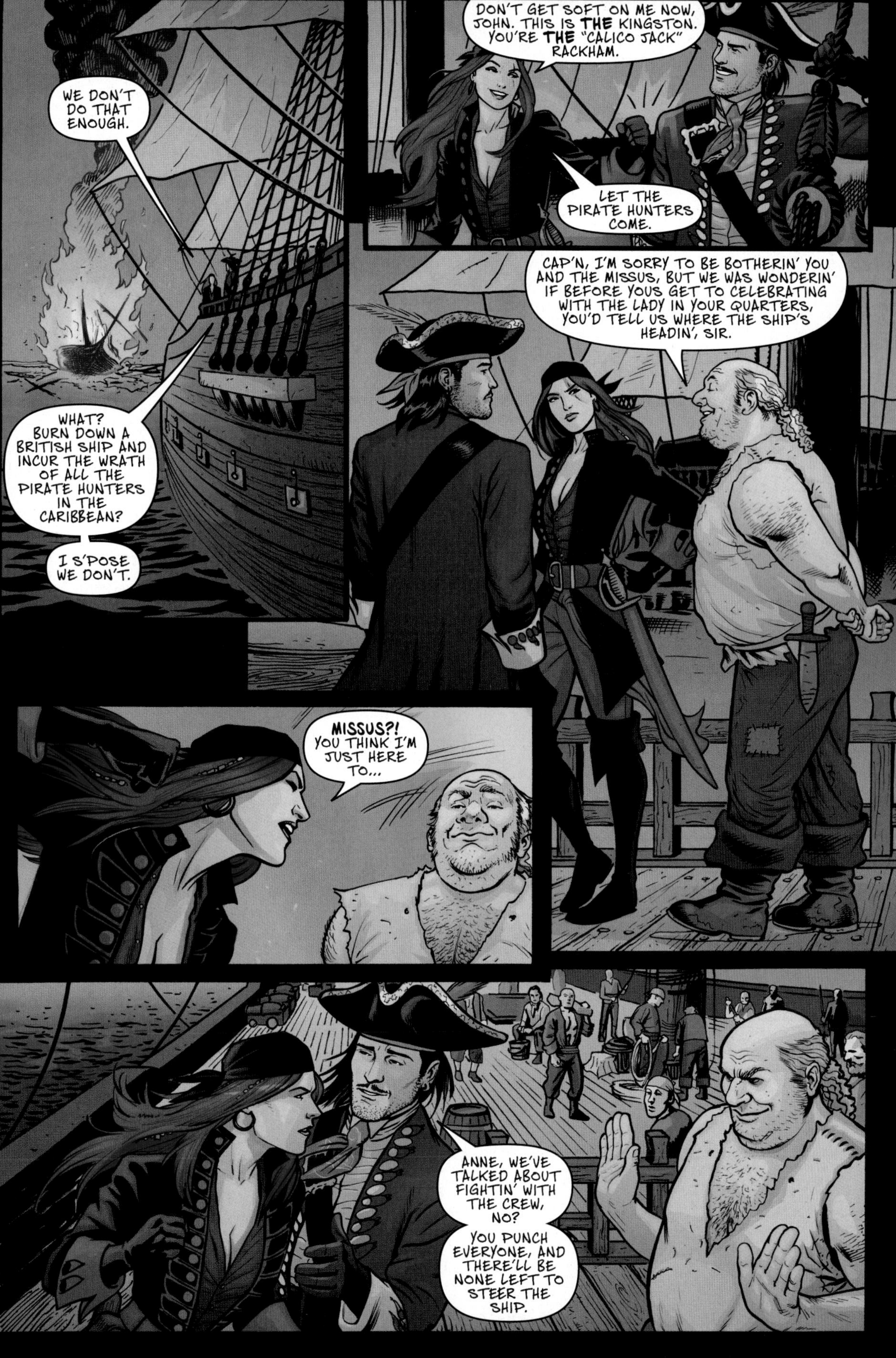
WE DON'T DO THAT ENOUGH.
DON'T GET SOFT ON ME NOW, JOHN. THIS IS **THE** KINGSTON. YOU'RE **THE** "CALICO JACK" RACKHAM.
LET THE PIRATE HUNTERS COME.
WHAT? BURN DOWN A BRITISH SHIP AND INCUR THE WRATH OF ALL THE PIRATE HUNTERS IN THE CARIBBEAN?
I S'POSE WE DON'T.
CAP'N, I'M SORRY TO BE BOTHERIN' YOU AND THE MISSUS, BUT WE WAS WONDERIN' IF BEFORE YOUS GET TO CELEBRATING WITH THE LADY IN YOUR QUARTERS, YOU'D TELL US WHERE THE SHIP'S HEADIN', SIR.
MISSUS?! YOU THINK I'M JUST HERE TO...
ANNE, WE'VE TALKED ABOUT FIGHTIN' WITH THE CREW, NO?
YOU PUNCH EVERYONE, AND THERE'LL BE NONE LEFT TO STEER THE SHIP.

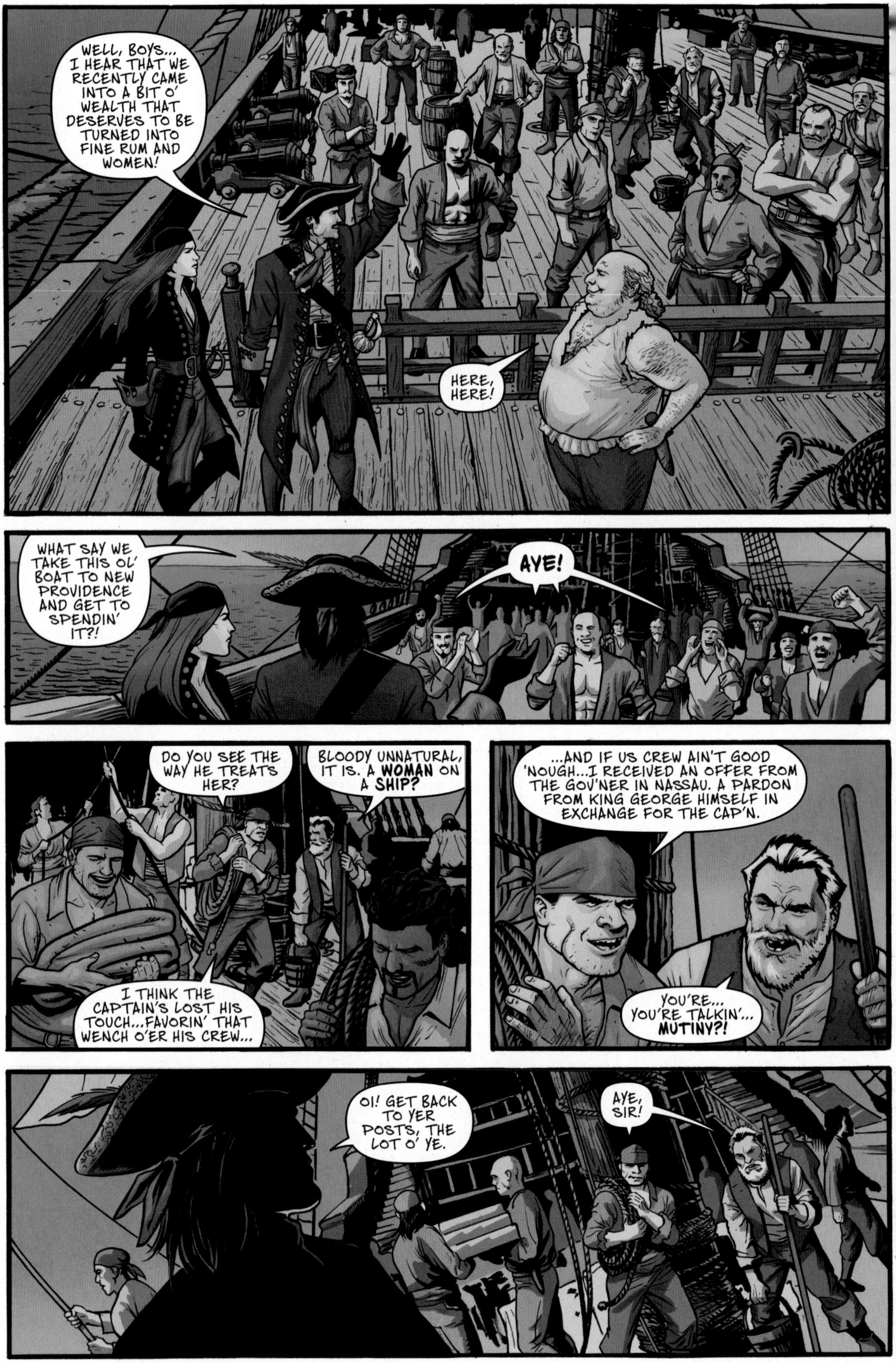
WELL, BOYS... I HEAR THAT WE RECENTLY CAME INTO A BIT O' WEALTH THAT DESERVES TO BE TURNED INTO FINE RUM AND WOMEN!
HERE, HERE!
WHAT SAY WE TAKE THIS OL' BOAT TO NEW PROVIDENCE AND GET TO SPENDIN' IT?!
AYE!
DO YOU SEE THE WAY HE TREATS HER?
BLOODY UNNATURAL, IT IS. A WOMAN ON A SHIP?
I THINK THE CAPTAIN'S LOST HIS TOUCH...FAVORIN' THAT WENCH O'ER HIS CREW...
...AND IF US CREW AIN'T GOOD 'NOUGH...I RECEIVED AN OFFER FROM THE GOV'NER IN NASSAU. A PARDON FROM KING GEORGE HIMSELF IN EXCHANGE FOR THE CAP'N.
YOU'RE... YOU'RE TALKIN'... MUTINY?!
OI! GET BACK TO YER POSTS, THE LOT O' YE.
AYE, SIR!

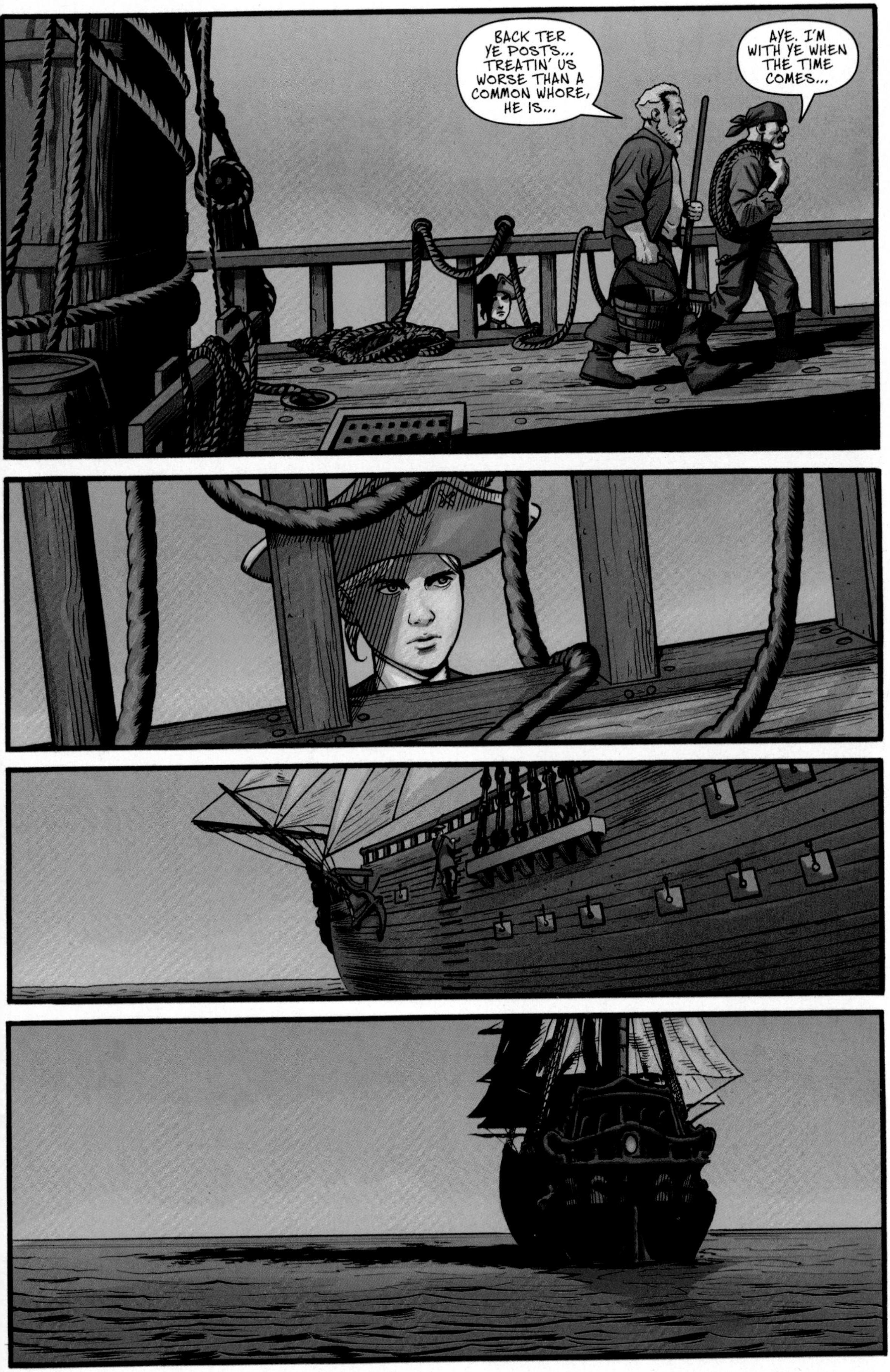
BACK TER YE POSTS... TREATIN' US WORSE THAN A COMMON WHORE, HE IS...
AYE. I'M WITH YE WHEN THE TIME COMES...

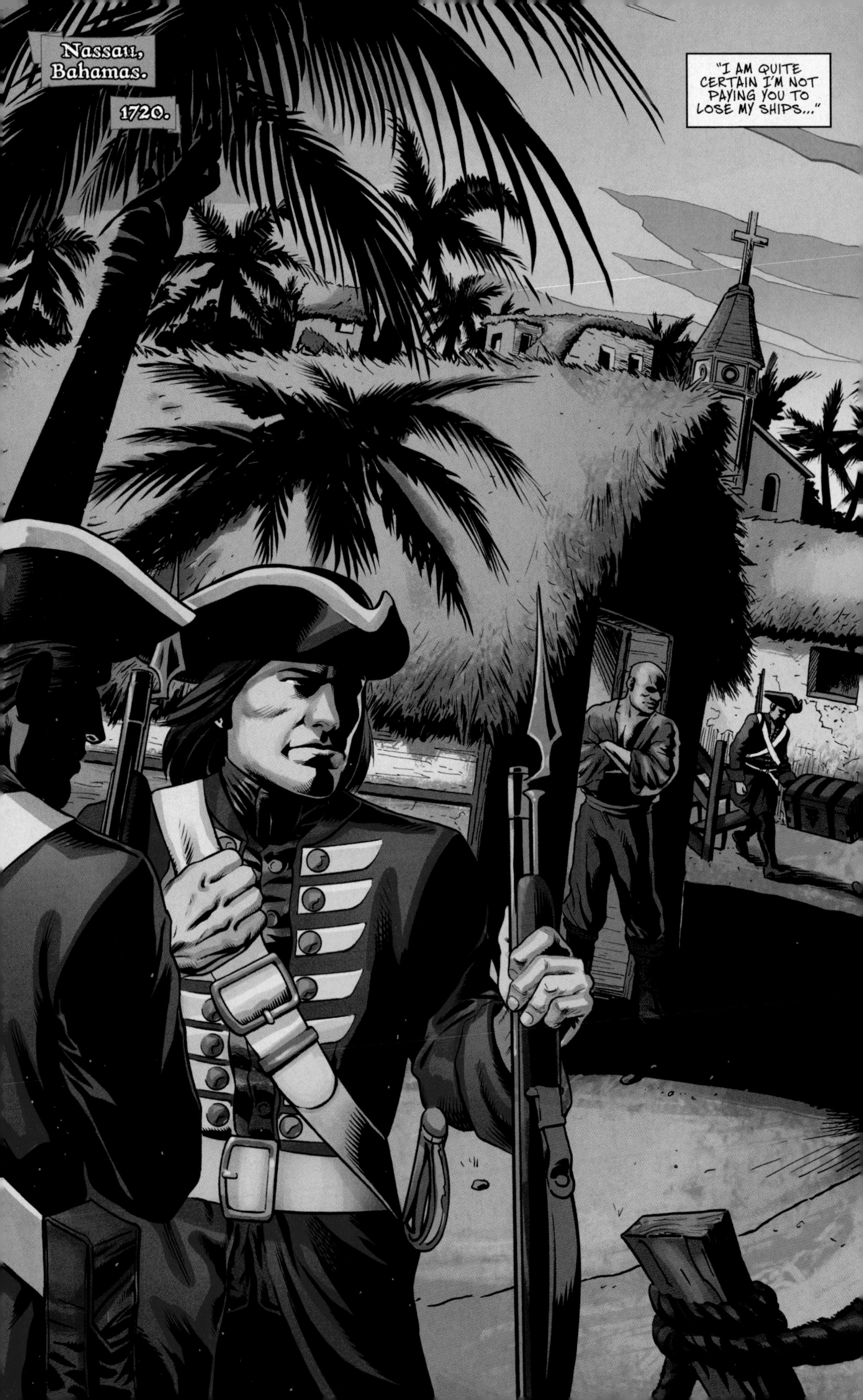
Nassau, Bahamas.
1720.
"I AM QUITE CERTAIN I'M NOT PAYING YOU TO LOSE MY SHIPS..."

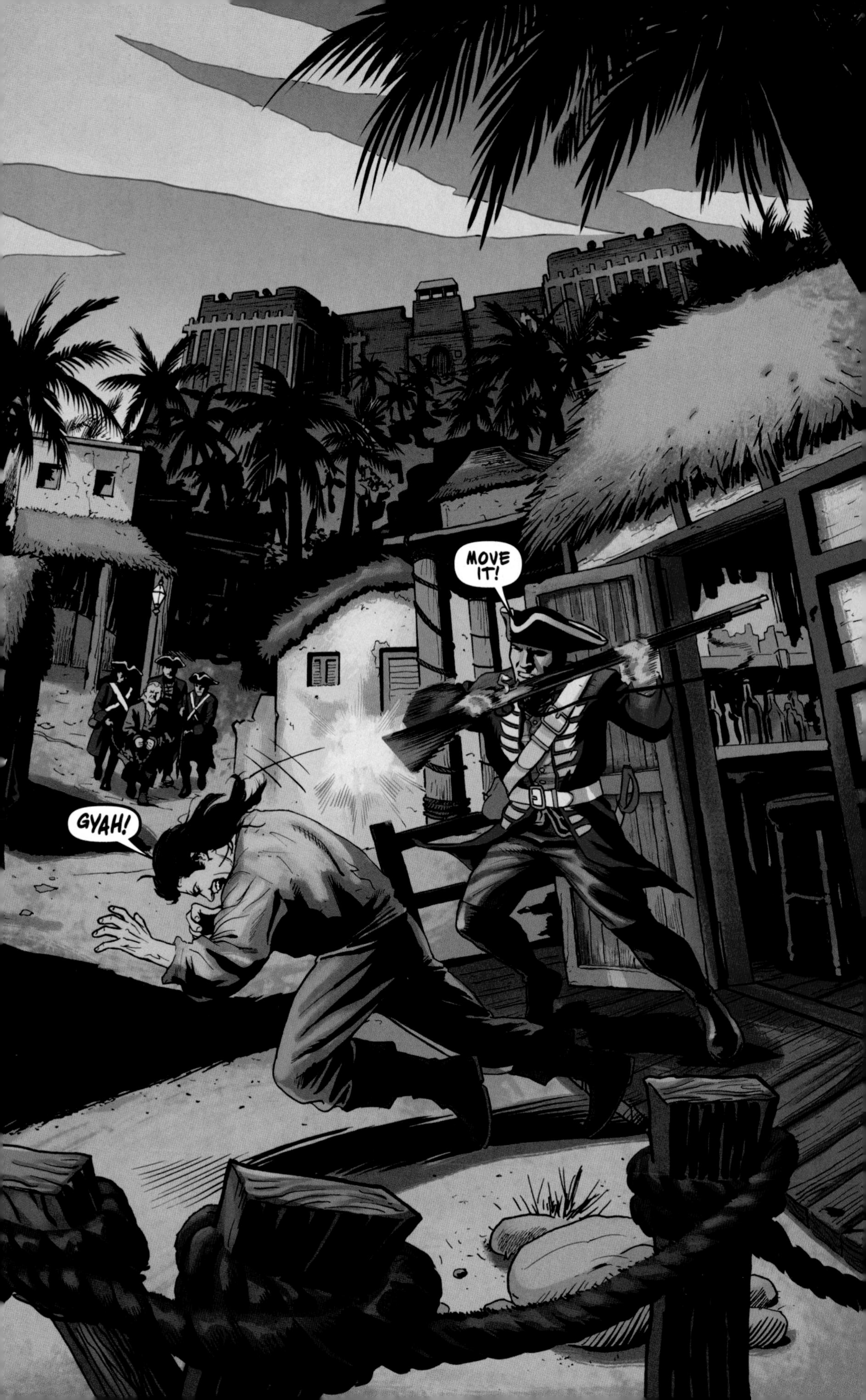
MOVE IT!
GYAH!

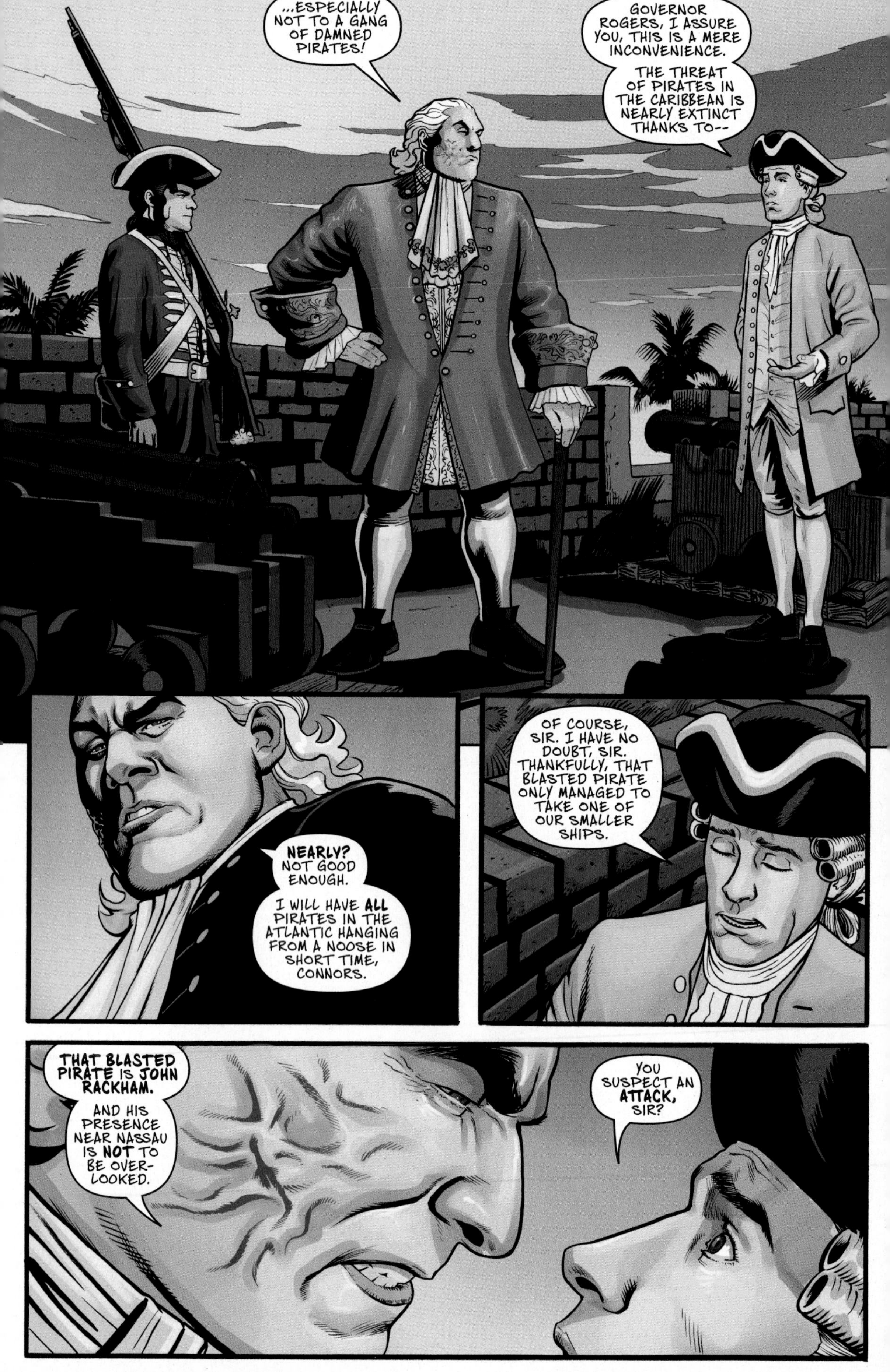
...ESPECIALLY NOT TO A GANG OF DAMNED PIRATES!
GOVERNOR ROGERS, I ASSURE YOU, THIS IS A MERE INCONVENIENCE.
THE THREAT OF PIRATES IN THE CARIBBEAN IS NEARLY EXTINCT THANKS TO--
NEARLY? NOT GOOD ENOUGH.
I WILL HAVE ALL PIRATES IN THE ATLANTIC HANGING FROM A NOOSE IN SHORT TIME, CONNORS.
OF COURSE, SIR. I HAVE NO DOUBT, SIR. THANKFULLY, THAT BLASTED PIRATE ONLY MANAGED TO TAKE ONE OF OUR SMALLER SHIPS.
THAT BLASTED PIRATE IS JOHN RACKHAM.
AND HIS PRESENCE NEAR NASSAU IS NOT TO BE OVER-LOOKED.
YOU SUSPECT AN ATTACK, SIR?

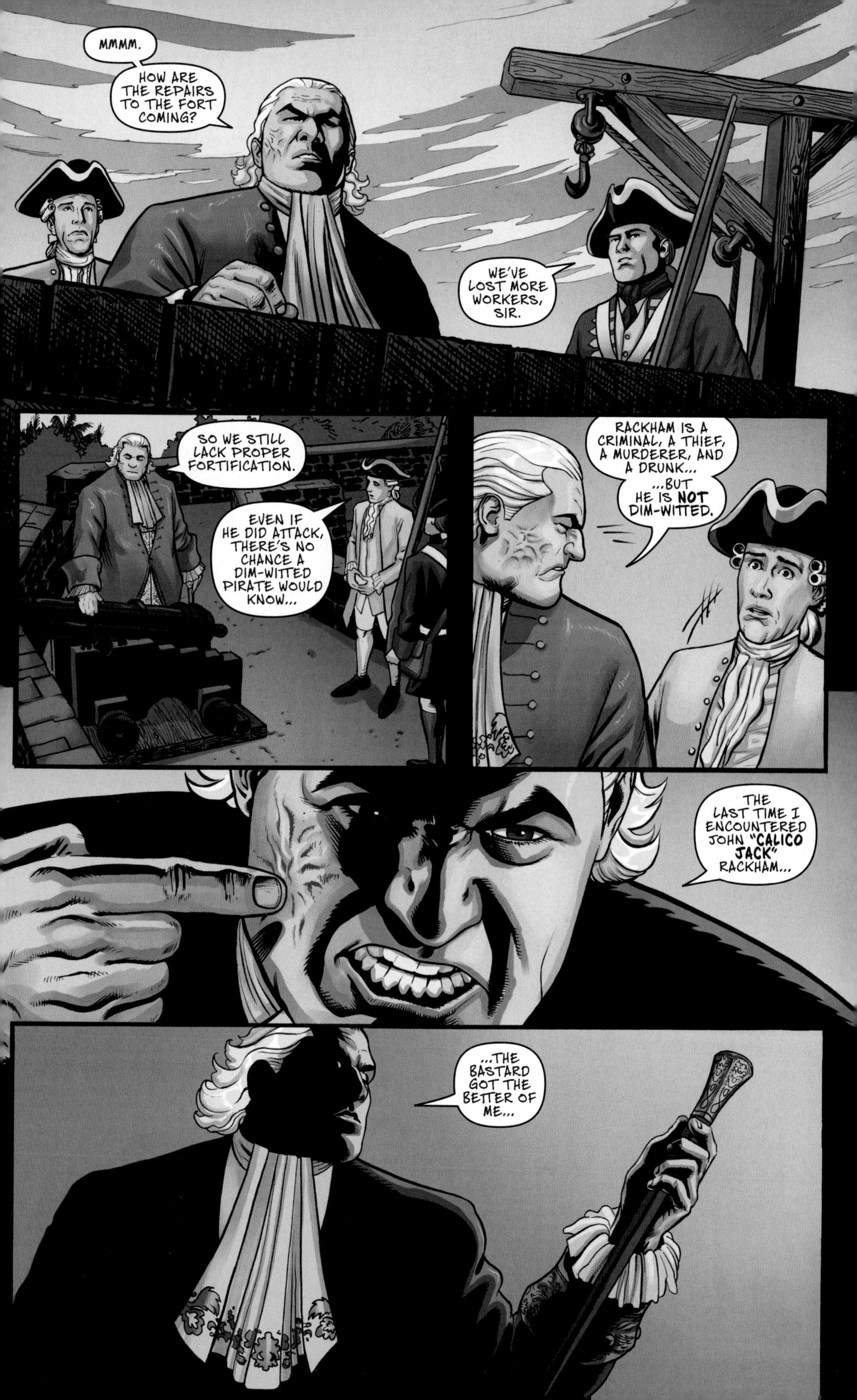
MMMM.
HOW ARE THE REPAIRS TO THE FORT COMING?
WE'VE LOST MORE WORKERS, SIR.
SO WE STILL LACK PROPER FORTIFICATION.
EVEN IF HE DID ATTACK, THERE'S NO CHANCE A DIM-WITTED PIRATE WOULD KNOW...
RACKHAM IS A CRIMINAL, A THIEF, A MURDERER, AND A DRUNK...
...BUT HE IS **NOT** DIM-WITTED.
THE LAST TIME I ENCOUNTERED JOHN **"CALICO JACK"** RACKHAM...
...THE BASTARD GOT THE BETTER OF ME...

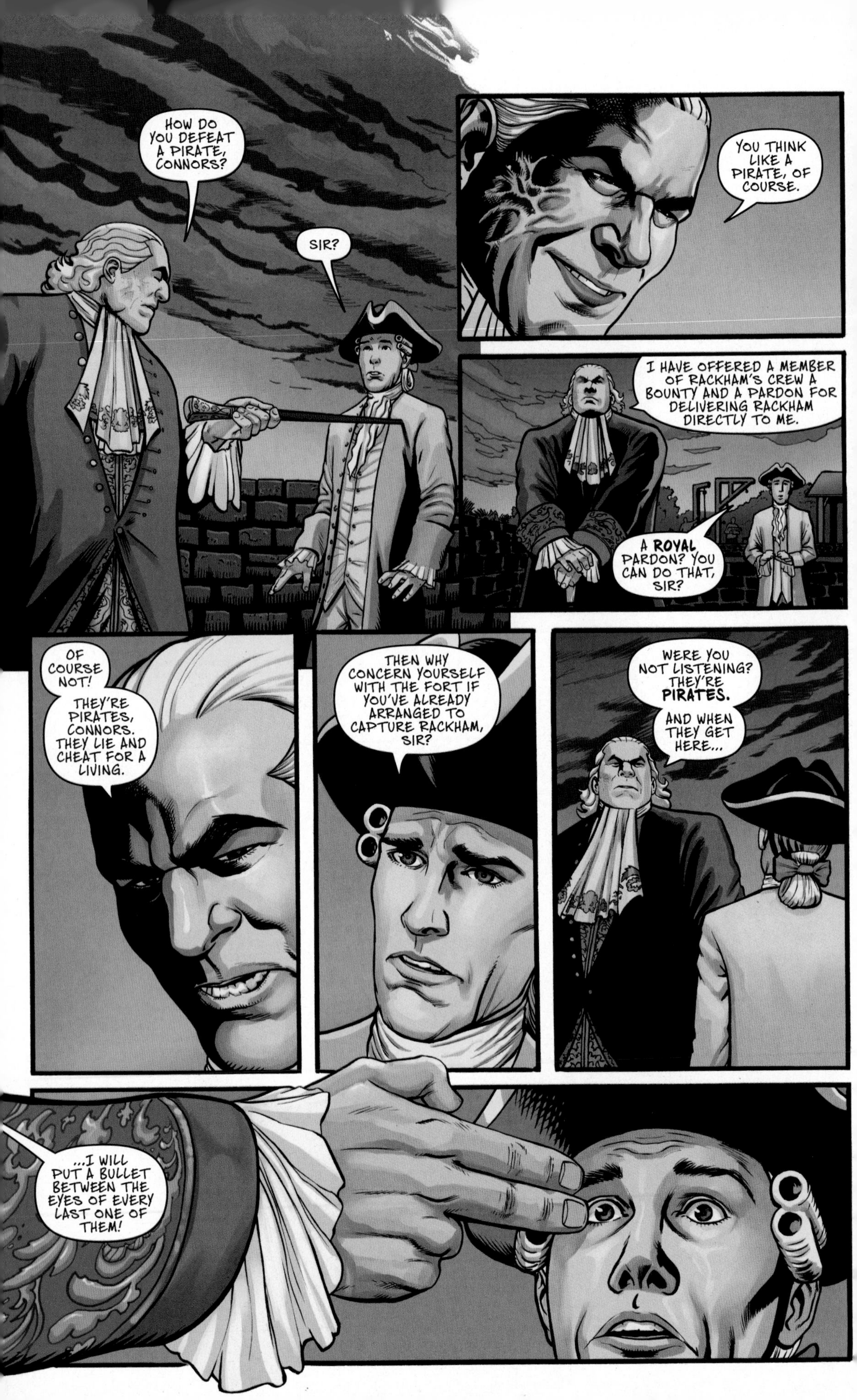
HOW DO YOU DEFEAT A PIRATE, CONNORS?
SIR?
YOU THINK LIKE A PIRATE, OF COURSE.
I HAVE OFFERED A MEMBER OF RACKHAM'S CREW A BOUNTY AND A PARDON FOR DELIVERING RACKHAM DIRECTLY TO ME.
A ROYAL PARDON? YOU CAN DO THAT, SIR?
OF COURSE NOT!
THEY'RE PIRATES, CONNORS. THEY LIE AND CHEAT FOR A LIVING.
THEN WHY CONCERN YOURSELF WITH THE FORT IF YOU'VE ALREADY ARRANGED TO CAPTURE RACKHAM, SIR?
WERE YOU NOT LISTENING? THEY'RE PIRATES.
AND WHEN THEY GET HERE...
...I WILL PUT A BULLET BETWEEN THE EYES OF EVERY LAST ONE OF THEM!

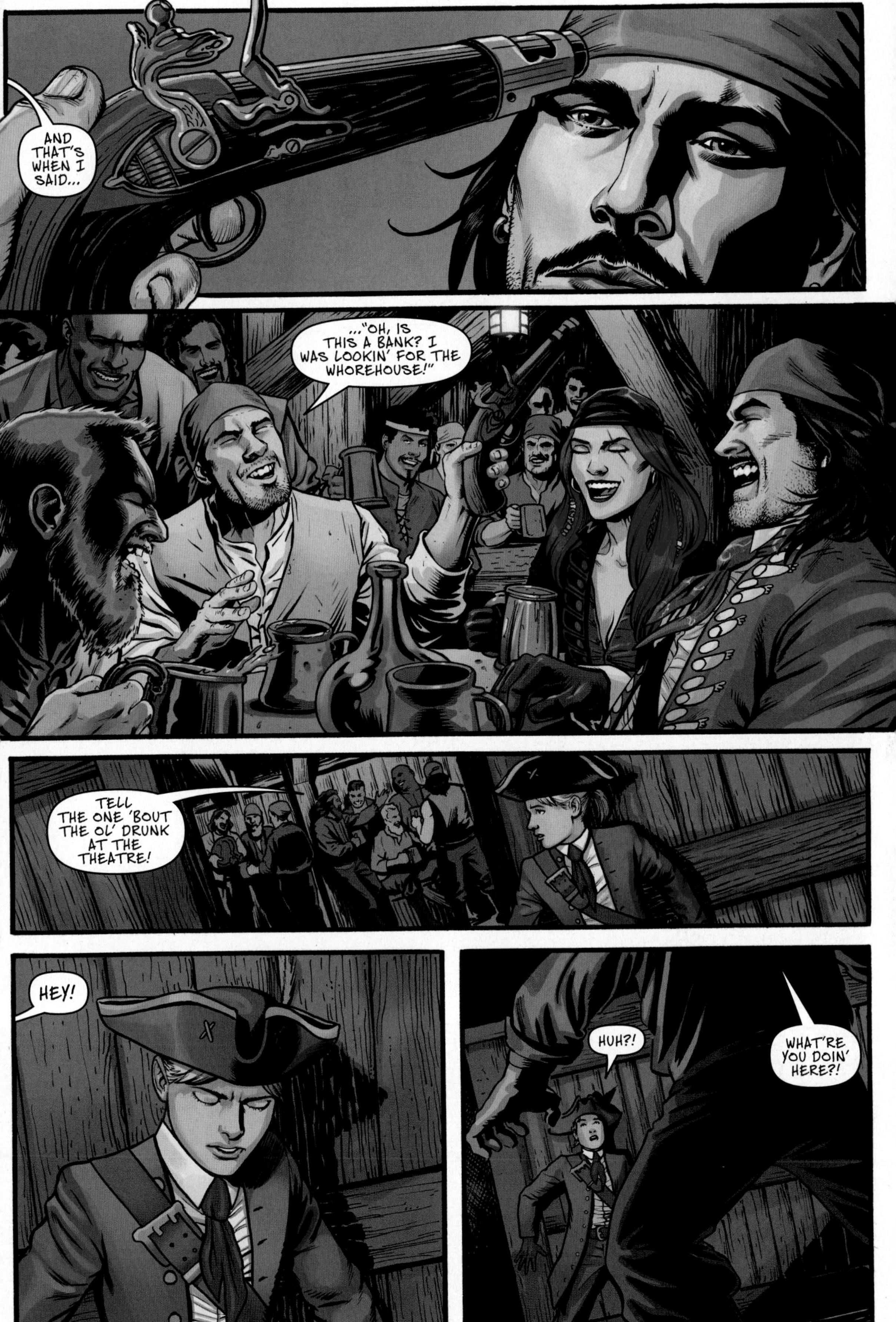

AND THAT'S WHEN I SAID...
..."OH, IS THIS A BANK? I WAS LOOKIN' FOR THE WHOREHOUSE!"
TELL THE ONE 'BOUT THE OL' DRUNK AT THE THEATRE!
HEY!
HUH?!
WHAT'RE YOU DOIN' HERE?!

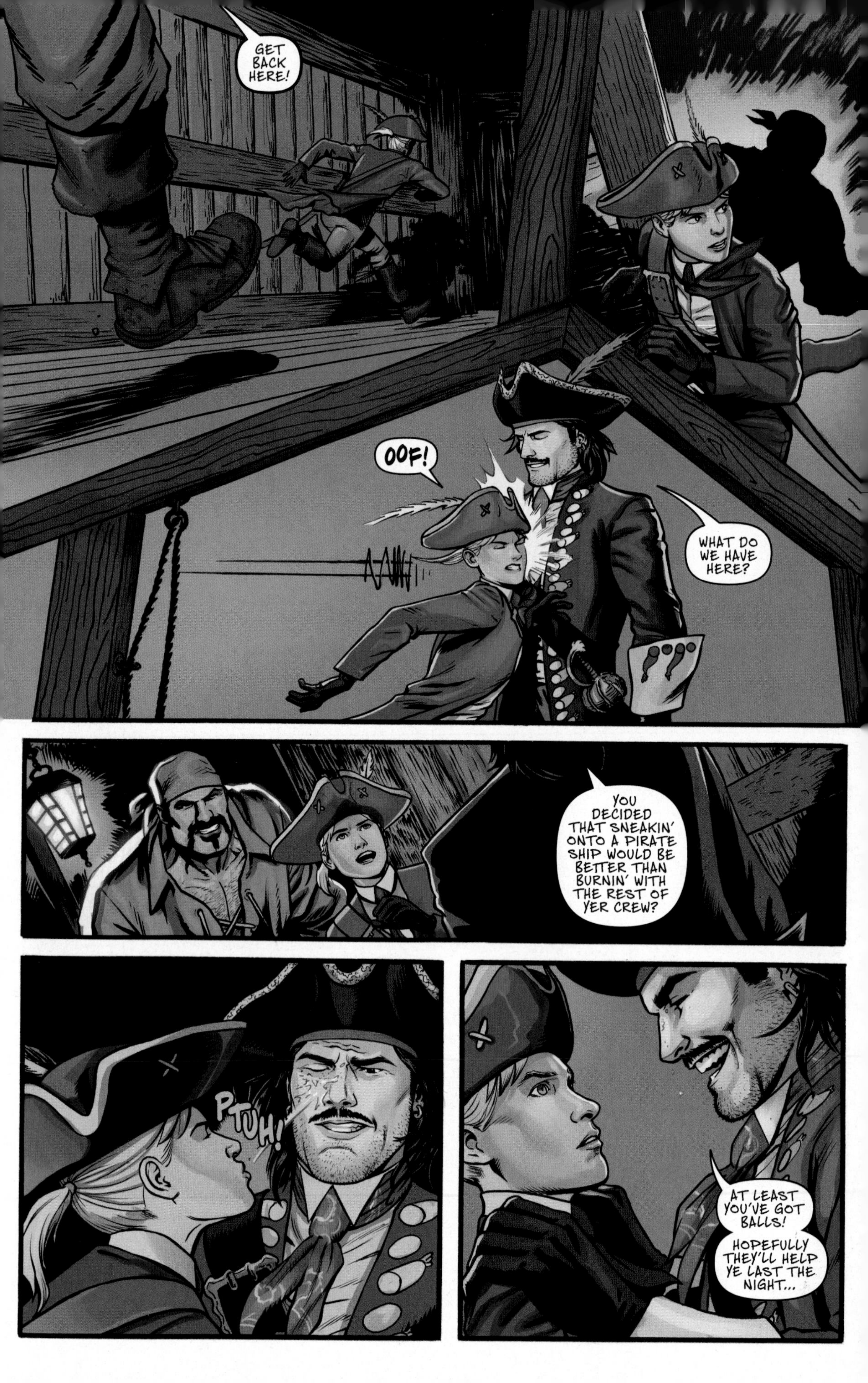
GET BACK HERE!
OOF!
WHAT DO WE HAVE HERE?
YOU DECIDED THAT SNEAKIN' ONTO A PIRATE SHIP WOULD BE BETTER THAN BURNIN' WITH THE REST OF YER CREW?
PTUH!
AT LEAST YOU'VE GOT BALLS!
HOPEFULLY THEY'LL HELP YE LAST THE NIGHT...

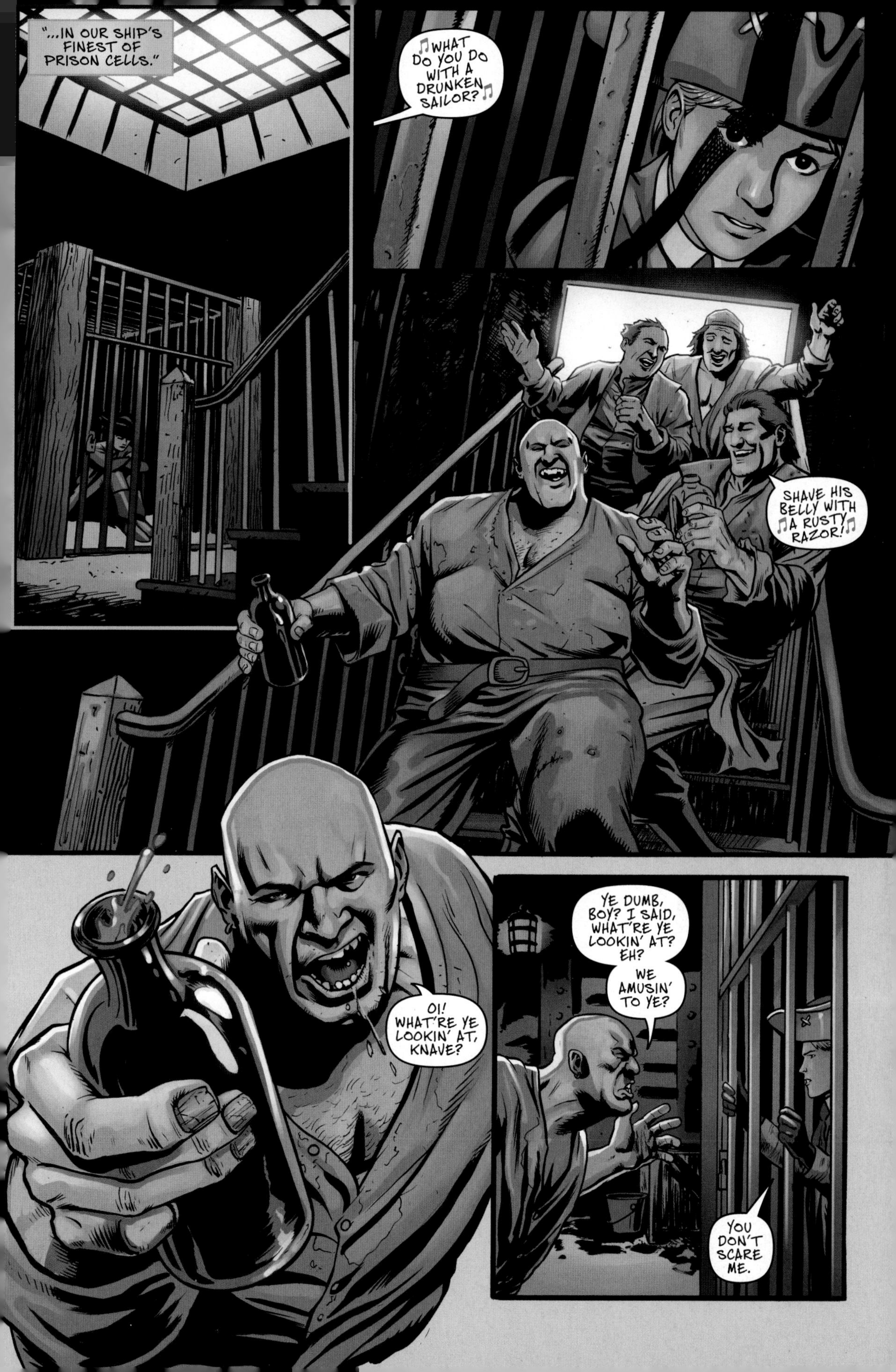
"...IN OUR SHIP'S FINEST OF PRISON CELLS."
♫WHAT DO YOU DO WITH A DRUNKEN SAILOR?♫
SHAVE HIS BELLY WITH ♫A RUSTY RAZOR!♫
OI! WHAT'RE YE LOOKIN' AT, KNAVE?
YE DUMB, BOY? I SAID, WHAT'RE YE LOOKIN' AT? EH?
WE AMUSIN' TO YE?
YOU DON'T SCARE ME.

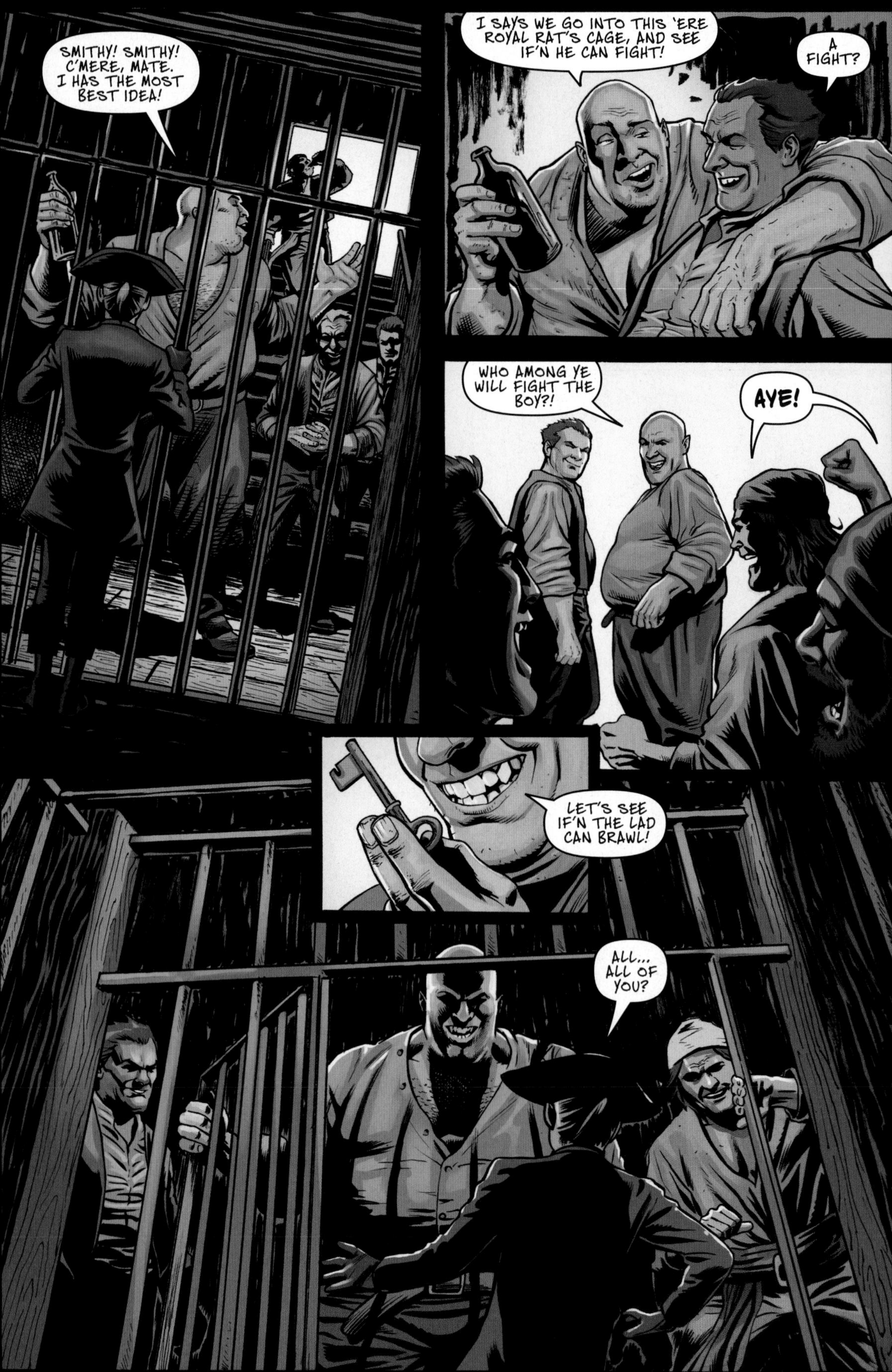
SMITHY! SMITHY! C'MERE, MATE. I HAS THE MOST BEST IDEA!
I SAYS WE GO INTO THIS 'ERE ROYAL RAT'S CAGE, AND SEE IF'N HE CAN FIGHT!
A FIGHT?
WHO AMONG YE WILL FIGHT THE BOY?!
AYE!
LET'S SEE IF'N THE LAD CAN BRAWL!
ALL... ALL OF YOU?

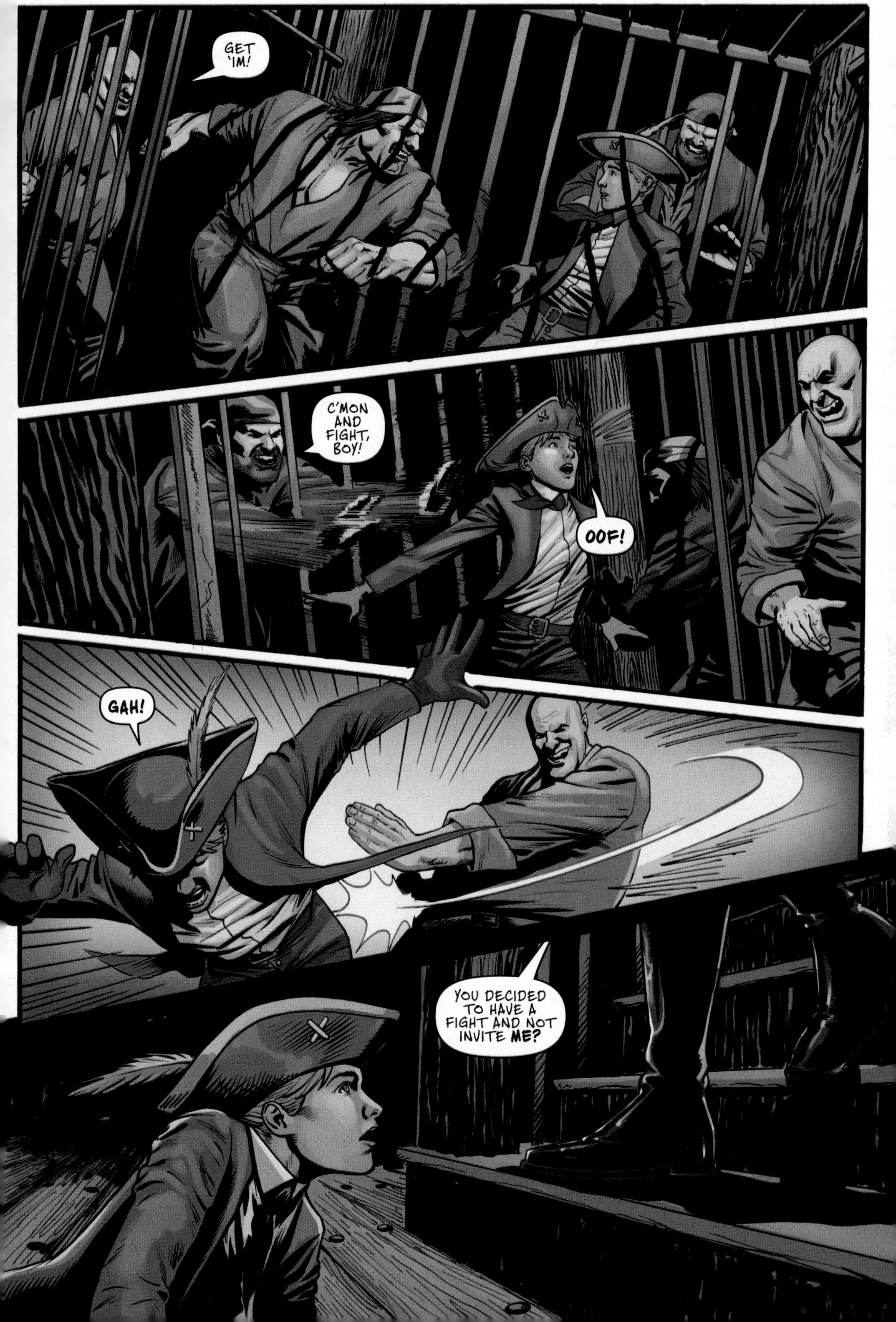
GET 'IM!
C'MON AND FIGHT, BOY!
OOF!
GAH!
YOU DECIDED TO HAVE A FIGHT AND NOT INVITE **ME?**

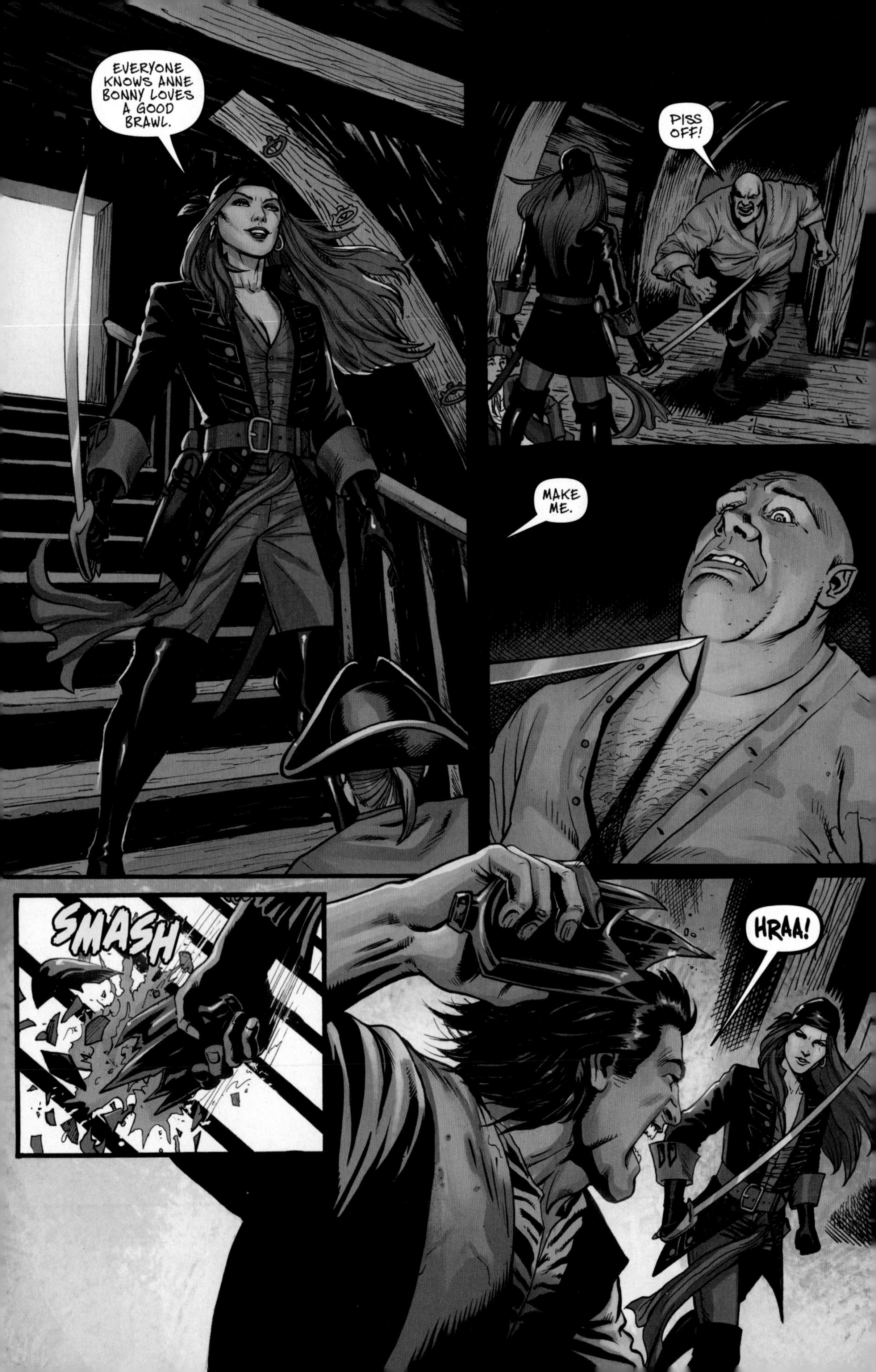
EVERYONE KNOWS ANNE BONNY LOVES A GOOD BRAWL.
PISS OFF!
MAKE ME.
SMASH
HRAA!

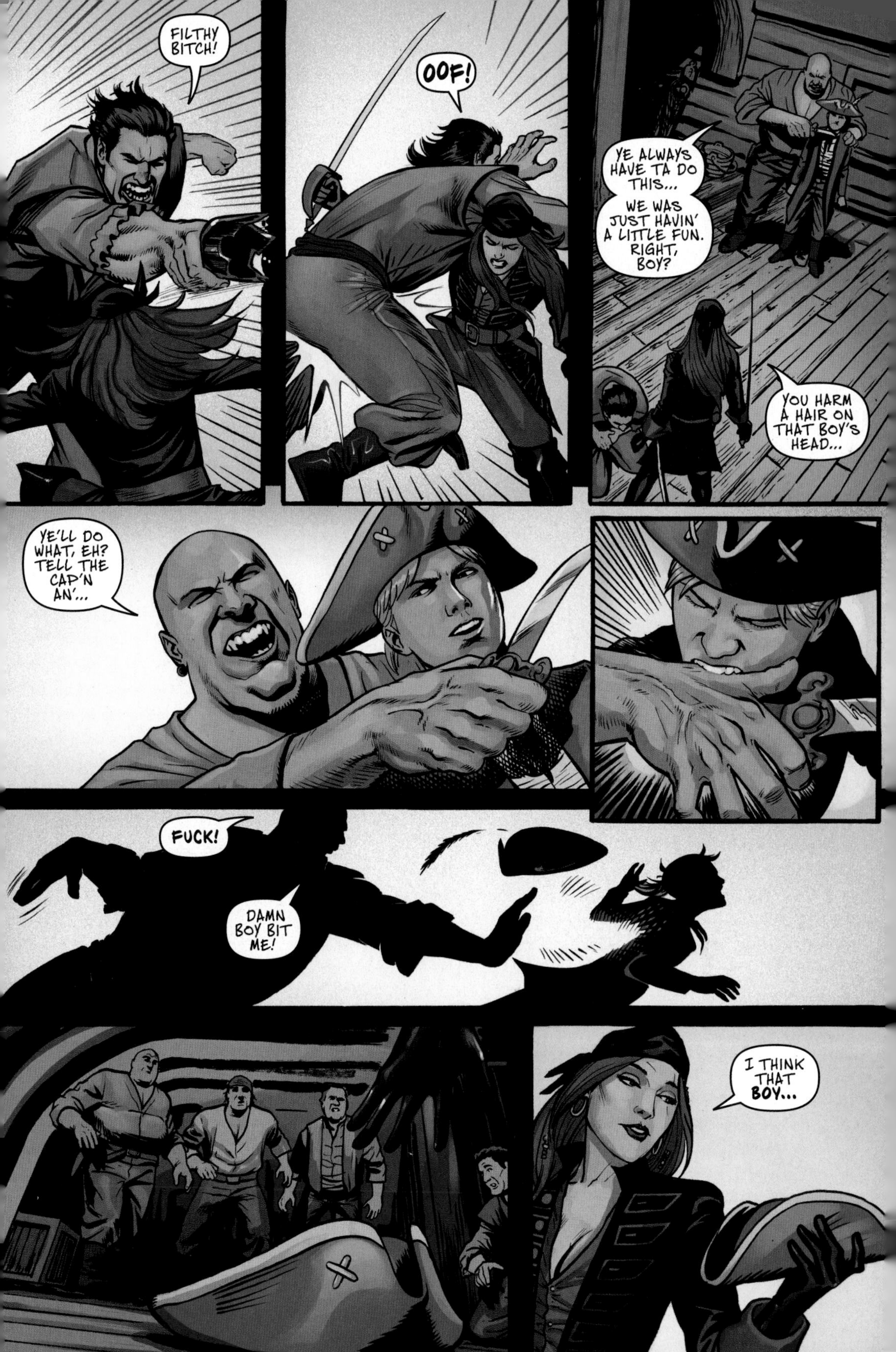
FILTHY BITCH!
OOF!
YE ALWAYS HAVE TA DO THIS...
WE WAS JUST HAVIN' A LITTLE FUN. RIGHT, BOY?
YOU HARM A HAIR ON THAT BOY'S HEAD...
YE'LL DO WHAT, EH? TELL THE CAP'N AN'...
FUCK!
DAMN BOY BIT ME!
I THINK THAT BOY...

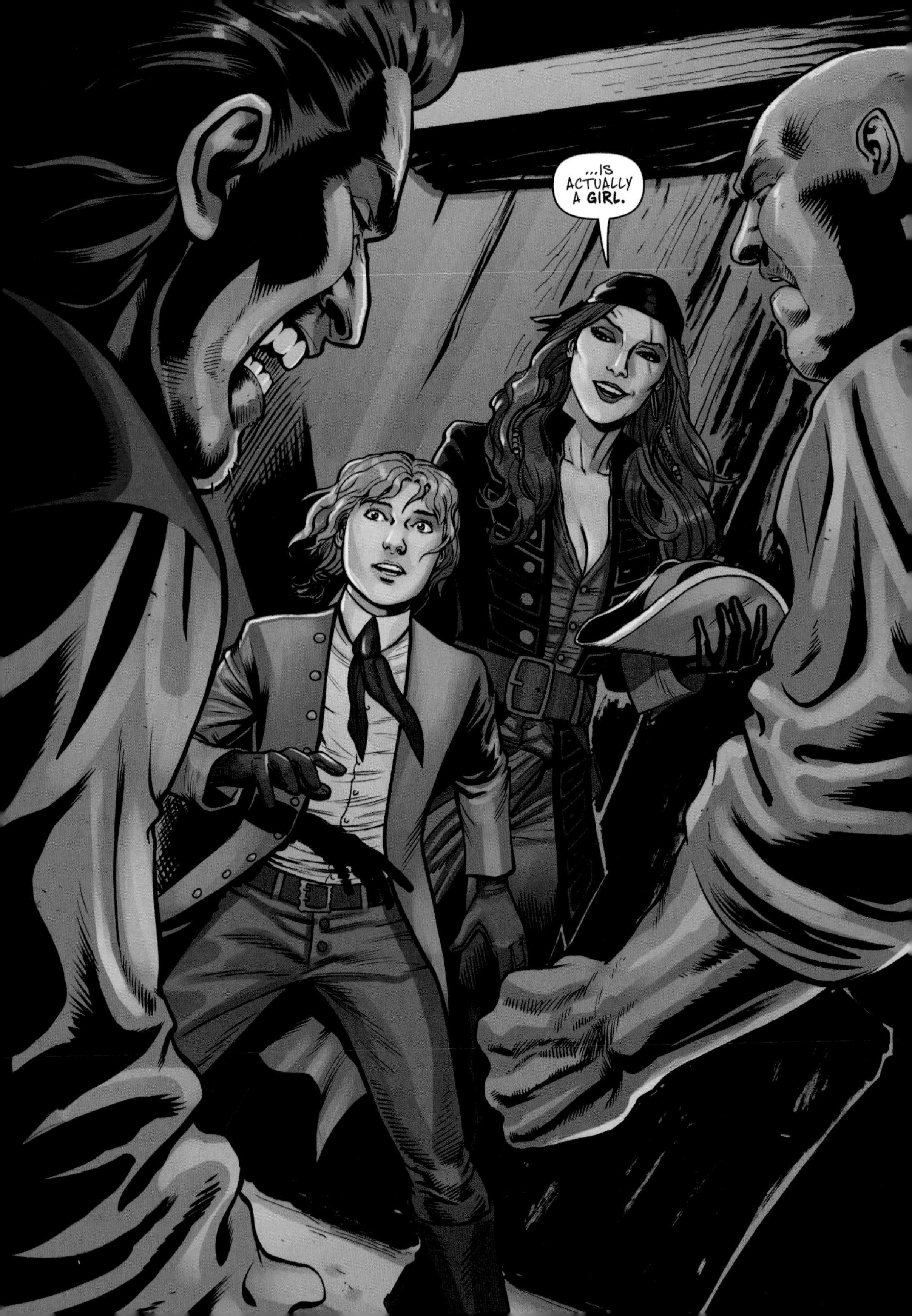
...IS ACTUALLY A GIRL.

Chapter 2

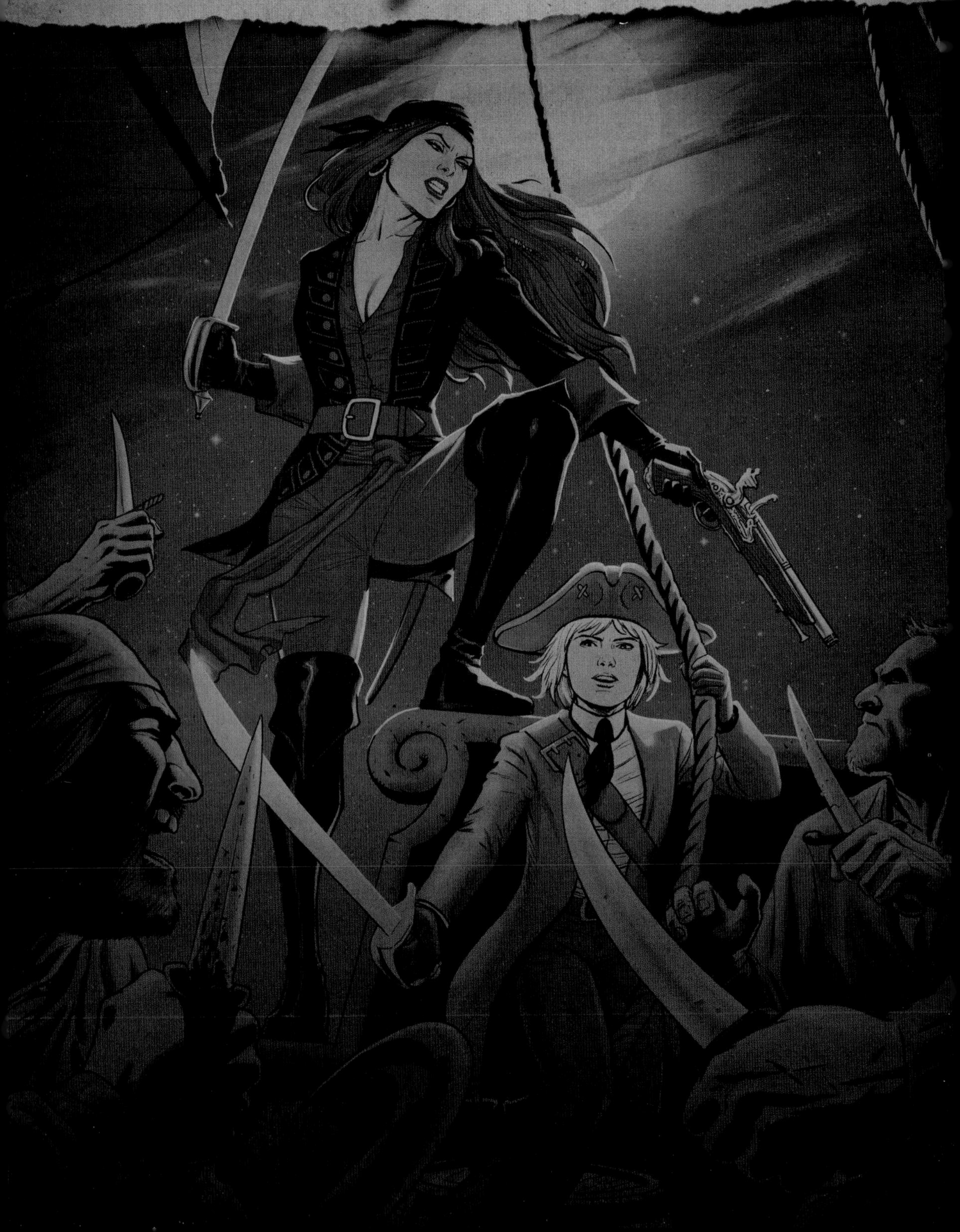

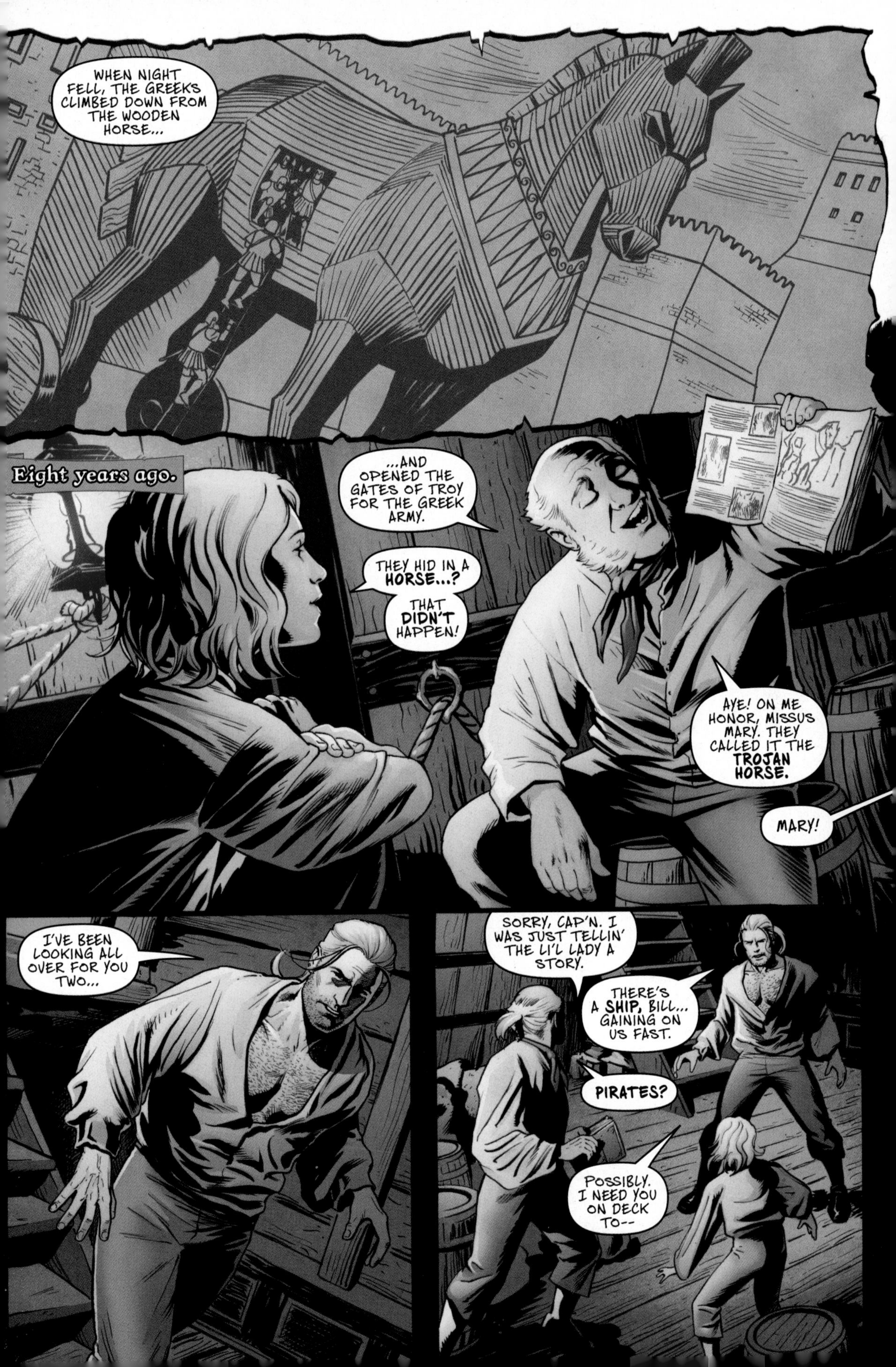
WHEN NIGHT FELL, THE GREEKS CLIMBED DOWN FROM THE WOODEN HORSE...
Eight years ago.
...AND OPENED THE GATES OF TROY FOR THE GREEK ARMY.
THEY HID IN A HORSE...?
THAT DIDN'T HAPPEN!
AYE! ON ME HONOR, MISSUS MARY. THEY CALLED IT THE TROJAN HORSE.
MARY!
I'VE BEEN LOOKING ALL OVER FOR YOU TWO...
SORRY, CAP'N. I WAS JUST TELLIN' THE LI'L LADY A STORY.
THERE'S A SHIP, BILL... GAINING ON US FAST.
PIRATES?
POSSIBLY. I NEED YOU ON DECK TO--

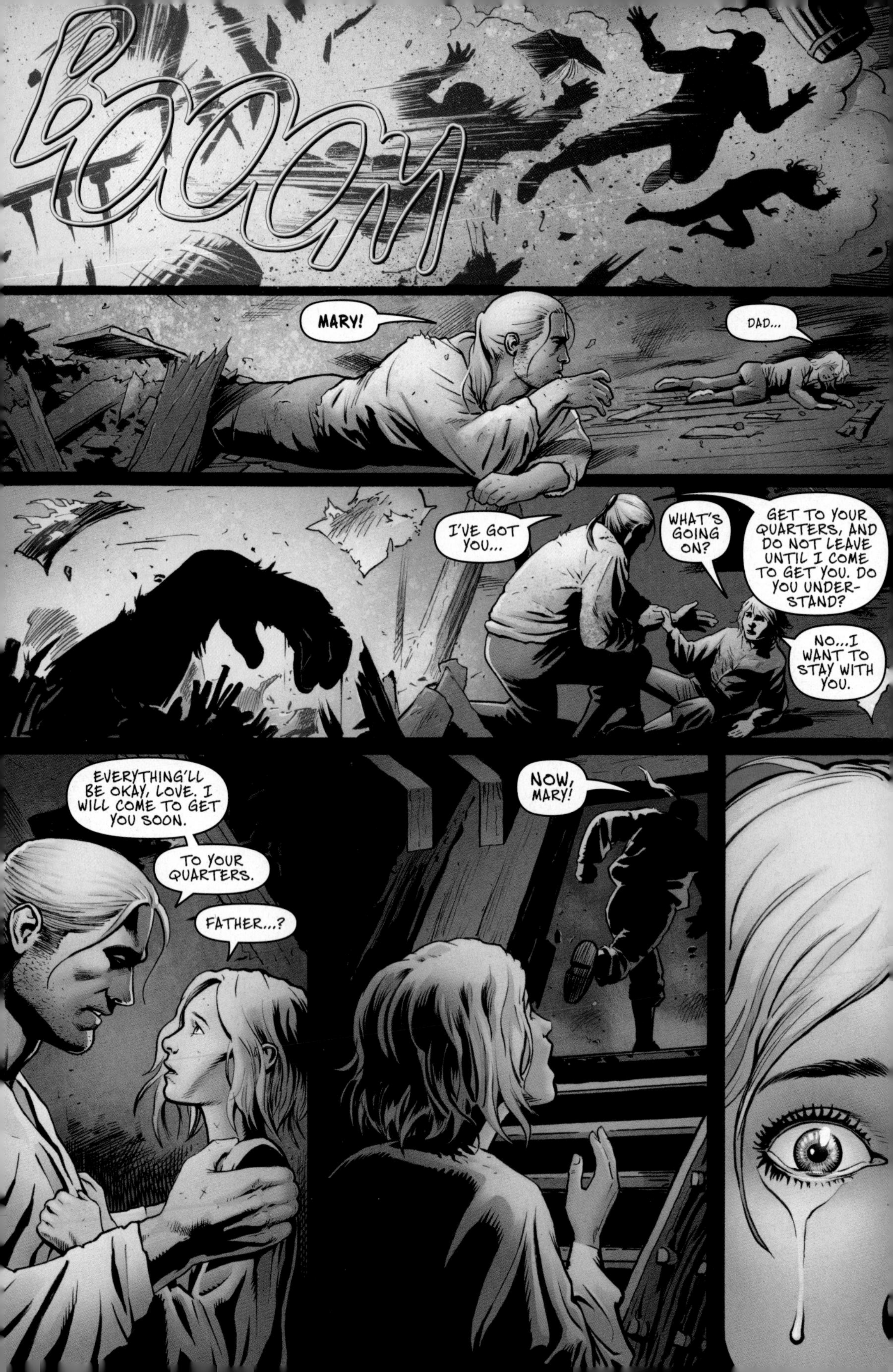
BOOOM
MARY!
DAD...
I'VE GOT YOU...
WHAT'S GOING ON?
GET TO YOUR QUARTERS, AND DO NOT LEAVE UNTIL I COME TO GET YOU. DO YOU UNDER-STAND?
NO...I WANT TO STAY WITH YOU.
EVERYTHING'LL BE OKAY, LOVE. I WILL COME TO GET YOU SOON.
TO YOUR QUARTERS.
FATHER...?
NOW, MARY!

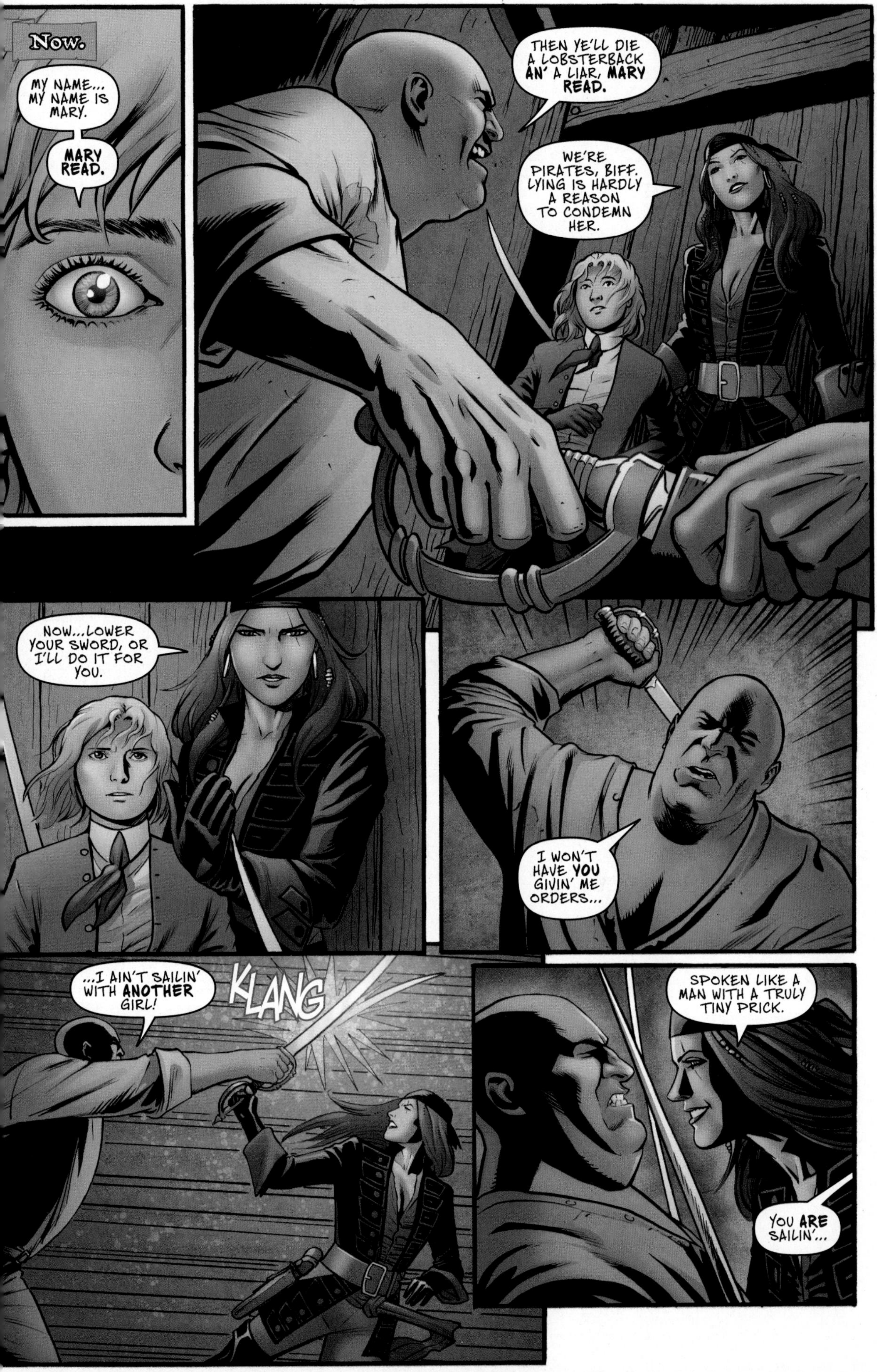
Now.
MY NAME... MY NAME IS MARY.
MARY READ.
THEN YE'LL DIE A LOBSTERBACK AN' A LIAR, MARY READ.
WE'RE PIRATES, BIFF. LYING IS HARDLY A REASON TO CONDEMN HER.
NOW...LOWER YOUR SWORD, OR I'LL DO IT FOR YOU.
I WON'T HAVE YOU GIVIN' ME ORDERS...
...I AIN'T SAILIN' WITH ANOTHER GIRL!
KLANG
SPOKEN LIKE A MAN WITH A TRULY TINY PRICK.
YOU ARE SAILIN'...

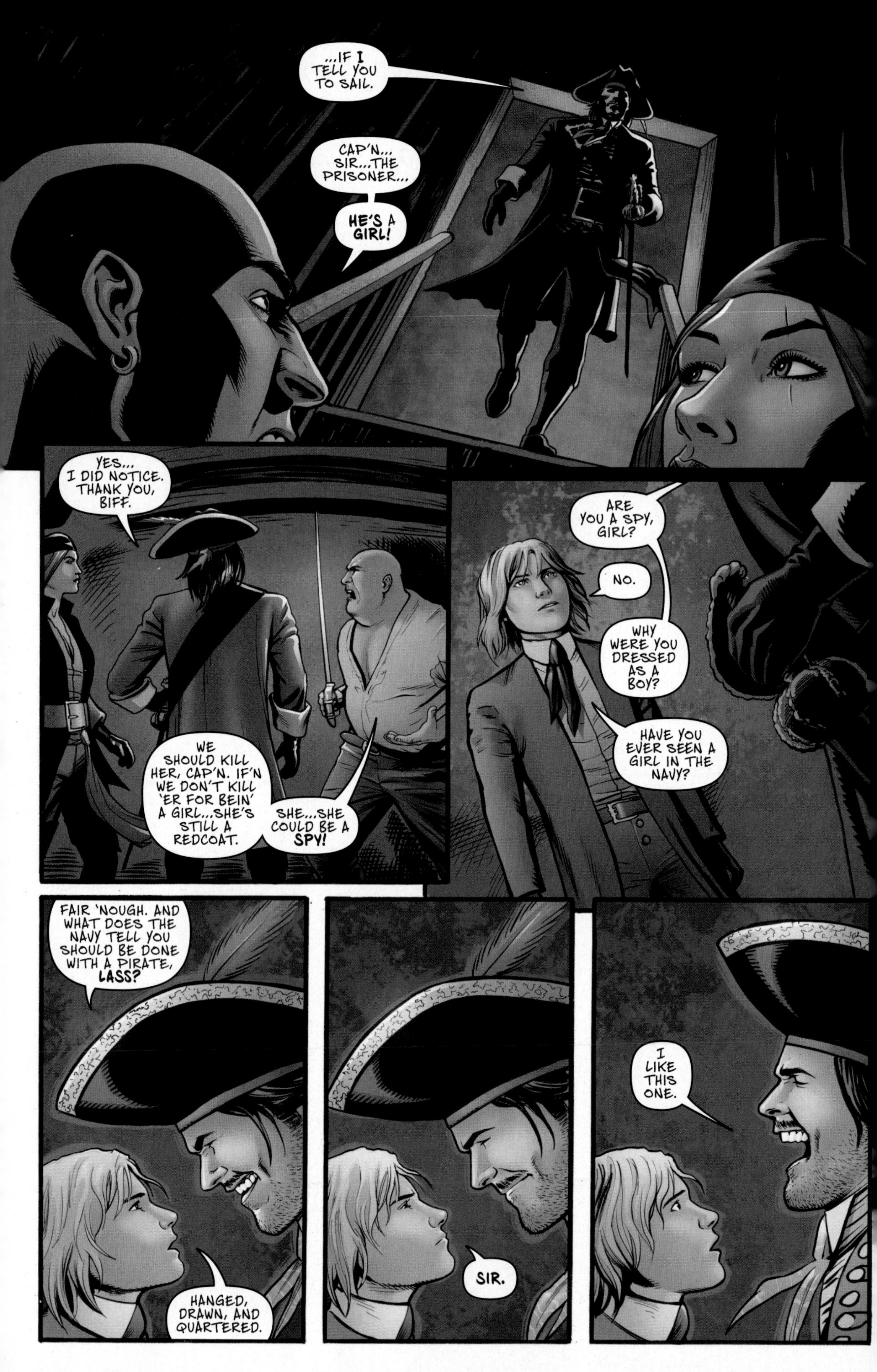
...IF I TELL YOU TO SAIL.
CAP'N... SIR...THE PRISONER...
HE'S A GIRL!
YES... I DID NOTICE. THANK YOU, BIFF.
WE SHOULD KILL HER, CAP'N. IF'N WE DON'T KILL 'ER FOR BEIN' A GIRL...SHE'S STILL A REDCOAT.
SHE...SHE COULD BE A SPY!
ARE YOU A SPY, GIRL?
NO.
WHY WERE YOU DRESSED AS A BOY?
HAVE YOU EVER SEEN A GIRL IN THE NAVY?
FAIR 'NOUGH. AND WHAT DOES THE NAVY TELL YOU SHOULD BE DONE WITH A PIRATE, LASS?
HANGED, DRAWN, AND QUARTERED.
SIR.
I LIKE THIS ONE.

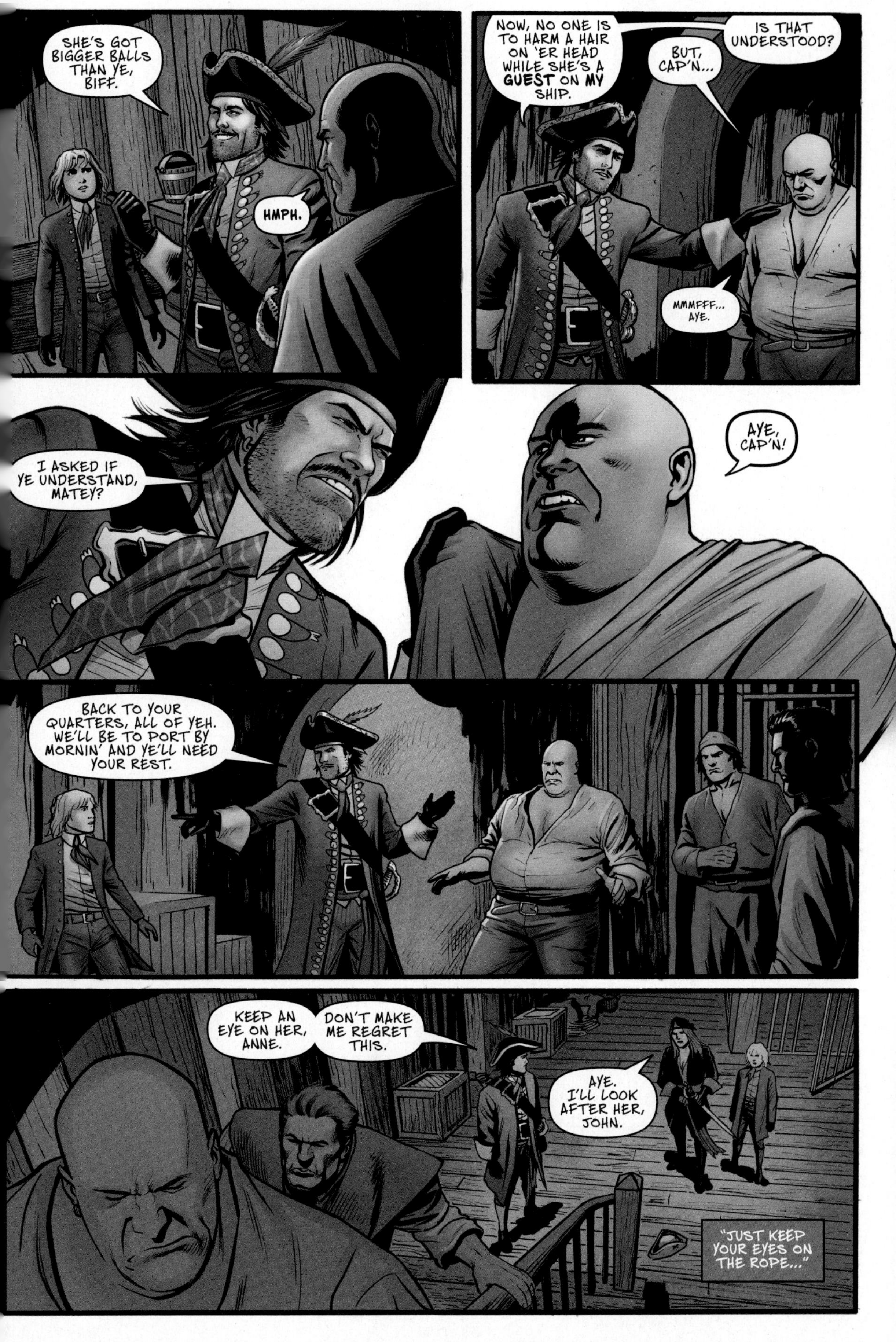
SHE'S GOT BIGGER BALLS THAN YE, BIFF.
HMPH.
NOW, NO ONE IS TO HARM A HAIR ON 'ER HEAD WHILE SHE'S A **GUEST** ON **MY** SHIP.
BUT, CAP'N...
IS THAT UNDERSTOOD?
MMMFFF... AYE.
I ASKED IF YE UNDERSTAND, MATEY?
AYE, CAP'N!
BACK TO YOUR QUARTERS, ALL OF YEH. WE'LL BE TO PORT BY MORNIN' AND YE'LL NEED YOUR REST.
KEEP AN EYE ON HER, ANNE.
DON'T MAKE ME REGRET THIS.
AYE. I'LL LOOK AFTER HER, JOHN.
"JUST KEEP YOUR EYES ON THE ROPE..."

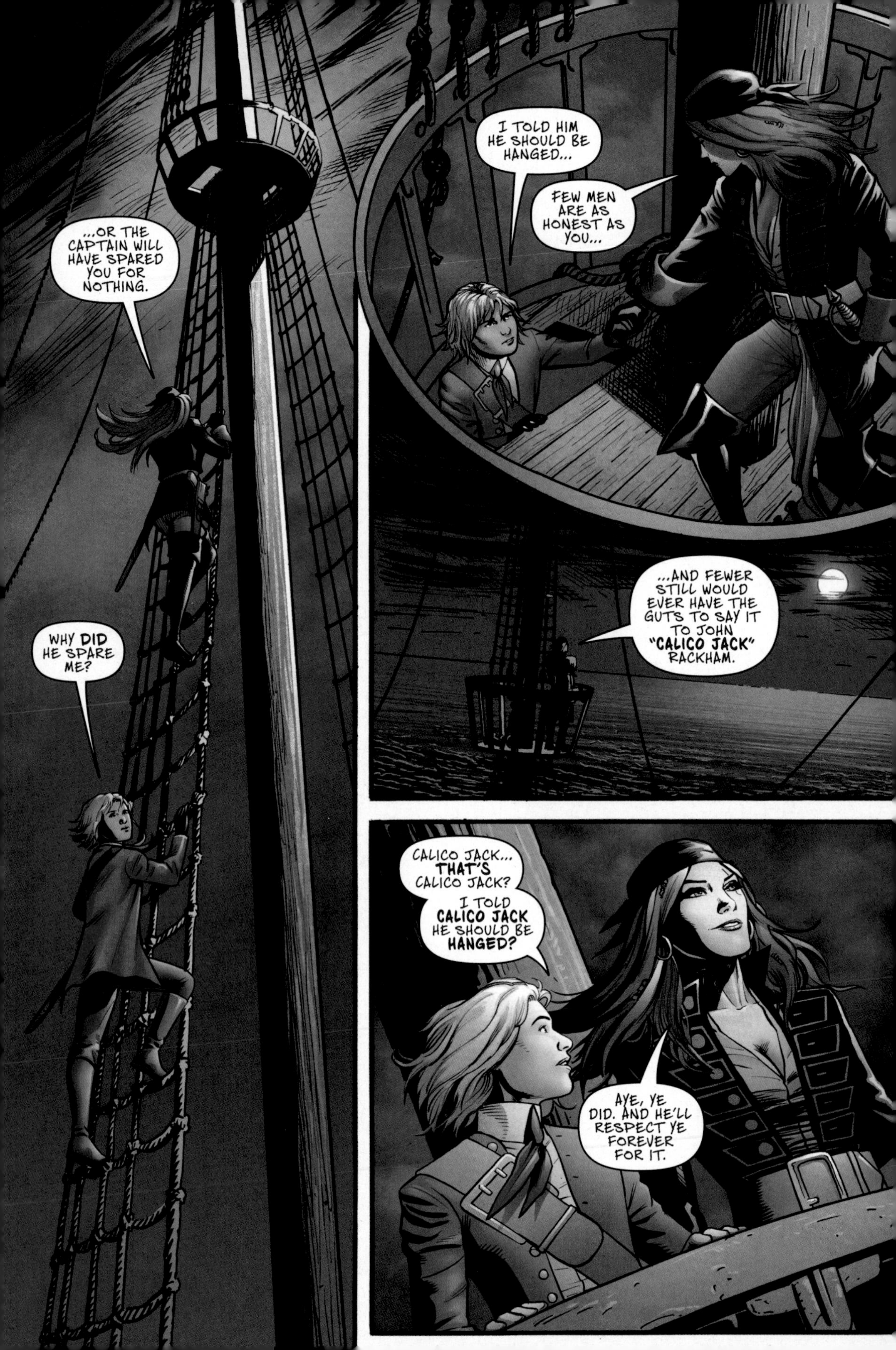
...OR THE CAPTAIN WILL HAVE SPARED YOU FOR NOTHING.
WHY DID HE SPARE ME?
I TOLD HIM HE SHOULD BE HANGED...
FEW MEN ARE AS HONEST AS YOU...
...AND FEWER STILL WOULD EVER HAVE THE GUTS TO SAY IT TO JOHN "CALICO JACK" RACKHAM.
CALICO JACK... THAT'S CALICO JACK?
I TOLD CALICO JACK HE SHOULD BE HANGED?
AYE, YE DID. AND HE'LL RESPECT YE FOREVER FOR IT.

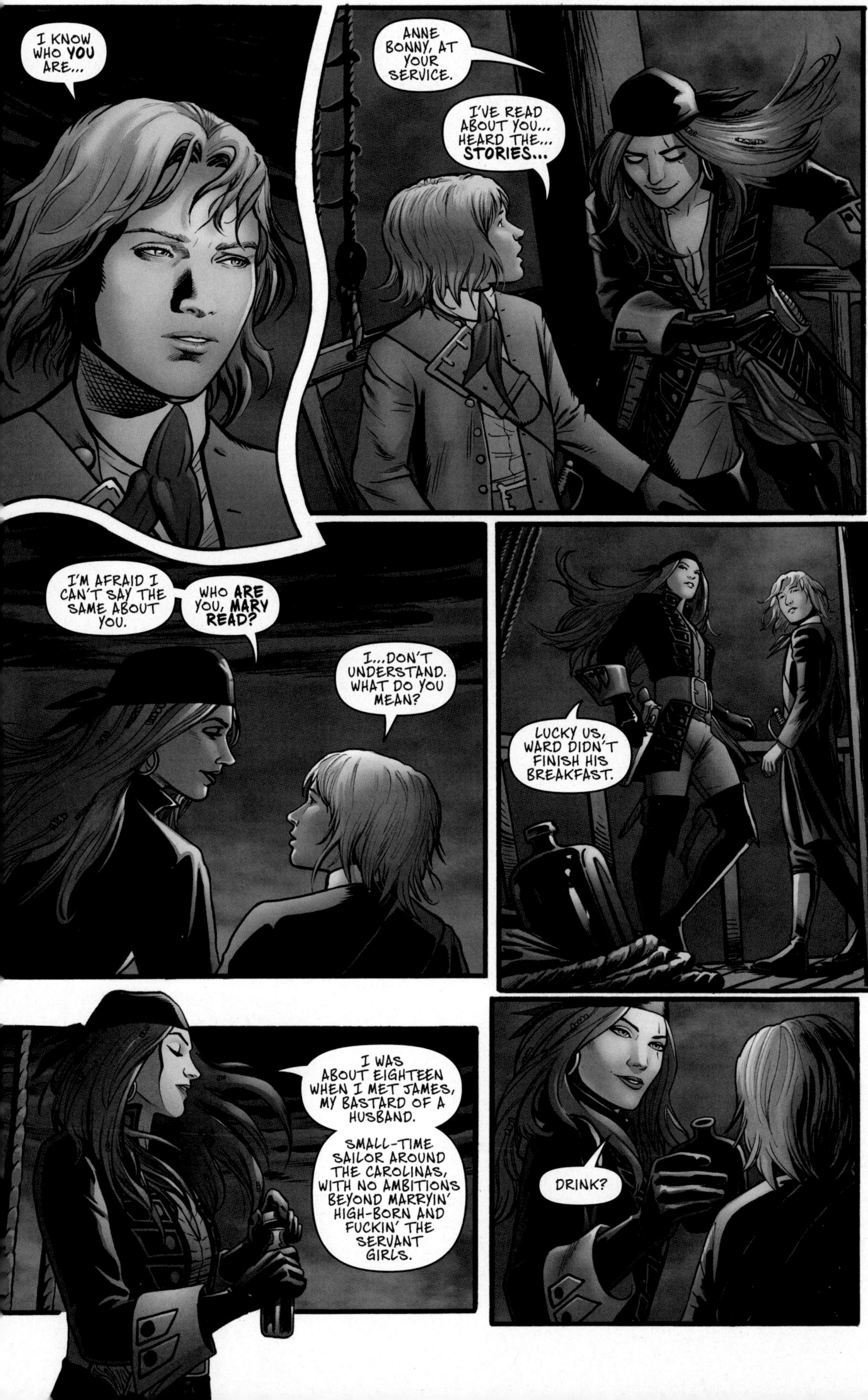
I KNOW WHO YOU ARE...
ANNE BONNY, AT YOUR SERVICE.
I'VE READ ABOUT YOU... HEARD THE... STORIES...
I'M AFRAID I CAN'T SAY THE SAME ABOUT YOU.
WHO ARE YOU, MARY READ?
I...DON'T UNDERSTAND. WHAT DO YOU MEAN?
LUCKY US, WARD DIDN'T FINISH HIS BREAKFAST.
I WAS ABOUT EIGHTEEN WHEN I MET JAMES, MY BASTARD OF A HUSBAND.
SMALL-TIME SAILOR AROUND THE CAROLINAS, WITH NO AMBITIONS BEYOND MARRYIN' HIGH-BORN AND FUCKIN' THE SERVANT GIRLS.
DRINK?

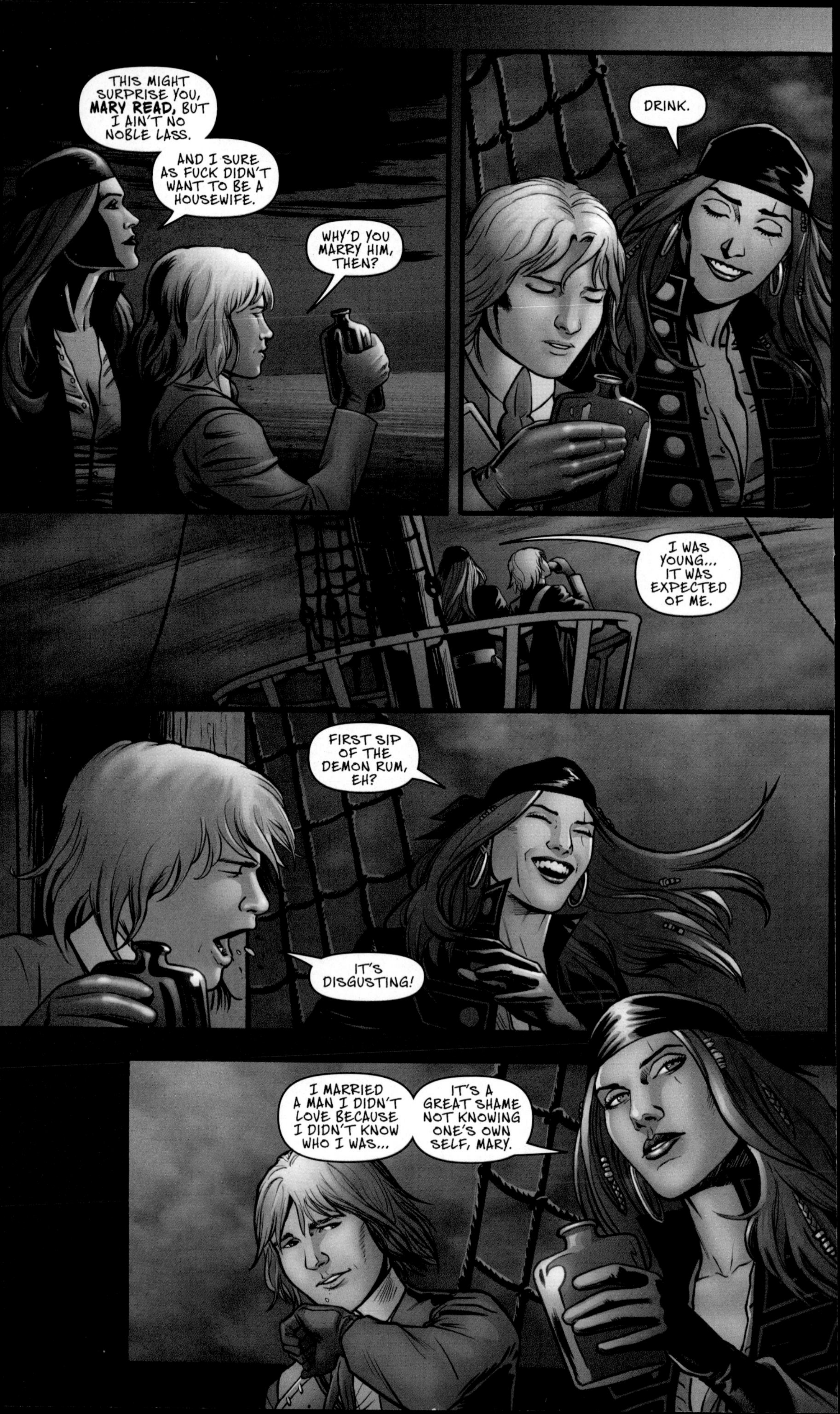
THIS MIGHT SURPRISE YOU, MARY READ, BUT I AIN'T NO NOBLE LASS.
AND I SURE AS FUCK DIDN'T WANT TO BE A HOUSEWIFE.
WHY'D YOU MARRY HIM, THEN?
DRINK.
I WAS YOUNG... IT WAS EXPECTED OF ME.
FIRST SIP OF THE DEMON RUM, EH?
IT'S DISGUSTING!
I MARRIED A MAN I DIDN'T LOVE BECAUSE I DIDN'T KNOW WHO I WAS...
IT'S A GREAT SHAME NOT KNOWING ONE'S OWN SELF, MARY.

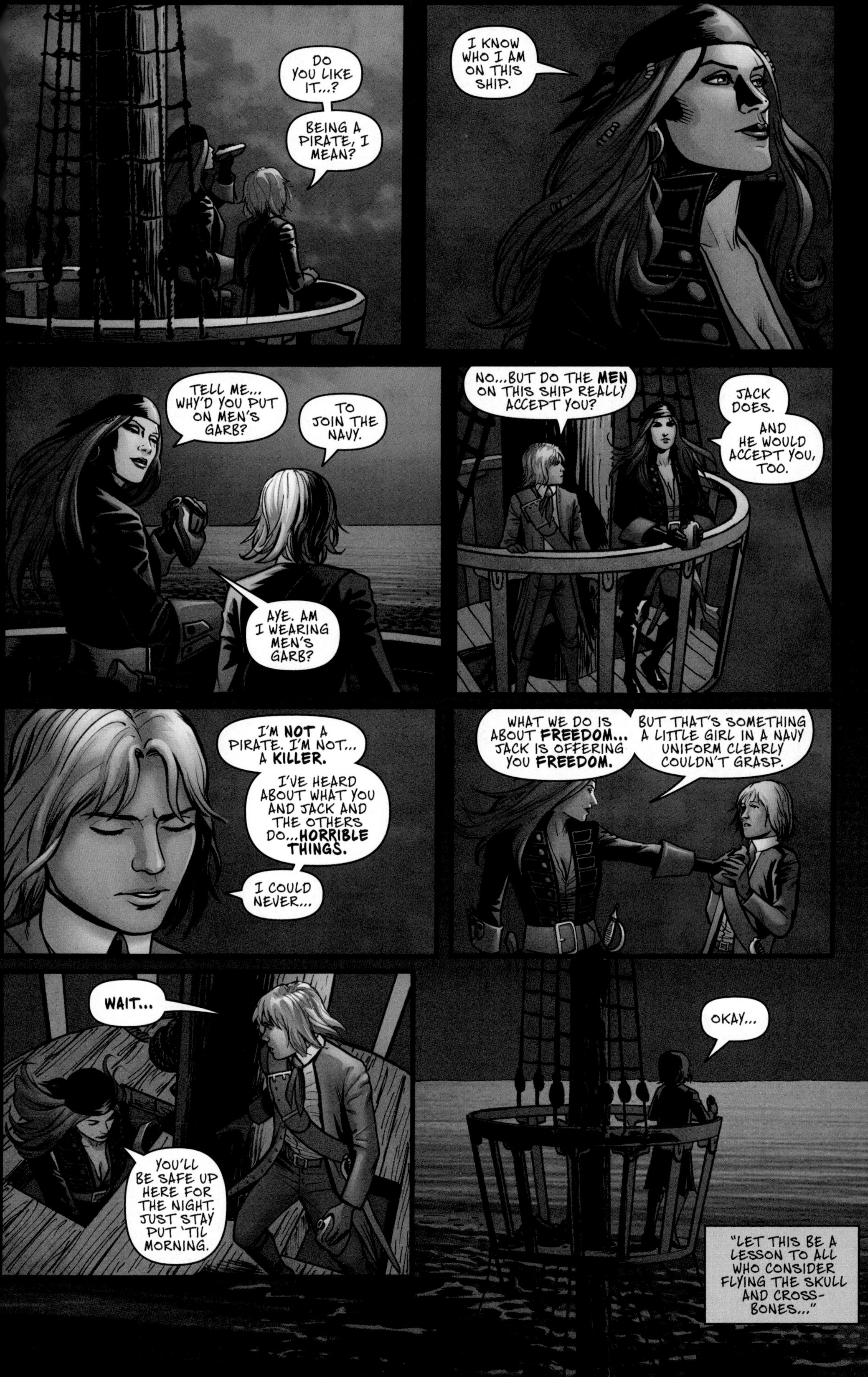
DO YOU LIKE IT...?
BEING A PIRATE, I MEAN?
I KNOW WHO I AM ON THIS SHIP.
TELL ME... WHY'D YOU PUT ON MEN'S GARB?
TO JOIN THE NAVY.
AYE. AM I WEARING MEN'S GARB?
NO...BUT DO THE **MEN** ON THIS SHIP REALLY ACCEPT YOU?
JACK DOES.
AND HE WOULD ACCEPT YOU, TOO.
I'M **NOT** A PIRATE. I'M NOT... A **KILLER.**
I'VE HEARD ABOUT WHAT YOU AND JACK AND THE OTHERS DO...**HORRIBLE THINGS.**
I COULD NEVER...
WHAT WE DO IS ABOUT **FREEDOM...** JACK IS OFFERING YOU **FREEDOM.**
BUT THAT'S SOMETHING A LITTLE GIRL IN A NAVY UNIFORM CLEARLY COULDN'T GRASP.
WAIT...
YOU'LL BE SAFE UP HERE FOR THE NIGHT. JUST STAY PUT 'TIL MORNING.
OKAY...
"LET THIS BE A LESSON TO ALL WHO CONSIDER FLYING THE SKULL AND CROSS-BONES..."

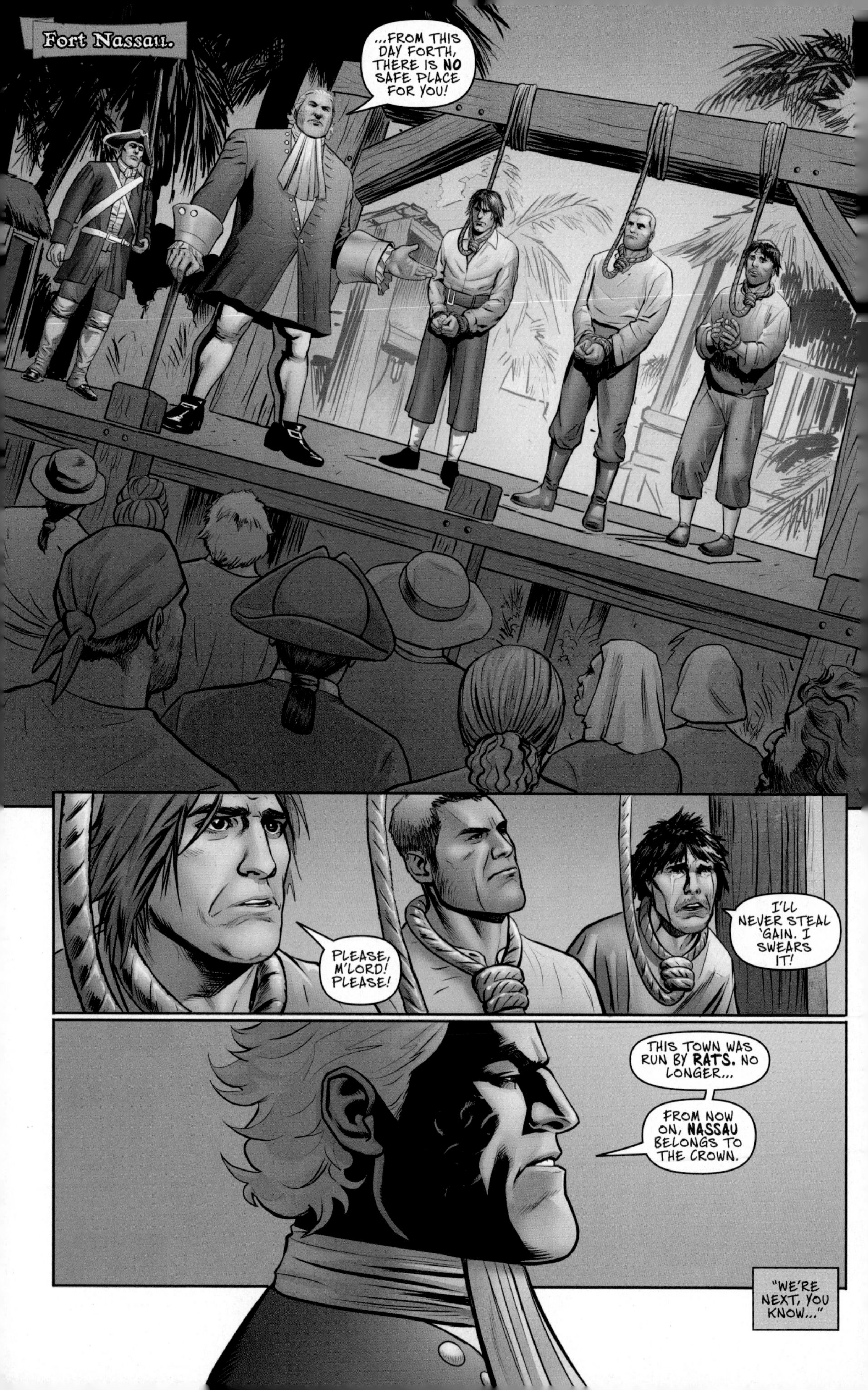
Fort Nassau.
...FROM THIS DAY FORTH, THERE IS NO SAFE PLACE FOR YOU!
PLEASE, M'LORD! PLEASE!
I'LL NEVER STEAL 'GAIN. I SWEARS IT!
THIS TOWN WAS RUN BY RATS. NO LONGER...
FROM NOW ON, NASSAU BELONGS TO THE CROWN.
"WE'RE NEXT, YOU KNOW..."

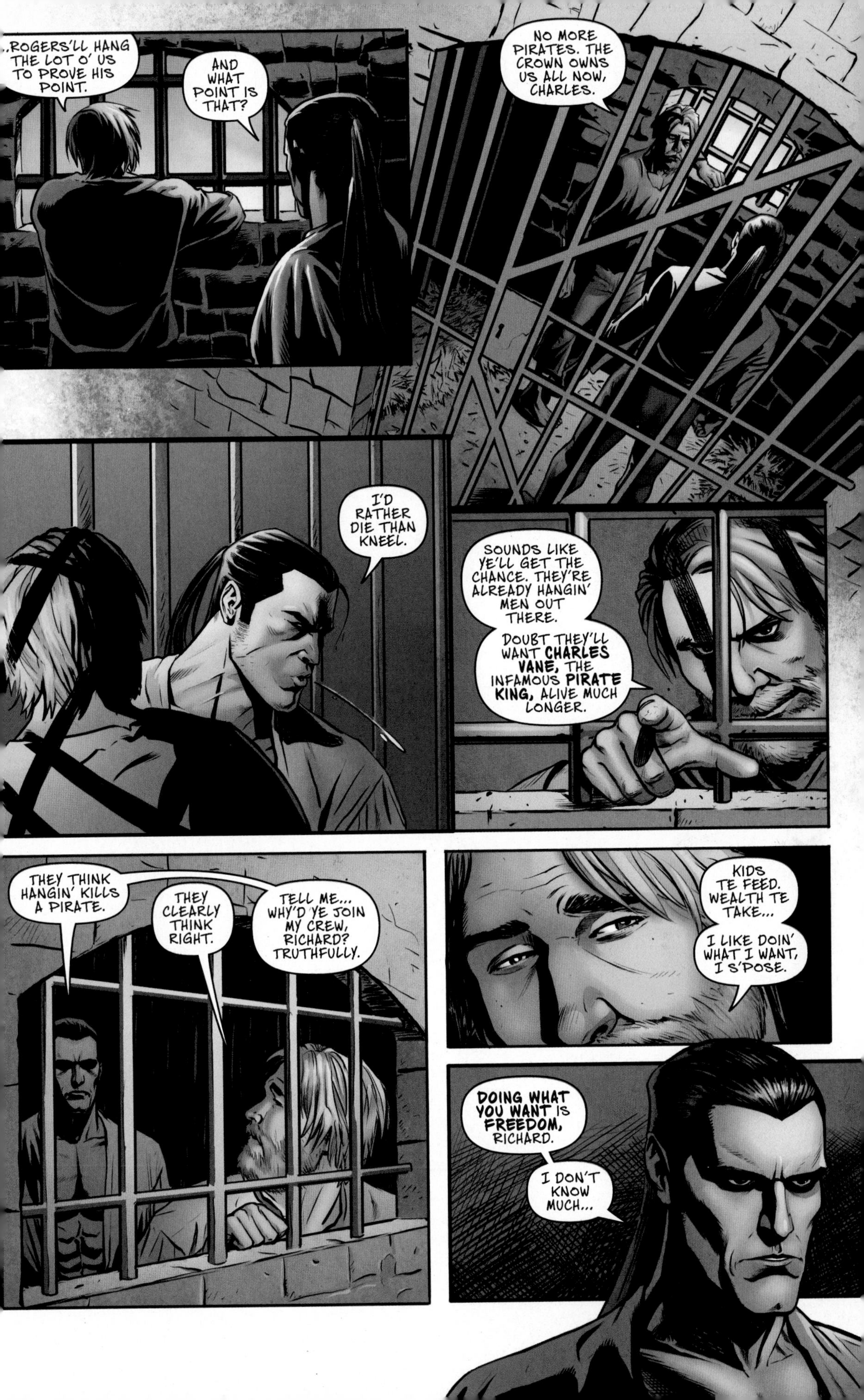
..ROGERS'LL HANG THE LOT O' US TO PROVE HIS POINT.
AND WHAT POINT IS THAT?
NO MORE PIRATES. THE CROWN OWNS US ALL NOW, CHARLES.
I'D RATHER DIE THAN KNEEL.
SOUNDS LIKE YE'LL GET THE CHANCE. THEY'RE ALREADY HANGIN' MEN OUT THERE.
DOUBT THEY'LL WANT CHARLES VANE, THE INFAMOUS PIRATE KING, ALIVE MUCH LONGER.
THEY THINK HANGIN' KILLS A PIRATE.
THEY CLEARLY THINK RIGHT.
TELL ME... WHY'D YE JOIN MY CREW, RICHARD? TRUTHFULLY.
KIDS TE FEED. WEALTH TE TAKE...
I LIKE DOIN' WHAT I WANT, I S'POSE.
DOING WHAT YOU WANT IS FREEDOM, RICHARD.
I DON'T KNOW MUCH...

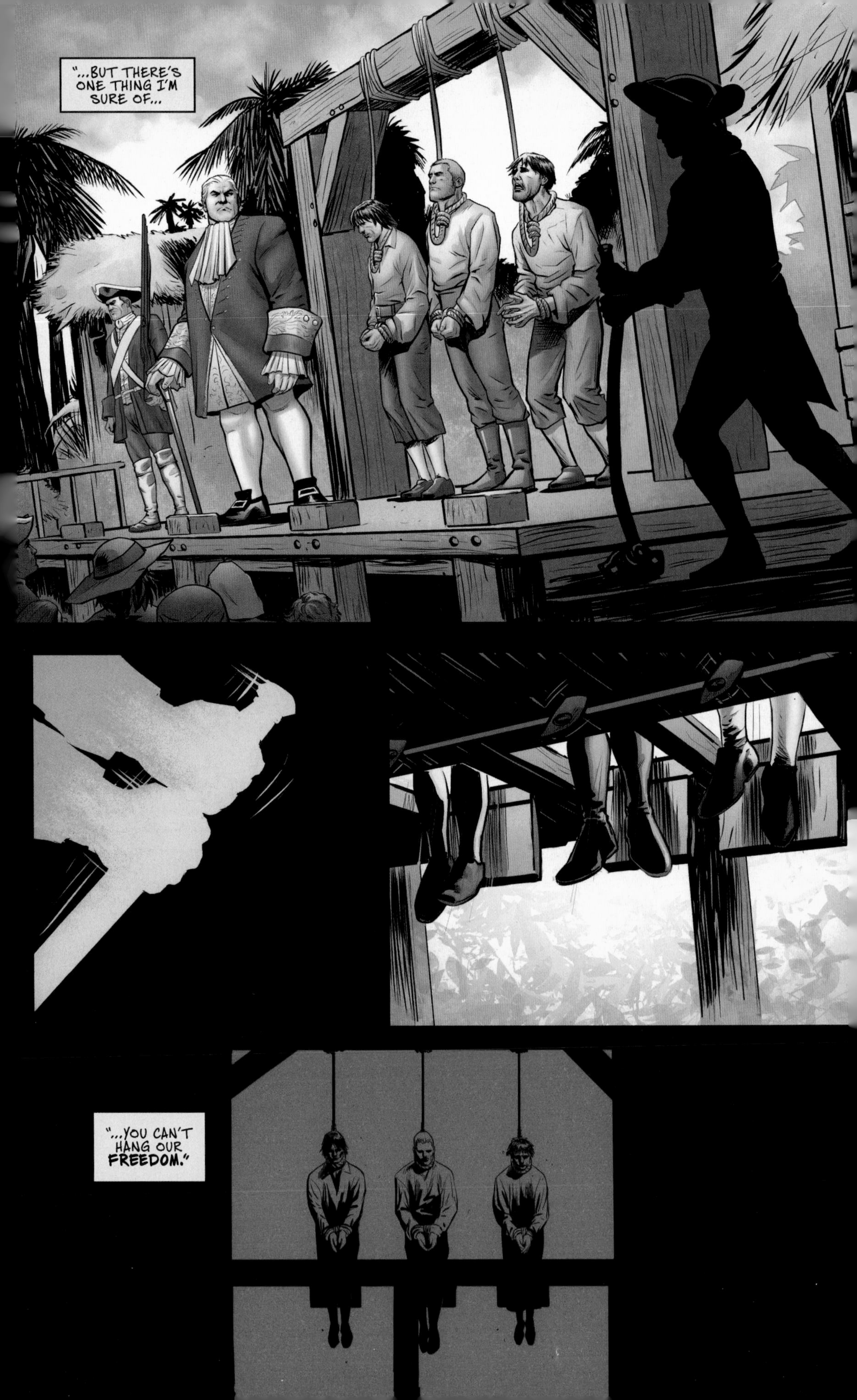
"...BUT THERE'S ONE THING I'M SURE OF...
"...YOU CAN'T HANG OUR FREEDOM."

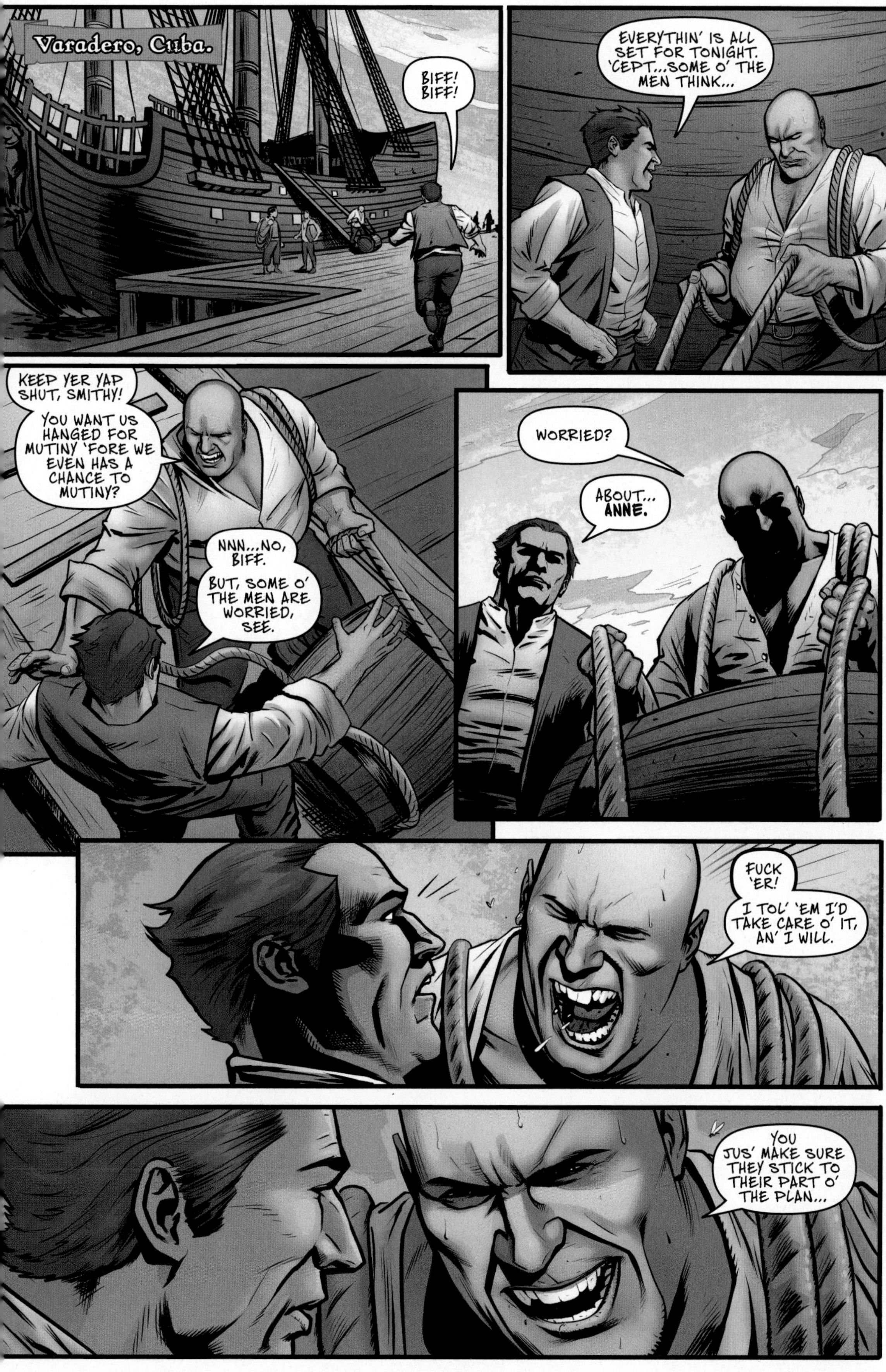
Varadero, Cuba.
BIFF! BIFF!
EVERYTHIN' IS ALL SET FOR TONIGHT. 'CEPT...SOME O' THE MEN THINK...
KEEP YER YAP SHUT, SMITHY!
YOU WANT US HANGED FOR MUTINY 'FORE WE EVEN HAS A CHANCE TO MUTINY?
NNN...NO, BIFF.
BUT, SOME O' THE MEN ARE WORRIED, SEE.
WORRIED?
ABOUT... **ANNE.**
FUCK 'ER!
I TOL' 'EM I'D TAKE CARE O' IT, AN' I WILL.
YOU JUS' MAKE SURE THEY STICK TO THEIR PART O' THE PLAN...

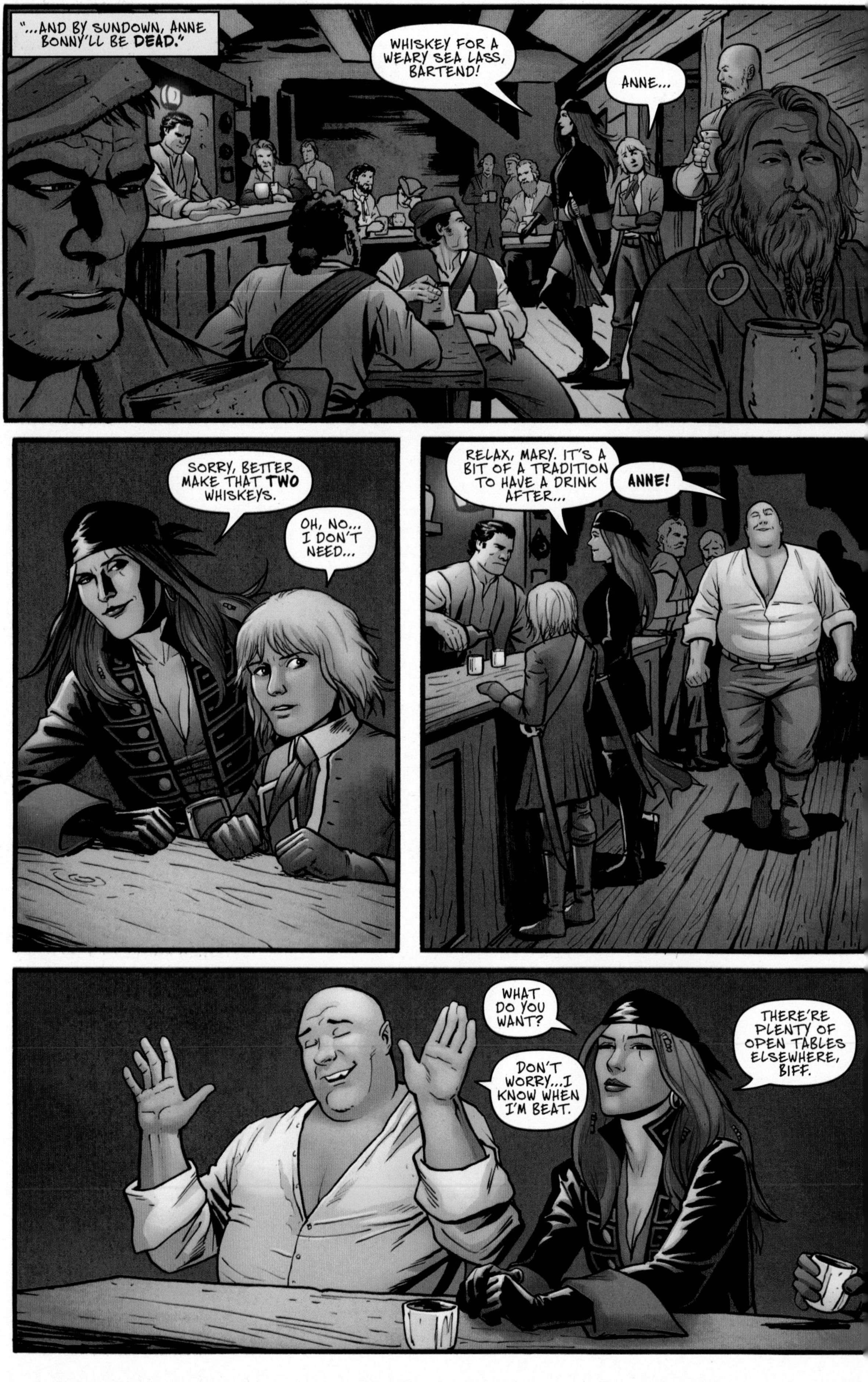
"...AND BY SUNDOWN, ANNE BONNY'LL BE **DEAD**."
WHISKEY FOR A WEARY SEA LASS, BARTEND!
ANNE...
SORRY, BETTER MAKE THAT **TWO** WHISKEYS.
OH, NO... I DON'T NEED...
RELAX, MARY. IT'S A BIT OF A TRADITION TO HAVE A DRINK AFTER...
ANNE!
WHAT DO YOU WANT?
DON'T WORRY...I KNOW WHEN I'M BEAT.
THERE'RE PLENTY OF OPEN TABLES ELSEWHERE, BIFF.

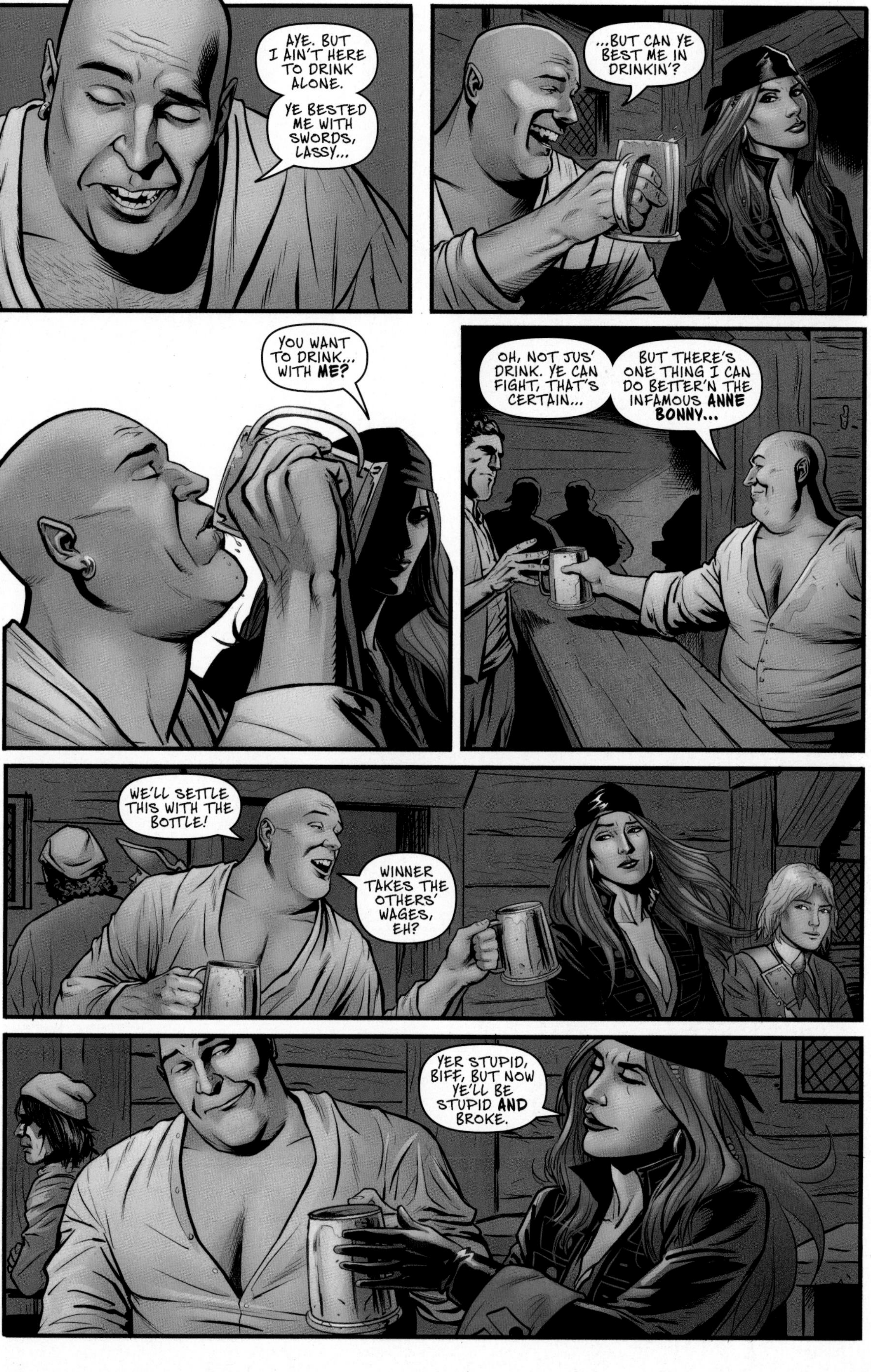
AYE. BUT I AIN'T HERE TO DRINK ALONE.
YE BESTED ME WITH SWORDS, LASSY...
...BUT CAN YE BEST ME IN DRINKIN'?
YOU WANT TO DRINK... WITH ME?
OH, NOT JUS' DRINK. YE CAN FIGHT, THAT'S CERTAIN...
BUT THERE'S ONE THING I CAN DO BETTER'N THE INFAMOUS ANNE BONNY...
WE'LL SETTLE THIS WITH THE BOTTLE!
WINNER TAKES THE OTHERS' WAGES, EH?
YER STUPID, BIFF, BUT NOW YE'LL BE STUPID AND BROKE.

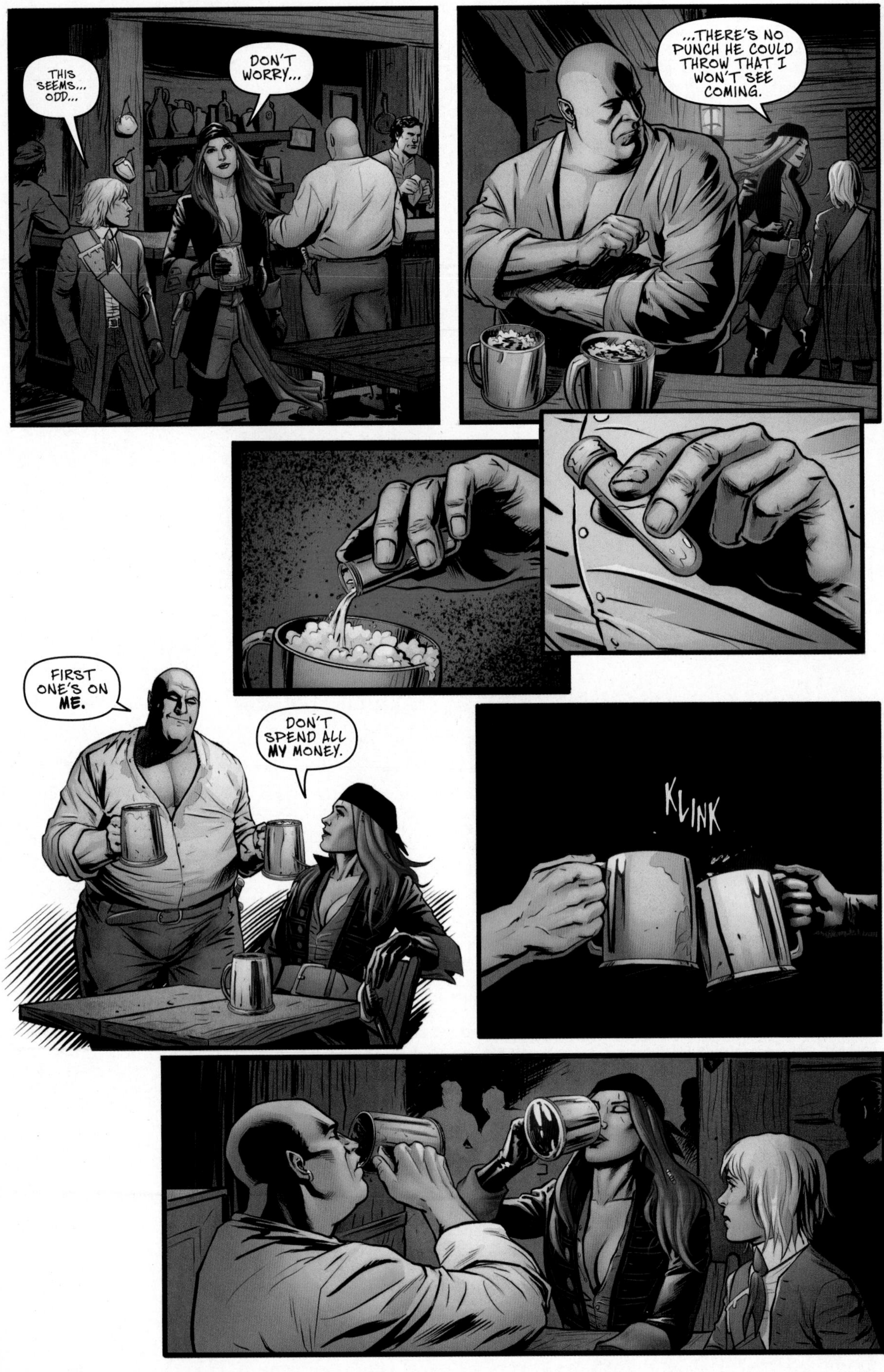
THIS SEEMS... ODD...
DON'T WORRY...
...THERE'S NO PUNCH HE COULD THROW THAT I WON'T SEE COMING.
FIRST ONE'S ON ME.
DON'T SPEND ALL MY MONEY.
KLINK

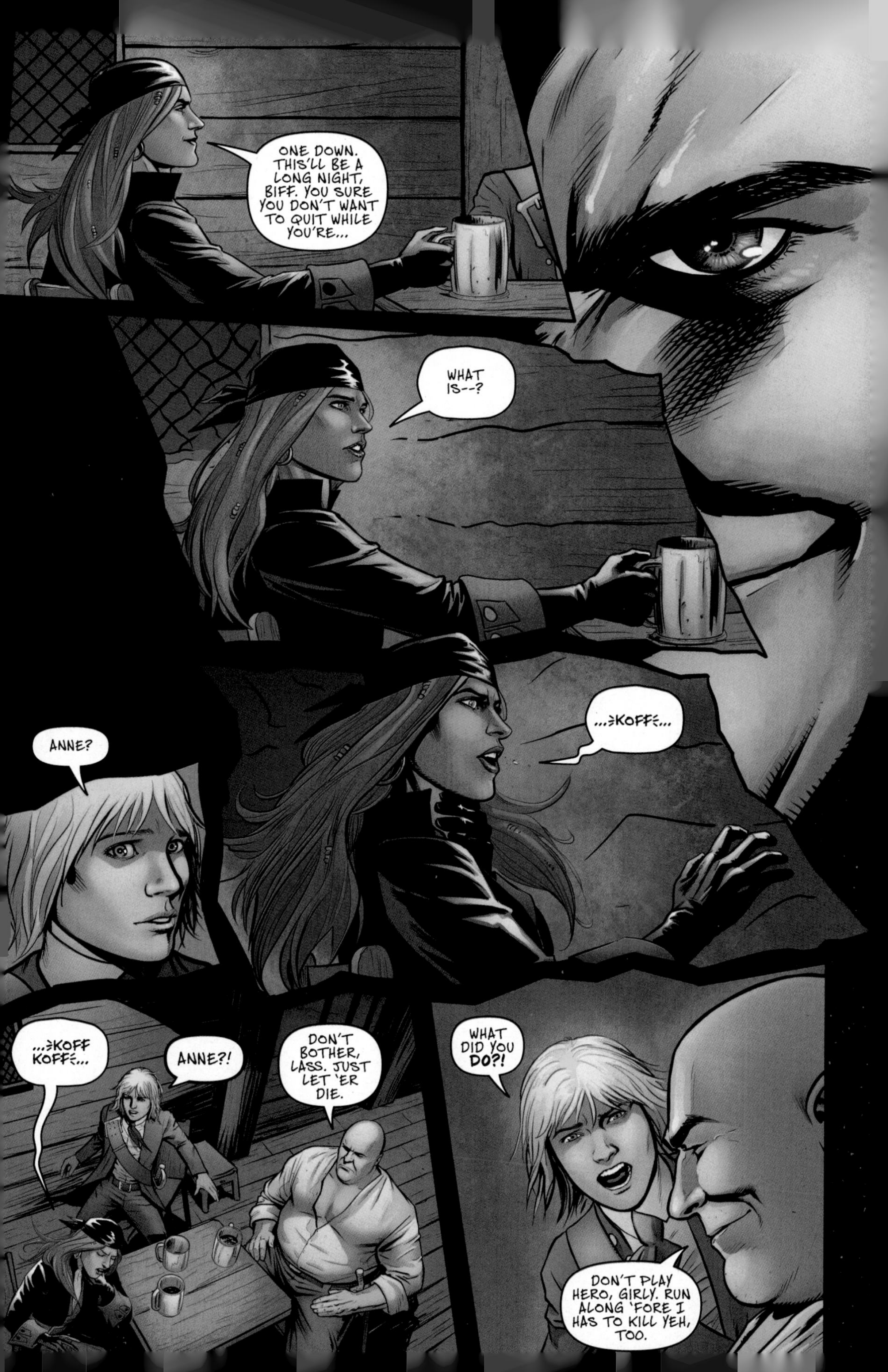
ONE DOWN. THIS'LL BE A LONG NIGHT, BIFF. YOU SURE YOU DON'T WANT TO QUIT WHILE YOU'RE...
WHAT IS--?
...KOFF...
ANNE?
...KOFF KOFF...
ANNE?!
DON'T BOTHER, LASS. JUST LET 'ER DIE.
WHAT DID YOU DO?!
DON'T PLAY HERO, GIRLY. RUN ALONG 'FORE I HAS TO KILL YEH, TOO.

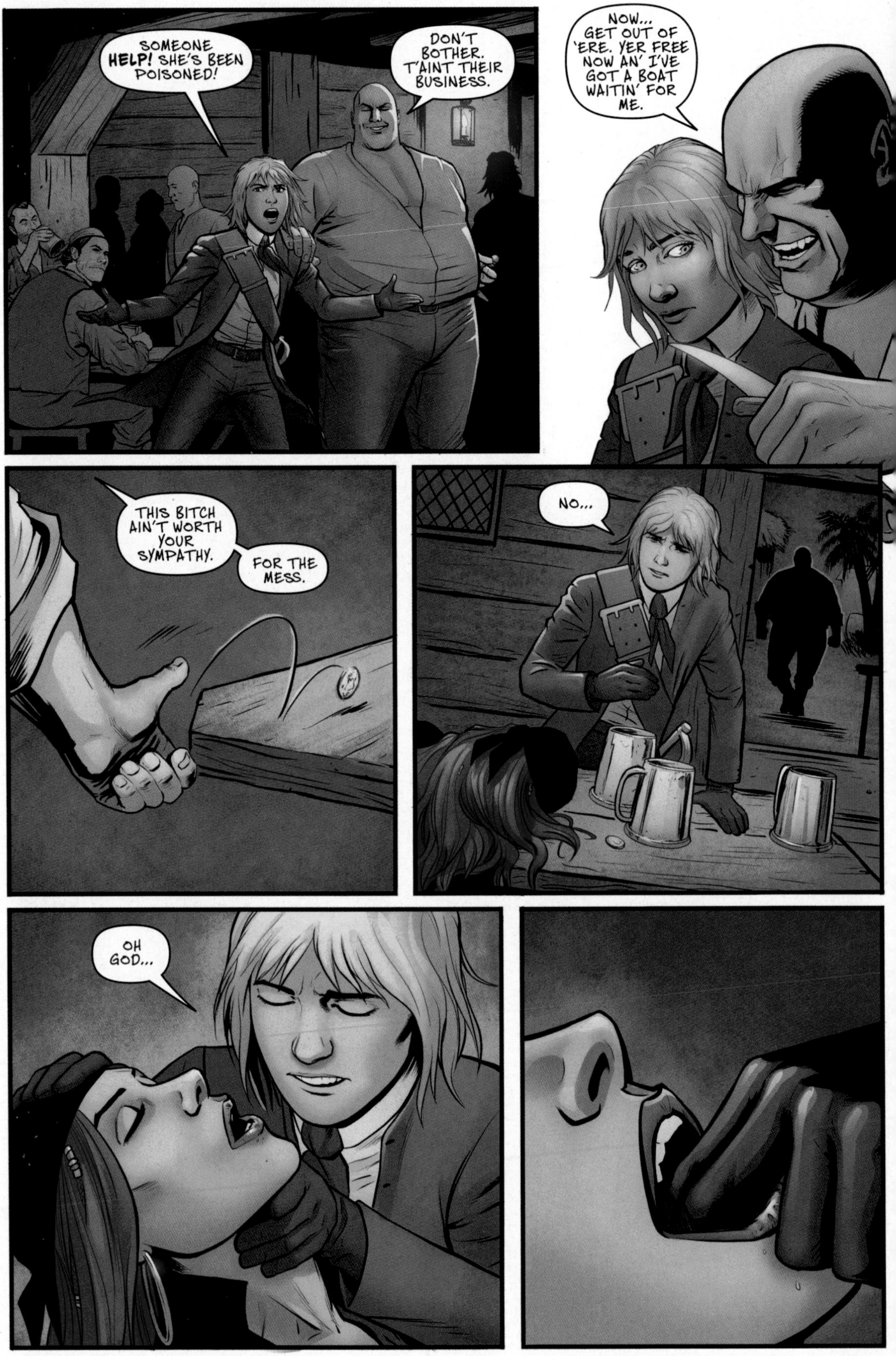
SOMEONE **HELP!** SHE'S BEEN POISONED!
DON'T BOTHER. T'AINT THEIR BUSINESS.
NOW... GET OUT OF 'ERE. YER FREE NOW AN' I'VE GOT A BOAT WAITIN' FOR ME.
THIS BITCH AIN'T WORTH YOUR SYMPATHY.
FOR THE MESS.
NO...
OH GOD...

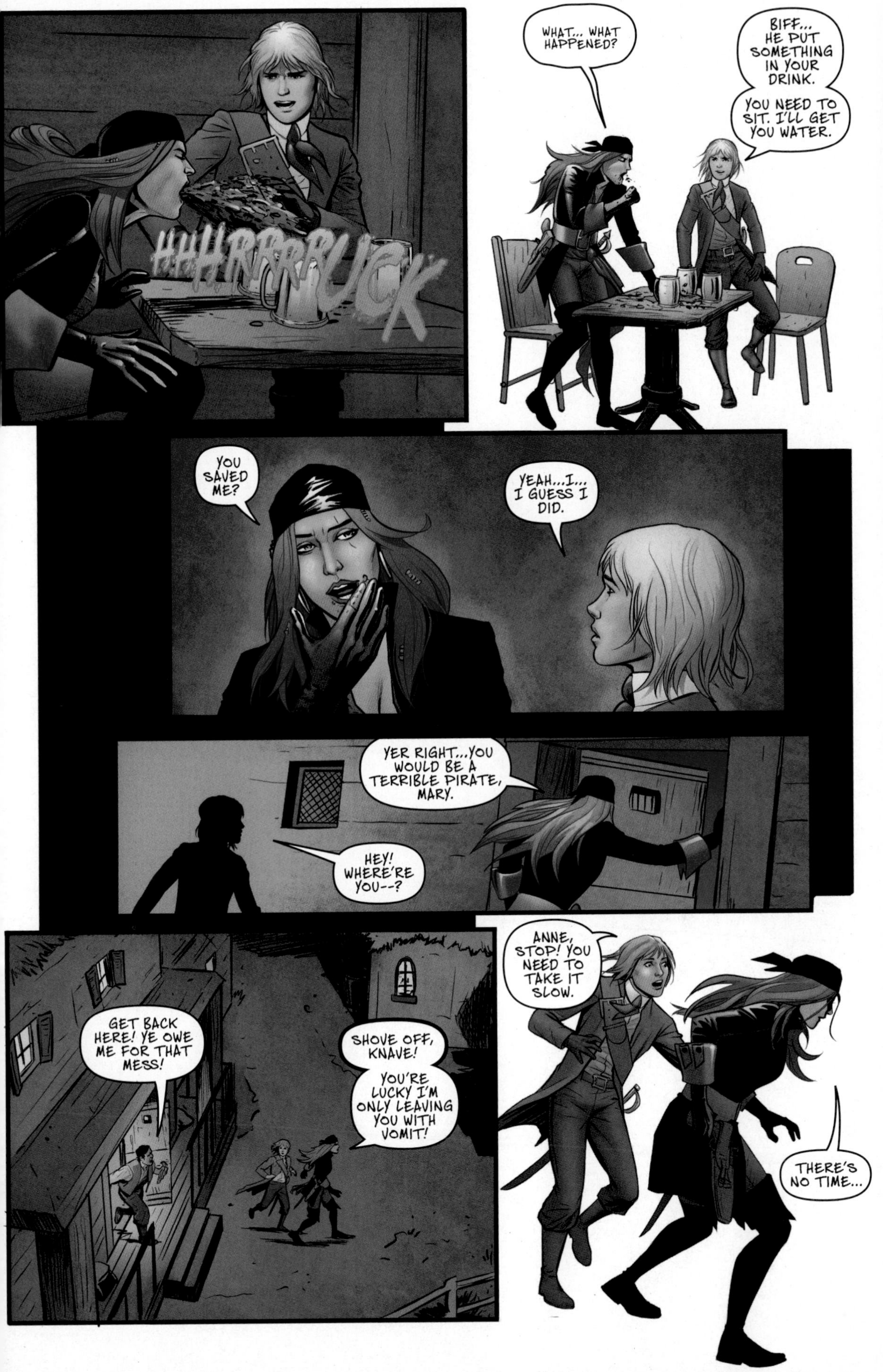
HHHRRRRRUCK
WHAT... WHAT HAPPENED?
BIFF... HE PUT SOMETHING IN YOUR DRINK.
YOU NEED TO SIT. I'LL GET YOU WATER.
YOU SAVED ME?
YEAH...I... I GUESS I DID.
YER RIGHT...YOU WOULD BE A TERRIBLE PIRATE, MARY.
HEY! WHERE'RE YOU--?
GET BACK HERE! YE OWE ME FOR THAT MESS!
SHOVE OFF, KNAVE!
YOU'RE LUCKY I'M ONLY LEAVING YOU WITH VOMIT!
ANNE, STOP! YOU NEED TO TAKE IT SLOW.
THERE'S NO TIME...

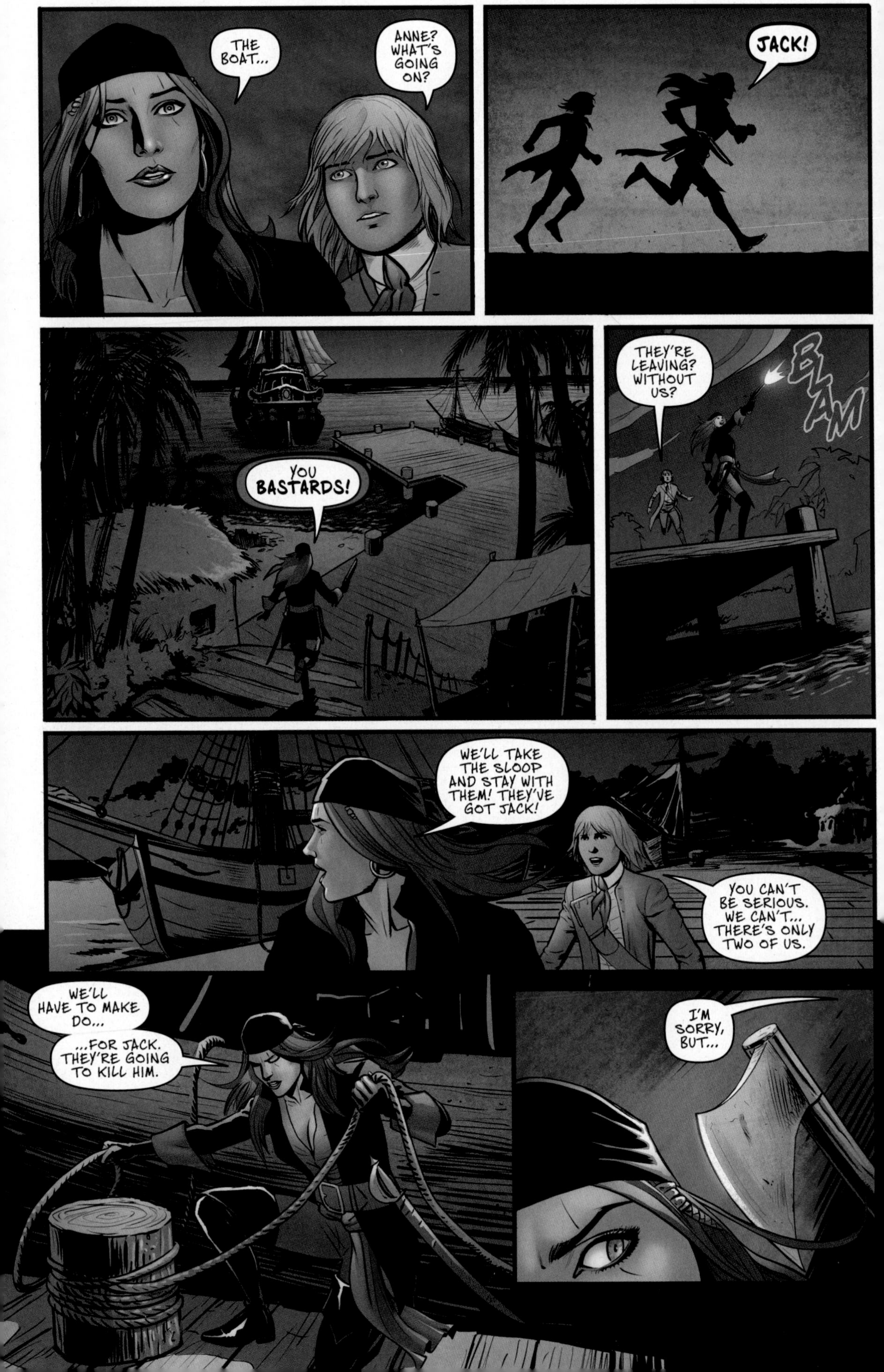
THE BOAT...
ANNE? WHAT'S GOING ON?
JACK!
YOU BASTARDS!
THEY'RE LEAVING? WITHOUT US?
BLAM
WE'LL TAKE THE SLOOP AND STAY WITH THEM! THEY'VE GOT JACK!
YOU CAN'T BE SERIOUS. WE CAN'T... THERE'S ONLY TWO OF US.
WE'LL HAVE TO MAKE DO...
...FOR JACK. THEY'RE GOING TO KILL HIM.
I'M SORRY, BUT...

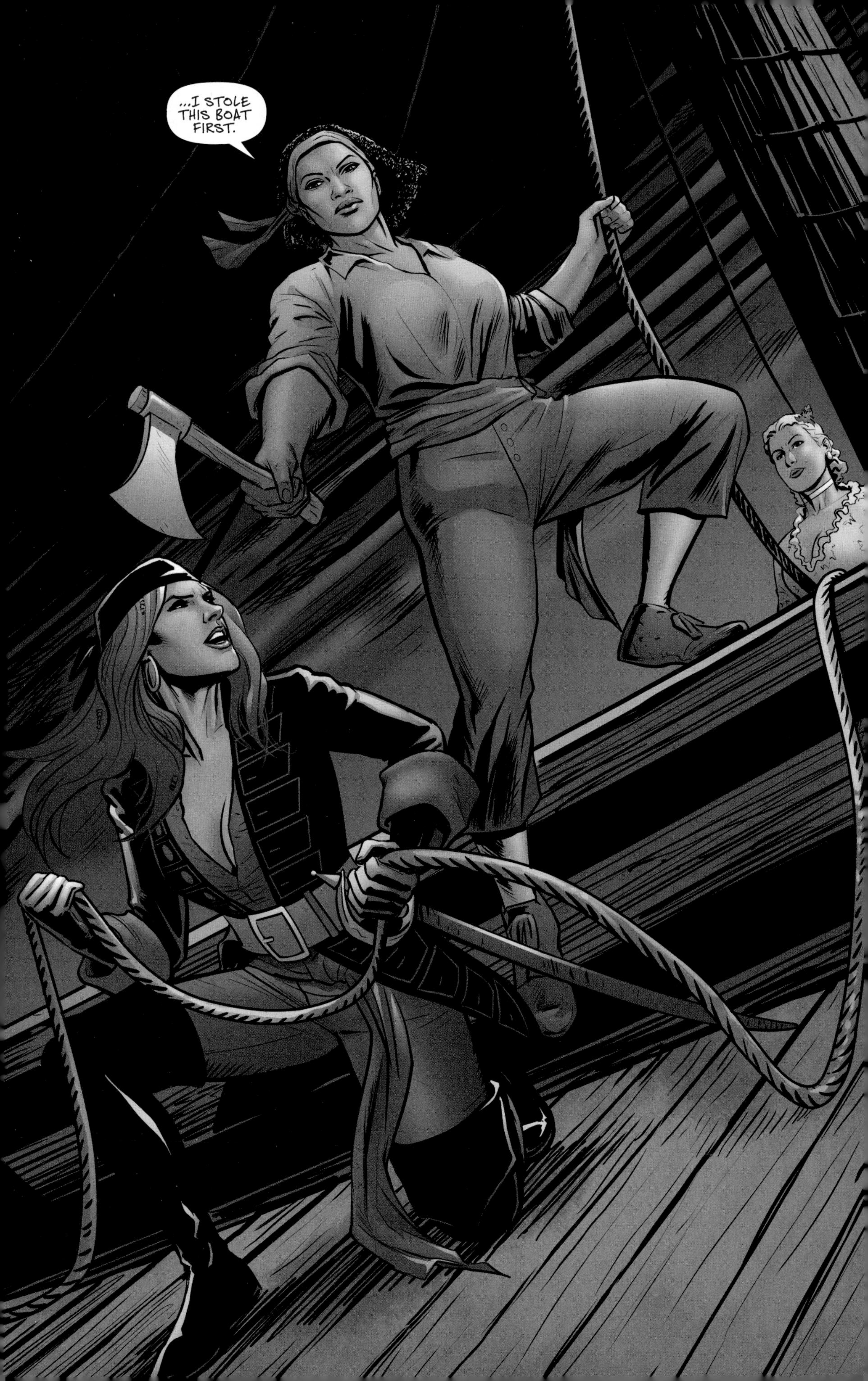
...I STOLE THIS BOAT FIRST.

Chapter 3

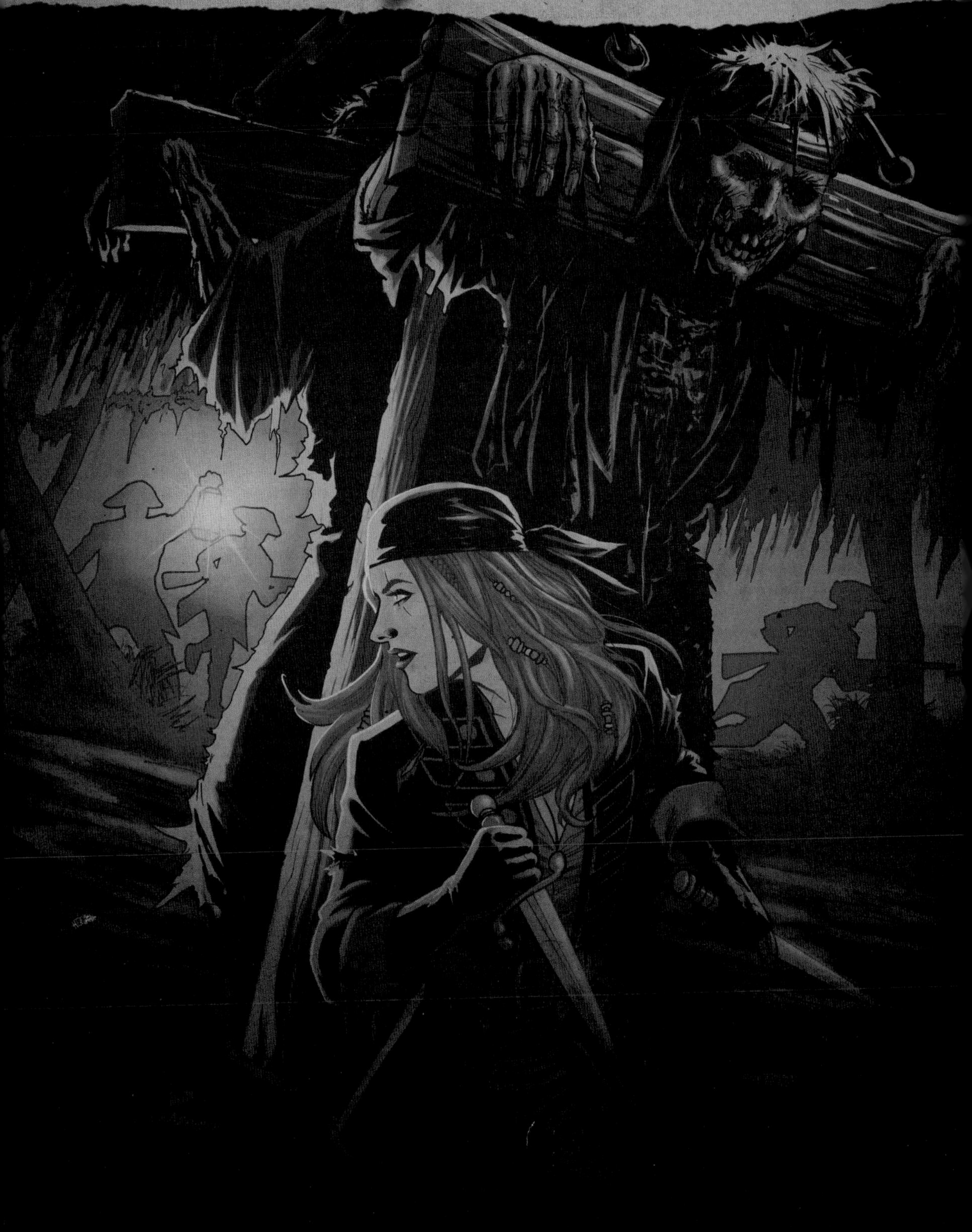

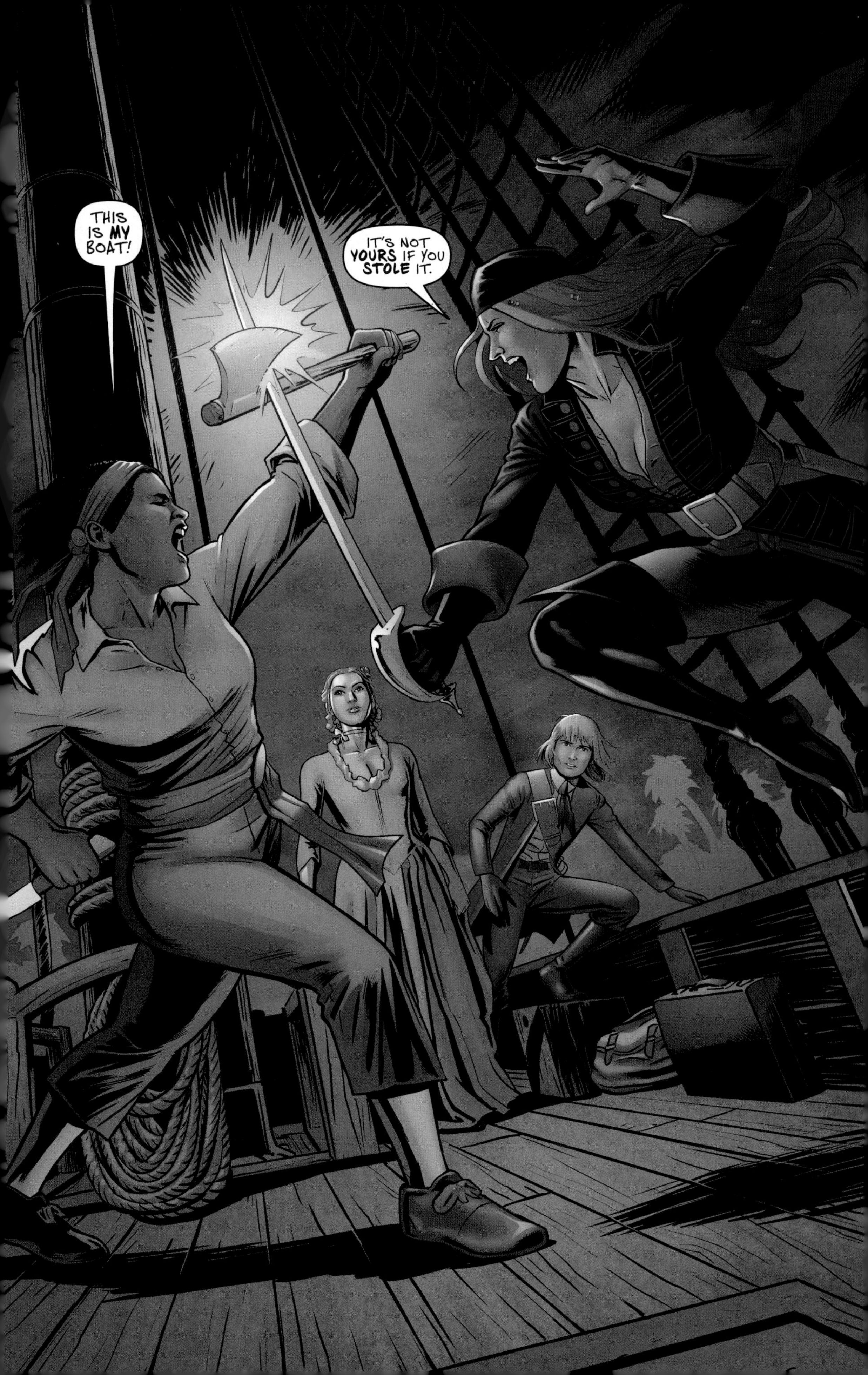
THIS IS MY BOAT!
IT'S NOT YOURS IF YOU STOLE IT.

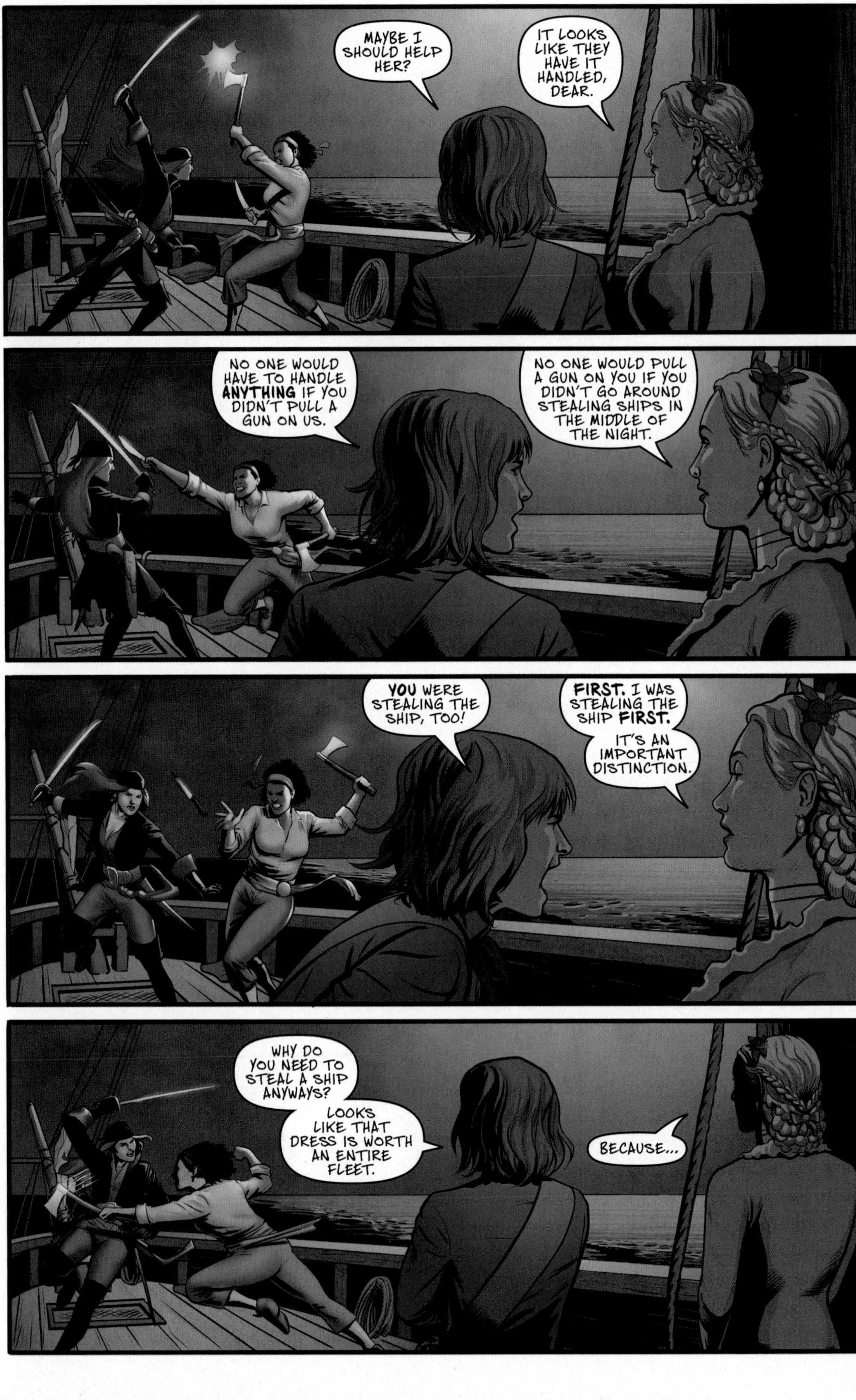
MAYBE I SHOULD HELP HER?
IT LOOKS LIKE THEY HAVE IT HANDLED, DEAR.
NO ONE WOULD HAVE TO HANDLE **ANYTHING** IF YOU DIDN'T PULL A GUN ON US.
NO ONE WOULD PULL A GUN ON YOU IF YOU DIDN'T GO AROUND STEALING SHIPS IN THE MIDDLE OF THE NIGHT.
YOU WERE STEALING THE SHIP, TOO!
FIRST. I WAS STEALING THE SHIP **FIRST.**
IT'S AN IMPORTANT DISTINCTION.
WHY DO YOU NEED TO STEAL A SHIP ANYWAYS?
LOOKS LIKE THAT DRESS IS WORTH AN ENTIRE FLEET.
BECAUSE...

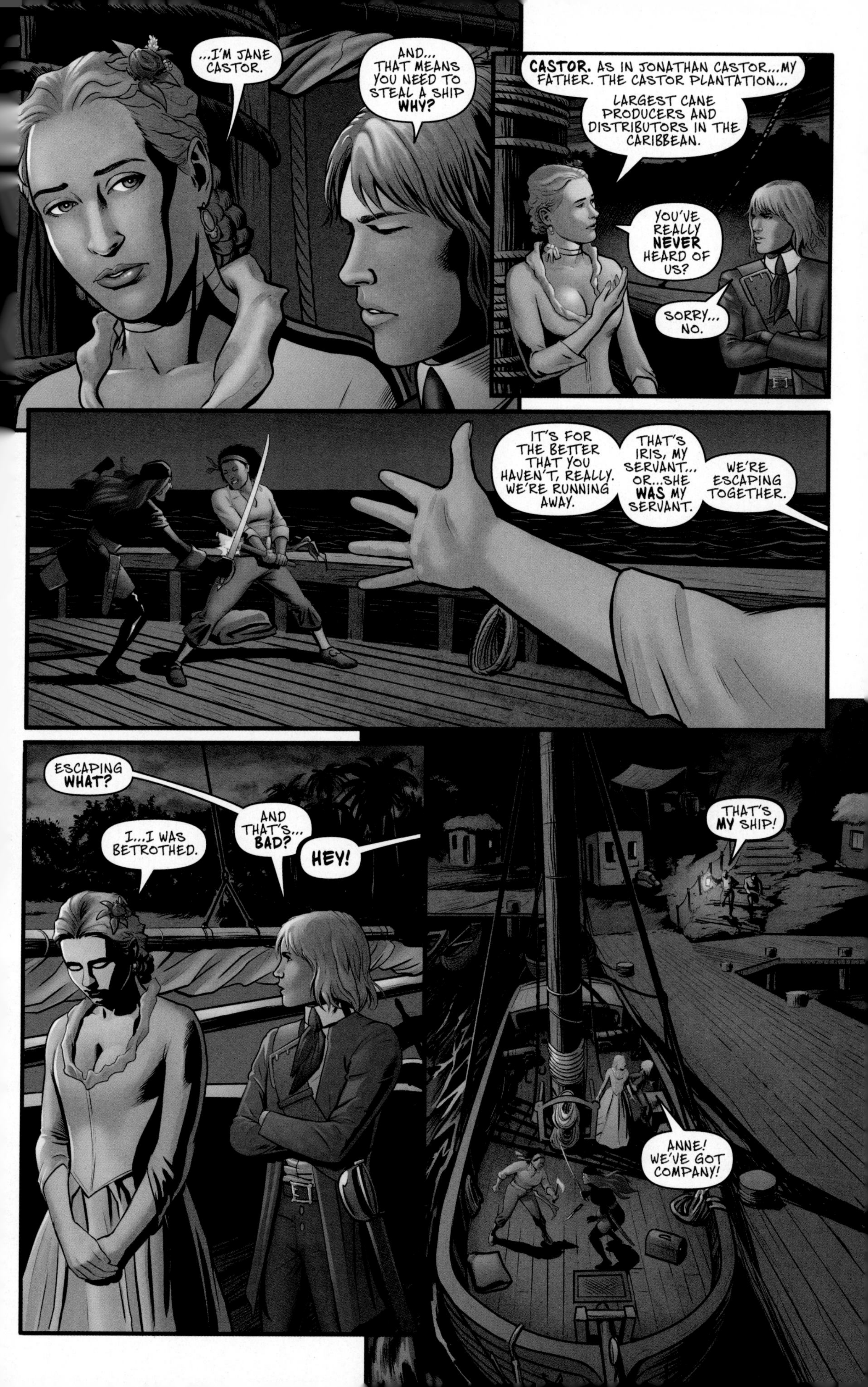
...I'M JANE CASTOR.
AND... THAT MEANS YOU NEED TO STEAL A SHIP **WHY?**
CASTOR. AS IN JONATHAN CASTOR...MY FATHER. THE CASTOR PLANTATION...
LARGEST CANE PRODUCERS AND DISTRIBUTORS IN THE CARIBBEAN.
YOU'VE REALLY **NEVER** HEARD OF US?
SORRY... NO.
IT'S FOR THE BETTER THAT YOU HAVEN'T, REALLY. WE'RE RUNNING AWAY.
THAT'S IRIS, MY SERVANT... OR...SHE **WAS** MY SERVANT.
WE'RE ESCAPING TOGETHER.
ESCAPING **WHAT?**
I...I WAS BETROTHED.
AND THAT'S... **BAD?**
HEY!
THAT'S **MY** SHIP!
ANNE! WE'VE GOT COMPANY!

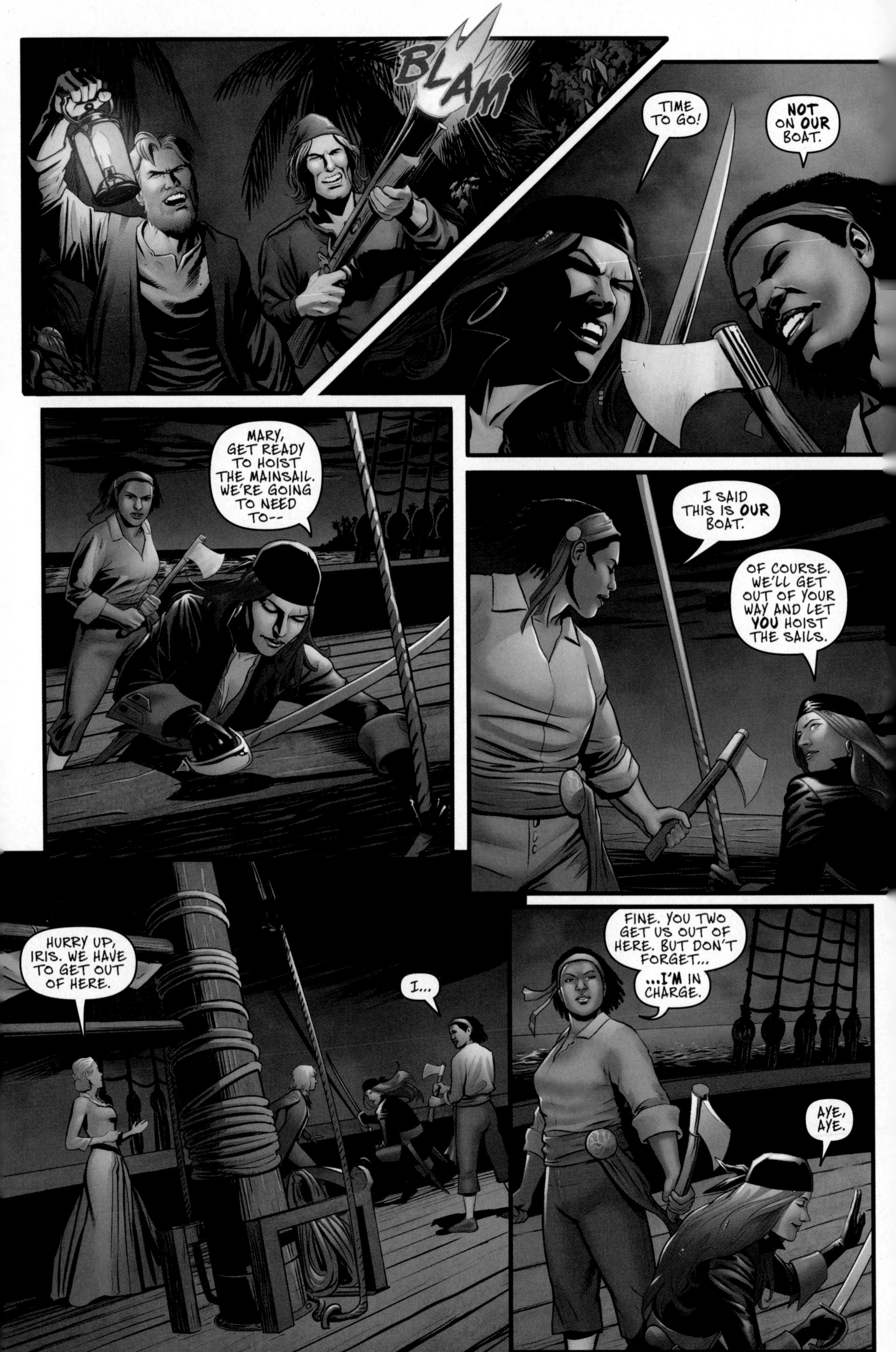
BLAM
TIME TO GO!
NOT ON OUR BOAT.
MARY, GET READY TO HOIST THE MAINSAIL. WE'RE GOING TO NEED TO--
I SAID THIS IS OUR BOAT.
OF COURSE. WE'LL GET OUT OF YOUR WAY AND LET YOU HOIST THE SAILS.
HURRY UP, IRIS. WE HAVE TO GET OUT OF HERE.
I...
FINE. YOU TWO GET US OUT OF HERE. BUT DON'T FORGET...
...I'M IN CHARGE.
AYE, AYE.

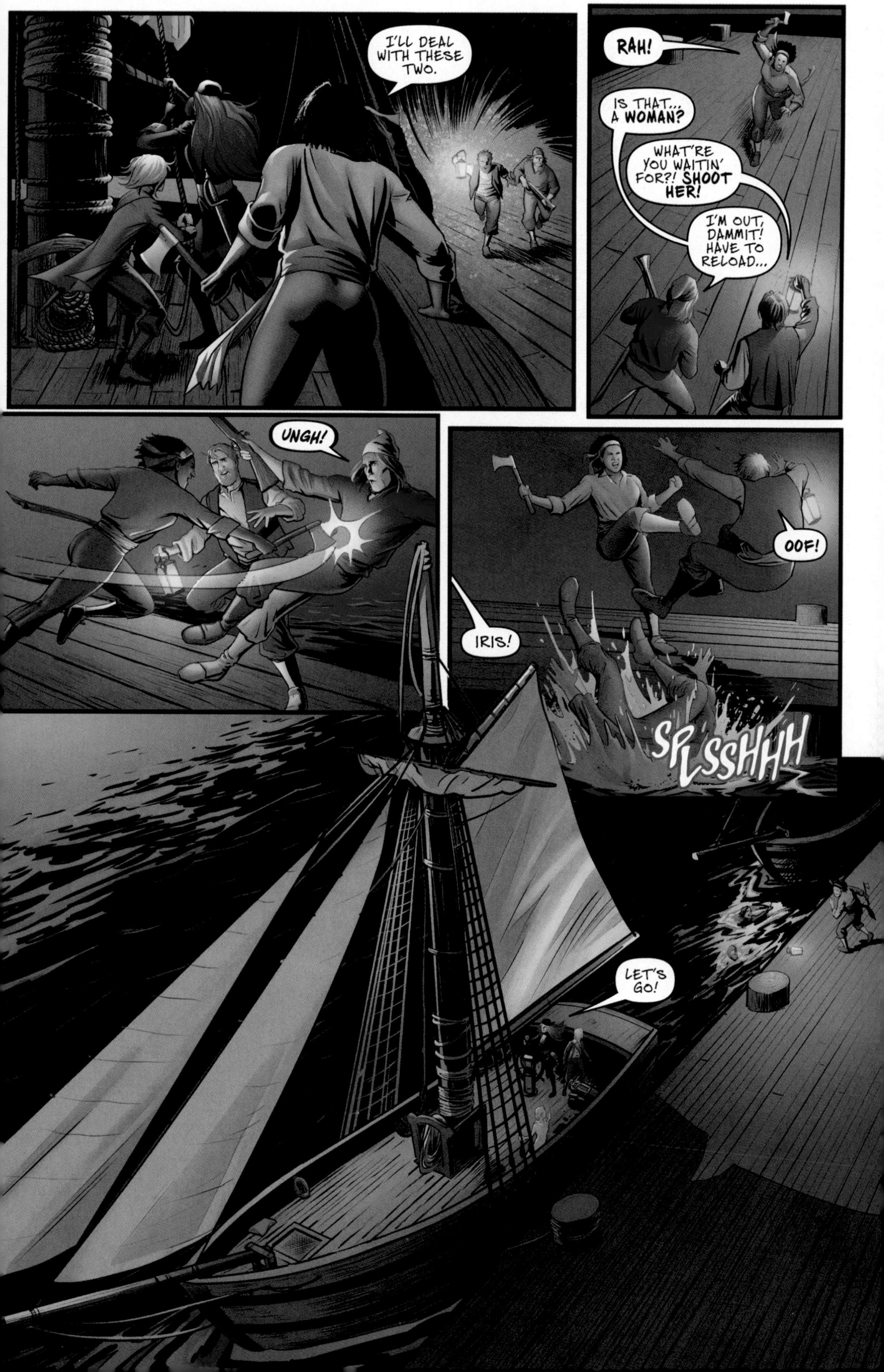
I'LL DEAL WITH THESE TWO.
RAH!
IS THAT... A WOMAN?
WHAT'RE YOU WAITIN' FOR?! SHOOT HER!
I'M OUT, DAMMIT! HAVE TO RELOAD...
UNGH!
IRIS!
OOF!
SPLSSHHH
LET'S GO!

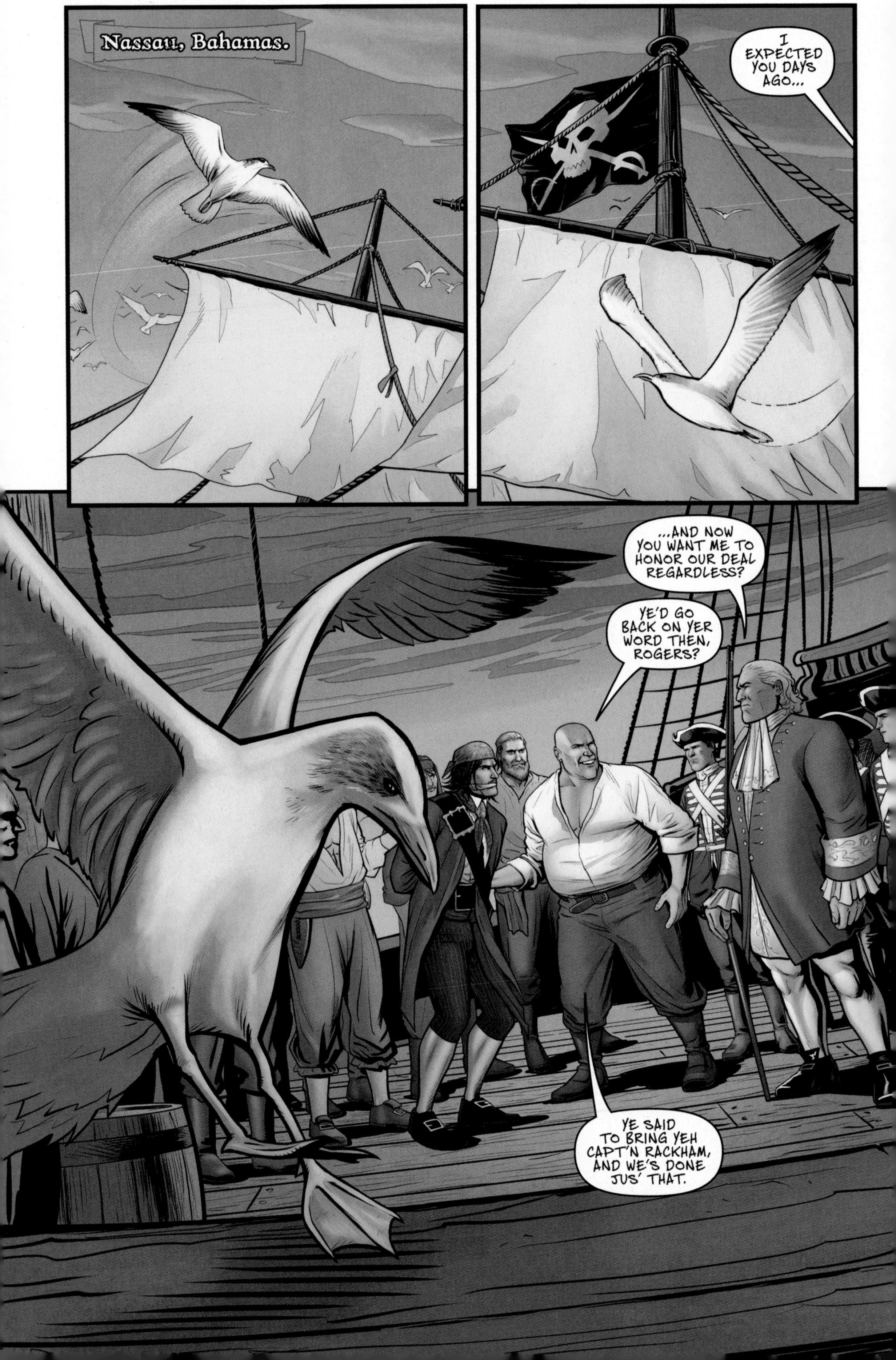
Nassau, Bahamas.
I EXPECTED YOU DAYS AGO...
...AND NOW YOU WANT ME TO HONOR OUR DEAL REGARDLESS?
YE'D GO BACK ON YER WORD THEN, ROGERS?
YE SAID TO BRING YEH CAPT'N RACKHAM, AND WE'S DONE JUS' THAT.

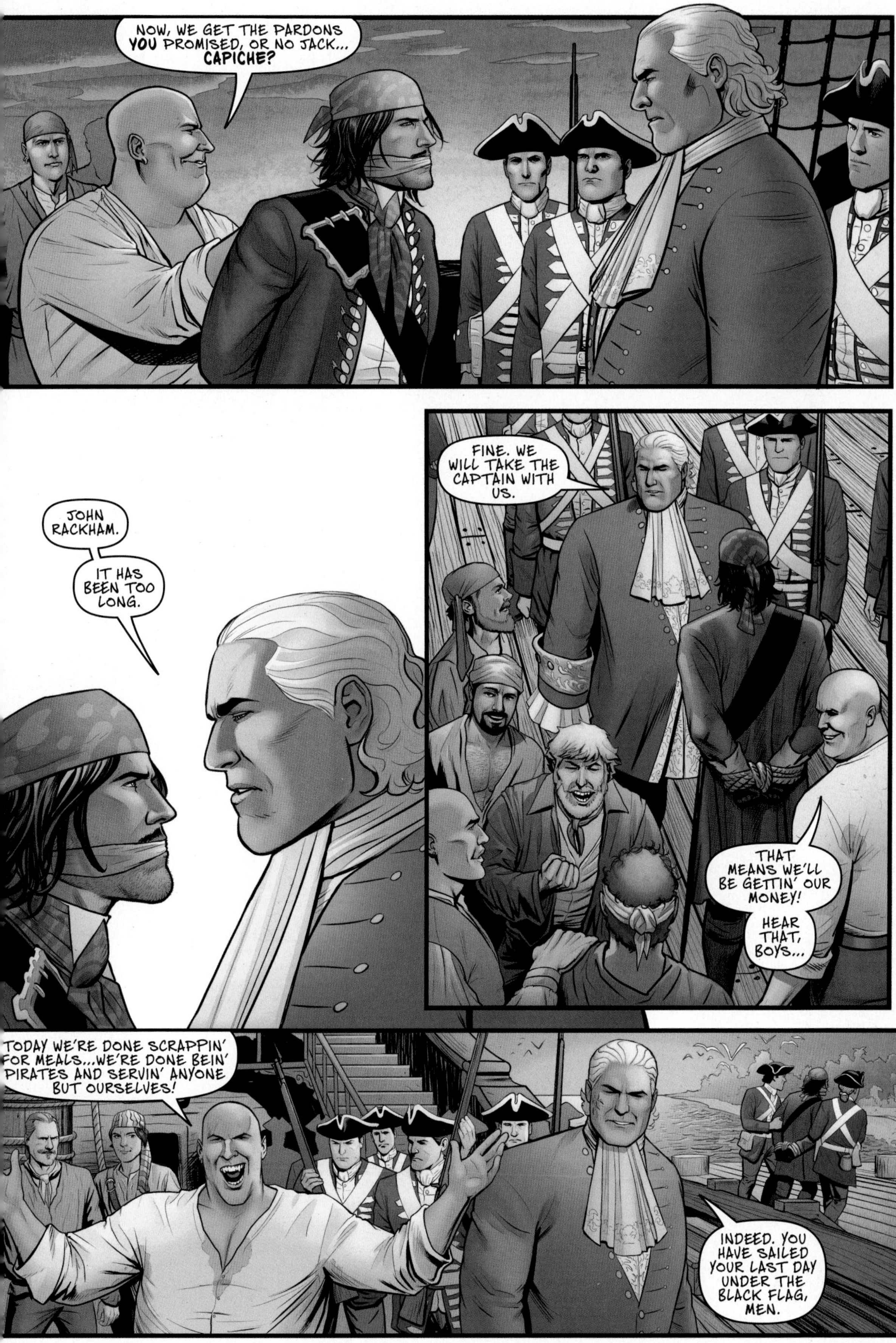
NOW, WE GET THE PARDONS YOU PROMISED, OR NO JACK... CAPICHE?
FINE. WE WILL TAKE THE CAPTAIN WITH US.
JOHN RACKHAM.
IT HAS BEEN TOO LONG.
THAT MEANS WE'LL BE GETTIN' OUR MONEY!
HEAR THAT, BOYS...
TODAY WE'RE DONE SCRAPPIN' FOR MEALS...WE'RE DONE BEIN' PIRATES AND SERVIN' ANYONE BUT OURSELVES!
INDEED. YOU HAVE SAILED YOUR LAST DAY UNDER THE BLACK FLAG, MEN.

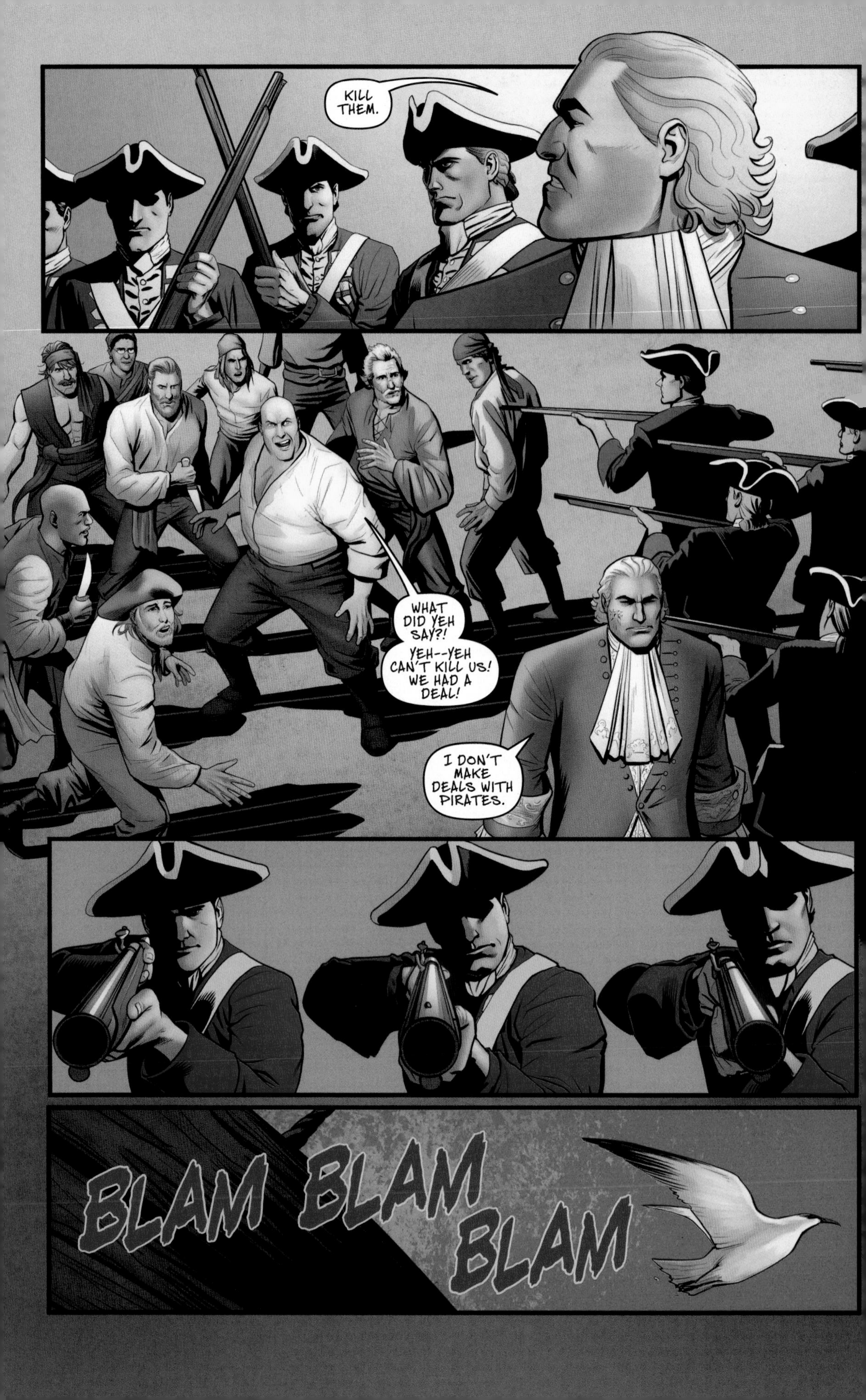
KILL THEM.
WHAT DID YEH SAY?!
YEH--YEH CAN'T KILL US! WE HAD A DEAL!
I DON'T MAKE DEALS WITH PIRATES.
BLAM BLAM BLAM

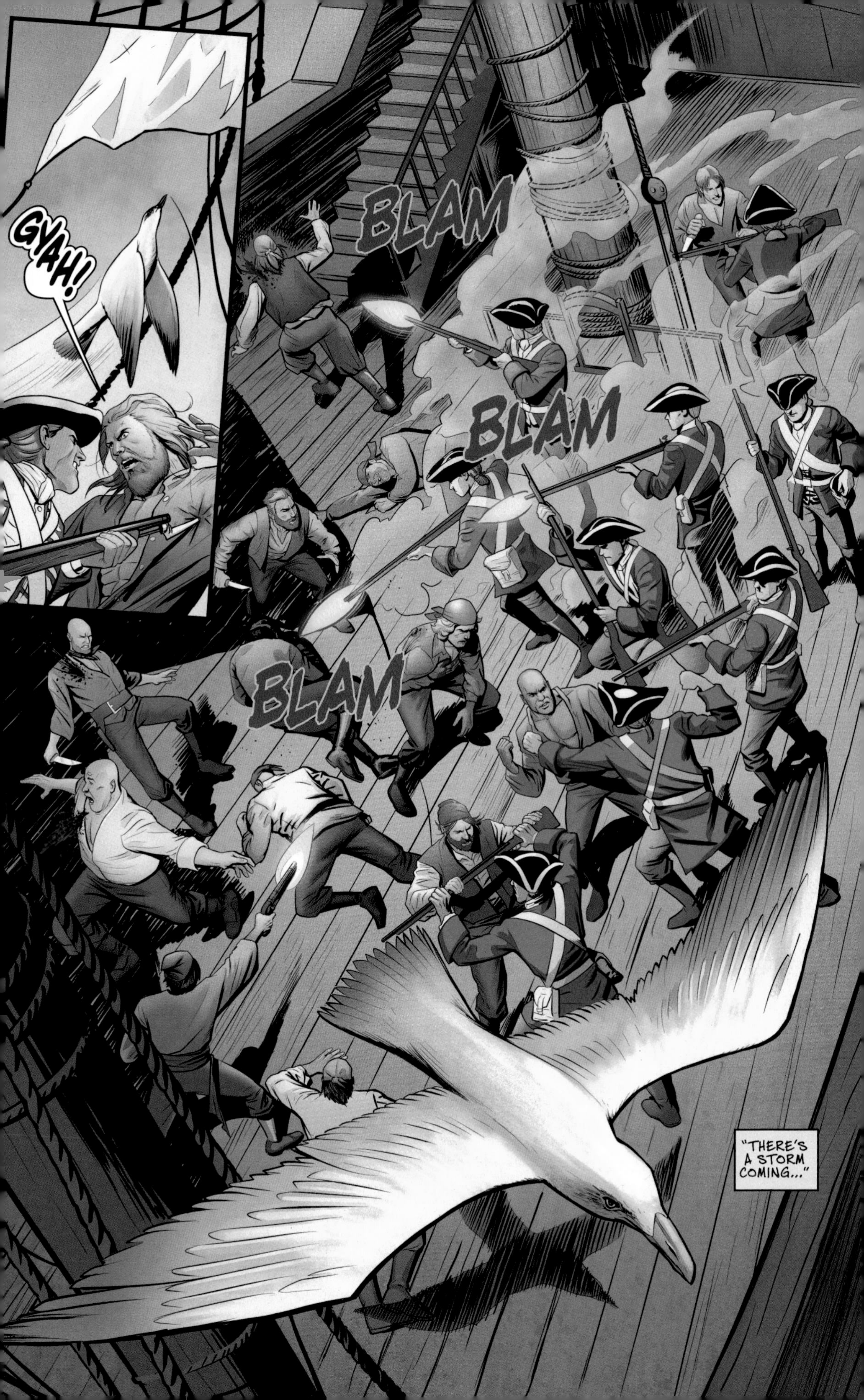
GYAH!
BLAM
BLAM
BLAM
"THERE'S A STORM COMING..."

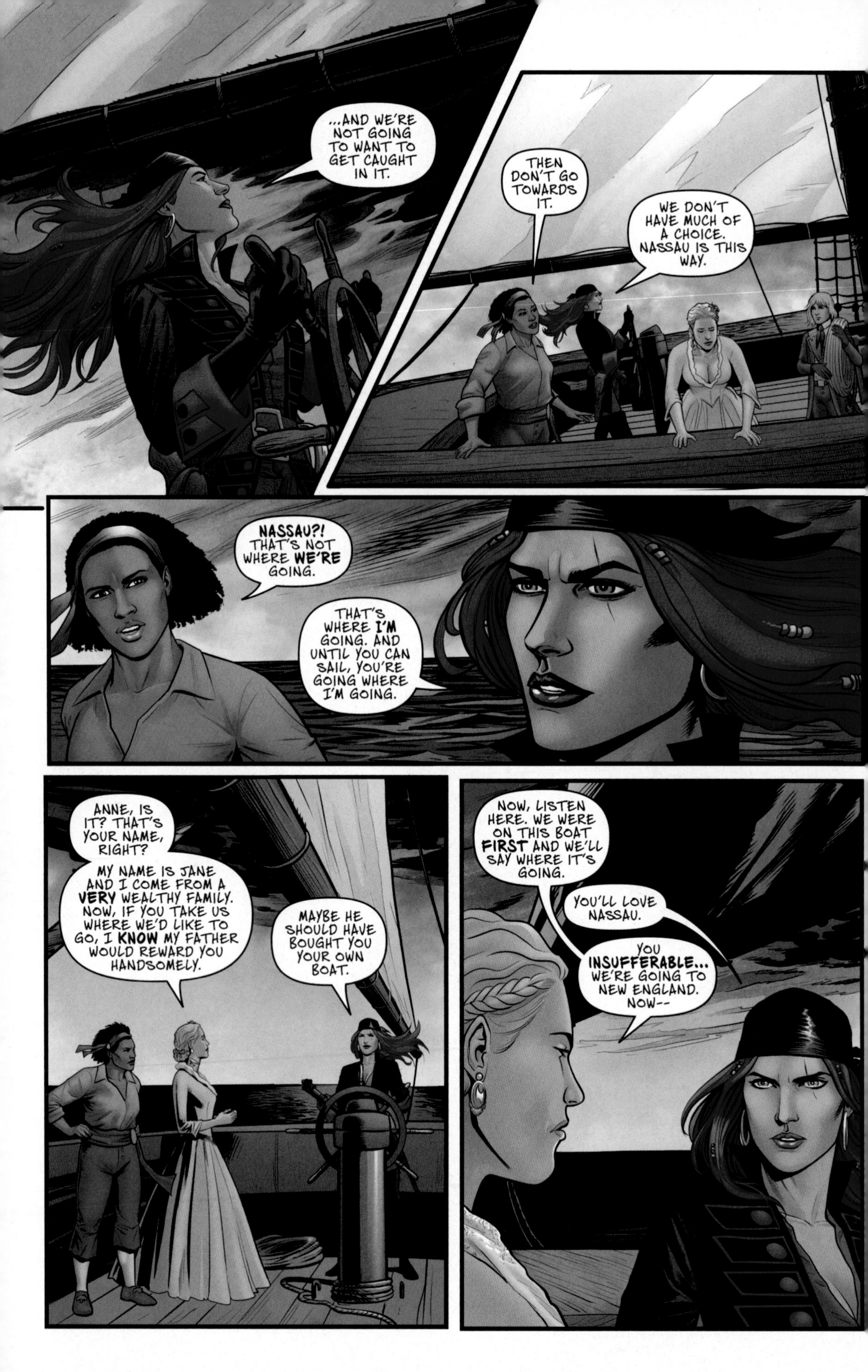
...AND WE'RE NOT GOING TO WANT TO GET CAUGHT IN IT.
THEN DON'T GO TOWARDS IT.
WE DON'T HAVE MUCH OF A CHOICE. NASSAU IS THIS WAY.
NASSAU?! THAT'S NOT WHERE WE'RE GOING.
THAT'S WHERE I'M GOING. AND UNTIL YOU CAN SAIL, YOU'RE GOING WHERE I'M GOING.
ANNE, IS IT? THAT'S YOUR NAME, RIGHT?
MY NAME IS JANE AND I COME FROM A VERY WEALTHY FAMILY. NOW, IF YOU TAKE US WHERE WE'D LIKE TO GO, I KNOW MY FATHER WOULD REWARD YOU HANDSOMELY.
MAYBE HE SHOULD HAVE BOUGHT YOU YOUR OWN BOAT.
NOW, LISTEN HERE. WE WERE ON THIS BOAT FIRST AND WE'LL SAY WHERE IT'S GOING.
YOU'LL LOVE NASSAU.
YOU INSUFFERABLE... WE'RE GOING TO NEW ENGLAND. NOW--

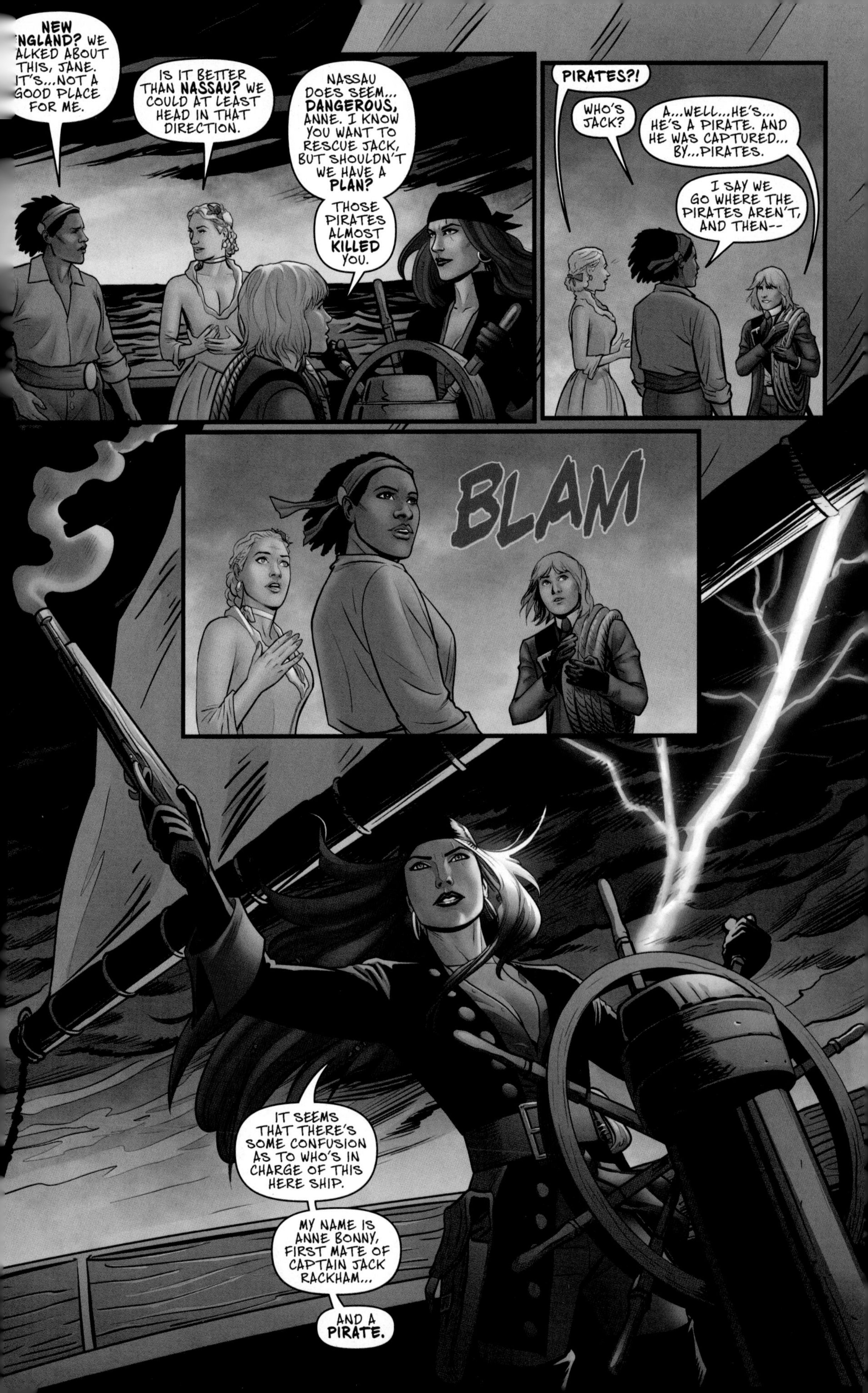
NEW ENGLAND? WE TALKED ABOUT THIS, JANE. IT'S...NOT A GOOD PLACE FOR ME.
IS IT BETTER THAN NASSAU? WE COULD AT LEAST HEAD IN THAT DIRECTION.
NASSAU DOES SEEM... DANGEROUS, ANNE. I KNOW YOU WANT TO RESCUE JACK, BUT SHOULDN'T WE HAVE A PLAN?
THOSE PIRATES ALMOST KILLED YOU.
PIRATES?!
WHO'S JACK?
A...WELL...HE'S... HE'S A PIRATE. AND HE WAS CAPTURED... BY...PIRATES.
I SAY WE GO WHERE THE PIRATES AREN'T, AND THEN--
BLAM
IT SEEMS THAT THERE'S SOME CONFUSION AS TO WHO'S IN CHARGE OF THIS HERE SHIP.
MY NAME IS ANNE BONNY, FIRST MATE OF CAPTAIN JACK RACKHAM...
AND A PIRATE.

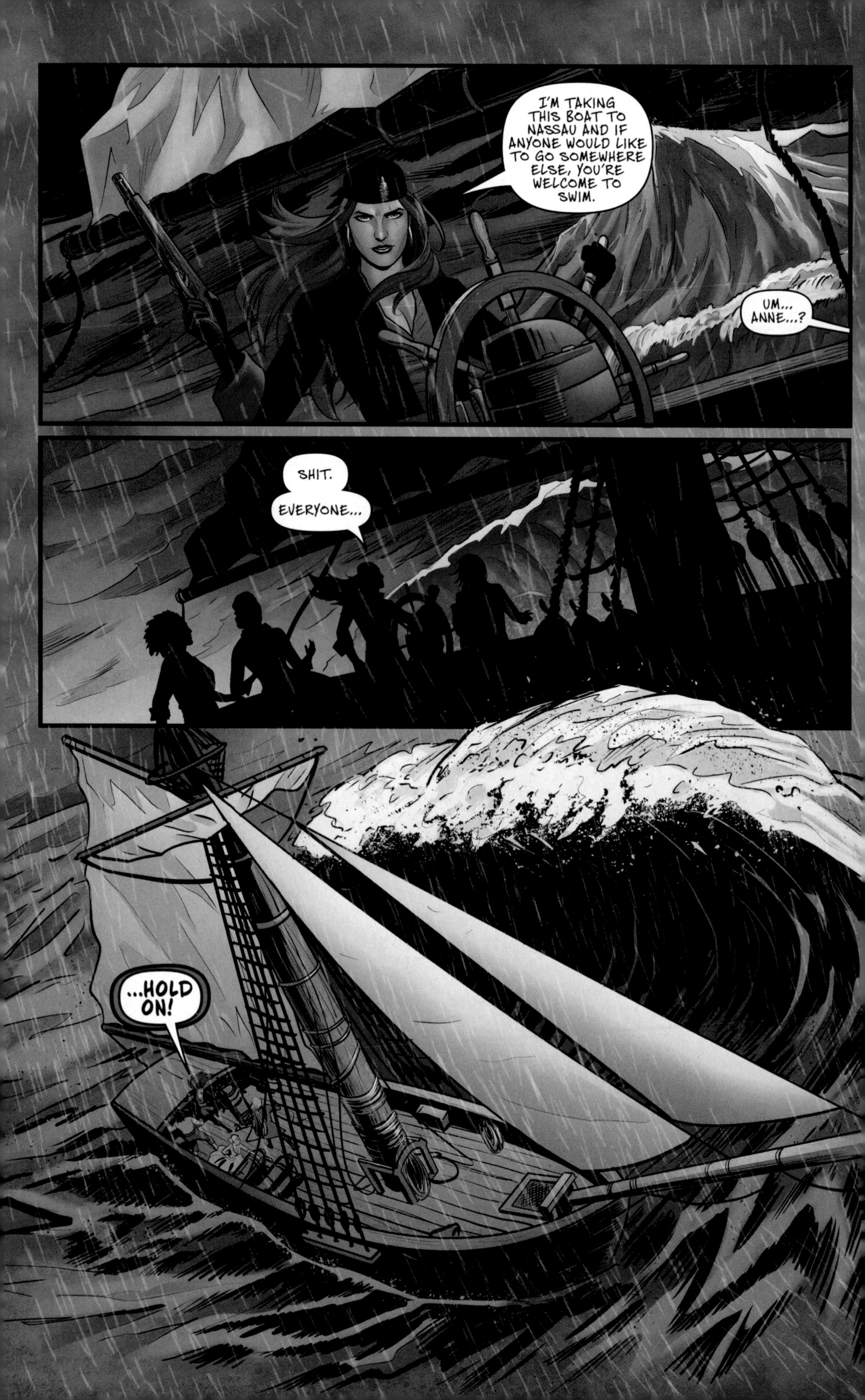
I'M TAKING THIS BOAT TO NASSAU AND IF ANYONE WOULD LIKE TO GO SOMEWHERE ELSE, YOU'RE WELCOME TO SWIM.
UM... ANNE...?
SHIT.
EVERYONE...
...HOLD ON!

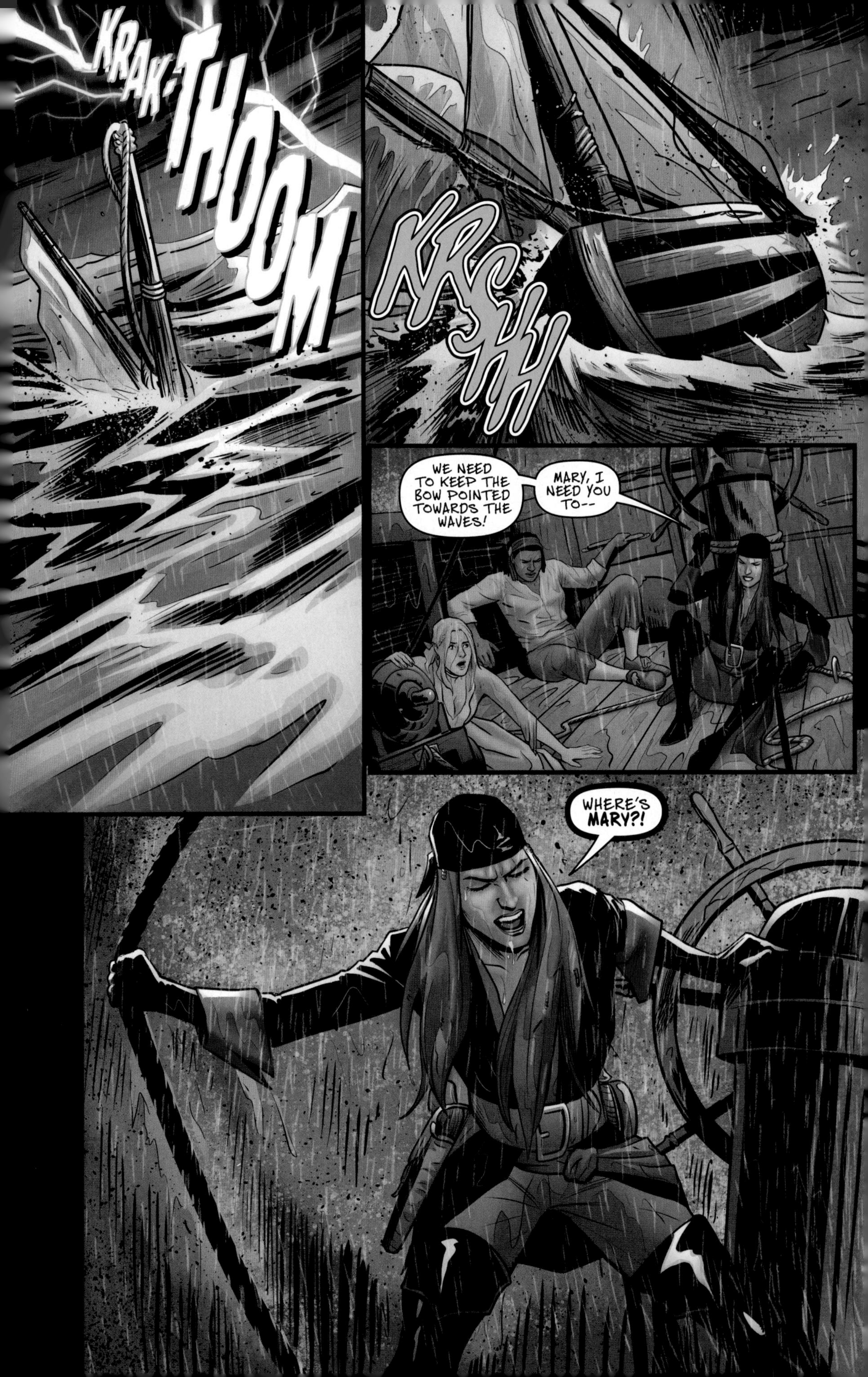
KRAK-THOOM
KRSHH
WE NEED TO KEEP THE BOW POINTED TOWARDS THE WAVES!
MARY, I NEED YOU TO--
WHERE'S MARY?!

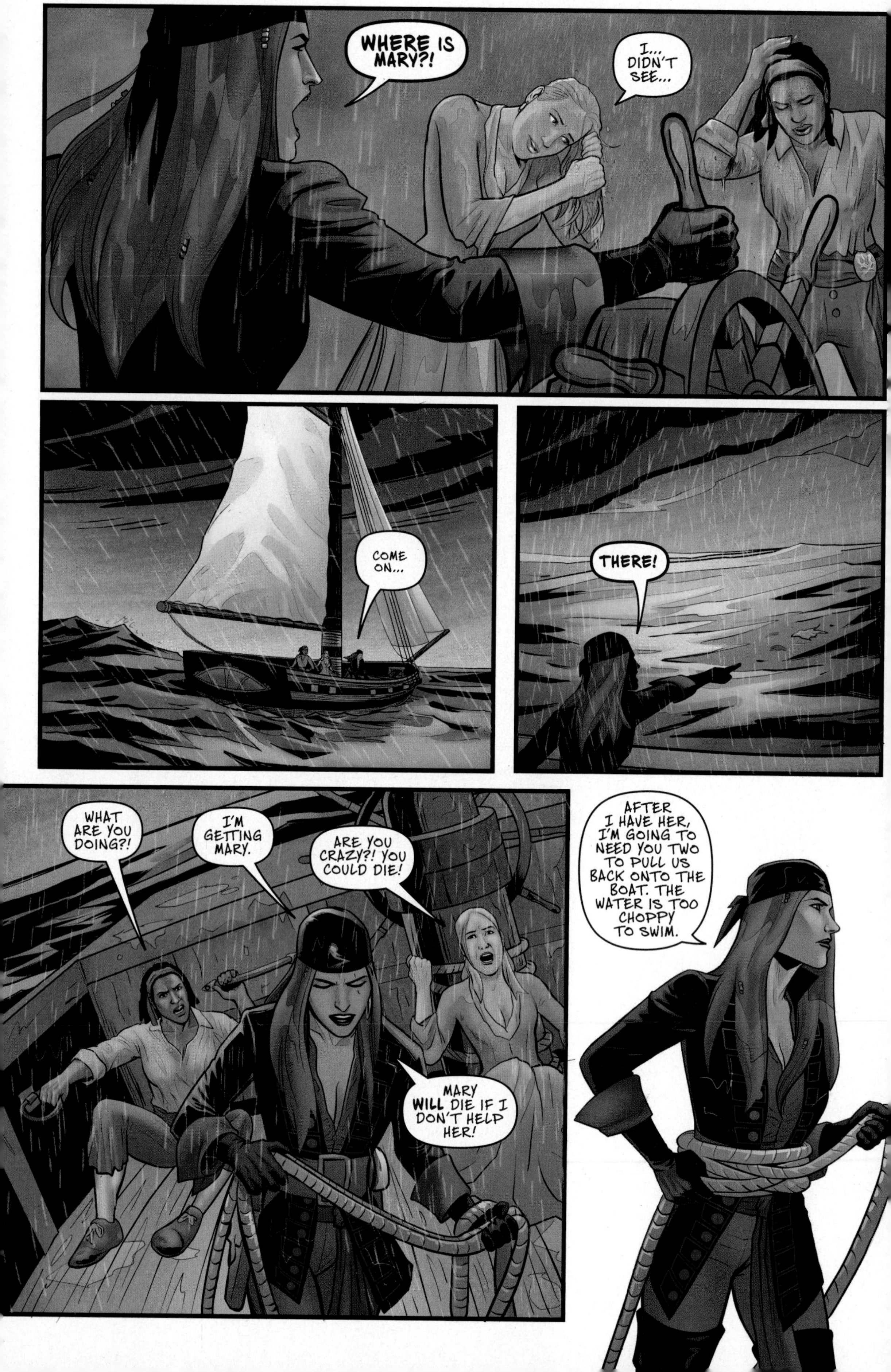
WHERE IS MARY?!
I... DIDN'T SEE...
COME ON...
THERE!
WHAT ARE YOU DOING?!
I'M GETTING MARY.
ARE YOU CRAZY?! YOU COULD DIE!
MARY WILL DIE IF I DON'T HELP HER!
AFTER I HAVE HER, I'M GOING TO NEED YOU TWO TO PULL US BACK ONTO THE BOAT. THE WATER IS TOO CHOPPY TO SWIM.

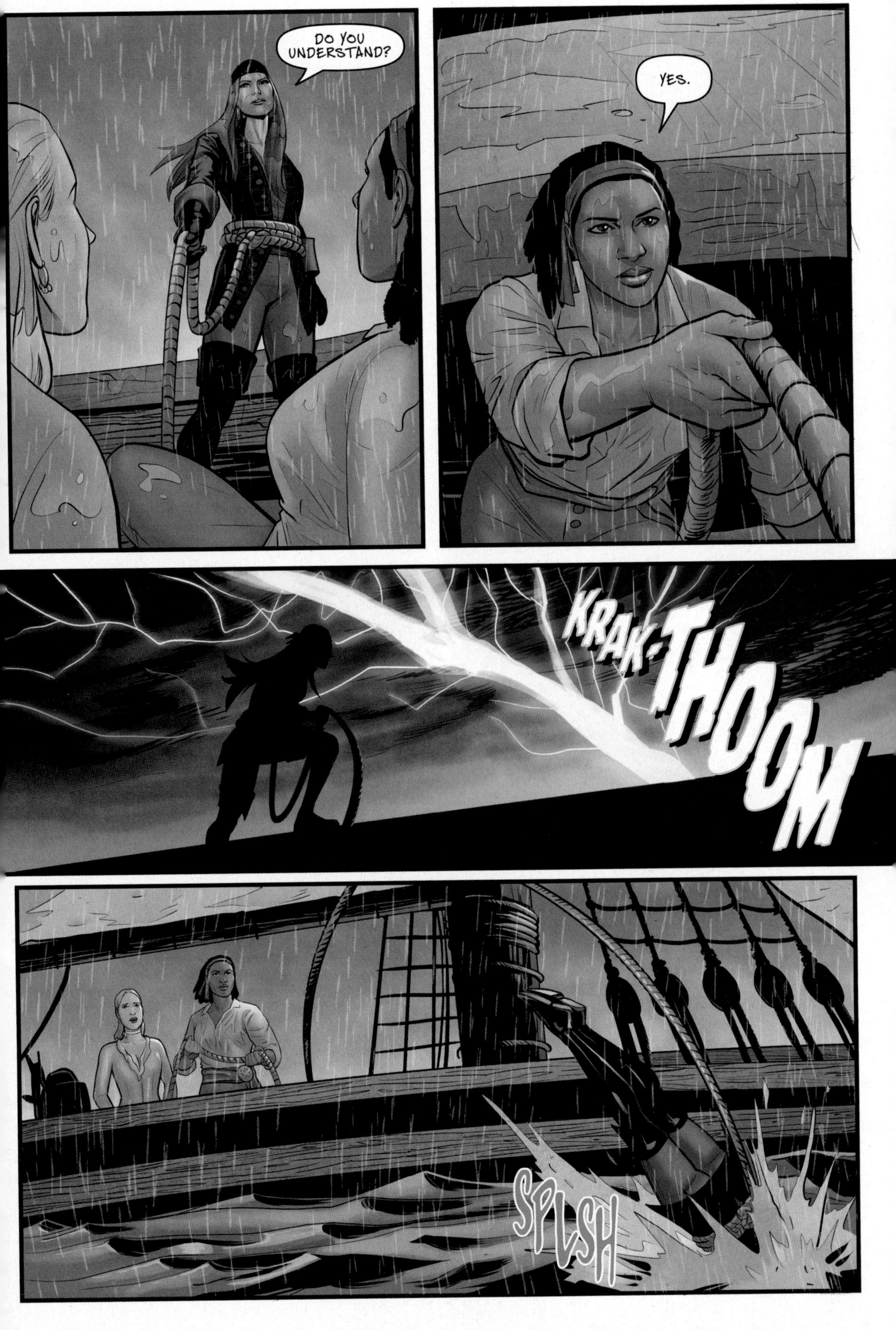
DO YOU UNDERSTAND?
YES.
KRAK-THOOM
SPLSH

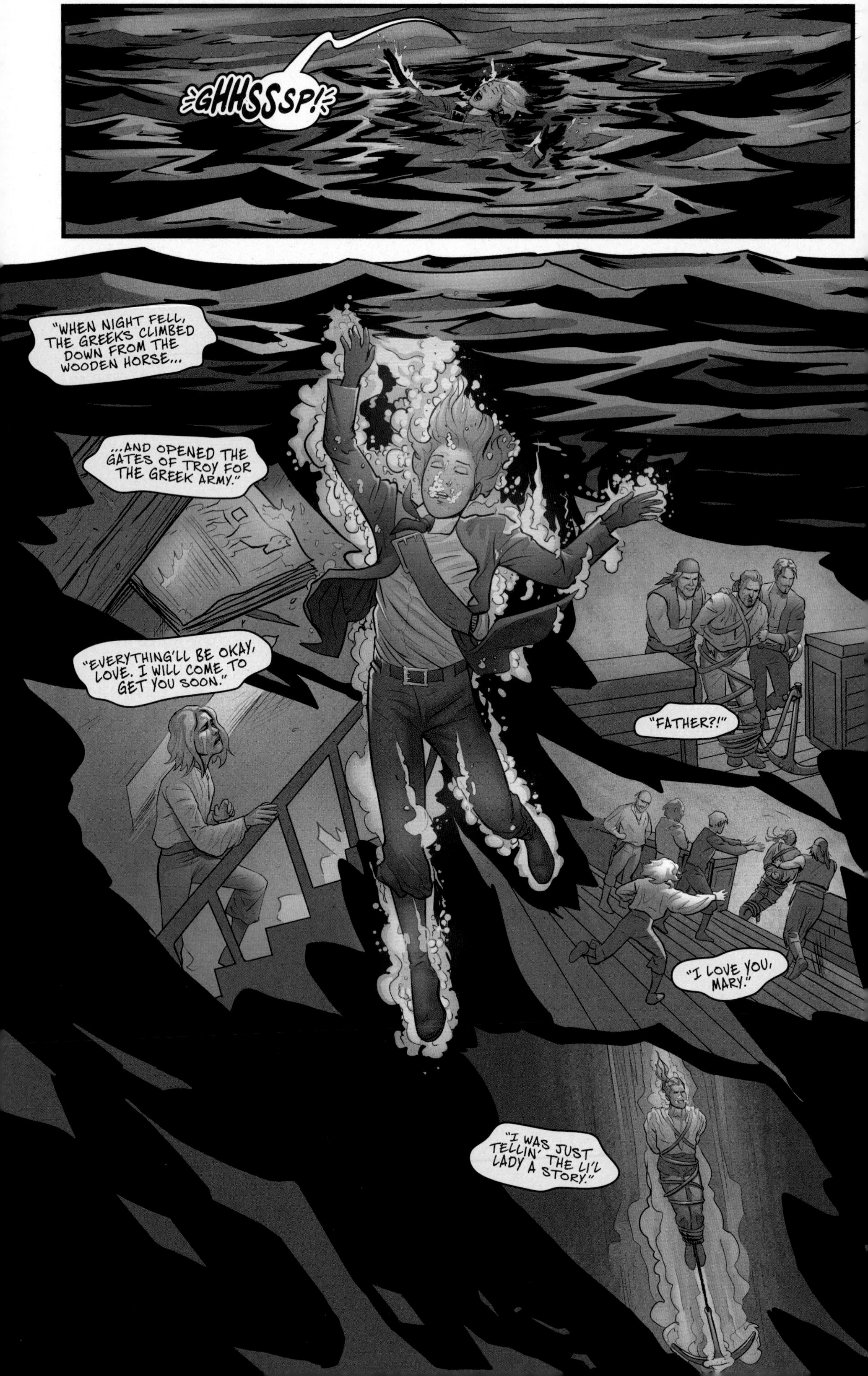
GHHSSSP!
"WHEN NIGHT FELL, THE GREEKS CLIMBED DOWN FROM THE WOODEN HORSE...
...AND OPENED THE GATES OF TROY FOR THE GREEK ARMY."
"EVERYTHING'LL BE OKAY, LOVE. I WILL COME TO GET YOU SOON."
"FATHER?!"
"I LOVE YOU, MARY."
"I WAS JUST TELLIN' THE LI'L LADY A STORY."

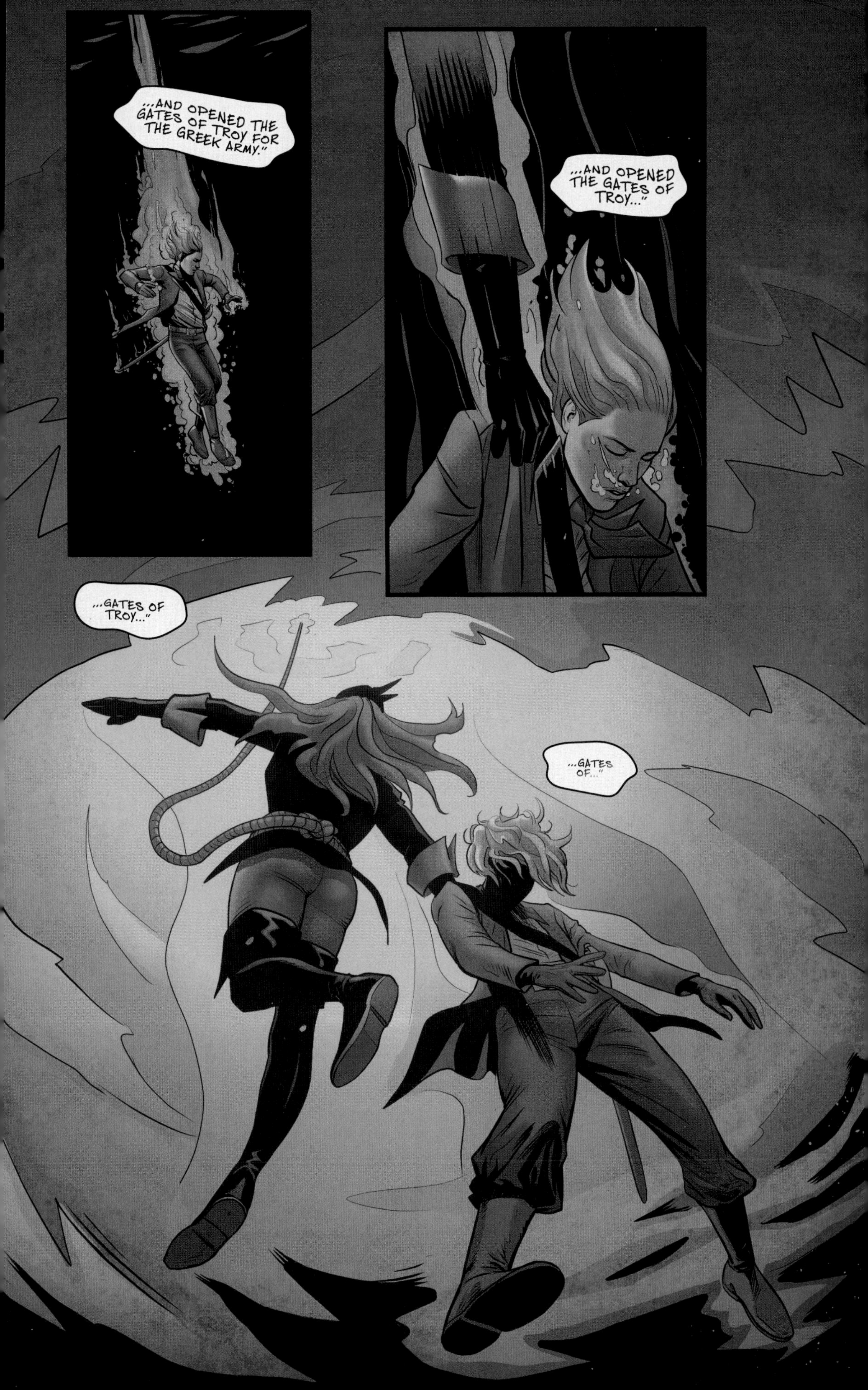
"...AND OPENED THE GATES OF TROY FOR THE GREEK ARMY."
"...AND OPENED THE GATES OF TROY..."
"...GATES OF TROY..."
"...GATES OF..."

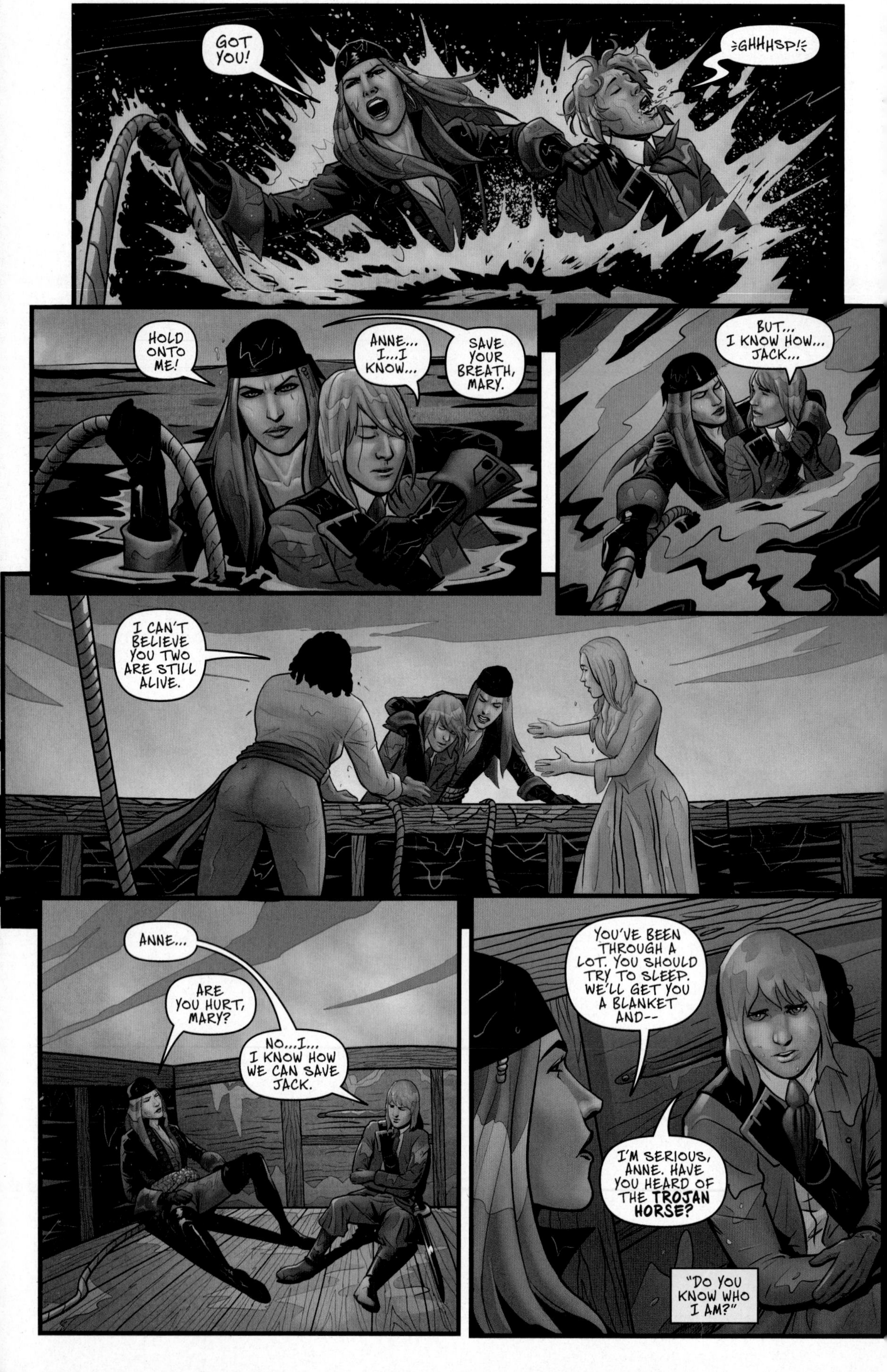
GOT YOU!
≈GHHHSP!≈
HOLD ONTO ME!
ANNE... I...I KNOW...
SAVE YOUR BREATH, MARY.
BUT... I KNOW HOW... JACK...
I CAN'T BELIEVE YOU TWO ARE STILL ALIVE.
ANNE...
ARE YOU HURT, MARY?
NO...I... I KNOW HOW WE CAN SAVE JACK.
YOU'VE BEEN THROUGH A LOT. YOU SHOULD TRY TO SLEEP. WE'LL GET YOU A BLANKET AND--
I'M SERIOUS, ANNE. HAVE YOU HEARD OF THE TROJAN HORSE?
"DO YOU KNOW WHO I AM?"

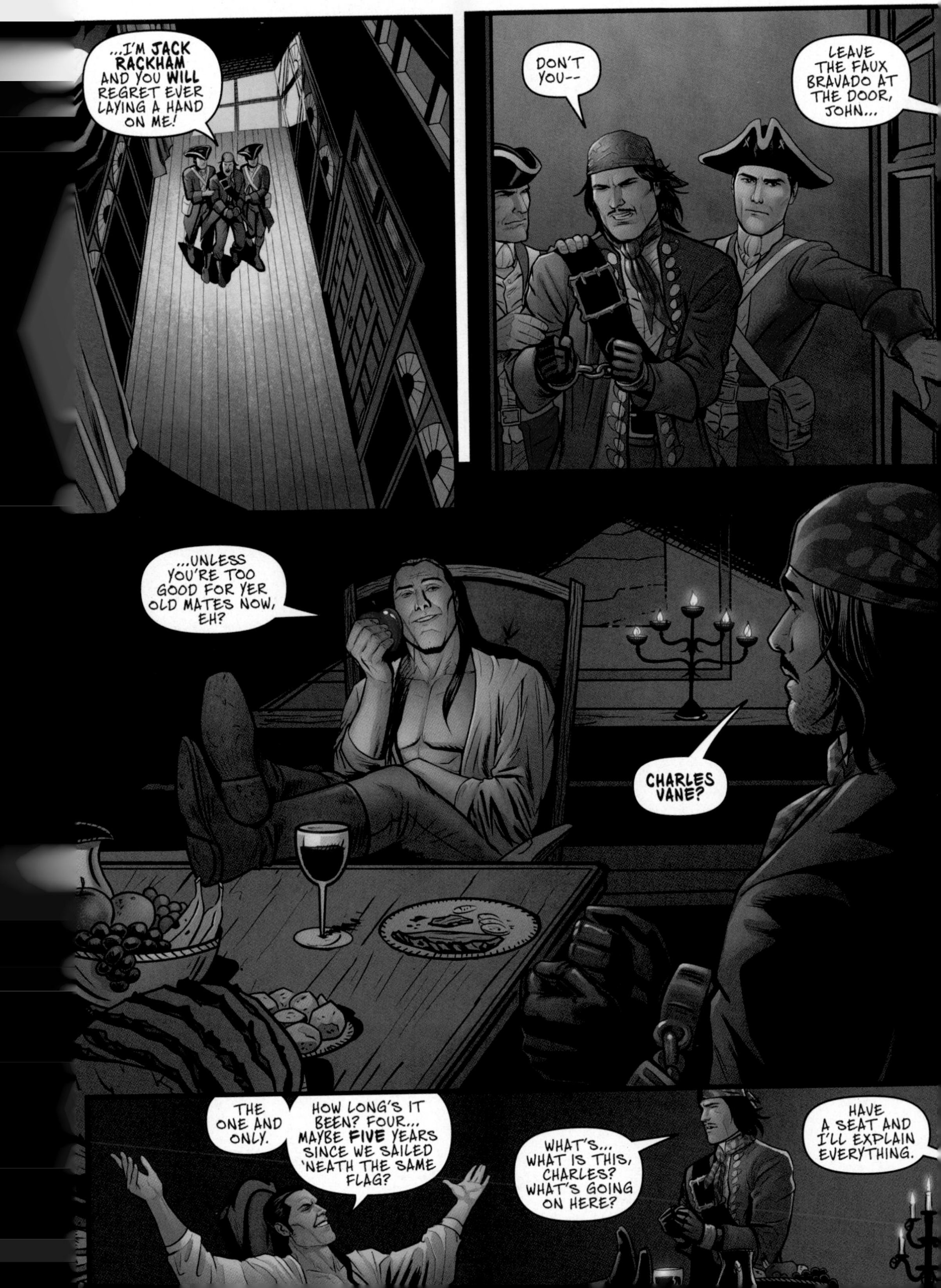
...I'M JACK RACKHAM AND YOU WILL REGRET EVER LAYING A HAND ON ME!
DON'T YOU--
LEAVE THE FAUX BRAVADO AT THE DOOR, JOHN...
...UNLESS YOU'RE TOO GOOD FOR YER OLD MATES NOW, EH?
CHARLES VANE?
THE ONE AND ONLY.
HOW LONG'S IT BEEN? FOUR... MAYBE FIVE YEARS SINCE WE SAILED 'NEATH THE SAME FLAG?
WHAT'S... WHAT IS THIS, CHARLES? WHAT'S GOING ON HERE?
HAVE A SEAT AND I'LL EXPLAIN EVERYTHING.

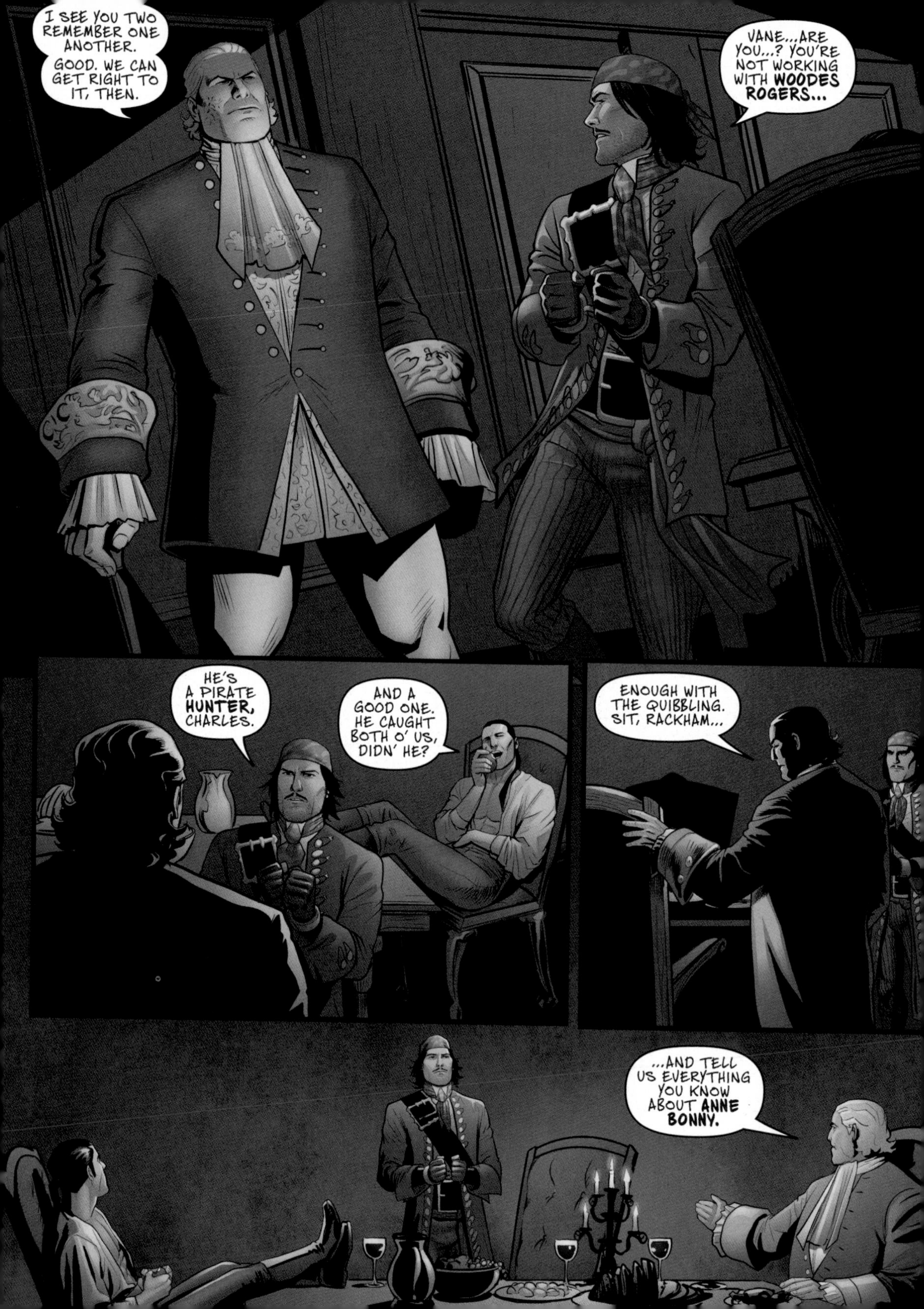
I SEE YOU TWO REMEMBER ONE ANOTHER.
GOOD. WE CAN GET RIGHT TO IT, THEN.
VANE...ARE YOU...? YOU'RE NOT WORKING WITH **WOODES ROGERS...**
HE'S A PIRATE **HUNTER,** CHARLES.
AND A GOOD ONE. HE CAUGHT BOTH O' US, DIDN' HE?
ENOUGH WITH THE QUIBBLING. SIT, RACKHAM...
...AND TELL US EVERYTHING YOU KNOW ABOUT **ANNE BONNY.**

Chapter 4

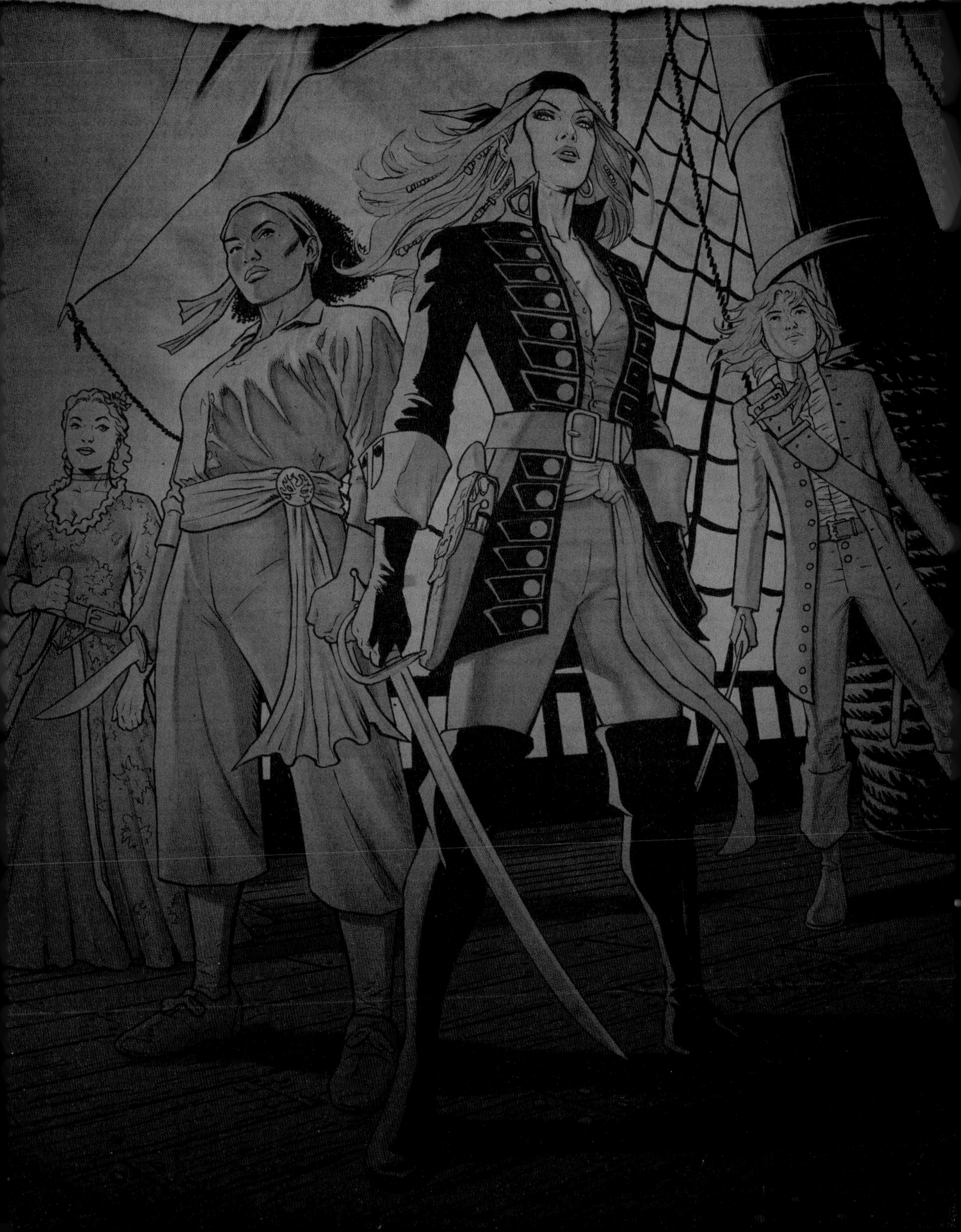

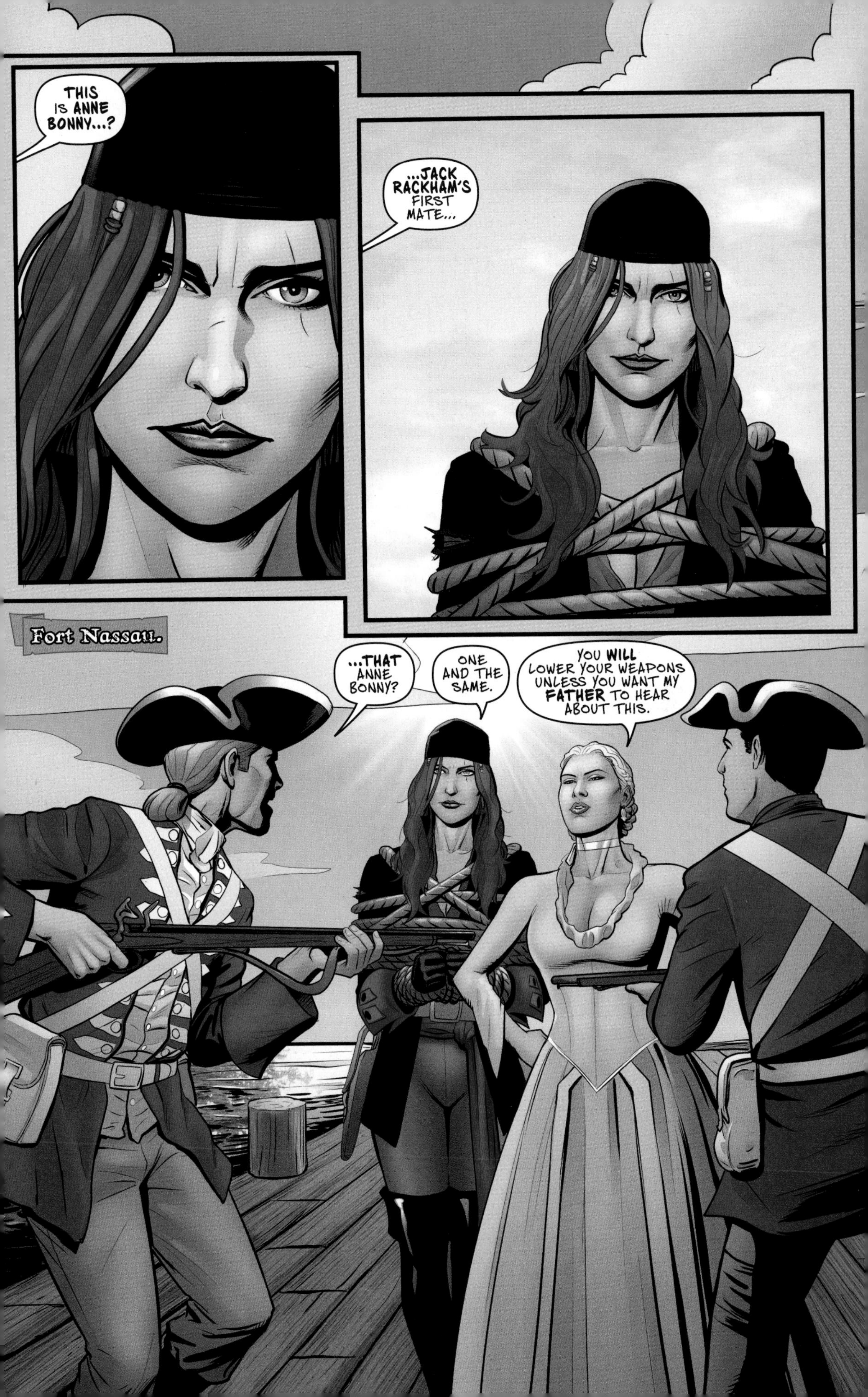
THIS IS ANNE BONNY...?
...JACK RACKHAM'S FIRST MATE...
Fort Nassau.
...THAT ANNE BONNY?
ONE AND THE SAME.
YOU WILL LOWER YOUR WEAPONS UNLESS YOU WANT MY FATHER TO HEAR ABOUT THIS.

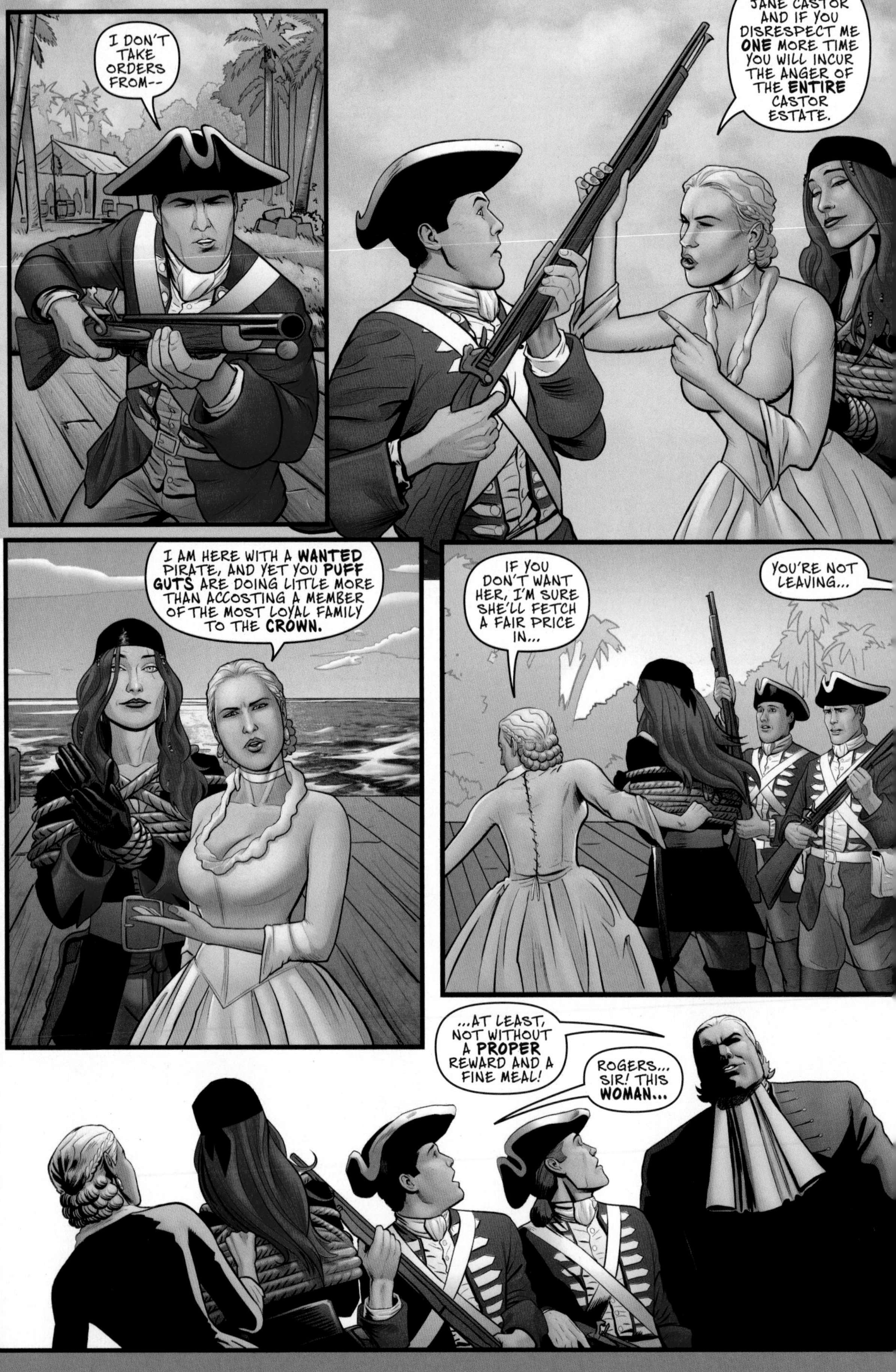
I DON'T TAKE ORDERS FROM--
MY NAME IS JANE CASTOR AND IF YOU DISRESPECT ME **ONE** MORE TIME YOU WILL INCUR THE ANGER OF THE **ENTIRE** CASTOR ESTATE.
I AM HERE WITH A **WANTED** PIRATE, AND YET YOU **PUFF GUTS** ARE DOING LITTLE MORE THAN ACCOSTING A MEMBER OF THE MOST LOYAL FAMILY TO THE **CROWN.**
IF YOU DON'T WANT HER, I'M SURE SHE'LL FETCH A FAIR PRICE IN...
YOU'RE NOT LEAVING...
...AT LEAST, NOT WITHOUT A **PROPER** REWARD AND A FINE MEAL!
ROGERS... SIR! THIS **WOMAN...**

THIS WOMAN IS **JANE CASTOR** AND IS **ALWAYS** A WELCOME GUEST HERE.

AND THIS... THIS IS SOMEONE I'VE BEEN JUST **DYING** TO MEET.

AND WHAT A PLEASURE IT IS. I'D SHAKE YER HAND BUT... WELL...

...I'M A LITTLE **TIED UP** AT THE MOMENT.

SEIZE THE PIRATE.

MISS CASTOR, MAY I HAVE THE HONOR OF YOUR PRESENCE FOR DINNER THIS EVENING AT THE GOVERNOR'S MANSION?

YES... YES, OF COURSE.

HRN... HEY...!

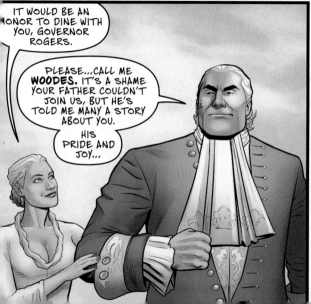

IT WOULD BE AN HONOR TO DINE WITH YOU, GOVERNOR ROGERS.

PLEASE...CALL ME **WOODES.** IT'S A SHAME YOUR FATHER COULDN'T JOIN US, BUT HE'S TOLD ME MANY A STORY ABOUT YOU.

HIS PRIDE AND JOY...

WE WILL HAVE THE **FINEST** ACCOMMODATIONS PREPARED AND PROVISIONS SENT TO YOUR SHIP FOR THE CREW.

YOUR HOSPITALITY IS MOST APPRECIATED, **WOODES.**

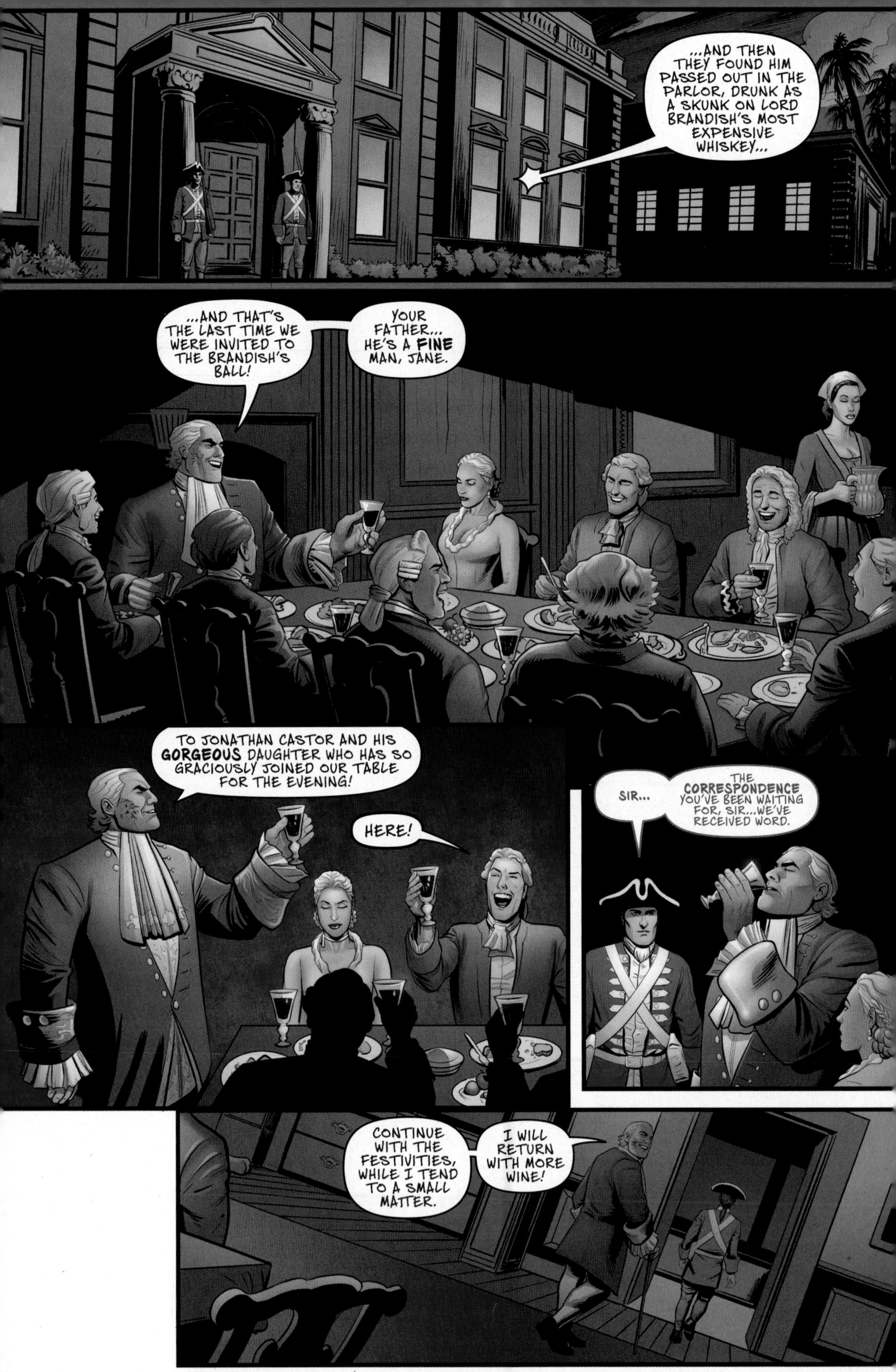
...AND THEN THEY FOUND HIM PASSED OUT IN THE PARLOR, DRUNK AS A SKUNK ON LORD BRANDISH'S MOST EXPENSIVE WHISKEY...
...AND THAT'S THE LAST TIME WE WERE INVITED TO THE BRANDISH'S BALL!
YOUR FATHER... HE'S A FINE MAN, JANE.
TO JONATHAN CASTOR AND HIS GORGEOUS DAUGHTER WHO HAS SO GRACIOUSLY JOINED OUR TABLE FOR THE EVENING!
HERE!
SIR...
THE CORRESPONDENCE YOU'VE BEEN WAITING FOR, SIR...WE'VE RECEIVED WORD.
CONTINUE WITH THE FESTIVITIES, WHILE I TEND TO A SMALL MATTER.
I WILL RETURN WITH MORE WINE!

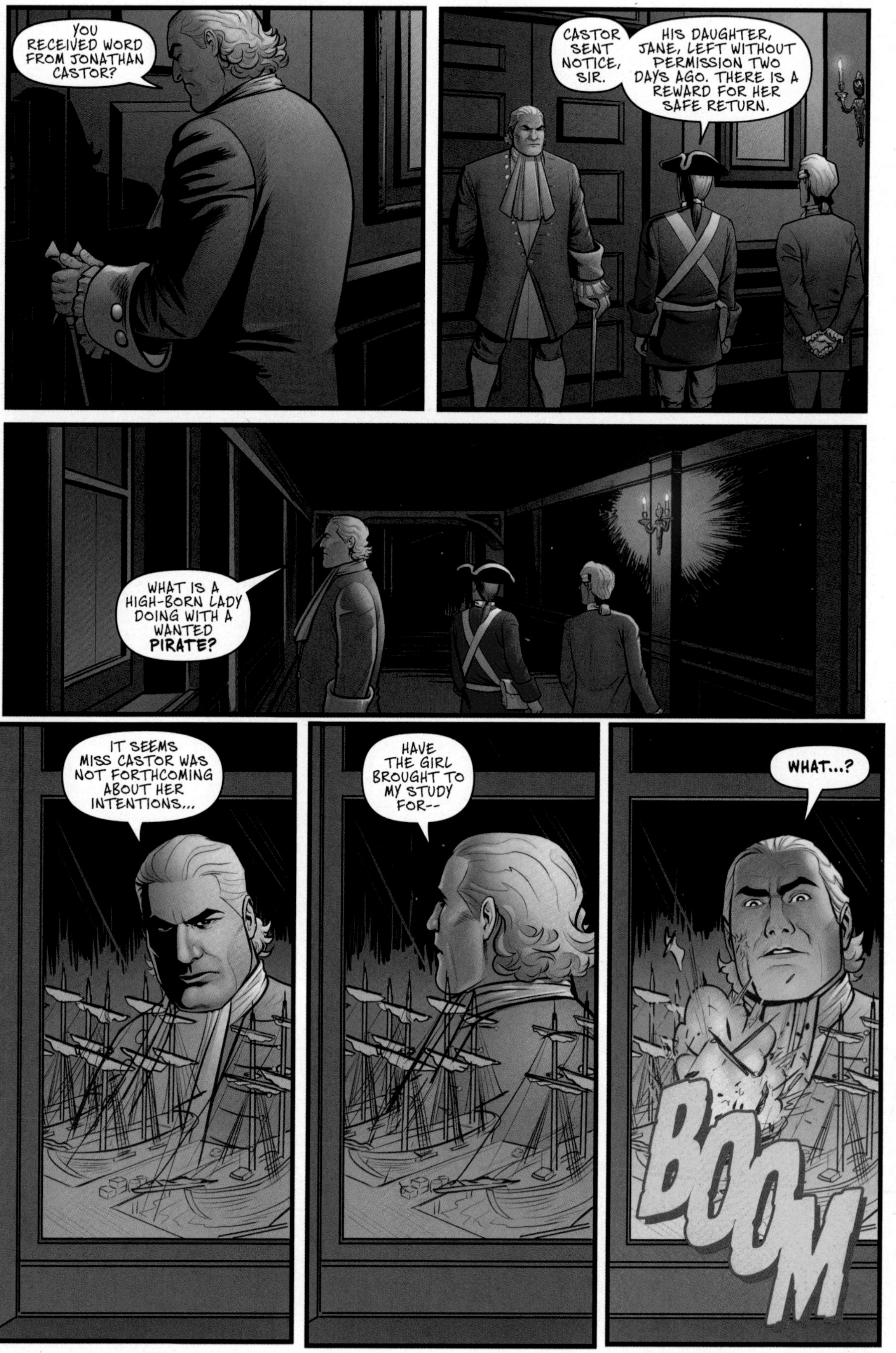
YOU RECEIVED WORD FROM JONATHAN CASTOR?
CASTOR SENT NOTICE, SIR.
HIS DAUGHTER, JANE, LEFT WITHOUT PERMISSION TWO DAYS AGO. THERE IS A REWARD FOR HER SAFE RETURN.
WHAT IS A HIGH-BORN LADY DOING WITH A WANTED **PIRATE?**
IT SEEMS MISS CASTOR WAS NOT FORTHCOMING ABOUT HER INTENTIONS...
HAVE THE GIRL BROUGHT TO MY STUDY FOR--
WHAT...?
BOOM

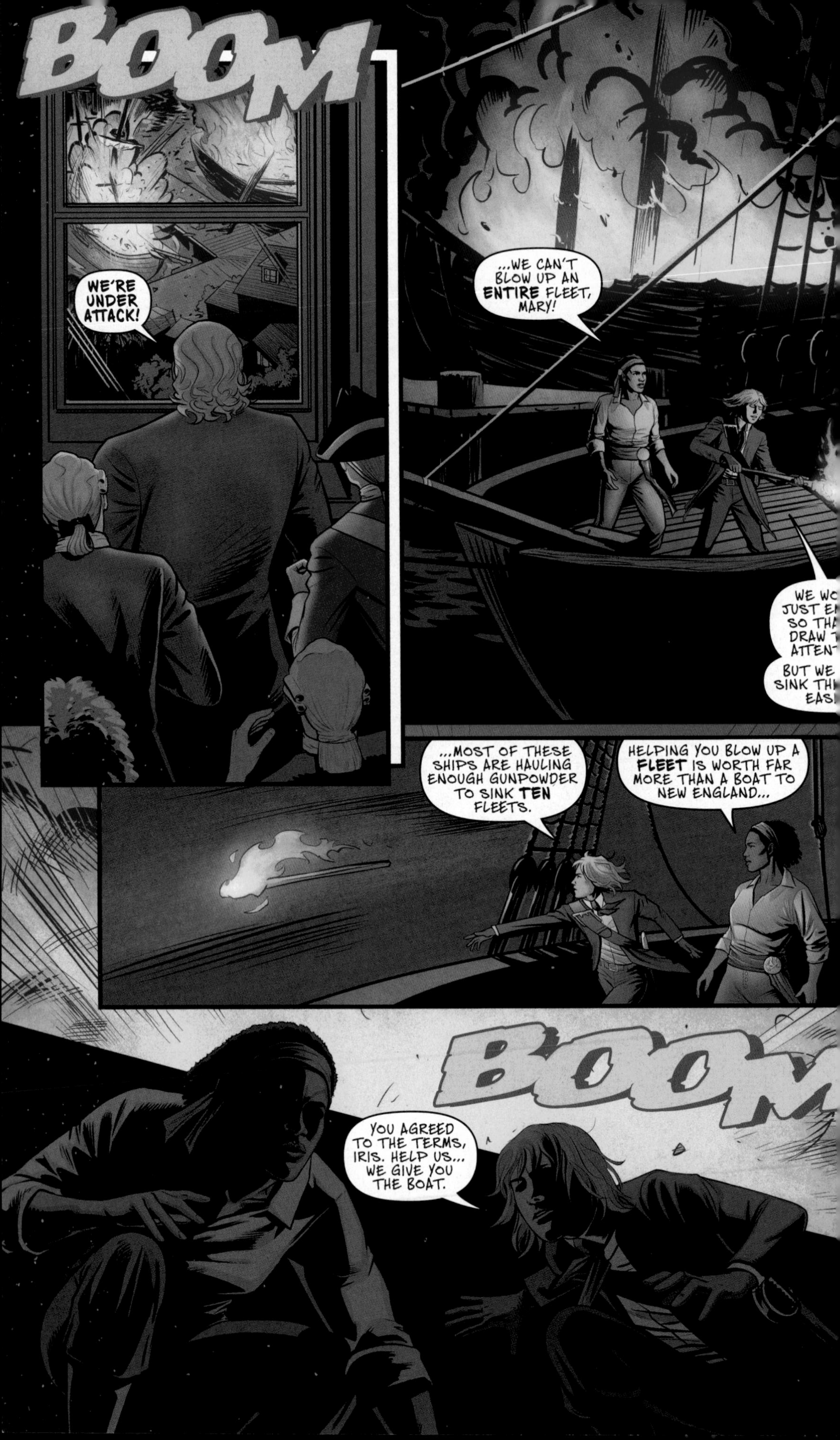
BOOM
WE'RE UNDER ATTACK!
...WE CAN'T BLOW UP AN ENTIRE FLEET, MARY!
...MOST OF THESE SHIPS ARE HAULING ENOUGH GUNPOWDER TO SINK TEN FLEETS.
HELPING YOU BLOW UP A FLEET IS WORTH FAR MORE THAN A BOAT TO NEW ENGLAND...
BOOM
YOU AGREED TO THE TERMS, IRIS. HELP US... WE GIVE YOU THE BOAT.

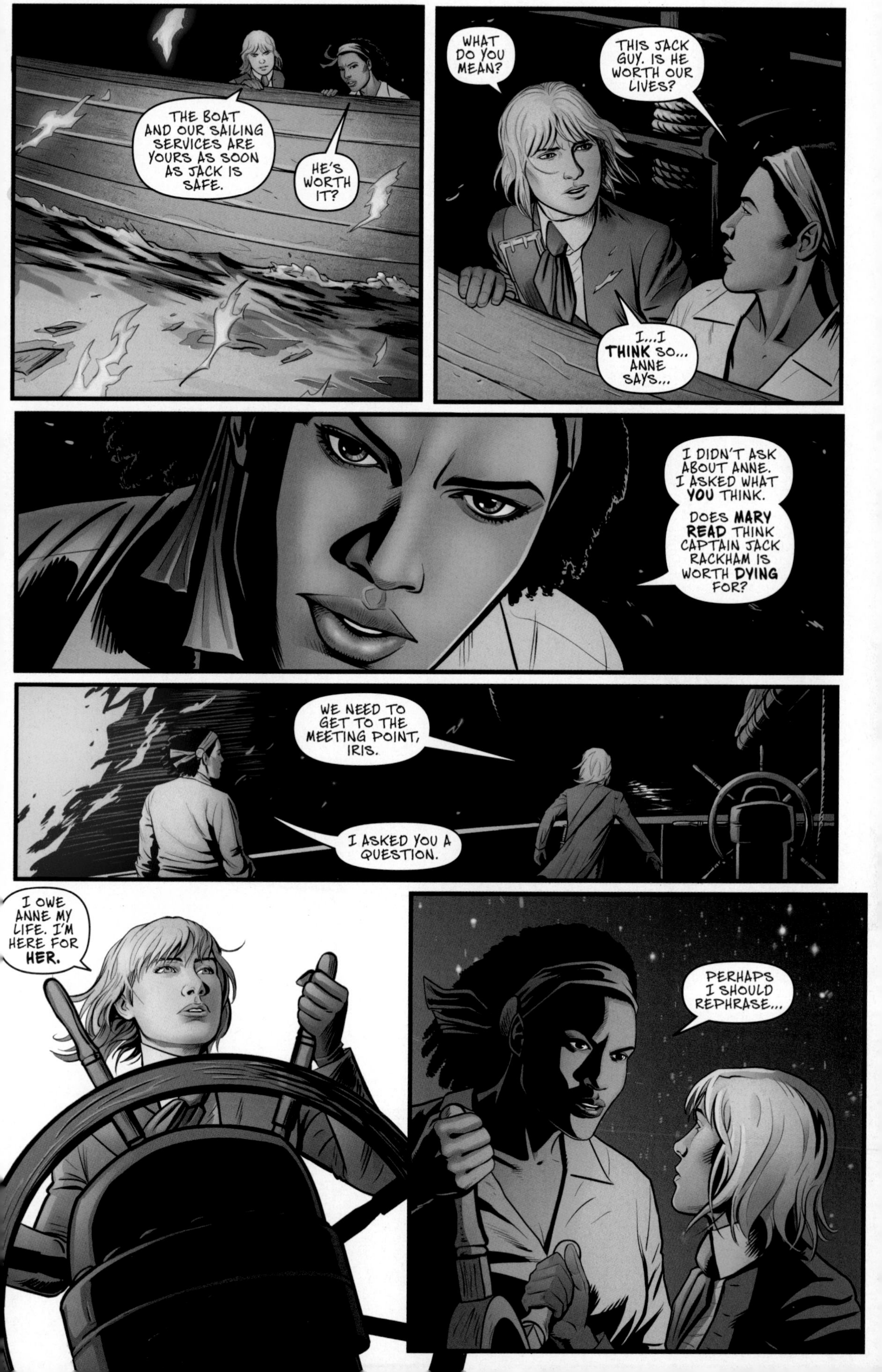
THE BOAT AND OUR SAILING SERVICES ARE YOURS AS SOON AS JACK IS SAFE.
HE'S WORTH IT?
WHAT DO YOU MEAN?
THIS JACK GUY. IS HE WORTH OUR LIVES?
I...I **THINK** SO... ANNE SAYS...
I DIDN'T ASK ABOUT ANNE. I ASKED WHAT **YOU** THINK.
DOES **MARY READ** THINK CAPTAIN JACK RACKHAM IS WORTH **DYING** FOR?
WE NEED TO GET TO THE MEETING POINT, IRIS.
I ASKED YOU A QUESTION.
I OWE ANNE MY LIFE. I'M HERE FOR **HER.**
PERHAPS I SHOULD REPHRASE...

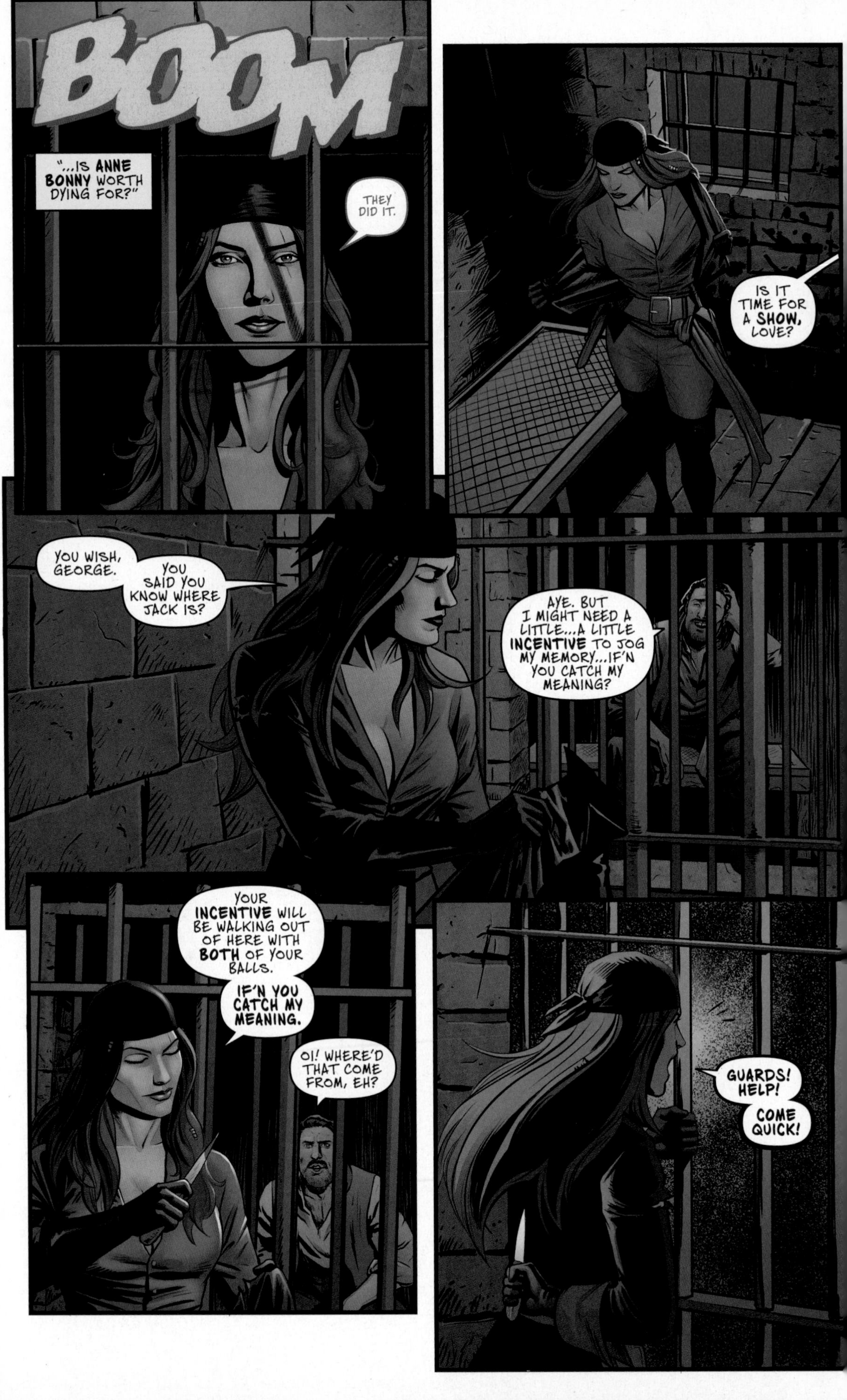
BOOM
"...IS ANNE BONNY WORTH DYING FOR?"
THEY DID IT.
IS IT TIME FOR A SHOW, LOVE?
YOU WISH, GEORGE.
YOU SAID YOU KNOW WHERE JACK IS?
AYE. BUT I MIGHT NEED A LITTLE...A LITTLE INCENTIVE TO JOG MY MEMORY...IF'N YOU CATCH MY MEANING?
YOUR INCENTIVE WILL BE WALKING OUT OF HERE WITH BOTH OF YOUR BALLS.
IF'N YOU CATCH MY MEANING.
OI! WHERE'D THAT COME FROM, EH?
GUARDS! HELP!
COME QUICK!

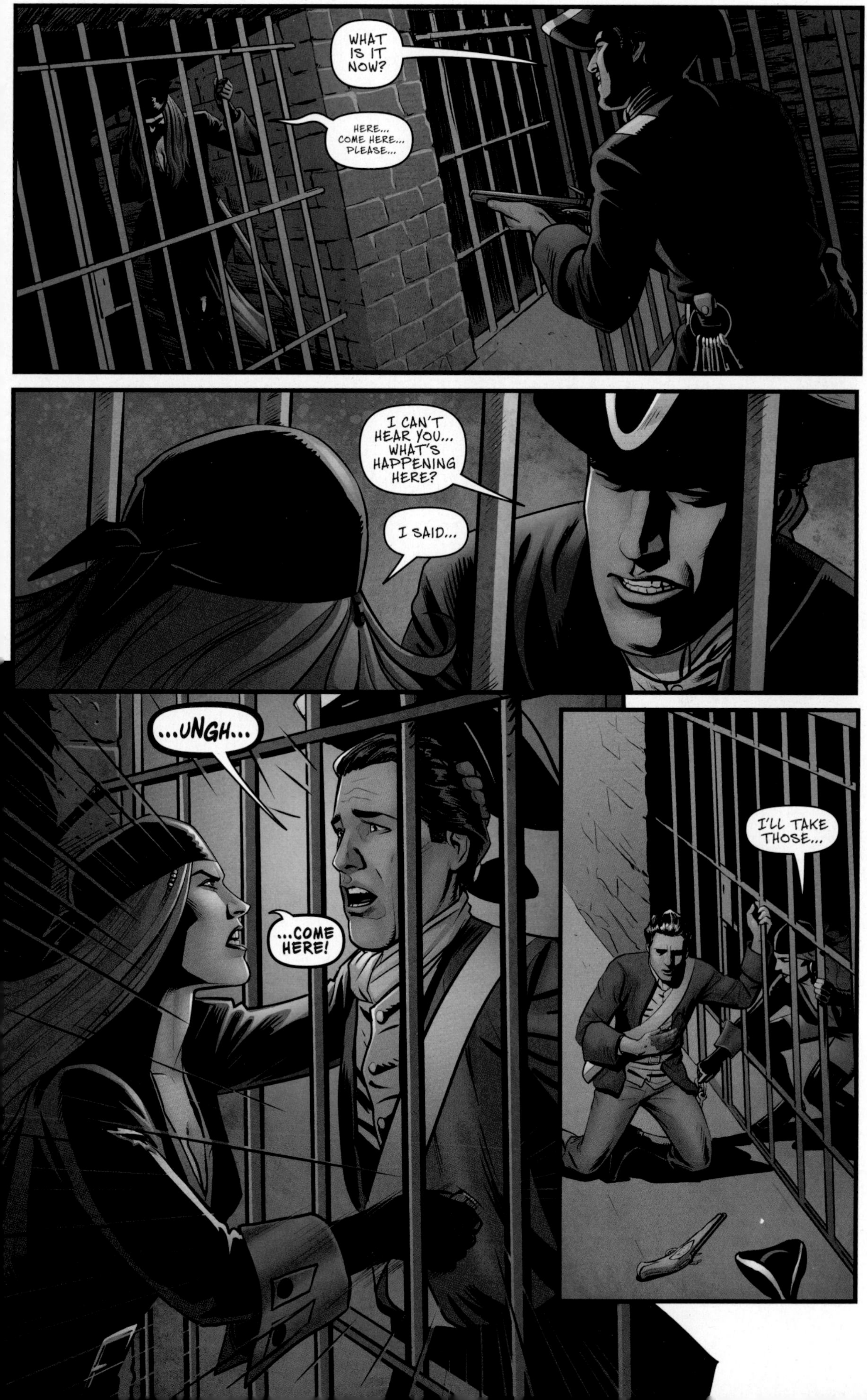
WHAT IS IT NOW?
HERE... COME HERE... PLEASE...
I CAN'T HEAR YOU... WHAT'S HAPPENING HERE?
I SAID...
...UNGH...
...COME HERE!
I'LL TAKE THOSE...

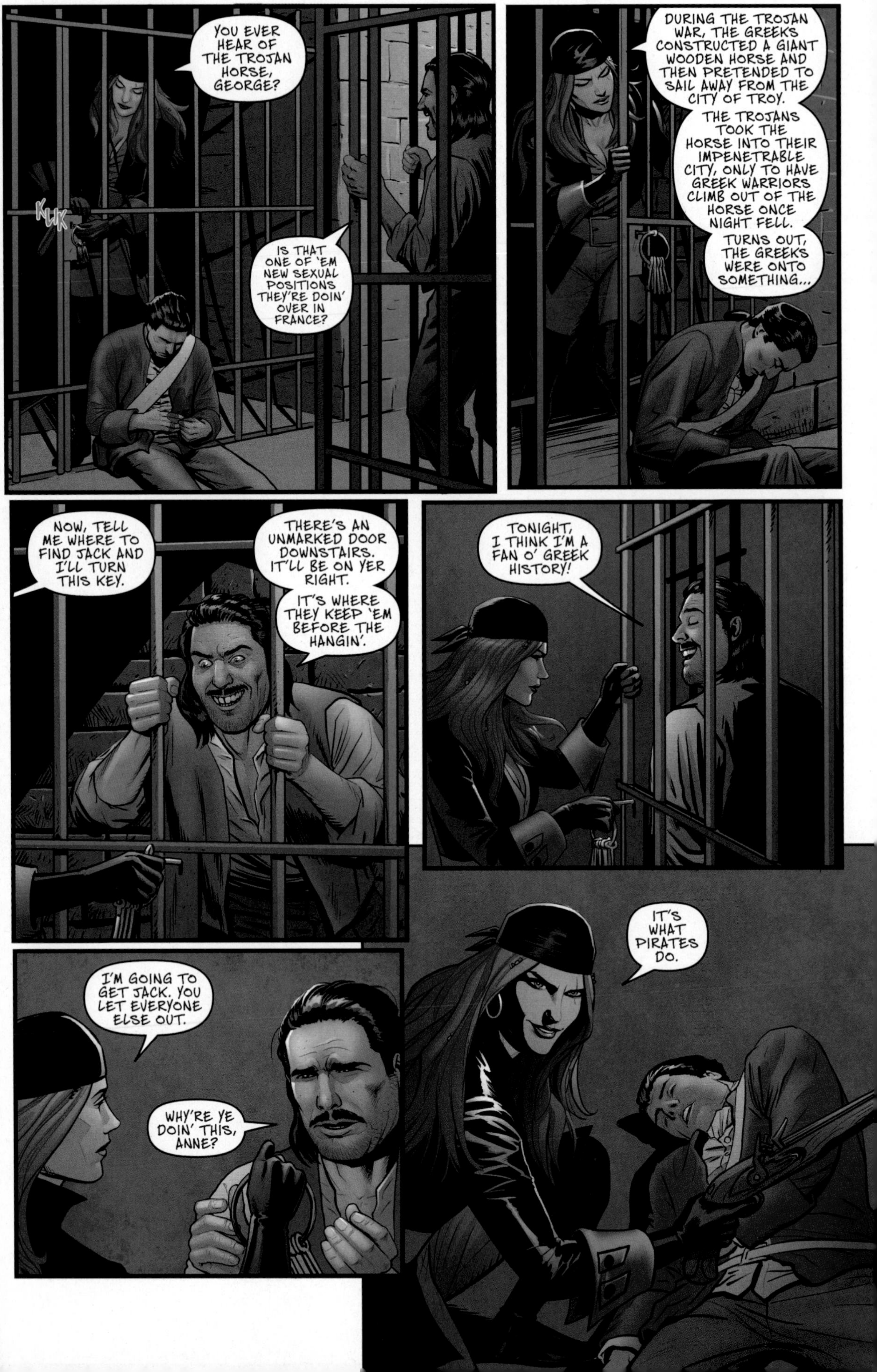
YOU EVER HEAR OF THE TROJAN HORSE, GEORGE?
KLIK
IS THAT ONE OF 'EM NEW SEXUAL POSITIONS THEY'RE DOIN' OVER IN FRANCE?
DURING THE TROJAN WAR, THE GREEKS CONSTRUCTED A GIANT WOODEN HORSE AND THEN PRETENDED TO SAIL AWAY FROM THE CITY OF TROY.
THE TROJANS TOOK THE HORSE INTO THEIR IMPENETRABLE CITY, ONLY TO HAVE GREEK WARRIORS CLIMB OUT OF THE HORSE ONCE NIGHT FELL.
TURNS OUT, THE GREEKS WERE ONTO SOMETHING...
NOW, TELL ME WHERE TO FIND JACK AND I'LL TURN THIS KEY.
THERE'S AN UNMARKED DOOR DOWNSTAIRS. IT'LL BE ON YER RIGHT.
IT'S WHERE THEY KEEP 'EM BEFORE THE HANGIN'.
TONIGHT, I THINK I'M A FAN O' GREEK HISTORY!
I'M GOING TO GET JACK. YOU LET EVERYONE ELSE OUT.
WHY'RE YE DOIN' THIS, ANNE?
IT'S WHAT PIRATES DO.

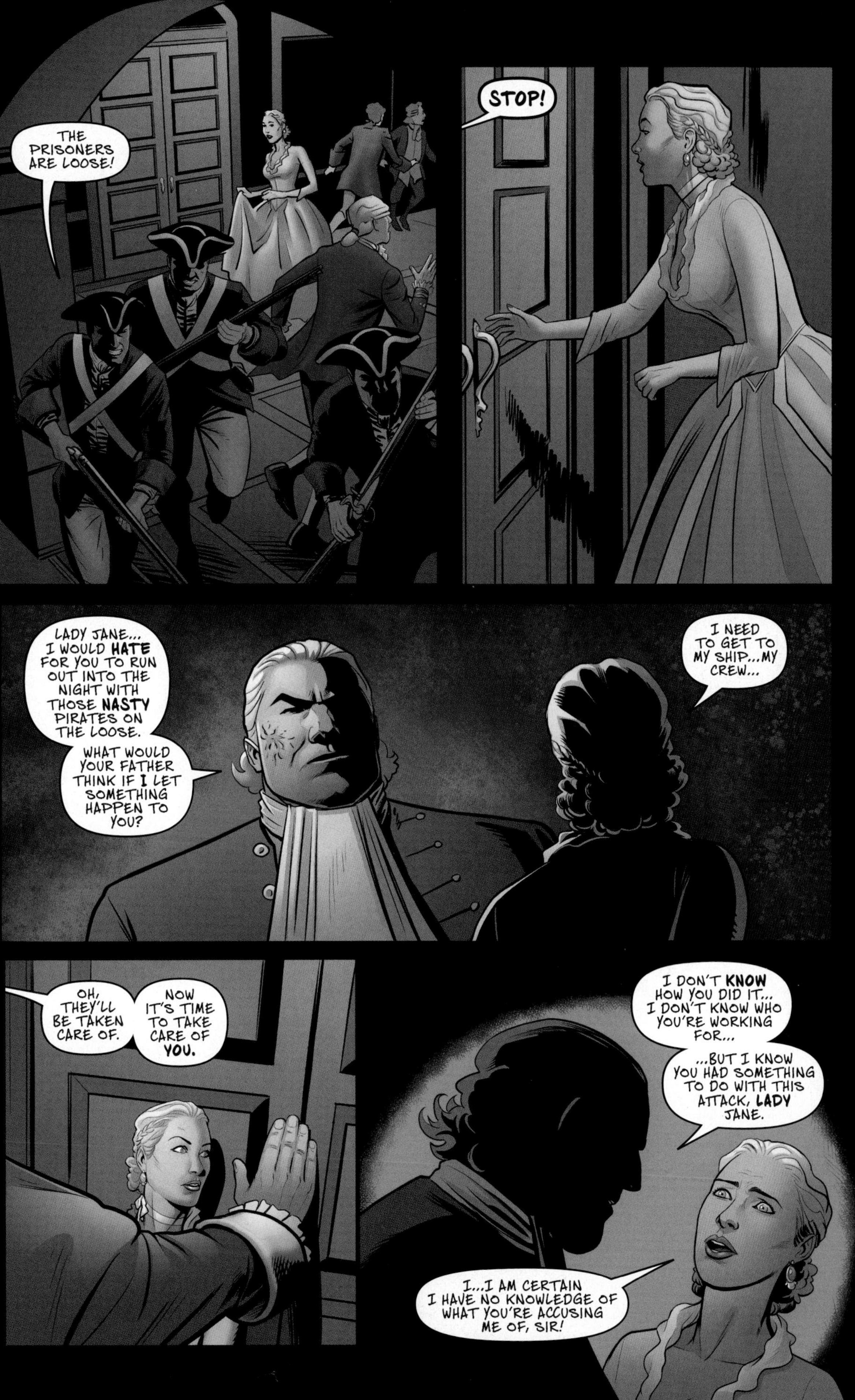
THE PRISONERS ARE LOOSE!
STOP!
LADY JANE... I WOULD HATE FOR YOU TO RUN OUT INTO THE NIGHT WITH THOSE NASTY PIRATES ON THE LOOSE.
WHAT WOULD YOUR FATHER THINK IF I LET SOMETHING HAPPEN TO YOU?
I NEED TO GET TO MY SHIP...MY CREW...
OH, THEY'LL BE TAKEN CARE OF.
NOW IT'S TIME TO TAKE CARE OF YOU.
I DON'T KNOW HOW YOU DID IT... I DON'T KNOW WHO YOU'RE WORKING FOR...
...BUT I KNOW YOU HAD SOMETHING TO DO WITH THIS ATTACK, LADY JANE.
I...I AM CERTAIN I HAVE NO KNOWLEDGE OF WHAT YOU'RE ACCUSING ME OF, SIR!

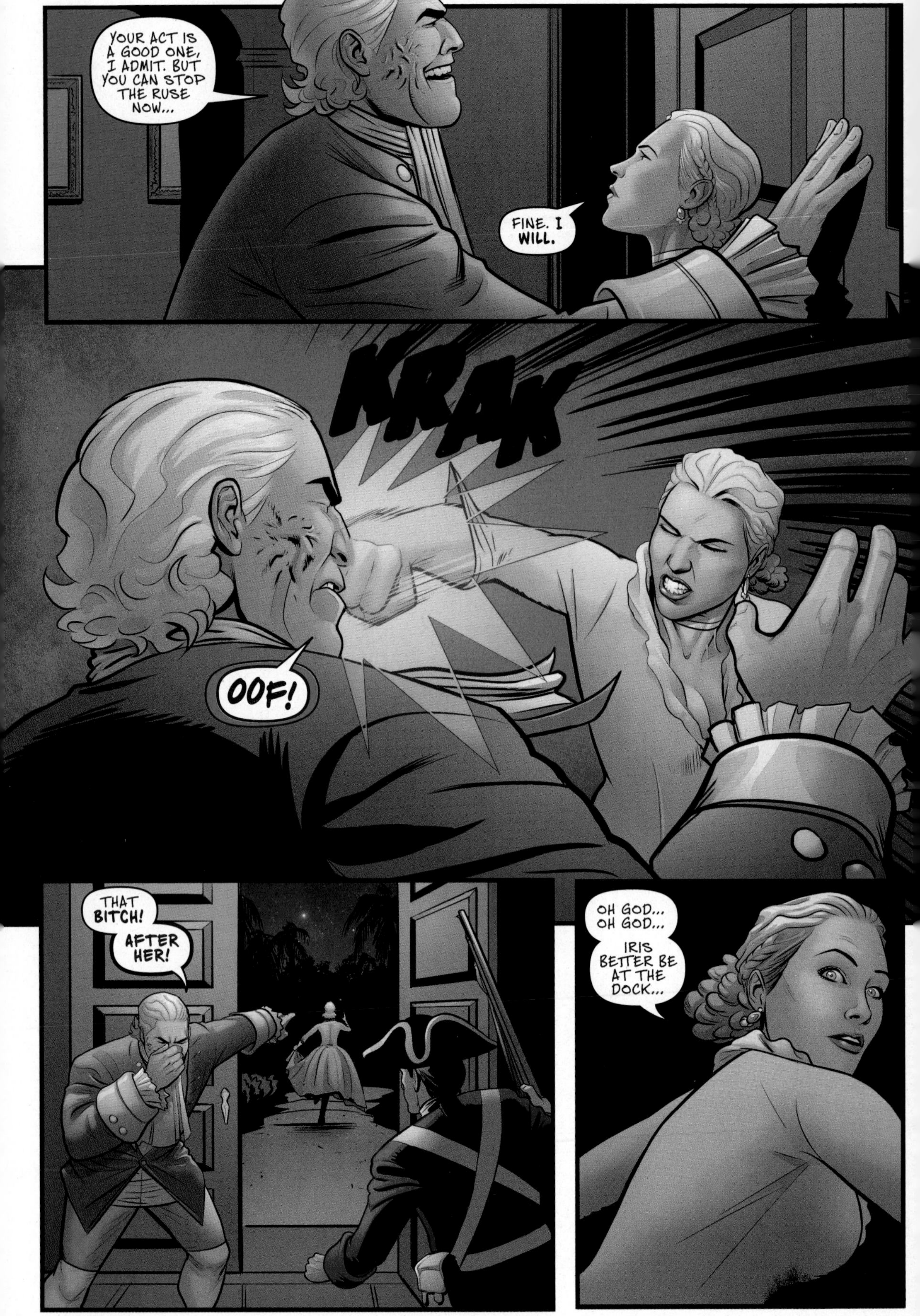
YOUR ACT IS A GOOD ONE, I ADMIT. BUT YOU CAN STOP THE RUSE NOW...
FINE. I WILL.
KRAK
OOF!
THAT BITCH!
AFTER HER!
OH GOD... OH GOD...
IRIS BETTER BE AT THE DOCK...

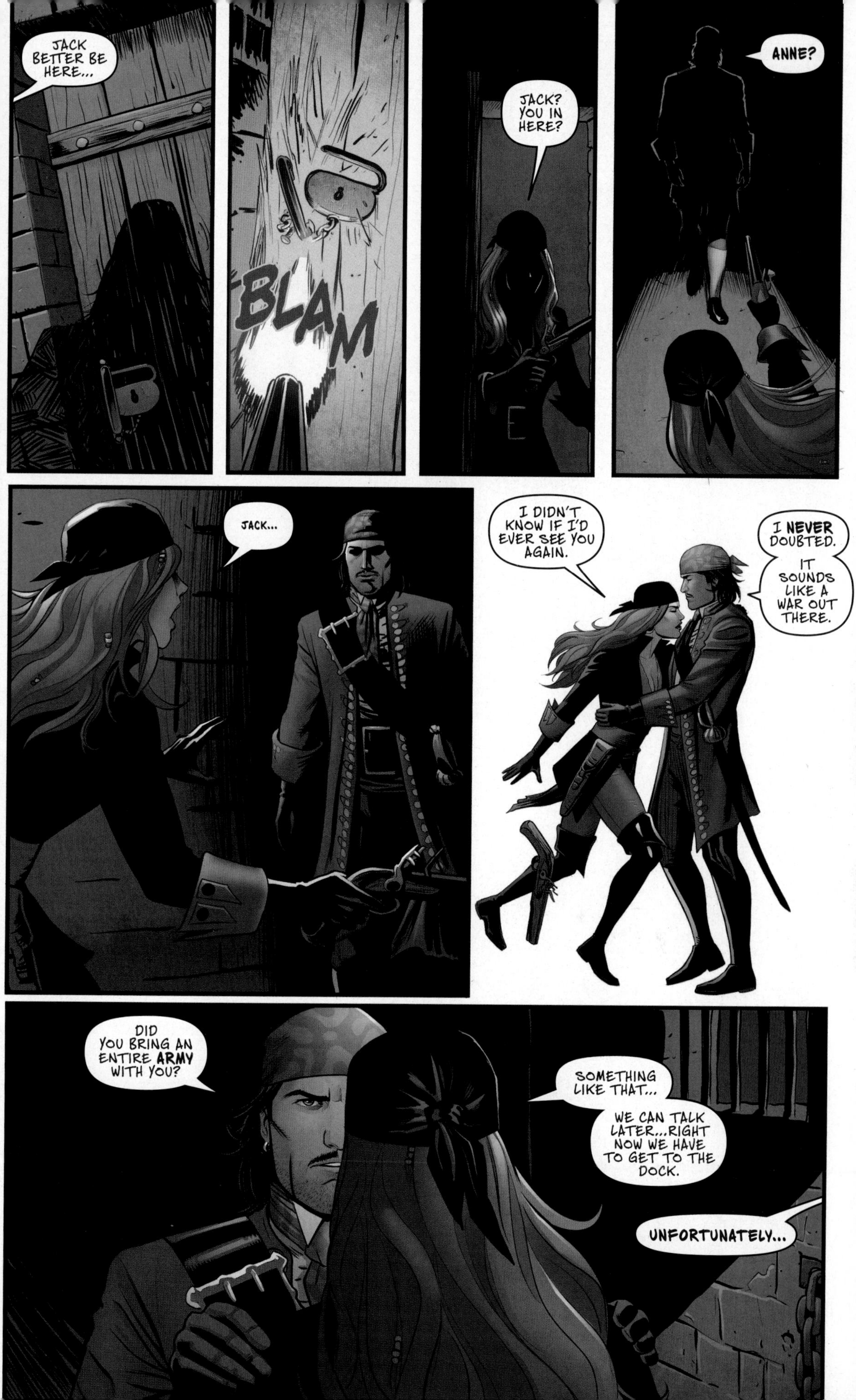
JACK BETTER BE HERE...
BLAM
JACK? YOU IN HERE?
ANNE?
JACK...
I DIDN'T KNOW IF I'D EVER SEE YOU AGAIN.
I NEVER DOUBTED.
IT SOUNDS LIKE A WAR OUT THERE.
DID YOU BRING AN ENTIRE ARMY WITH YOU?
SOMETHING LIKE THAT...
WE CAN TALK LATER...RIGHT NOW WE HAVE TO GET TO THE DOCK.
UNFORTUNATELY...

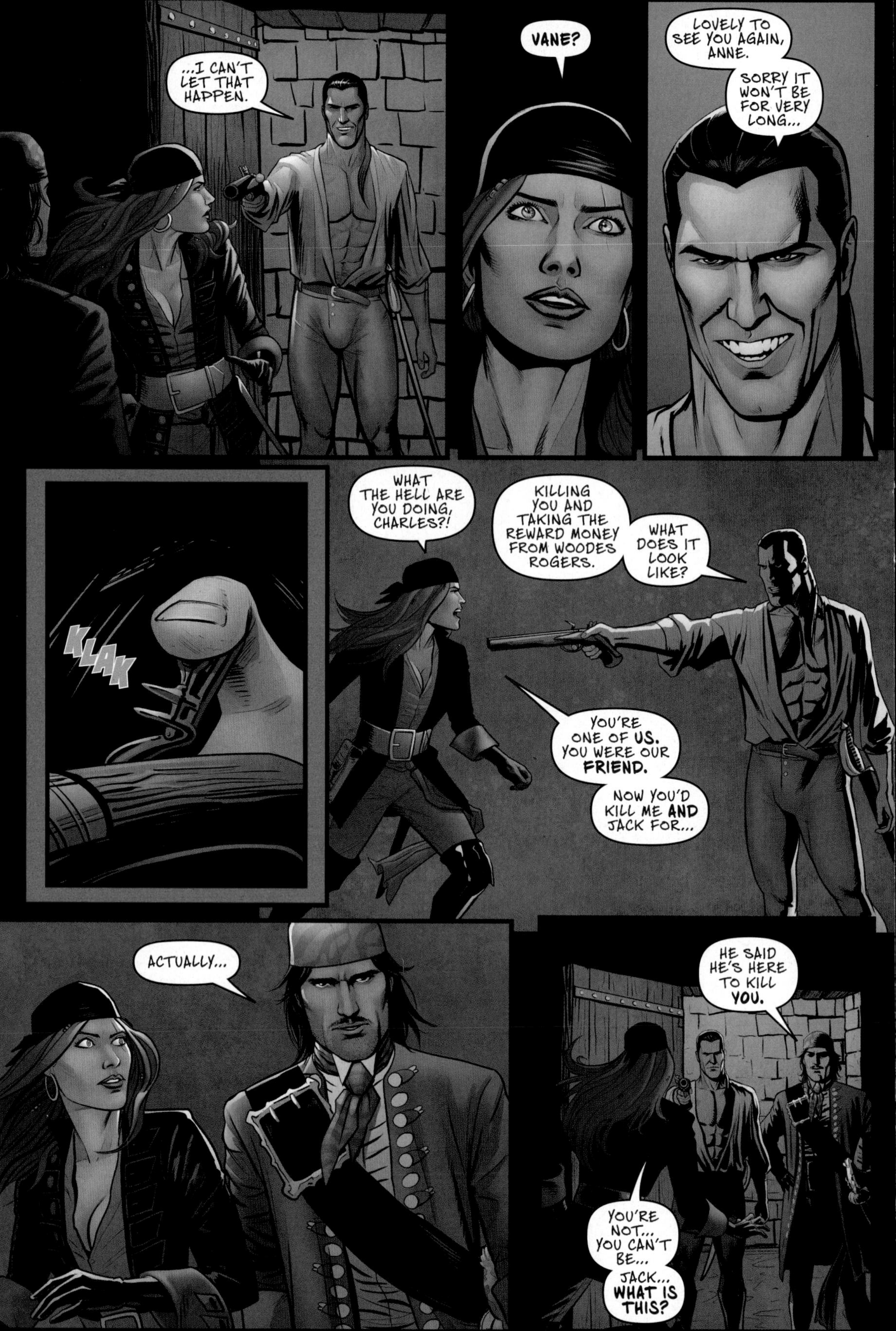
...I CAN'T LET THAT HAPPEN.
VANE?
LOVELY TO SEE YOU AGAIN, ANNE.
SORRY IT WON'T BE FOR VERY LONG...
KLAK
WHAT THE HELL ARE YOU DOING, CHARLES?!
KILLING YOU AND TAKING THE REWARD MONEY FROM WOODES ROGERS.
WHAT DOES IT LOOK LIKE?
YOU'RE ONE OF **US.** YOU WERE OUR **FRIEND.**
NOW YOU'D KILL ME **AND** JACK FOR...
ACTUALLY...
HE SAID HE'S HERE TO KILL **YOU.**
YOU'RE NOT... YOU CAN'T BE... JACK... **WHAT IS THIS?**

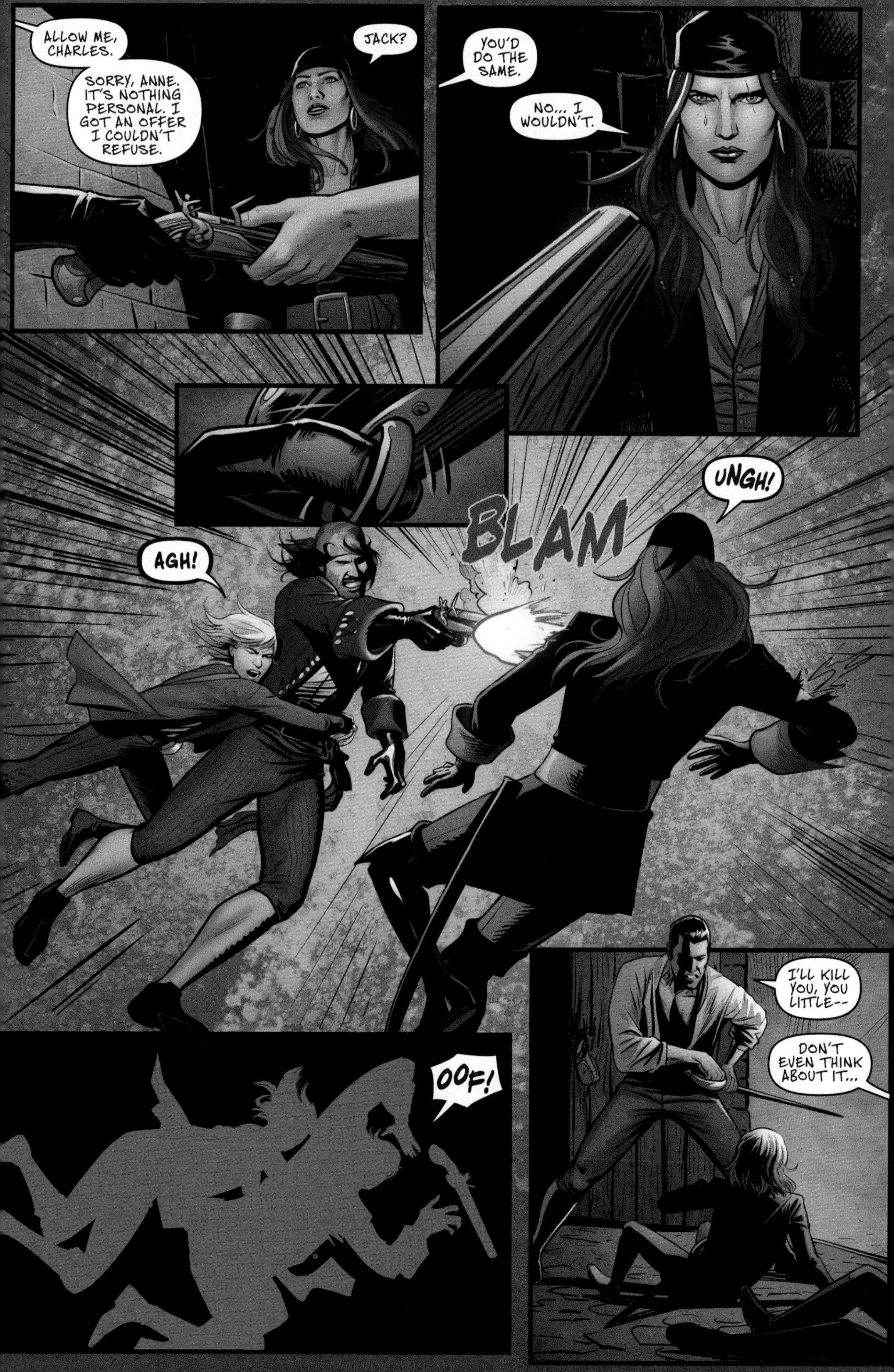
ALLOW ME, CHARLES.
JACK?
SORRY, ANNE. IT'S NOTHING PERSONAL. I GOT AN OFFER I COULDN'T REFUSE.
YOU'D DO THE SAME.
NO... I WOULDN'T.
BLAM
UNGH!
AGH!
OOF!
I'LL KILL YOU, YOU LITTLE--
DON'T EVEN THINK ABOUT IT...

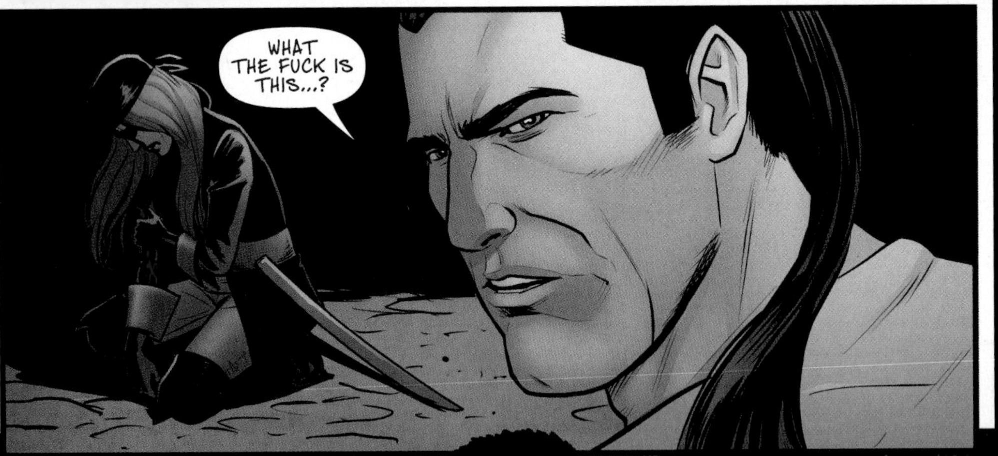
WHAT THE FUCK IS THIS...?

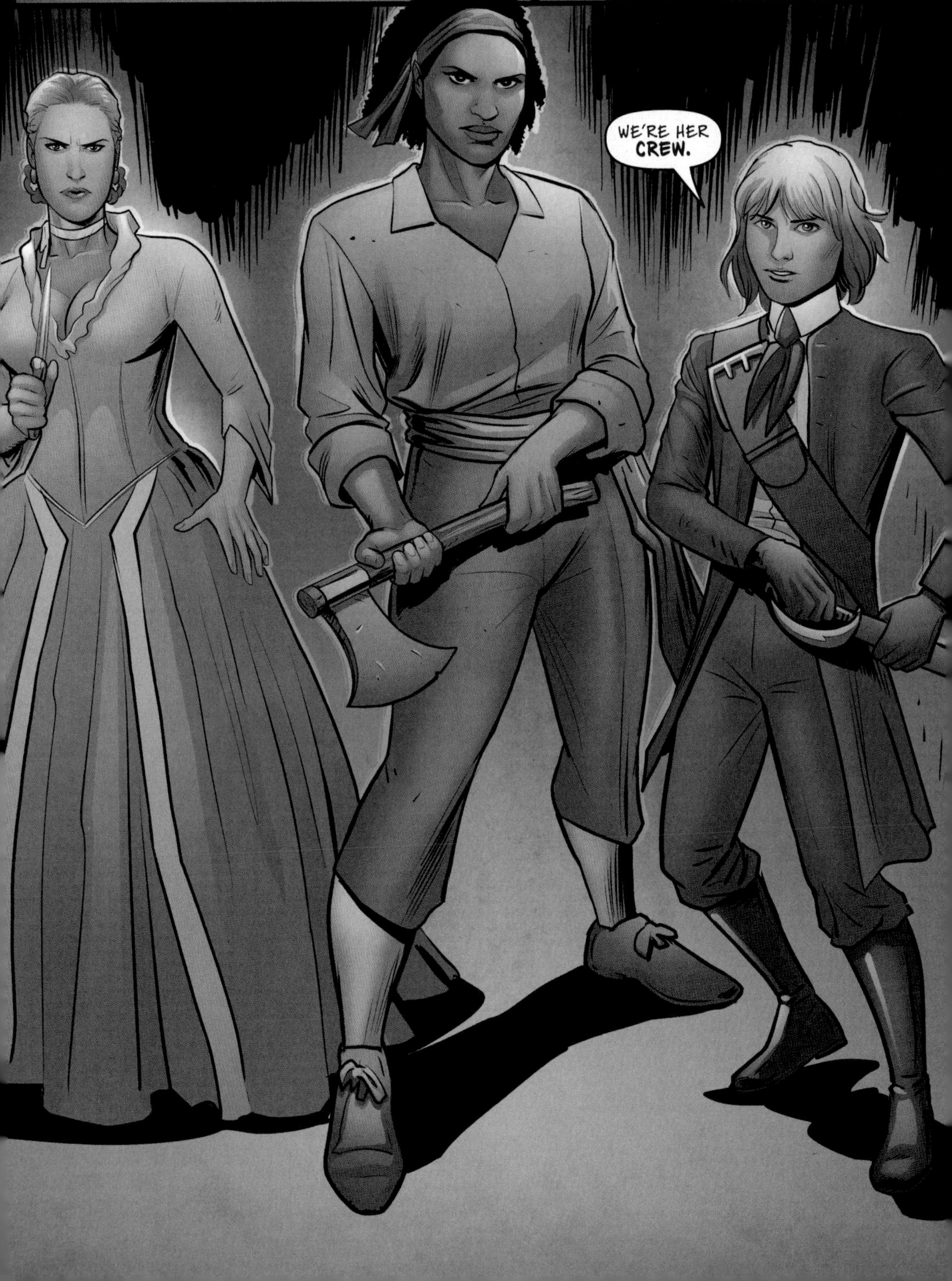
WE'RE HER **CREW.**

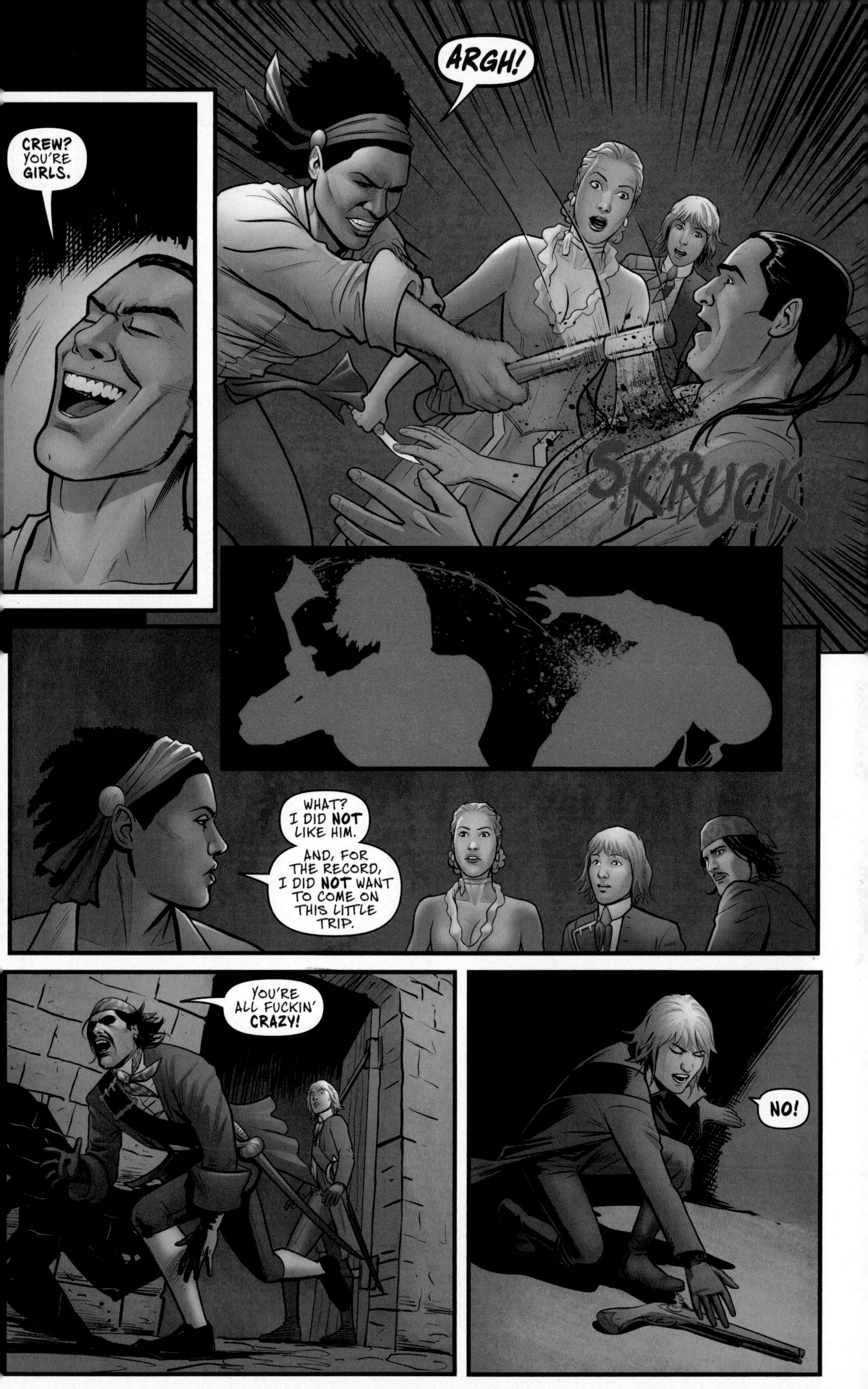
CREW? YOU'RE GIRLS.
ARGH!
SKRUCK
WHAT? I DID NOT LIKE HIM.
AND, FOR THE RECORD, I DID NOT WANT TO COME ON THIS LITTLE TRIP.
YOU'RE ALL FUCKIN' CRAZY!
NO!

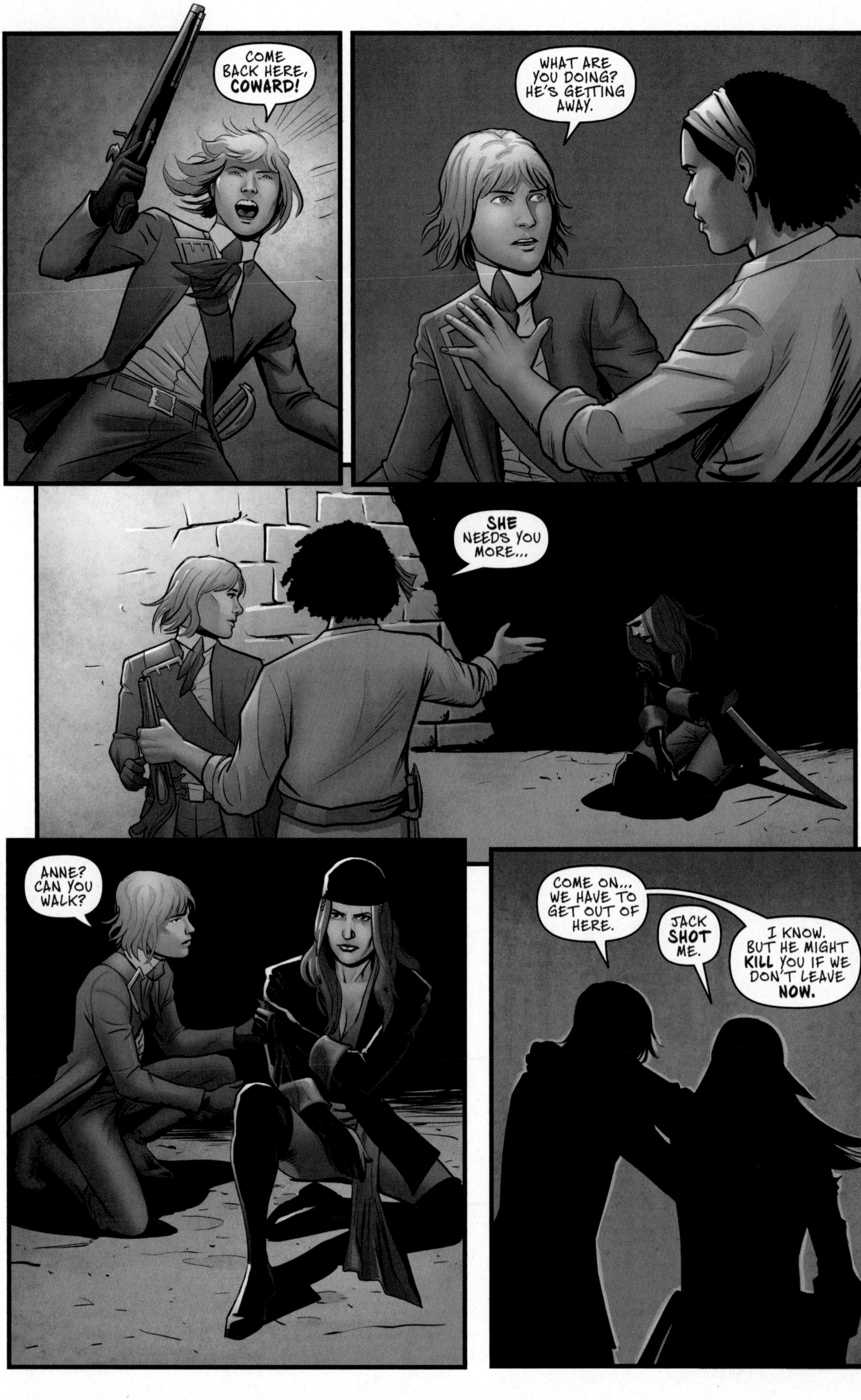
COME BACK HERE, **COWARD!**
WHAT ARE YOU DOING? HE'S GETTING AWAY.
SHE NEEDS YOU MORE...
ANNE? CAN YOU WALK?
COME ON... WE HAVE TO GET OUT OF HERE.
JACK **SHOT** ME.
I KNOW. BUT HE MIGHT **KILL** YOU IF WE DON'T LEAVE **NOW.**

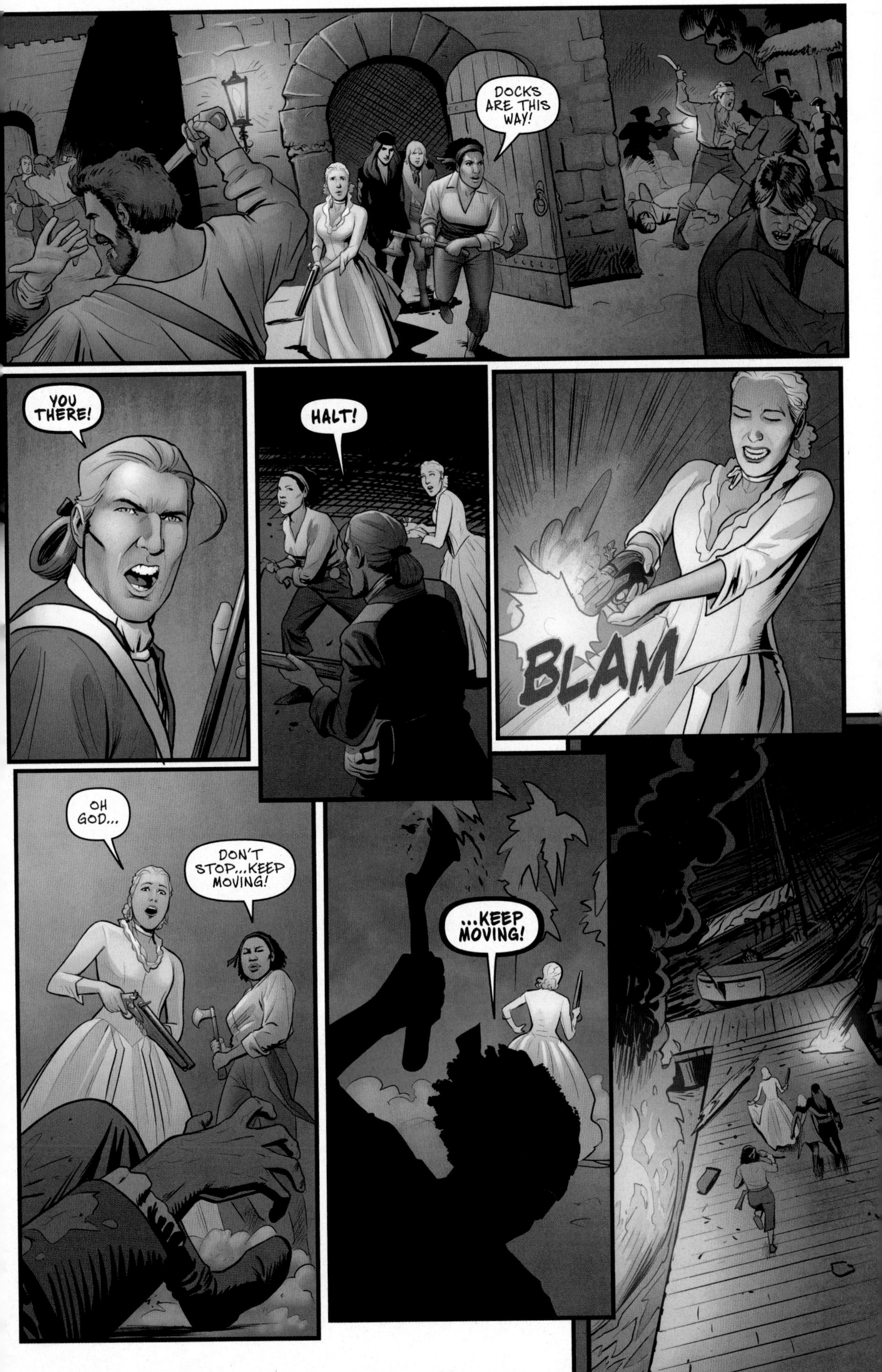
DOCKS ARE THIS WAY!
YOU THERE!
HALT!
BLAM
OH GOD...
DON'T STOP...KEEP MOVING!
...KEEP MOVING!

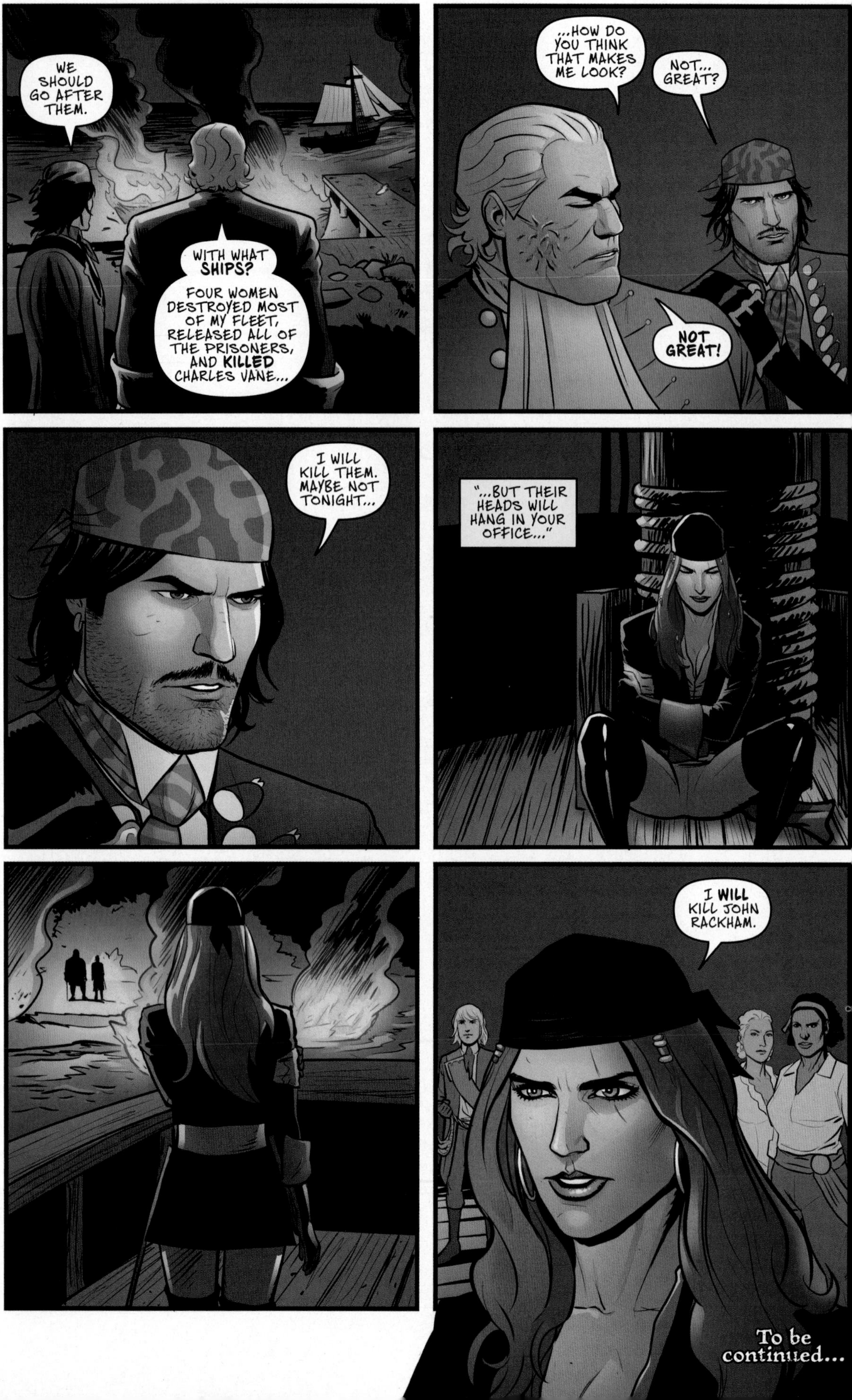
WE SHOULD GO AFTER THEM.
WITH WHAT SHIPS?
FOUR WOMEN DESTROYED MOST OF MY FLEET, RELEASED ALL OF THE PRISONERS, AND KILLED CHARLES VANE...
...HOW DO YOU THINK THAT MAKES ME LOOK?
NOT... GREAT?
NOT GREAT!
I WILL KILL THEM. MAYBE NOT TONIGHT...
"...BUT THEIR HEADS WILL HANG IN YOUR OFFICE..."
I WILL KILL JOHN RACKHAM.
To be continued...

Cover Gallery

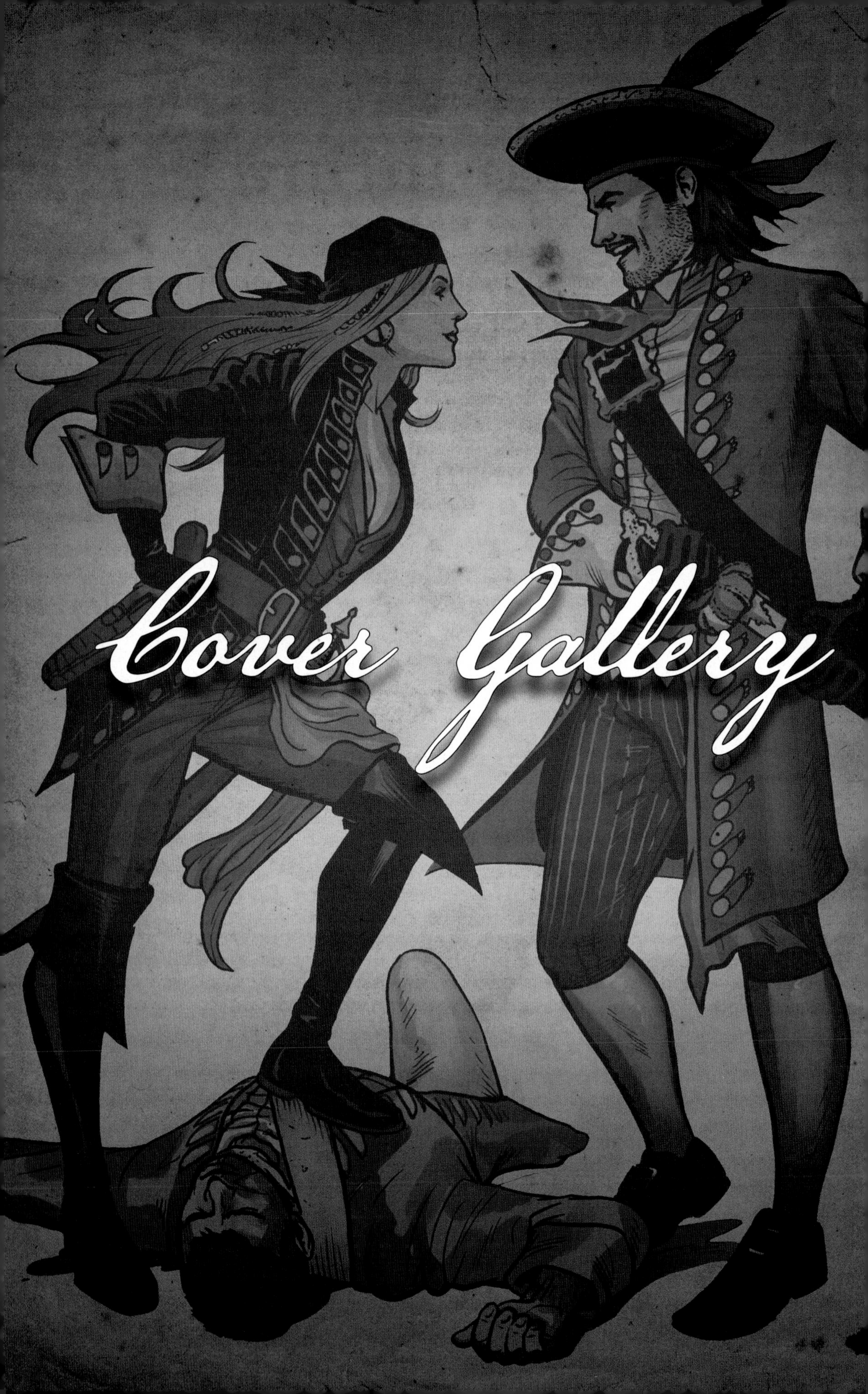

Issue №1 Cover A

Art by Craig Cermak

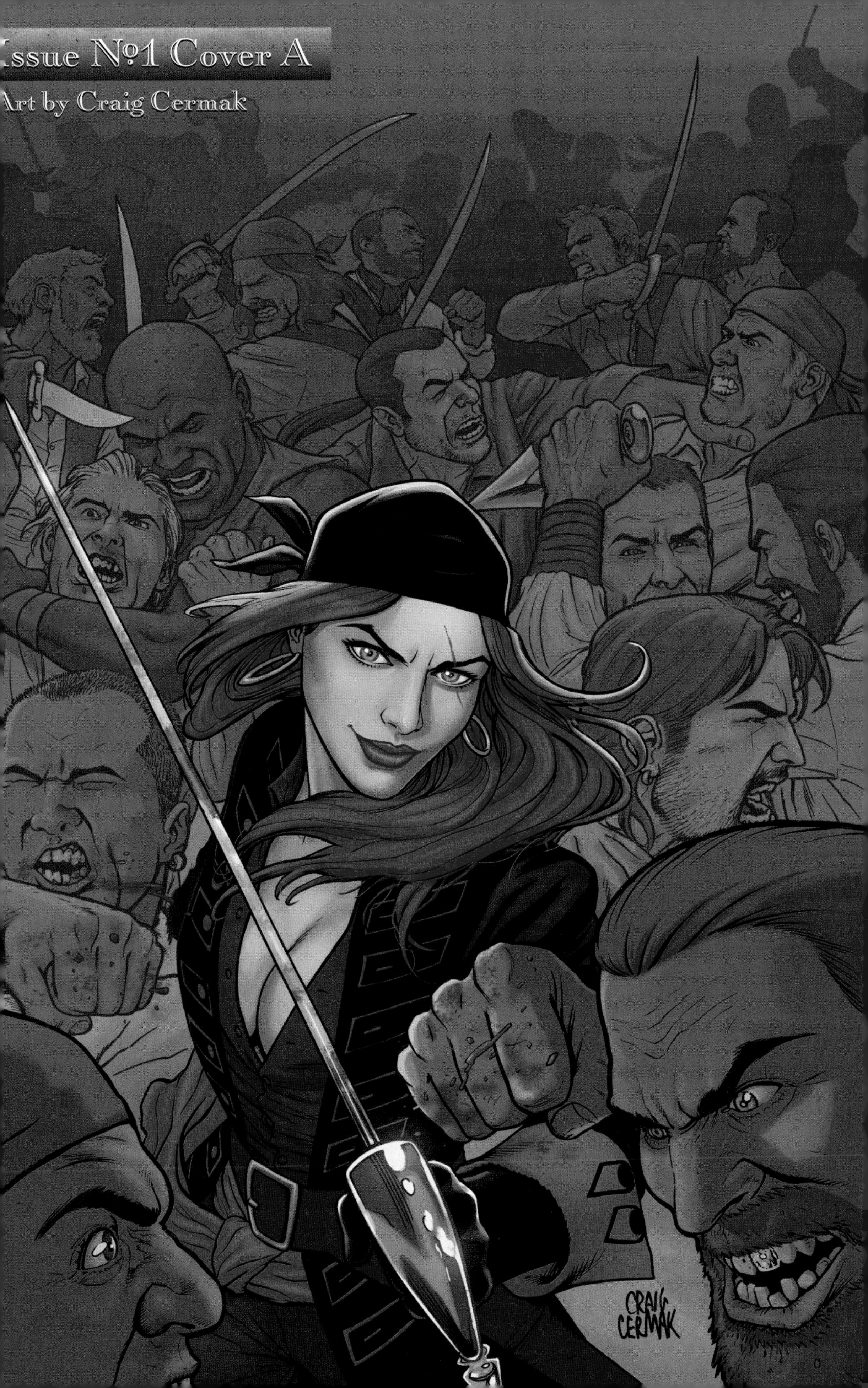
CRAIG CERMAK

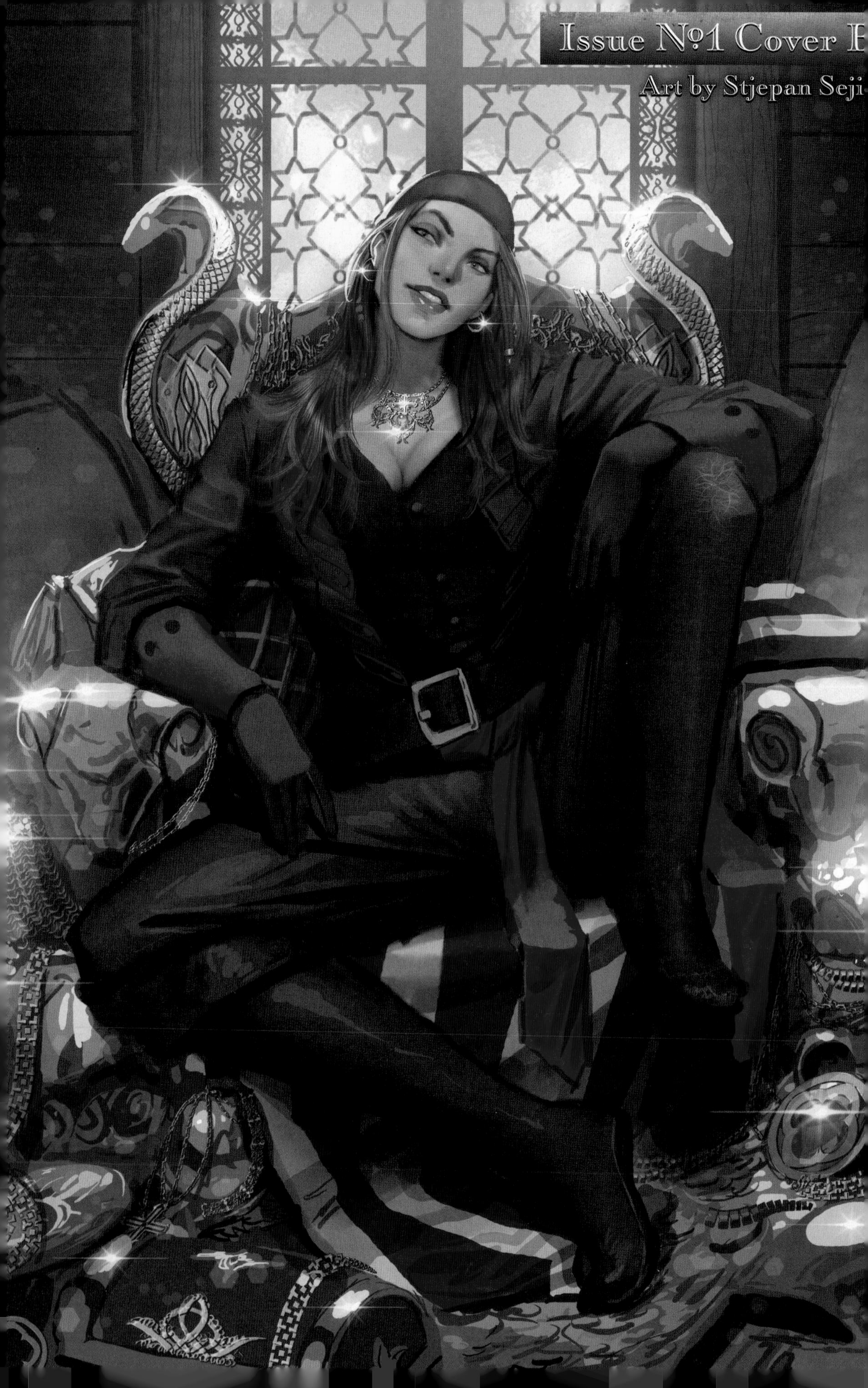
Issue №1 Cover
Art by Stjepan Seji

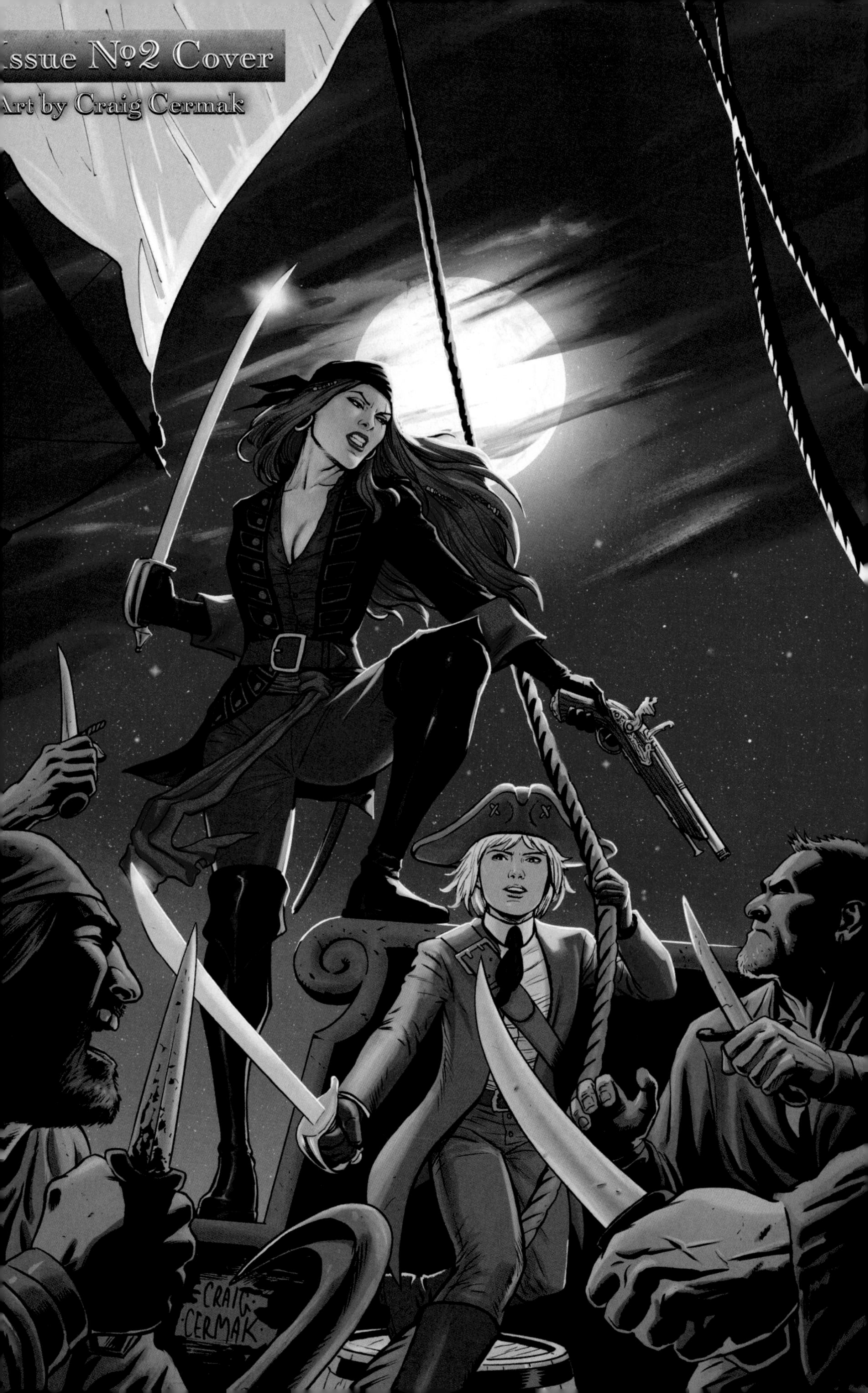
CRAIG
CERMAK
Issue №2 Cover
Art by Craig Cermak

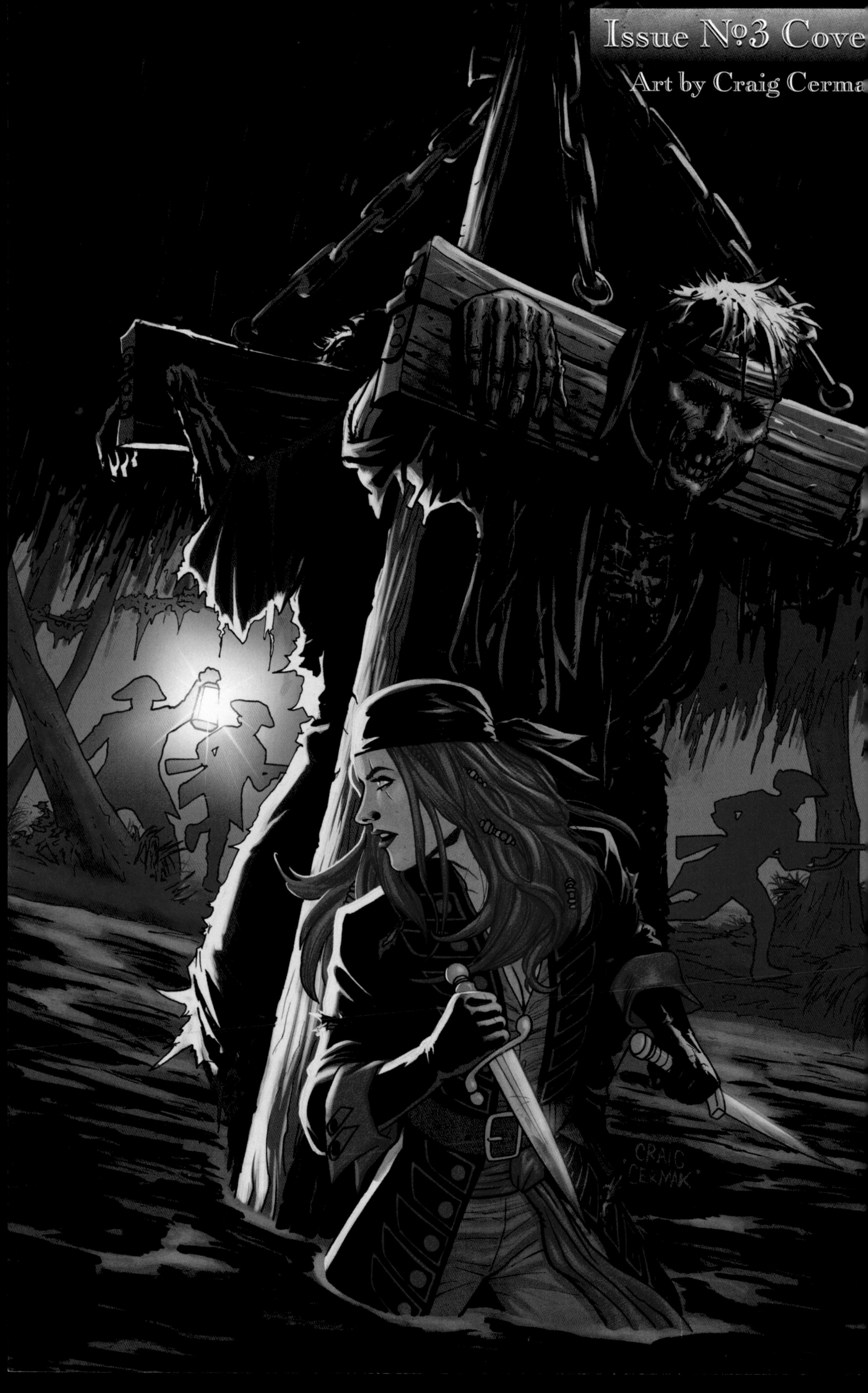
CRAIG
CERMAK

Issue №3 Cove

Art by Craig Cerma

Issue №4 Cover

Art by Craig Cermak

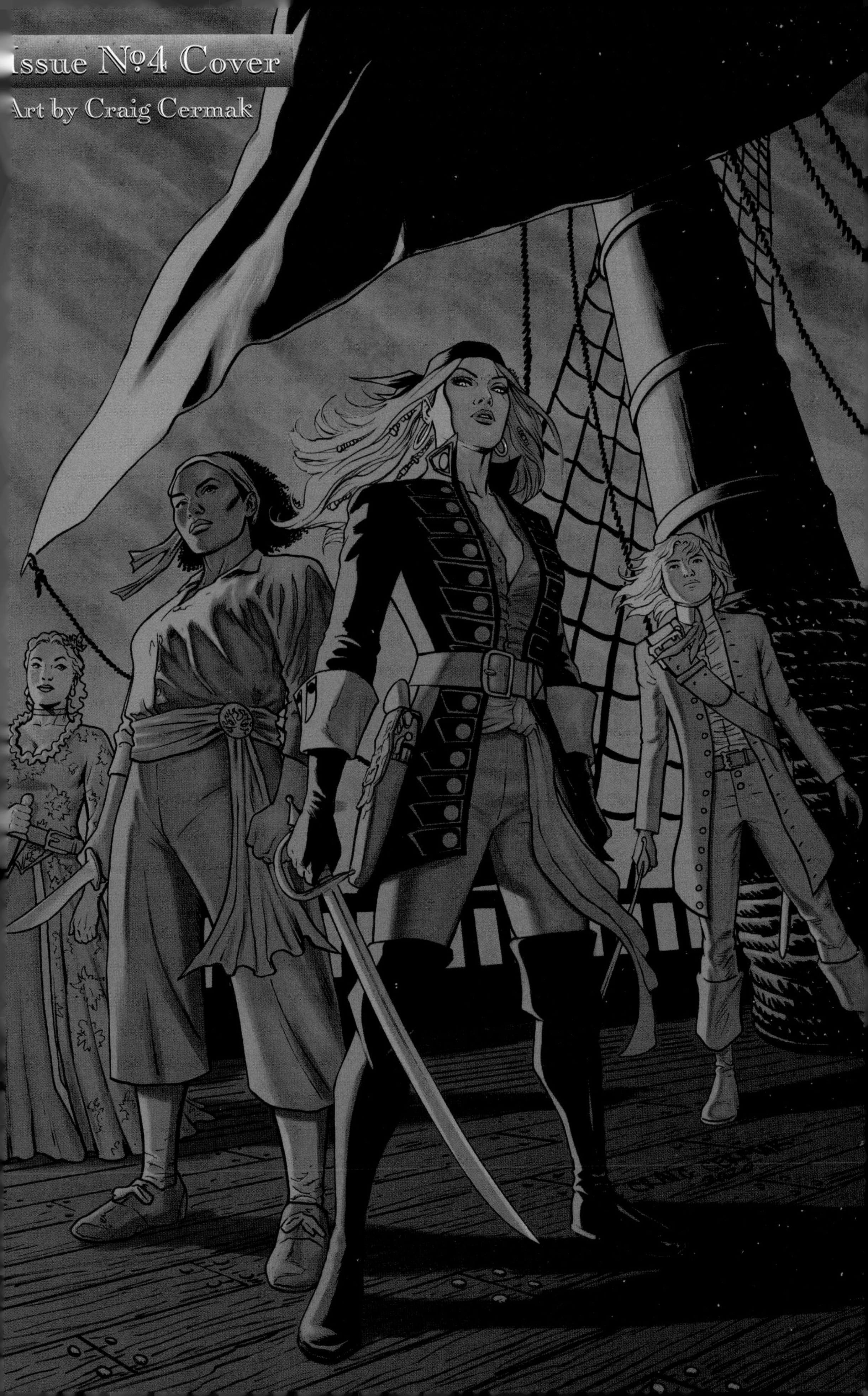

Dead Men Tell No Tales

I think everyone's hometown has a tradition or event of some kind that seems absolutely normal until you leave home and realize no one else has heard of this thing and thinks it sounds really odd. Well, I'm from **Tampa, FL** and we *really* like pirates. And I don't mean in a *"we named our football team the Buccaneers"* kind of way – I mean the kind of pirate obsession that spans week-long festivals with giant pirate parades, and models of pirate ships invading Tampa bay, and drunken Floridians dressed as pirates demanding the keys to the city from the mayor… Yeah, we call this tradition *Gasparilla* in honor of a pirate named Jose Gaspar (probably a fictitious pirate, by the way) who was said to wander the bay area. Pirates (and drunk people on boats throwing beads) … that's kind of our **thing**.

I mention Gasparilla because 1) it's really odd and funny, and 2) because I find it fascinating just how much pirate lore and mythology has invaded (hehe) our lives. Pirate *fact* is a bit tough to come by, but the legends and myths about these oftentimes larger-than-life rebels lives on in popular culture to ignite a sense of adventure for the audience. *Anne Bonny* is one such pirate legend who is definitely more myth than fact. Unlike Jose Gaspar, there is actually record that Bonny existed, but that record is pretty scarce.

What we do know comes from *A General History of the Pyrates* written by *Captain Charles Johnson*. Or, was it? Some accounts cite that this book was actually written by Daniel Defoe. So, this very trustworthy source by one of the aforementioned authors tells us that Anne Bonny was born in Ireland somewhere around 1700. After getting married, she moved to Nassau with her husband where she met *Captain "Calico Jack" Rackham* and ran off with him as his lover and partner.

Some accounts say that Anne had red hair. Some say she didn't.

Some sources say that Anne liked to flash her breasts at men before killing them, just so they *knew* their life was ended by a woman. But still others claim that Anne preferred to dress only in men's clothing and conceal her sex.

Others say Anne had a relationship with her female companion *Mary Read*, not Jack.

After the capture of Anne and Mary, some legends state that the women staved off the noose by citing pregnancies.

While it's unfortunate that not more is **known** about the most notorious female pirate of all time, I think this is what makes her such an interesting character to write about, especially when we consider the time period she lived and what we do know that she chose as her vocation – piracy. Sure, pirates are often portrayed in pop culture as drunk, savage, ruthless, dirty, cunning… and afraid of crocodiles, but there is so much more to *choosing* a life of piracy. And that's exactly what Anne did. Choose.

uring a time when women had no rights in the newly formed British empire, Anne Bonny chose to eave her husband and make a name for herself on a pirate ship. Let's not forget that it was also taboo to ave a woman on a ship in the first place. Piracy offered Anne, and all others that chose the life, a form of esistance against the crown. Flying the skull and crossbones was a revolt – indentured servants, runaway aves, disgruntled sailors, and even women. Despite race, religion, nationality, and language, these pirates l found a community aboard their ships that life in the empire denied them. Many of these pirates were ven politically motivated, using their ships and influence to cut off supply lines, and severing the trade outes of slaves to the sugar plantations of America and the West Indies. While initially trying to catch irates, the Royal Navy eventually came to fear them and hope to avoid encounters.

f course, legends were spun about the murdering pirates that would torture all men, women, and hildren they came in contact with. It was all the great British Empire could do to disillusion anyone siding vith these motley rebels or, worse, thinking of joining them. Despite these wildly exaggerated rumors out demonic pirates, many ordinary people thought of pirates as a kind of folk hero. There was not place for them in the society that the British Empire was creating, so they fought to create their own aces and, along with it, fortunes.

ur story begins at the **end** of this Golden age of piracy, at a time when the crown had simply had nough. Pirates were wreaking extreme havoc, and something (or **someone**) needed to stop them. Cue *Voodes Rogers*, the man sent to bring peace to the Bahamas and a war hero from England's most recent var with France and Spain. Interestingly, Woodes served as a privateer during the war and felt he had general understanding of how pirates thought and operated. Rogers was devoted to his King and ountry in every way possible, and he was not willing to fail in his task of pacifying the seas (or, really, just eturning supremacy to the Royal Navy and not a motley assortment of roguish criminals).

Man Among Ye is an attempt at living on the edge of fact and fiction. We don't know what the dventures of Anne, Mary, and Jack really look like, but we know the time period they lived in and the inds of issues that pirates were dealing with. More importantly, we know **WHY** these three and their rews would choose a life under the black flag and why, despite Rogers' best efforts, they would fight ooth and nail to hang onto that lifestyle.

o, we hope you enjoy this tale and feel a little inspired to add some adventure and rebellion to your life ust so long as you maintain social distancing).

our Co-Captain and Gunner (because I wanna fire the canons!)

Stephanie

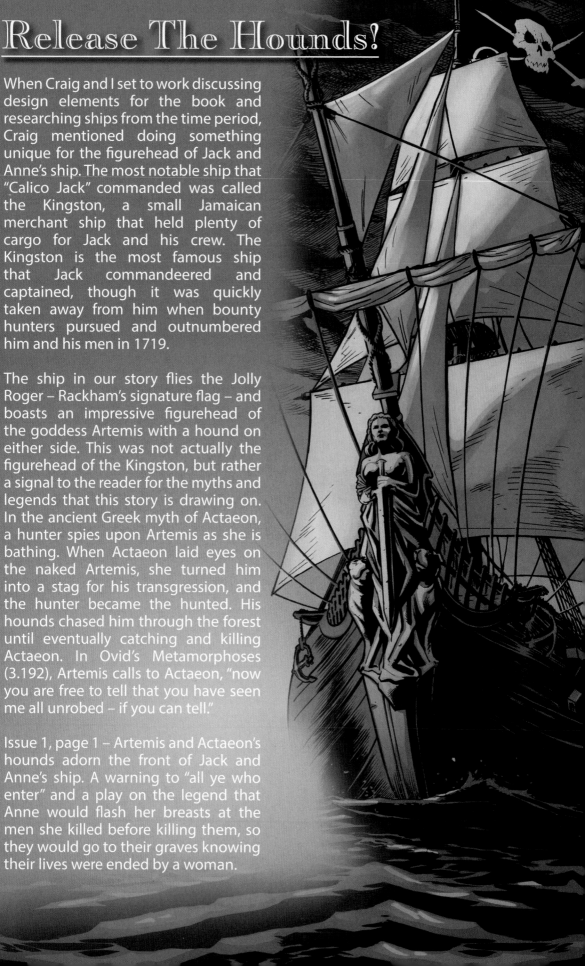

Release The Hounds!

When Craig and I set to work discussing design elements for the book and researching ships from the time period, Craig mentioned doing something unique for the figurehead of Jack and Anne's ship. The most notable ship that "Calico Jack" commanded was called the Kingston, a small Jamaican merchant ship that held plenty of cargo for Jack and his crew. The Kingston is the most famous ship that Jack commandeered and captained, though it was quickly taken away from him when bounty hunters pursued and outnumbered him and his men in 1719.

The ship in our story flies the Jolly Roger – Rackham's signature flag – and boasts an impressive figurehead of the goddess Artemis with a hound on either side. This was not actually the figurehead of the Kingston, but rather a signal to the reader for the myths and legends that this story is drawing on. In the ancient Greek myth of Actaeon, a hunter spies upon Artemis as she is bathing. When Actaeon laid eyes on the naked Artemis, she turned him into a stag for his transgression, and the hunter became the hunted. His hounds chased him through the forest until eventually catching and killing Actaeon. In Ovid's Metamorphoses (3.192), Artemis calls to Actaeon, "now you are free to tell that you have seen me all unrobed – if you can tell."

Issue 1, page 1 – Artemis and Actaeon's hounds adorn the front of Jack and Anne's ship. A warning to "all ye who enter" and a play on the legend that Anne would flash her breasts at the men she killed before killing them, so they would go to their graves knowing their lives were ended by a woman.

A Glimpse into the process of creating A MAN AMONG YE №1

Character Designs by Craig Cermak

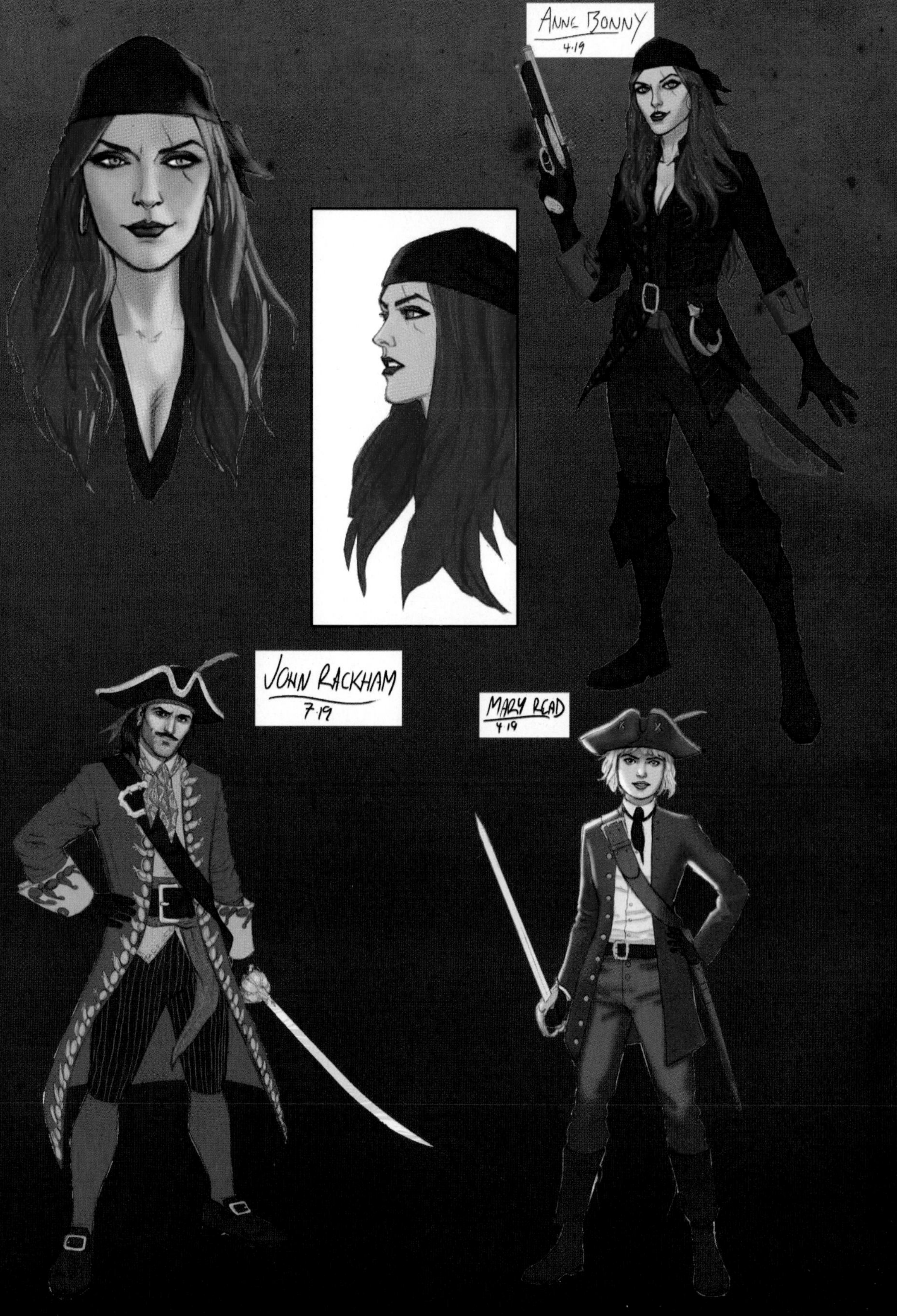
ANNE BONNY
4.19
JOHN RACKHAM
7.19
MARY READ
4.19

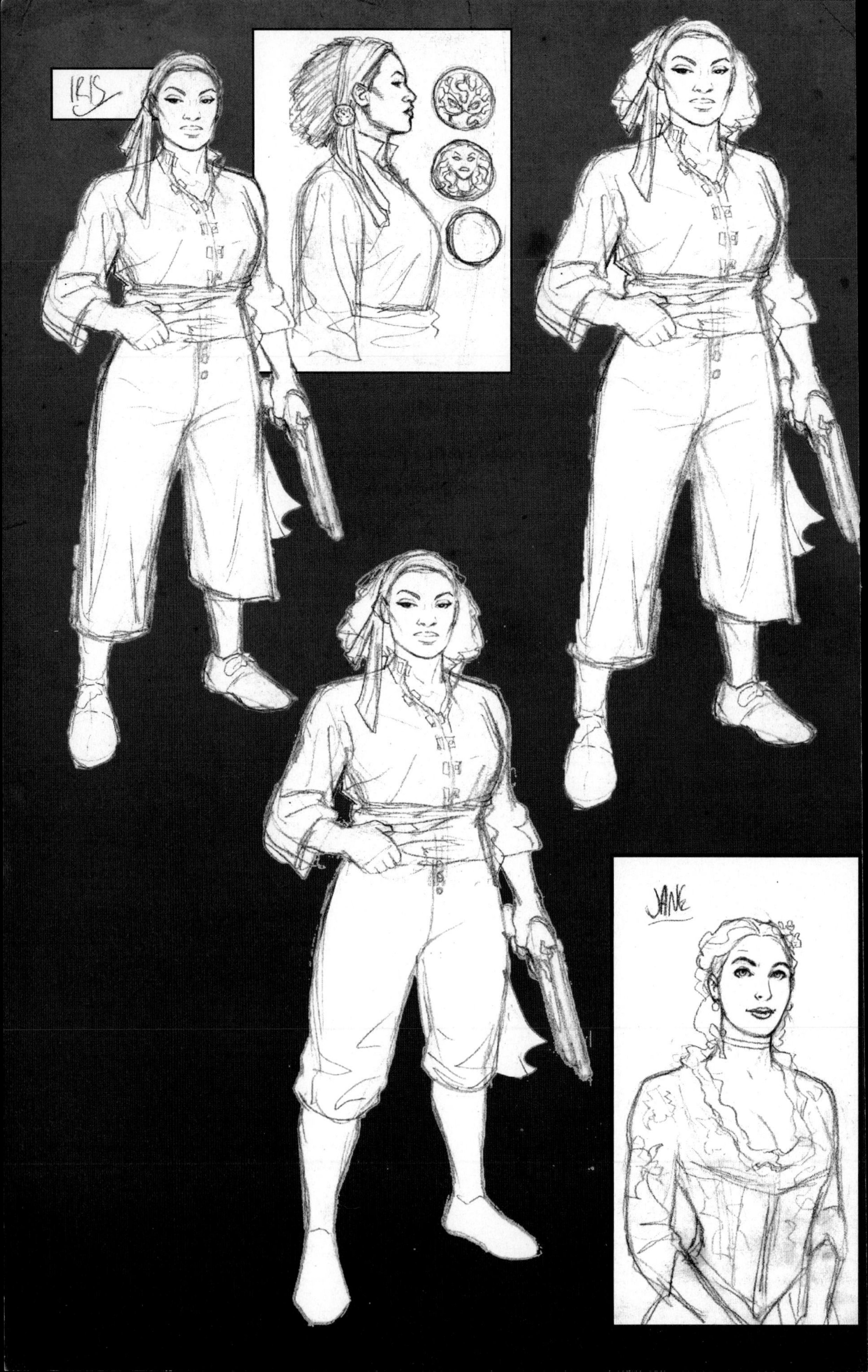
IRIS
JANE

Kingston Ship Process Art

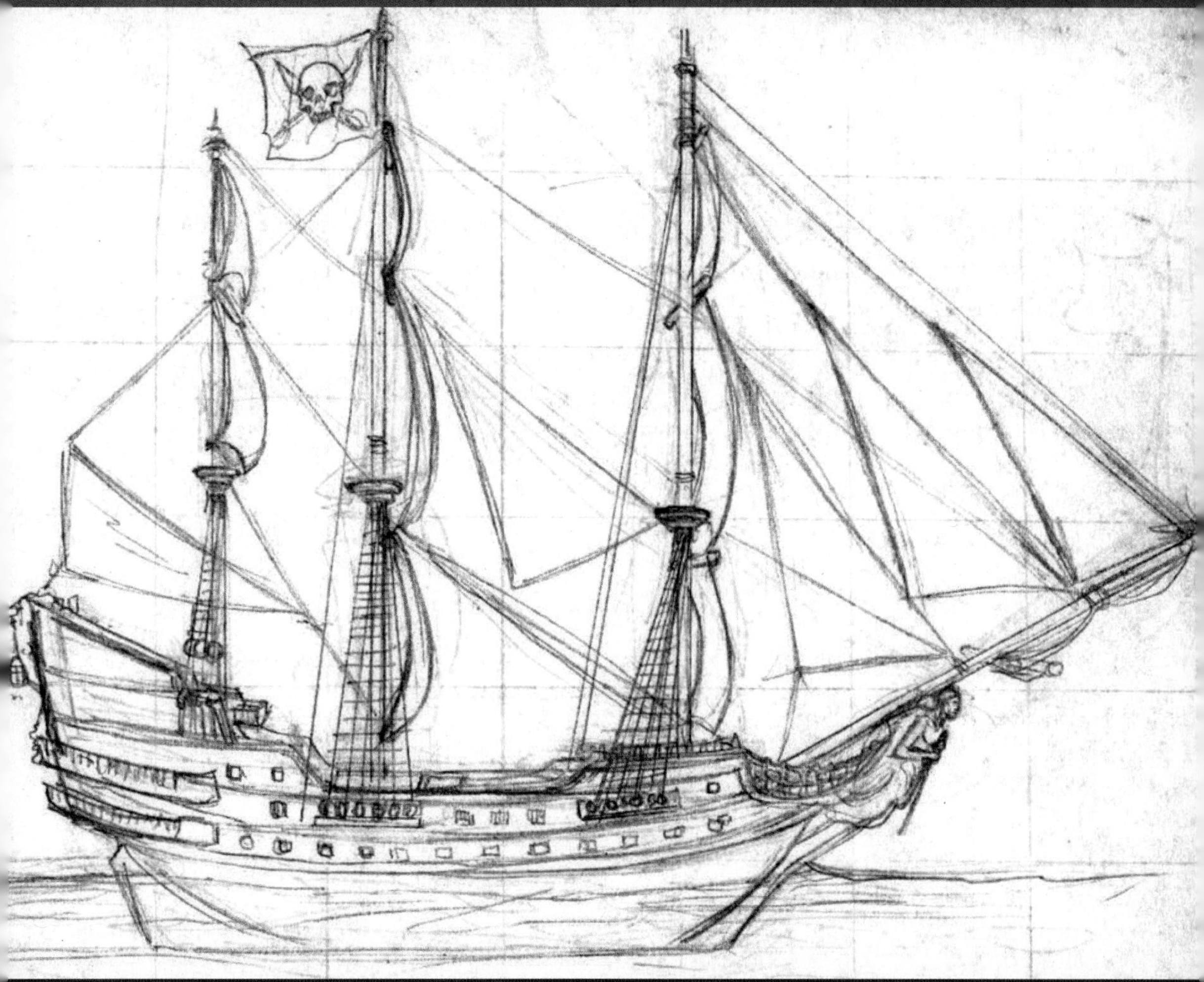

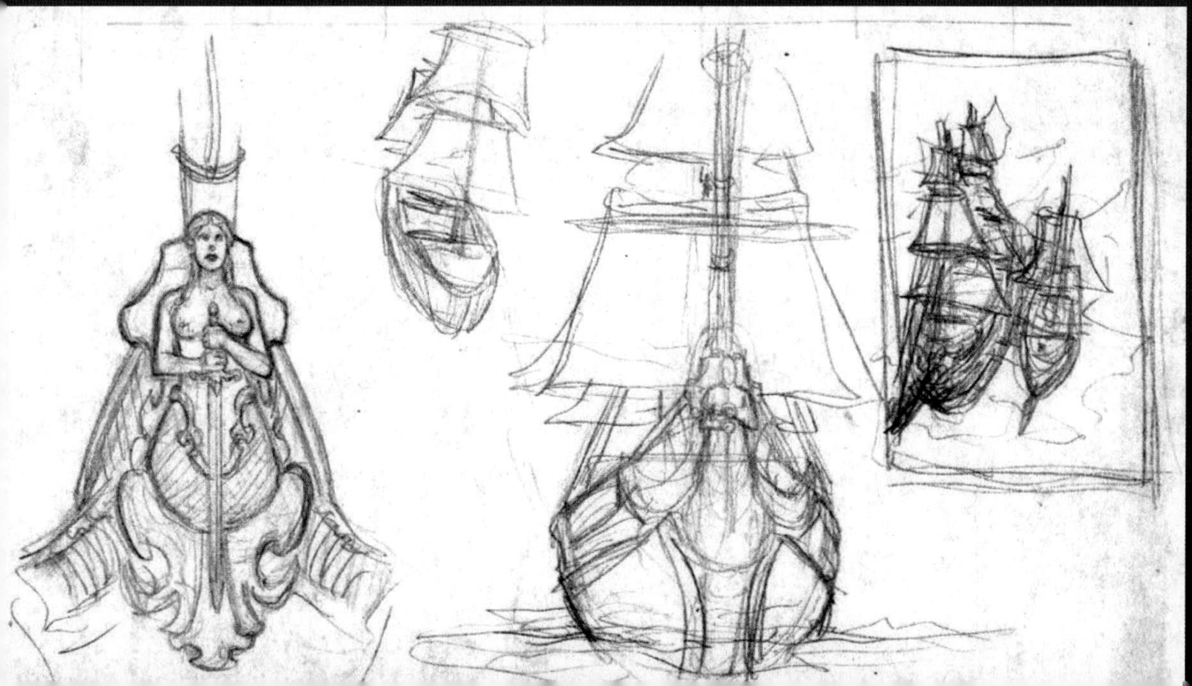

Issue №1 Cover Process Art

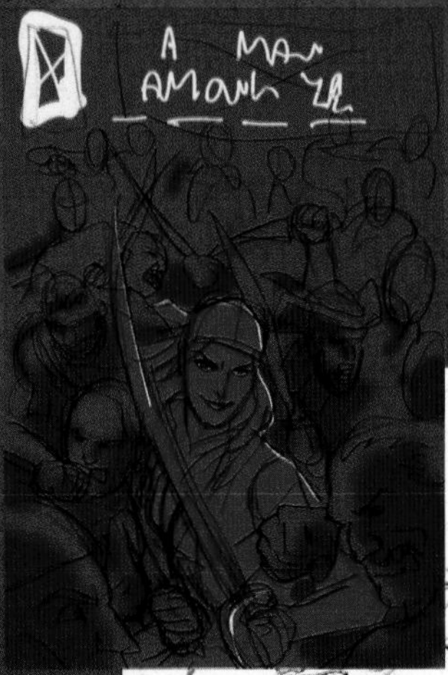
A MAN
AMONG YE

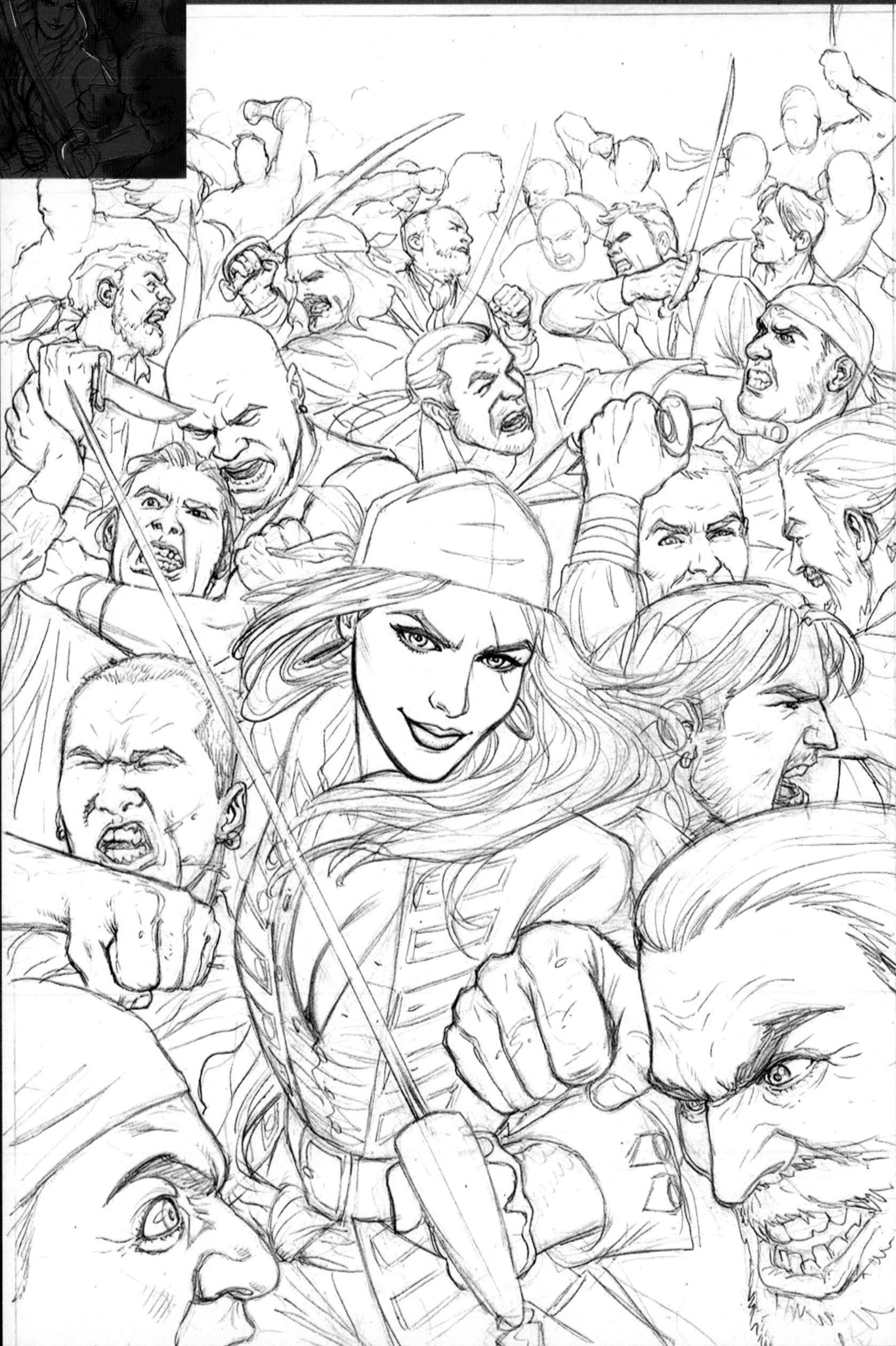

Issue №1 Cover Inks

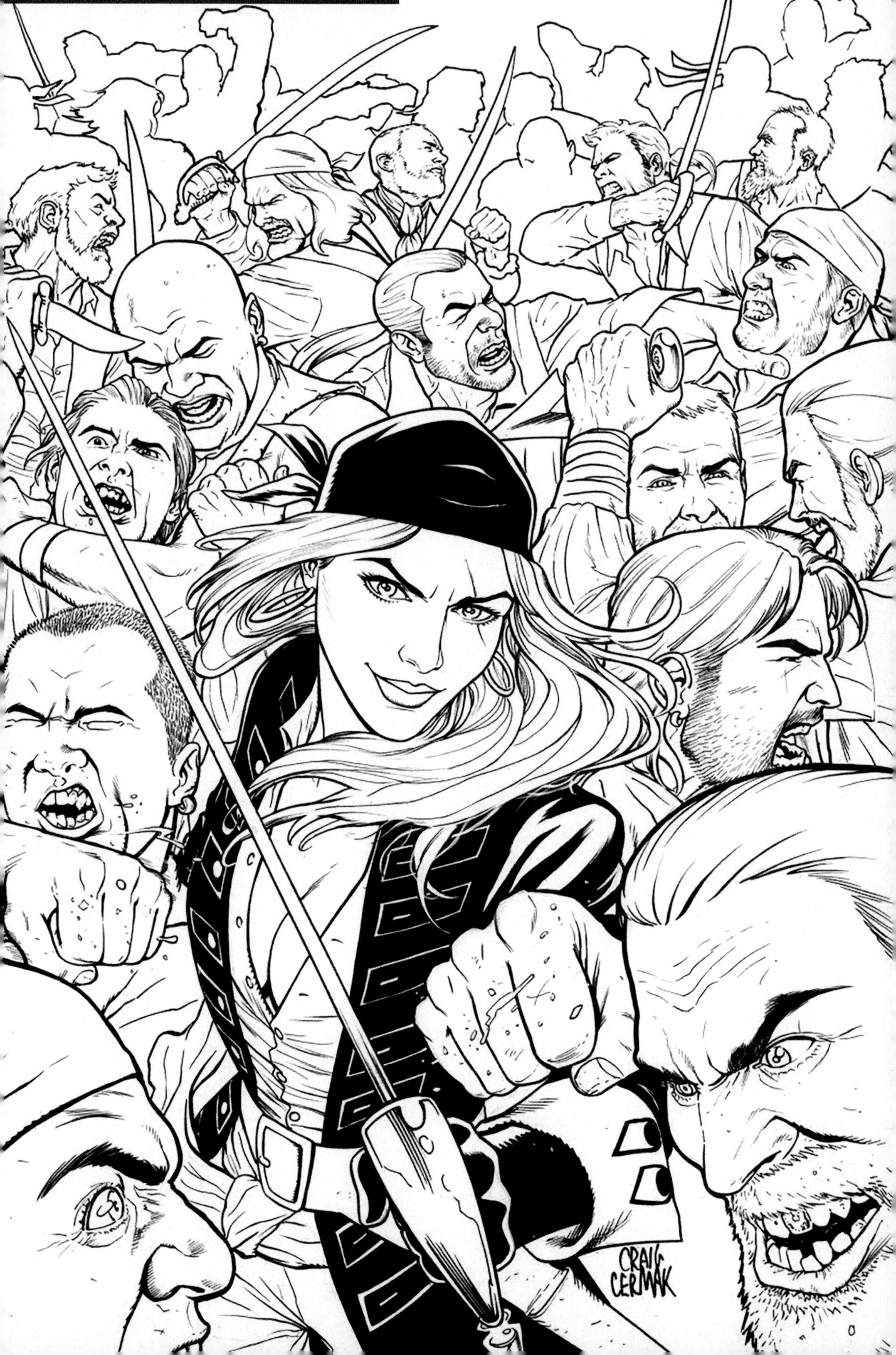
CRAIG CERMAK

Issue №2 Cover Process Art

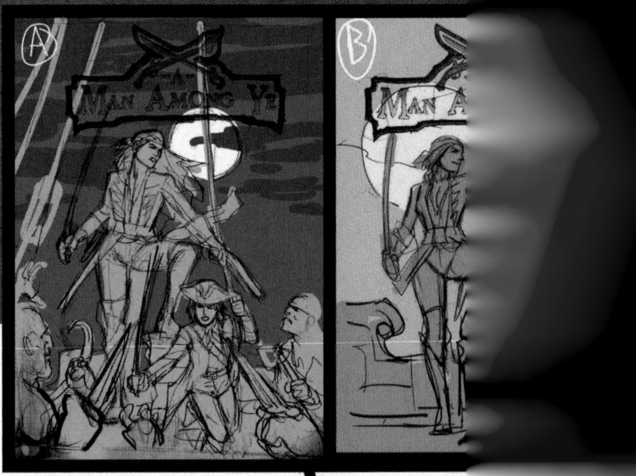

A
A
Man Among Ye
B
Man A

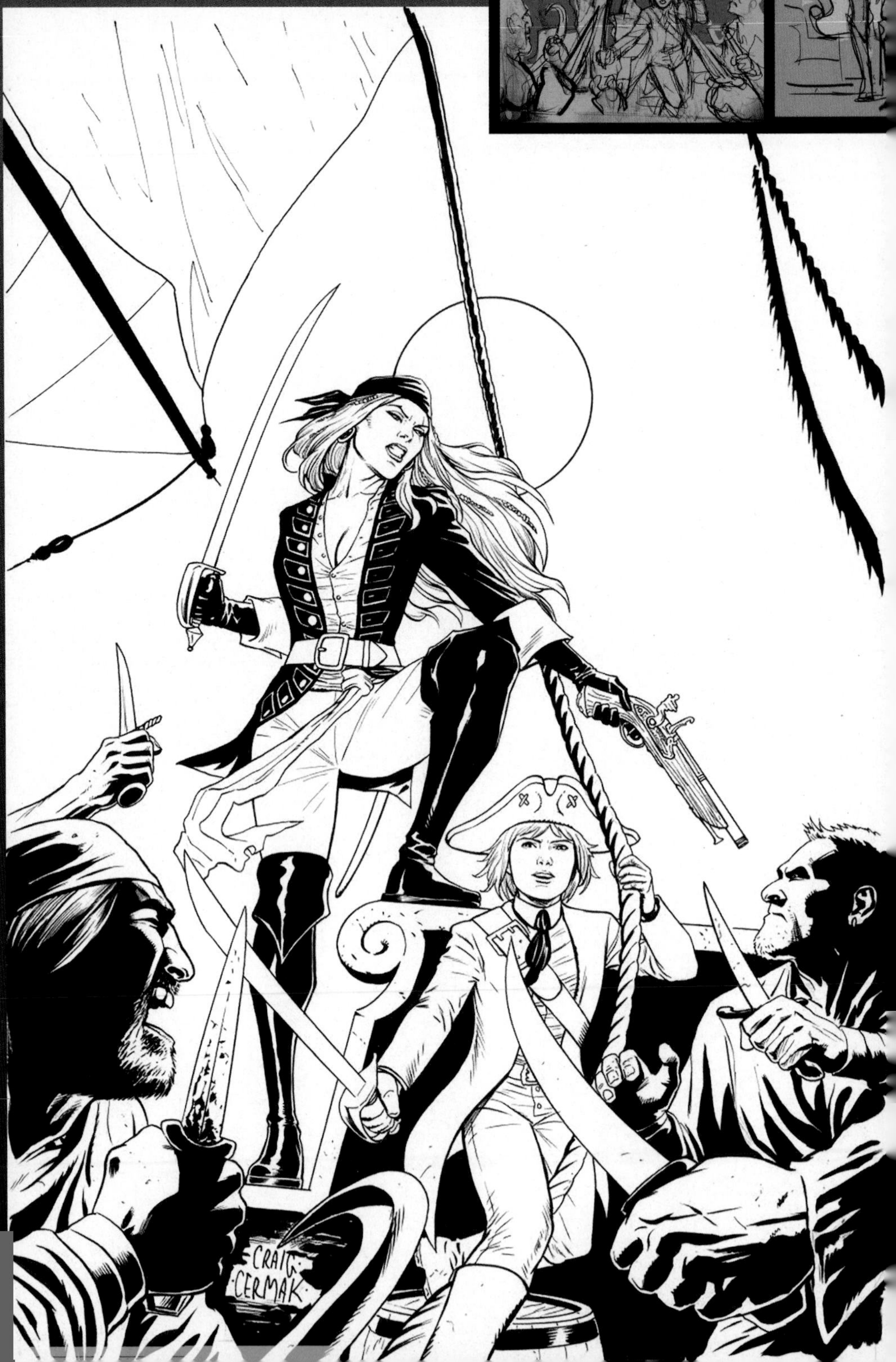

CRAIG CERMAK

Issue №3 Cover Process

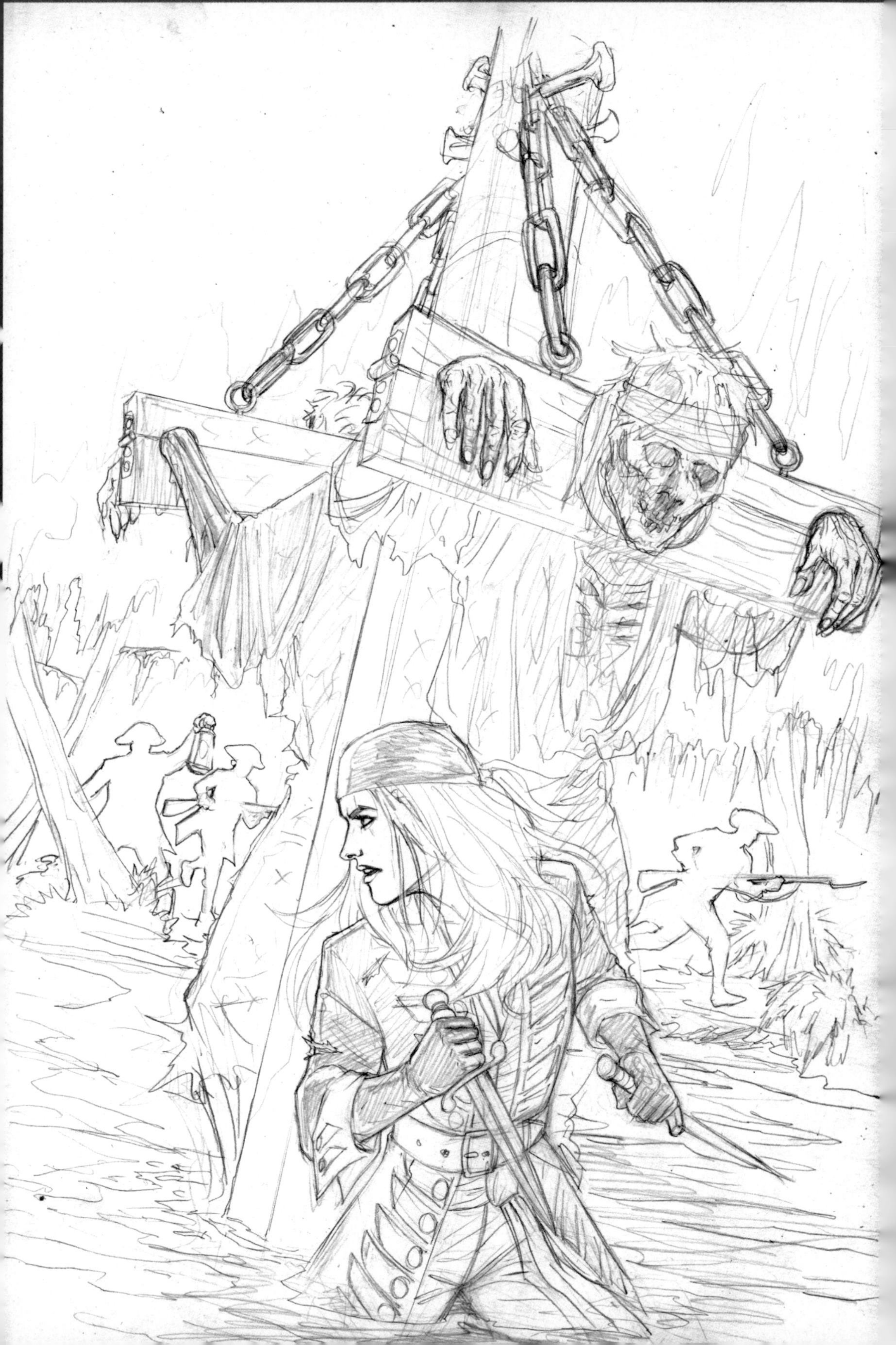

Issue №3 Cover Inks

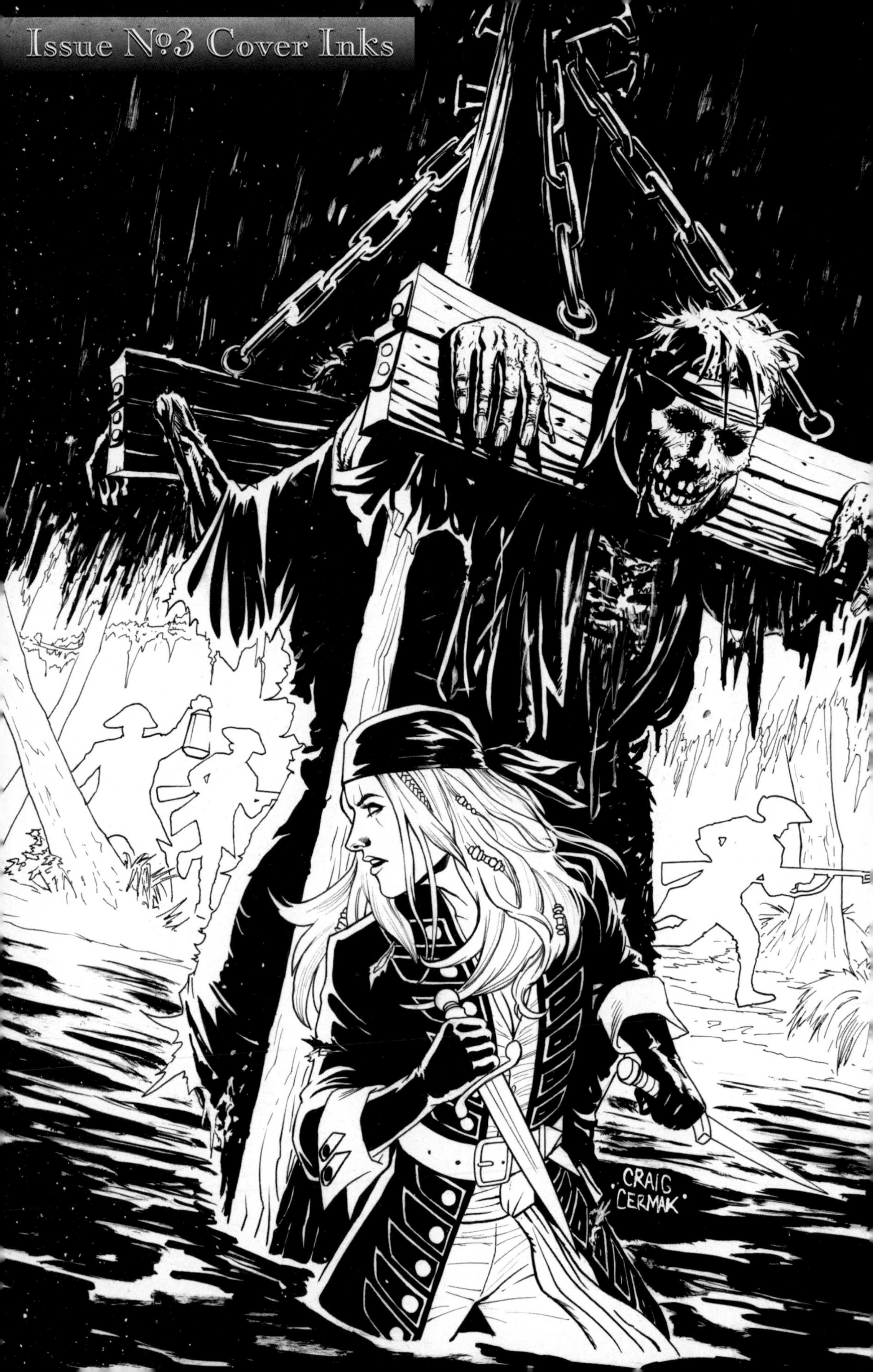
CRAIG CERMAK

Issue №3 Cover Color Process

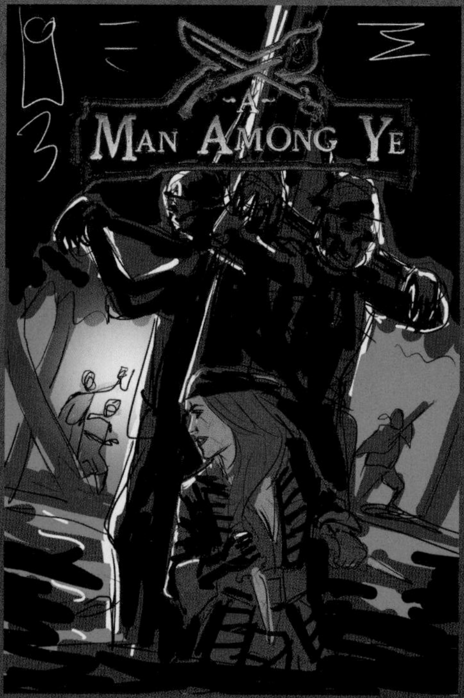

A
MAN AMONG YE

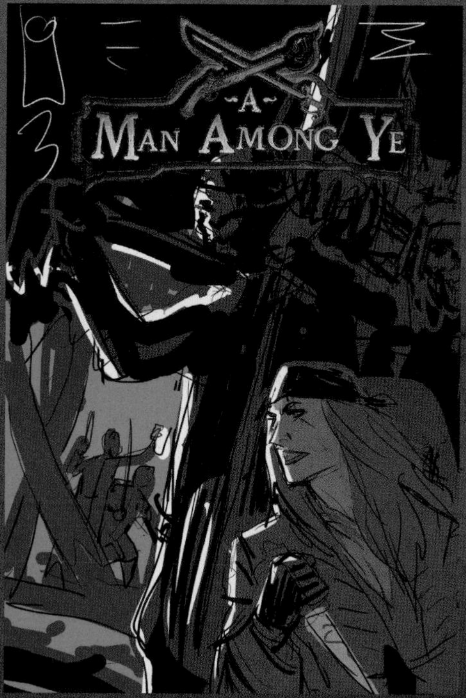

A
MAN AMONG YE

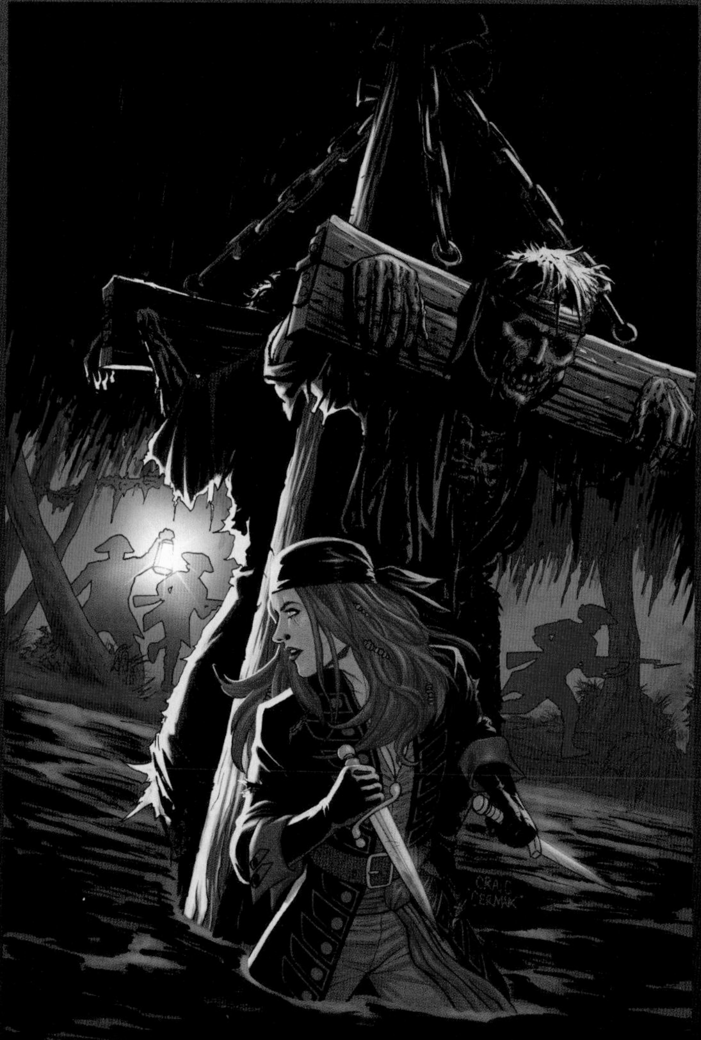

CRAIG CERMAK

Issue №4 Cover Thumbnails

A

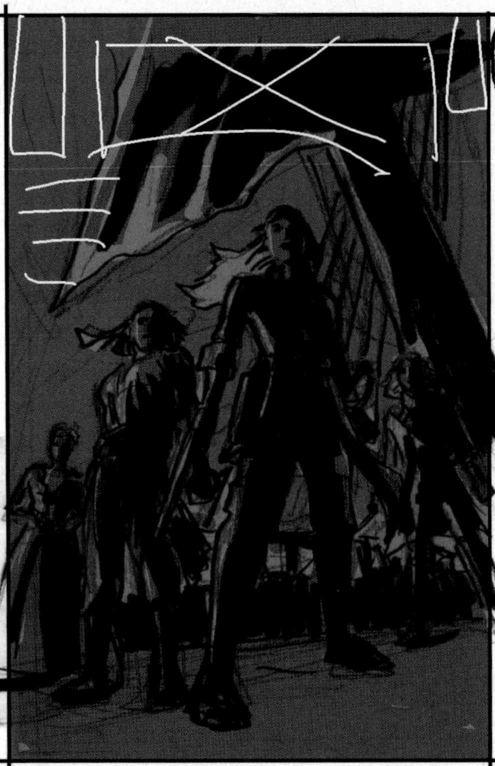

B

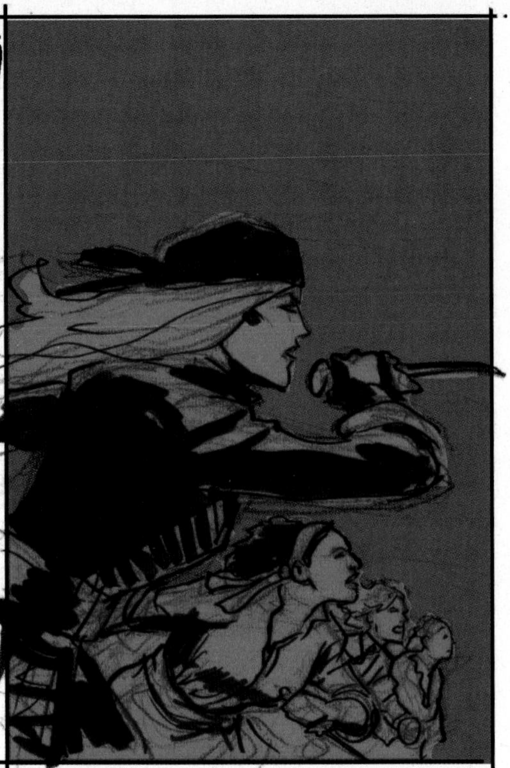

C

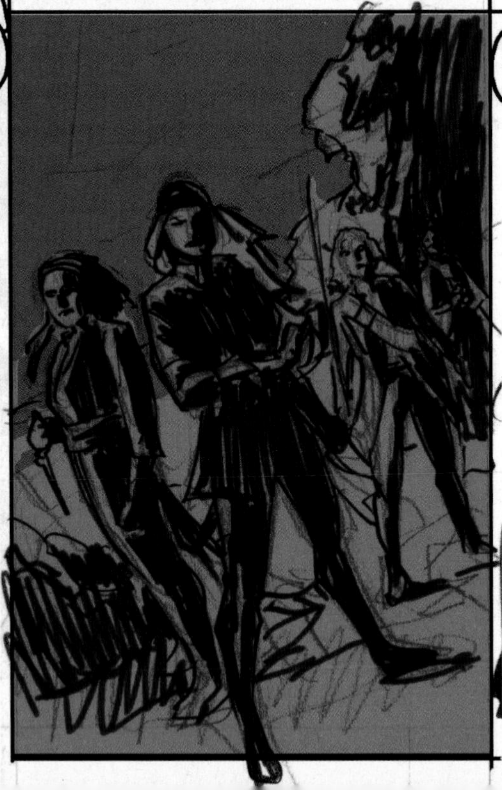

D

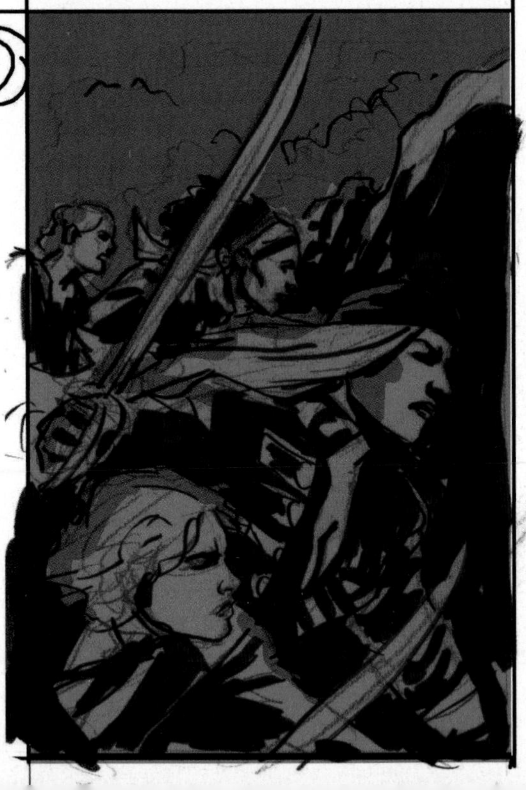

Issue №4 Cover Layout

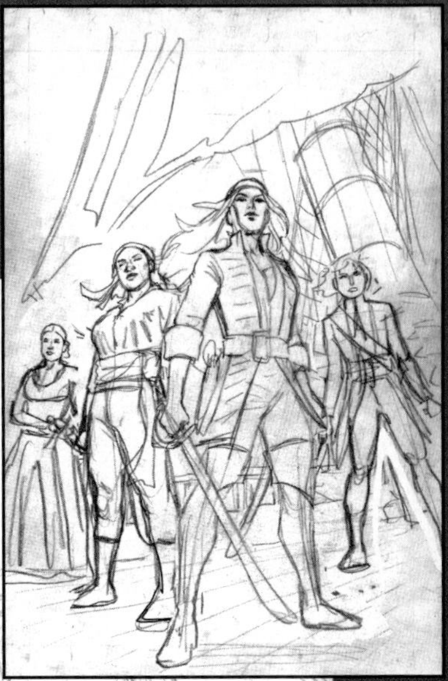

Issue №4 Cover Pencils

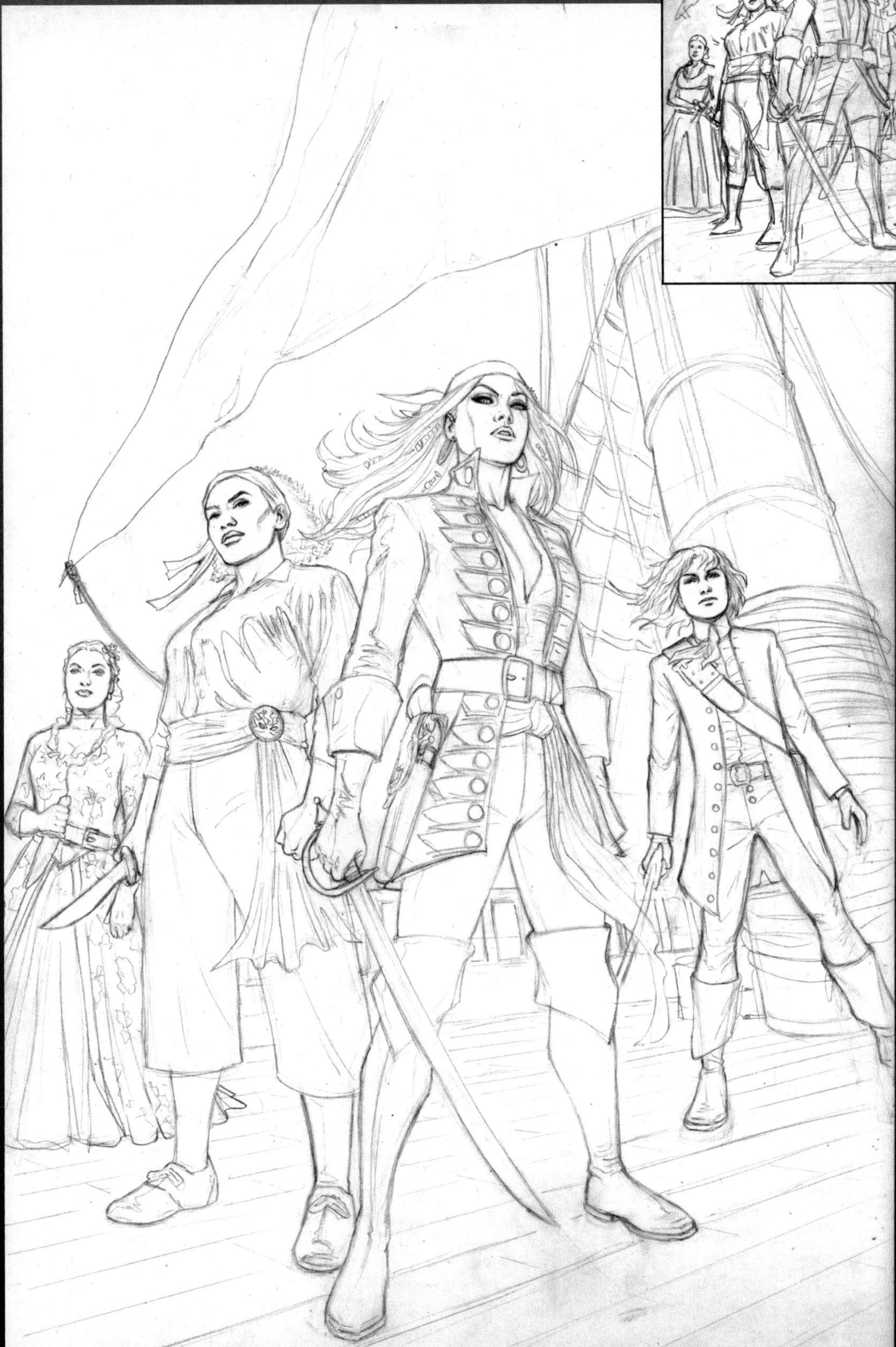

Issue №4 Cover Inks

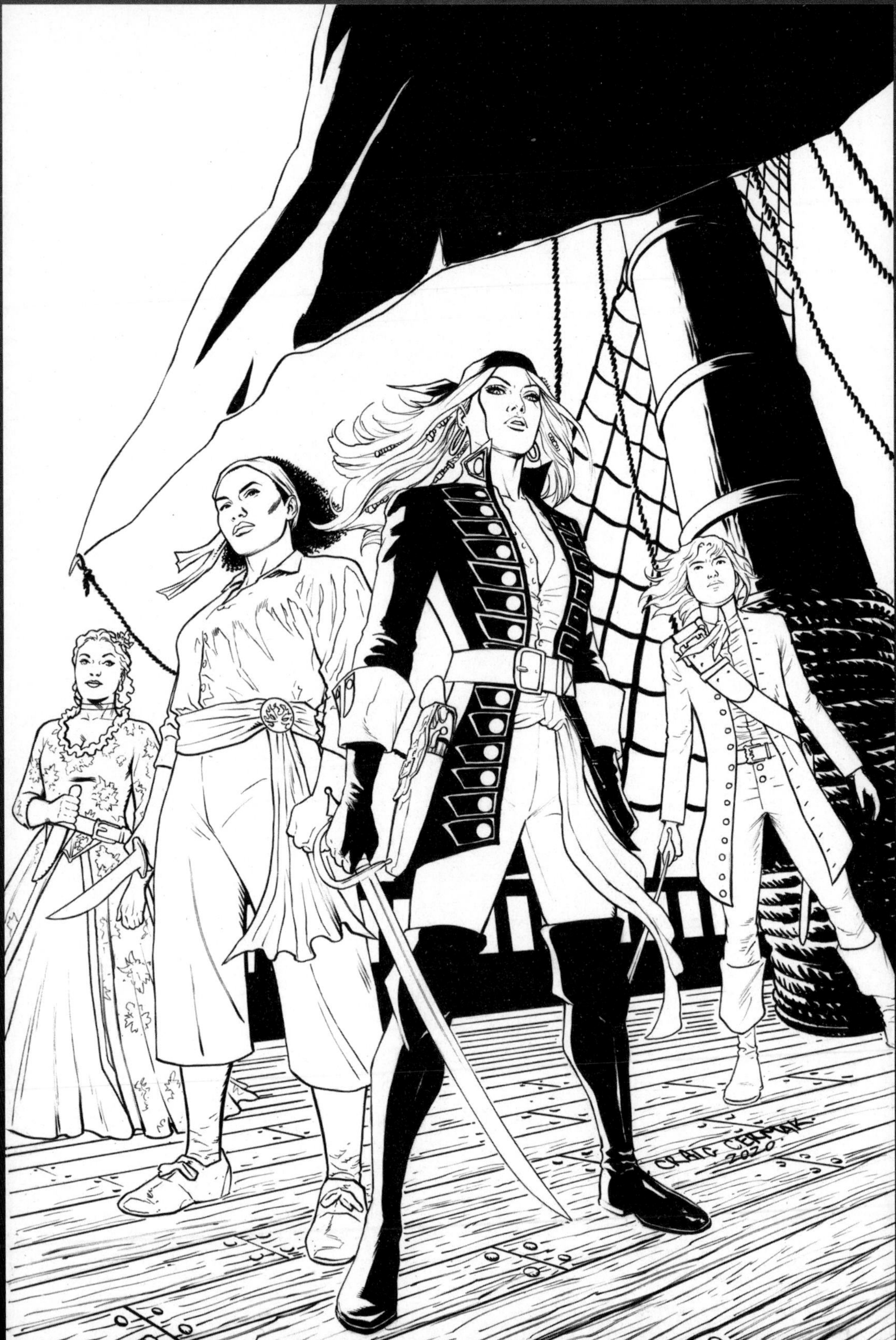
CRAIG CERMAK
2020

1, Page 4 process art by Craig Cermak

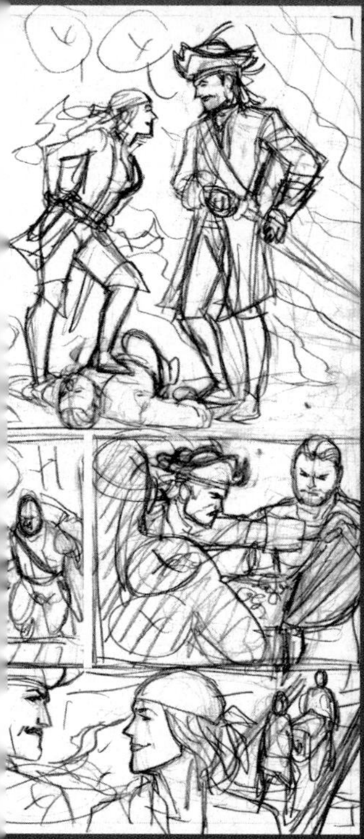

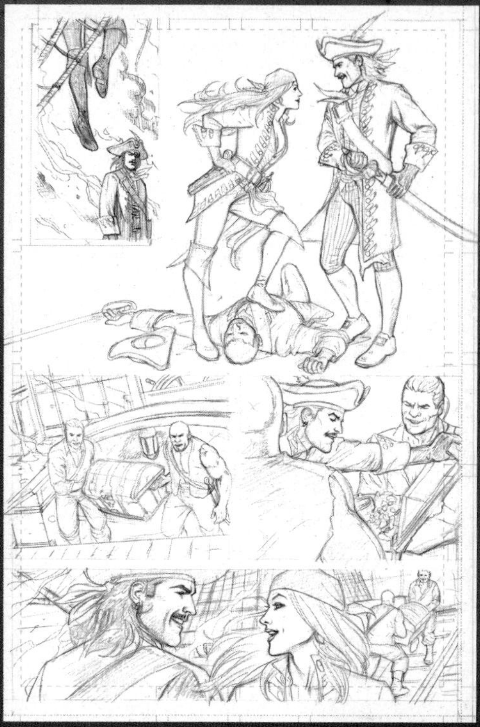

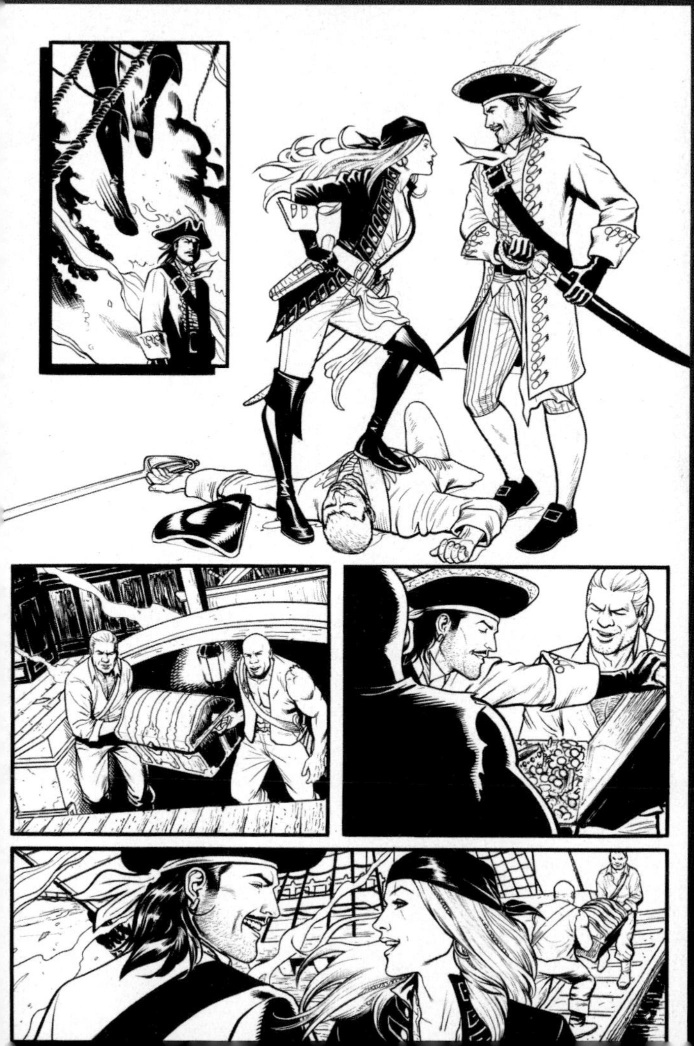

Issue 1, Page 17 process art by Craig Cermak

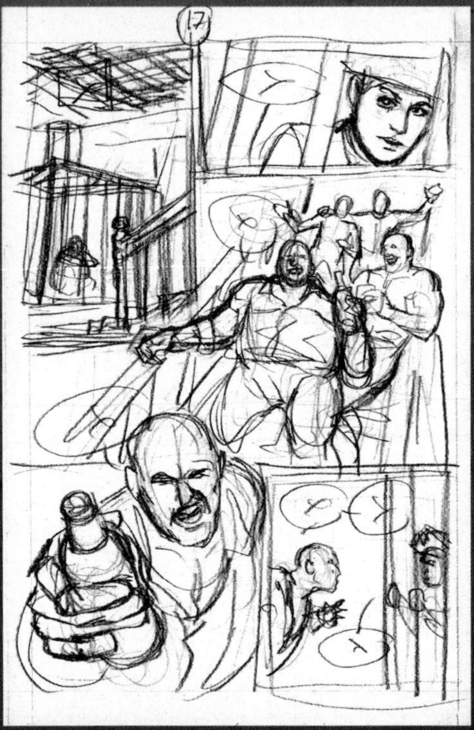

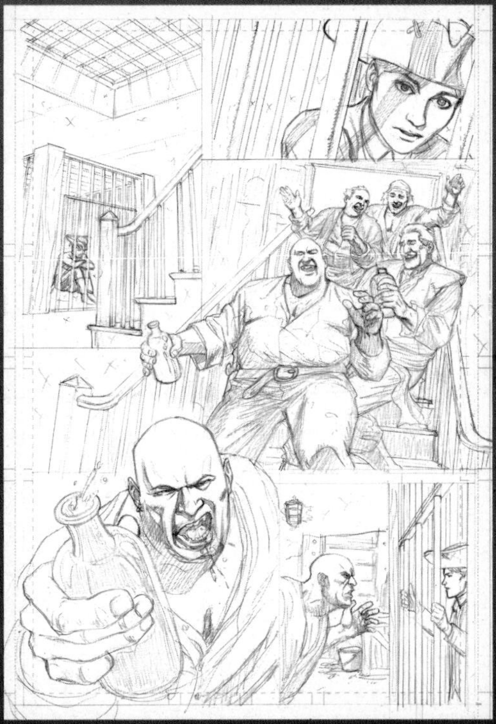

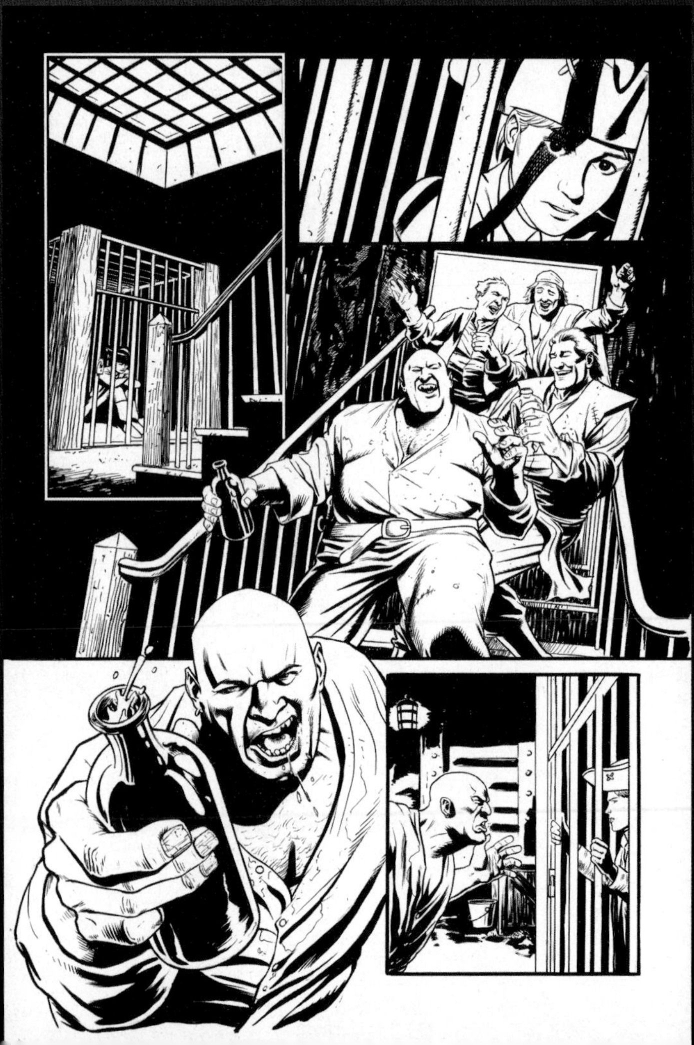

Issue 3, Page 1 process art by Craig Cermak

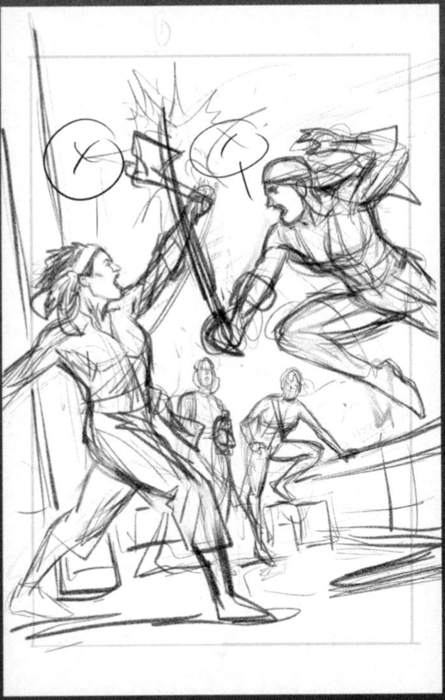

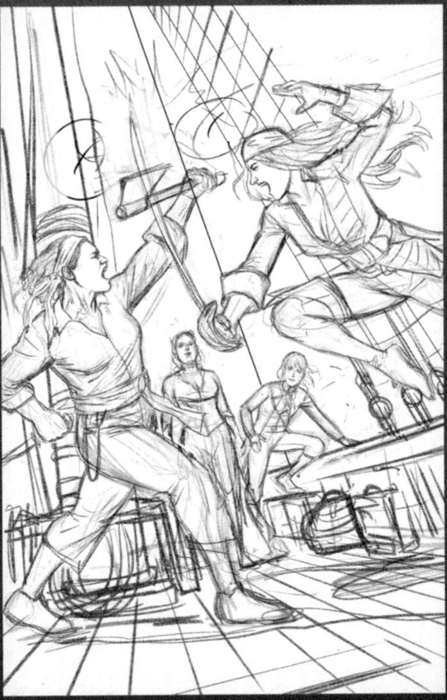

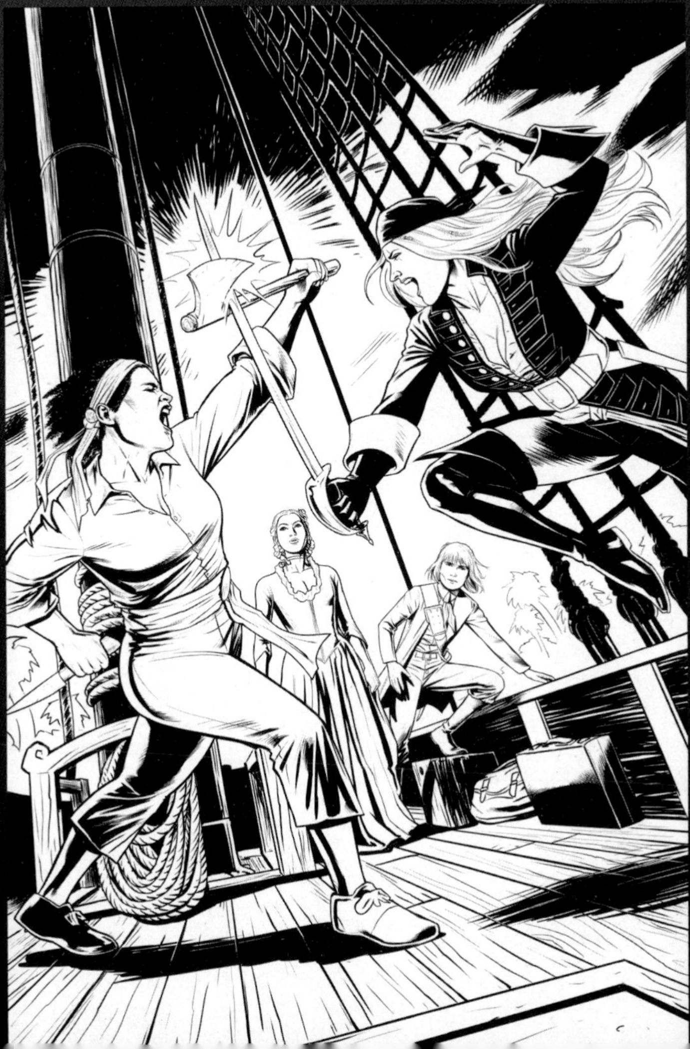

Issue 3, Page 3 process art by Craig Cermak

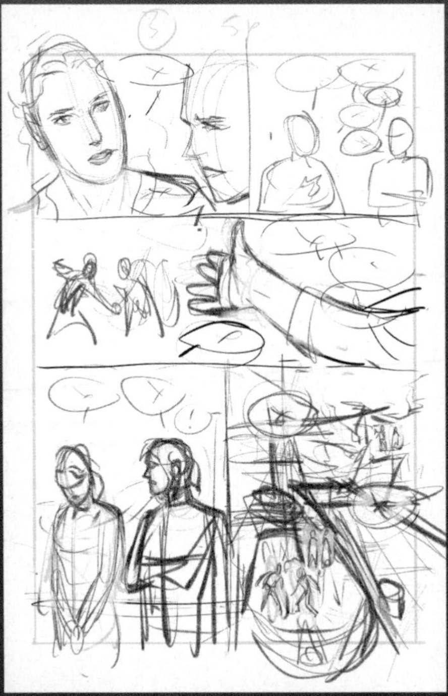

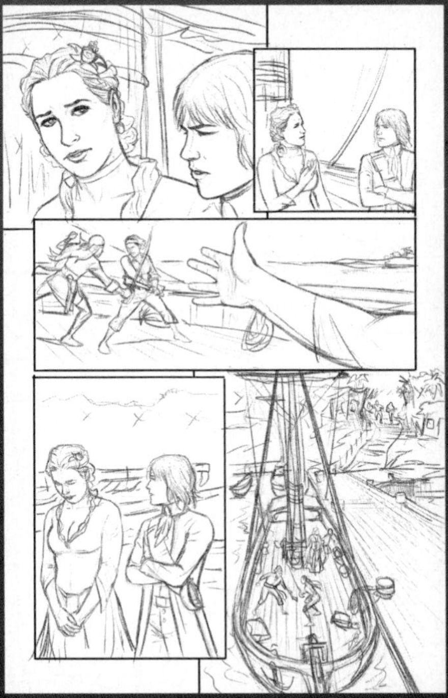

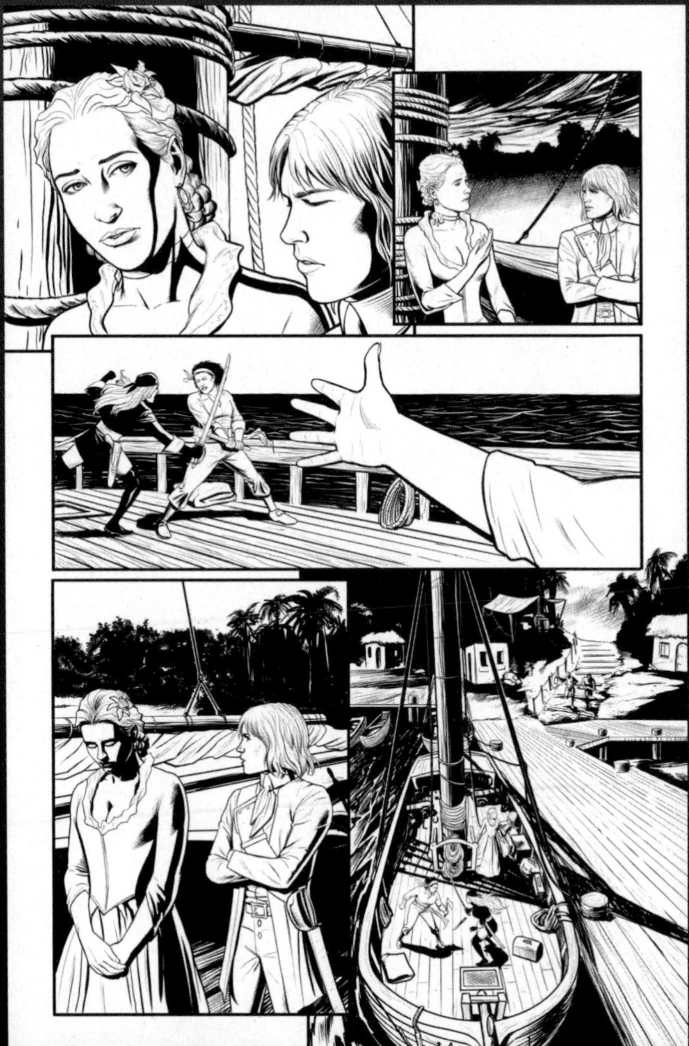

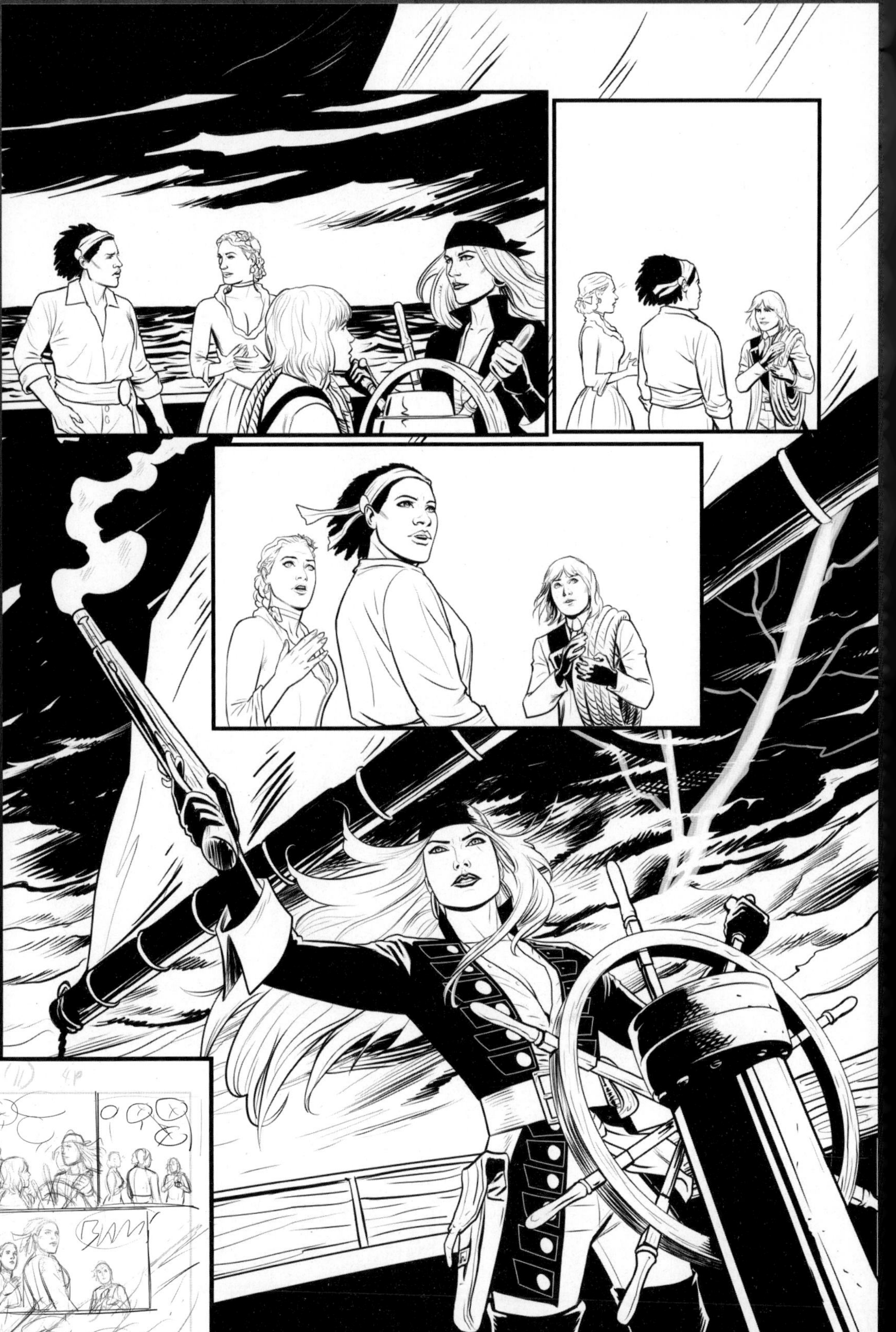

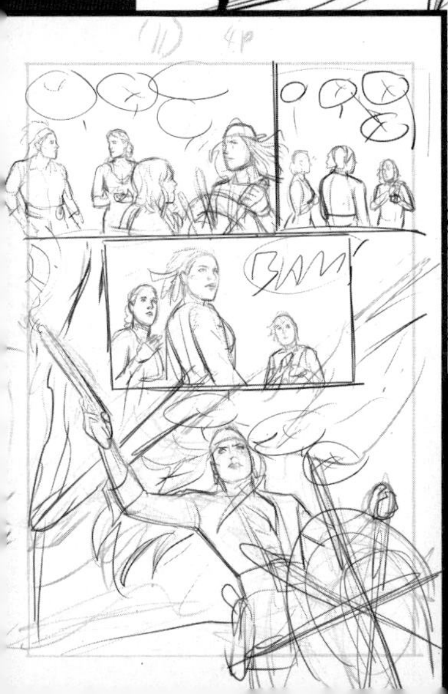
BAM

Issue 3, Page 11 process art
by Craig Cermak

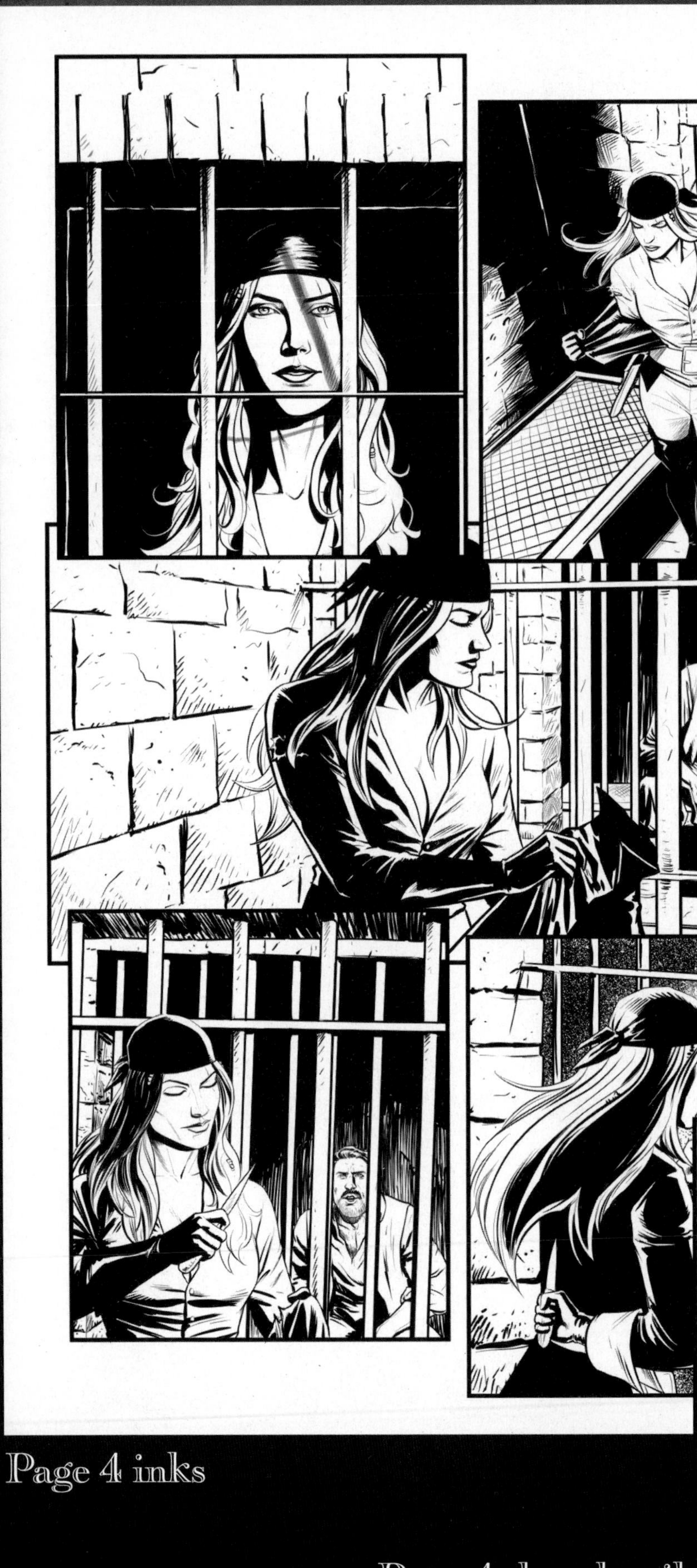

Page 4 inks

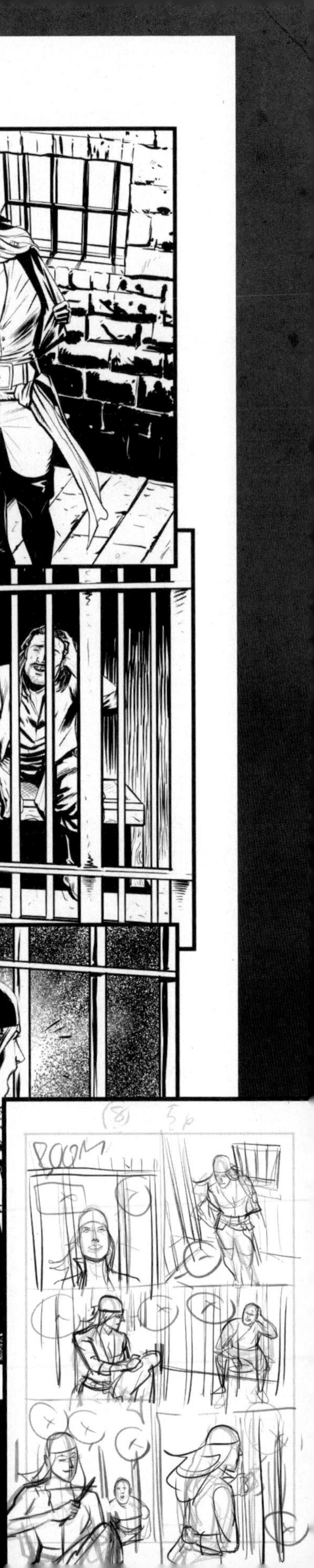

Page 4 thumbnail

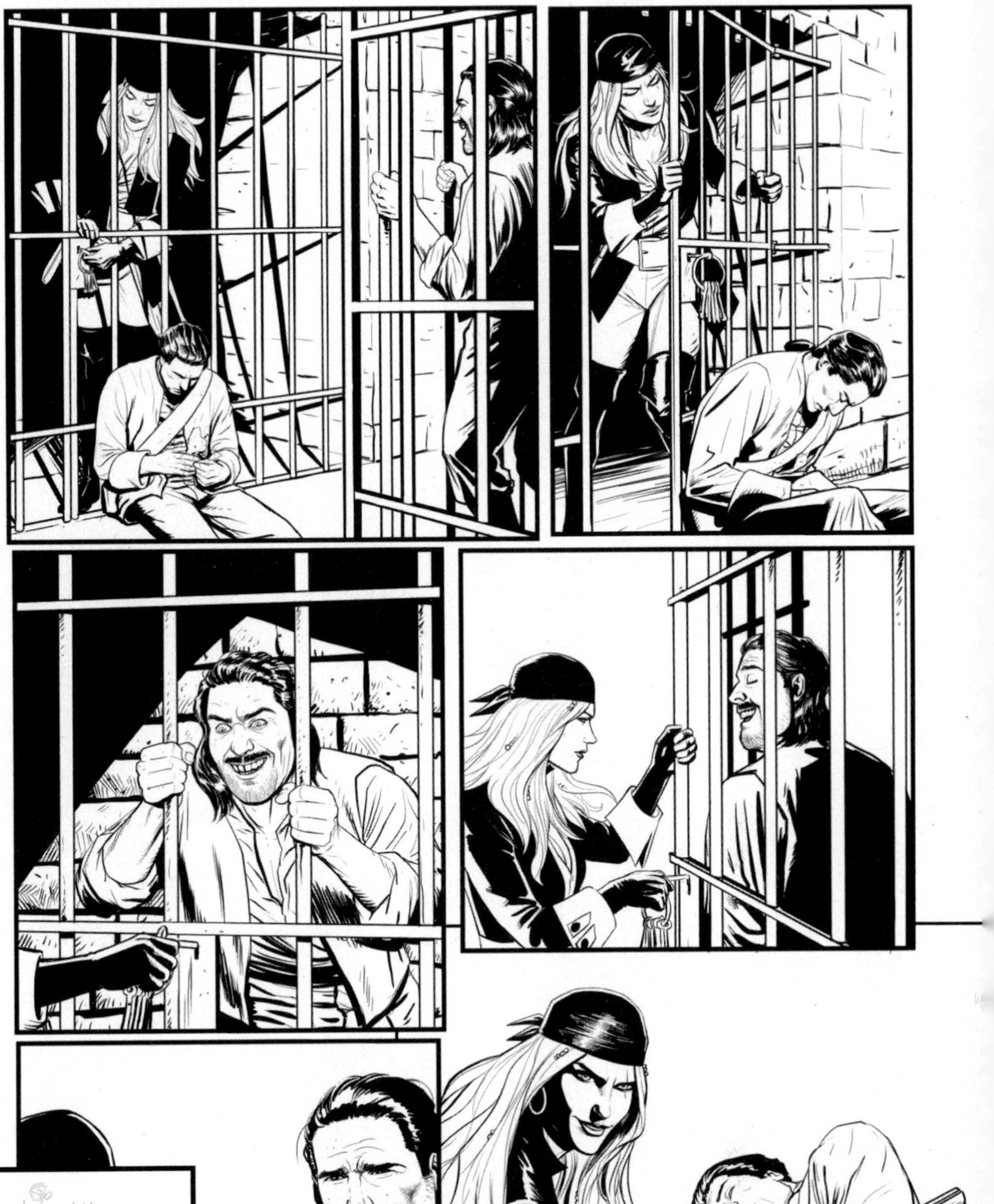

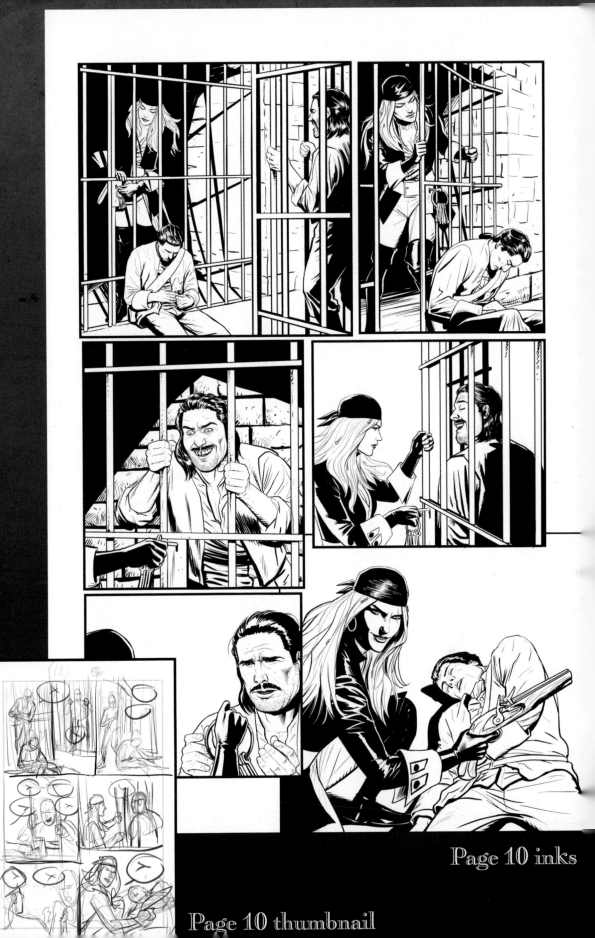

Page 10 inks

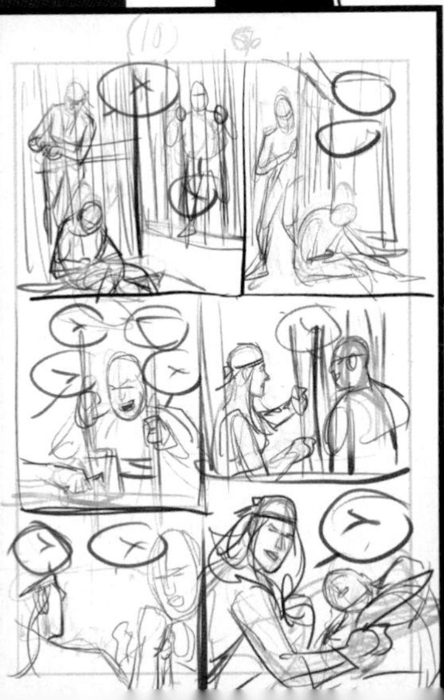

Page 10 thumbnail

Page 16 pencils

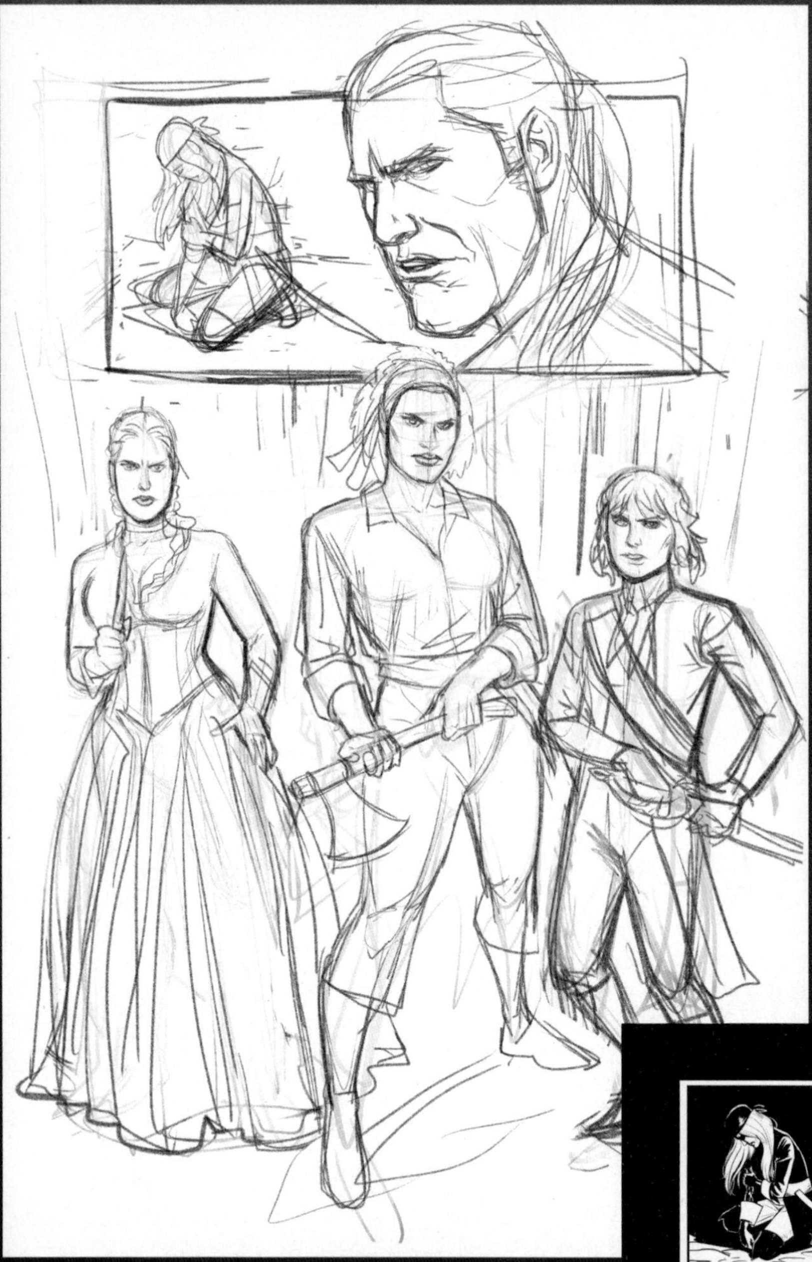

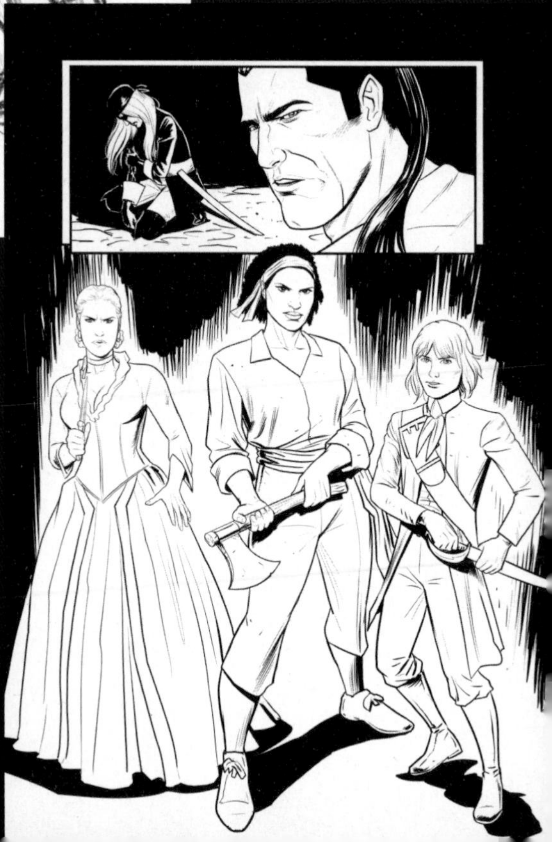

Page 16 inks

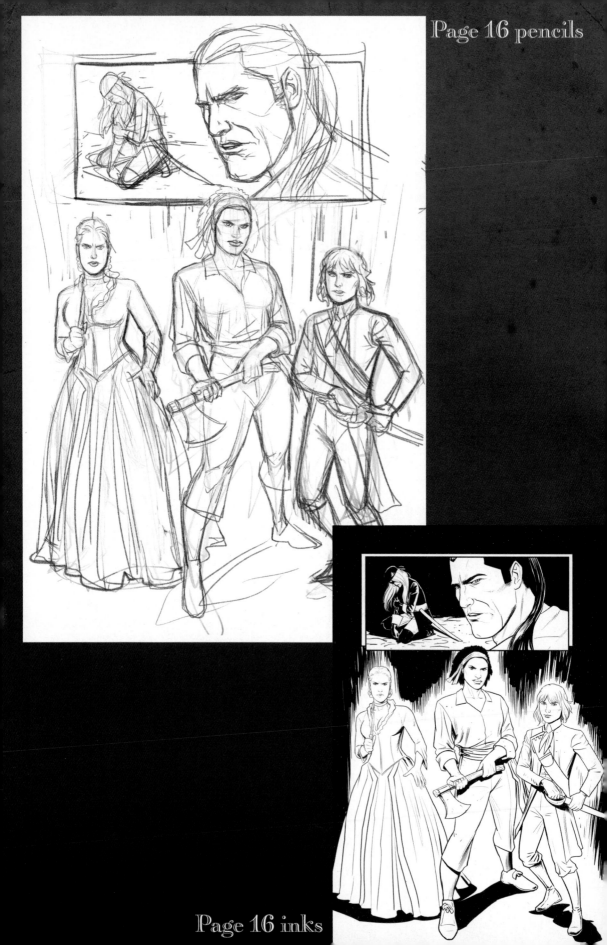

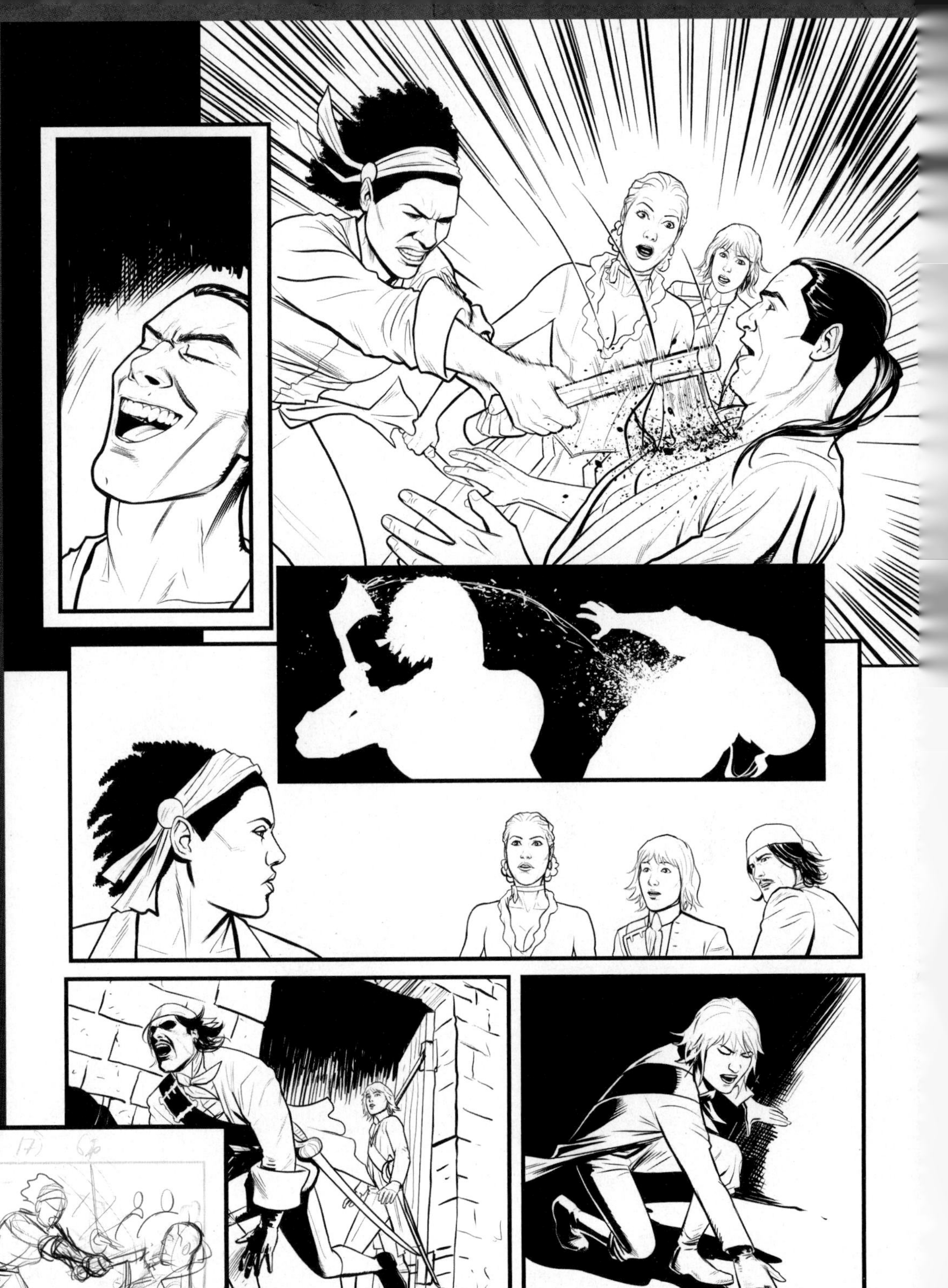

Page 17 inks

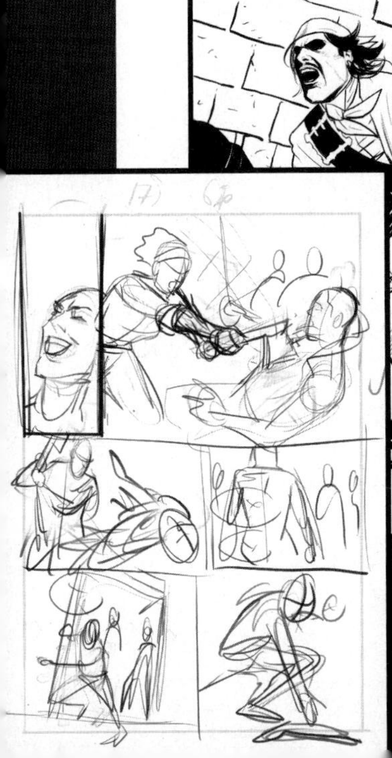

Page 17 thumbnail

Meet The Crew

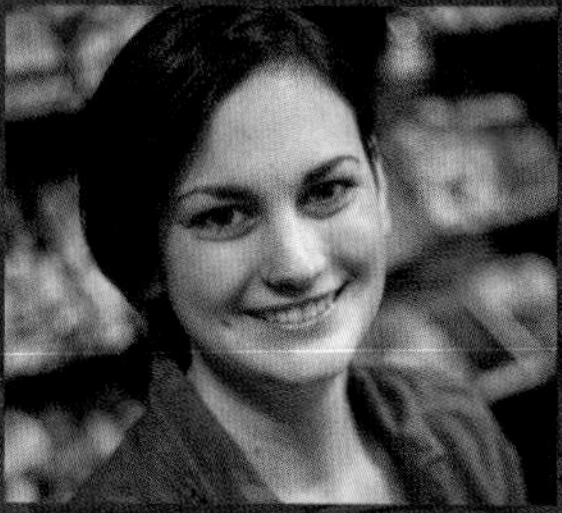

Stephanie Phillips

An American author and creator of comics and graphic novels such as *The Butcher of Paris*, *Artemis and the Assassin*, and *Descendent*. Her stories and comics have appeared with DC, Dark Horse, Heavy Metal, AfterShock, Black Mask, and more.

Craig Cermak

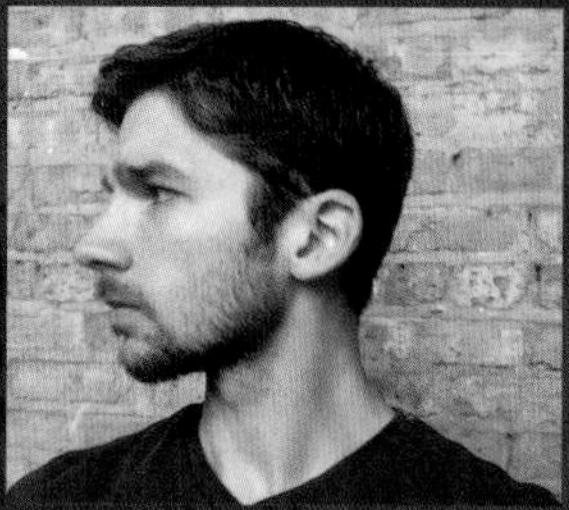

Craig has drawn *Elvira*, *Bettie Page*, *Voltron: Year One*, and was co-creator of *Red Team* (Dynamite Comics), as well as the soon-to-be-released title *Nursery* (First Comics). He's also been working on an original sci-fi project titled *Carnus*. His days and nights are spent at the drawing table on the North Side of Chicago, aided by dark chocolate and green tea, and his trusty cat, Barda.

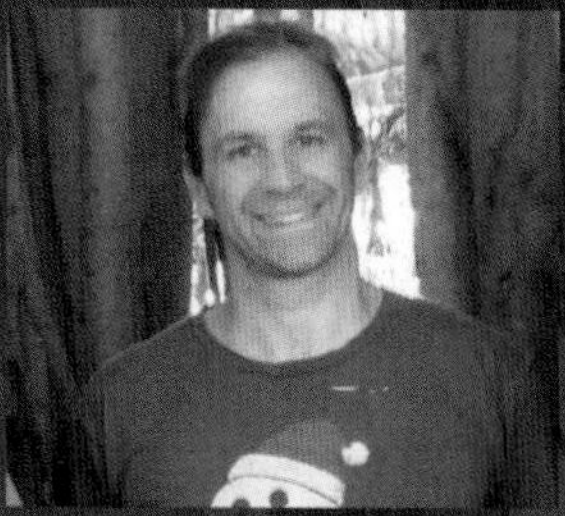

John Kalisz

John has been coloring comics for nearly thirty years, working on *Avengers*, *Zatanna*, and everything in between!

Brittany Pezzillo

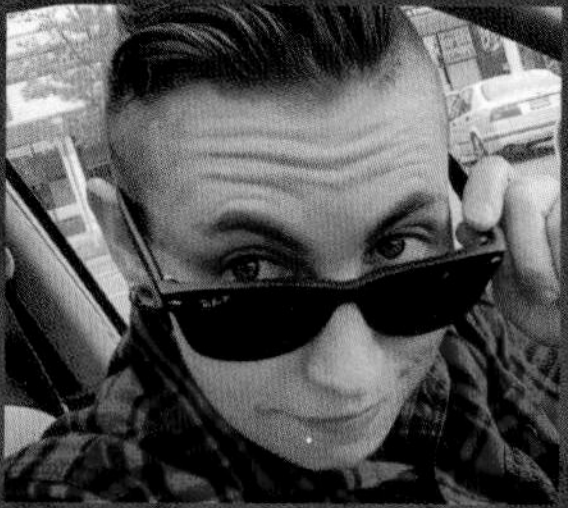

Brittany is an illustrator and can often be found coloring inside the lines with reckless abandon to bring great comic books to fruition. They've worked on wonderful games such as *Marvel: Crisis Protocol*, *Humblewood 5e* as well as done a plethora of coloring work for Dynamite, IDW and Marvel. When not social distancing they can be found in Philadelphia, PA furiously scribbling creator projects like *Galaxy Shark and EyeGuy*, sculpting, skateboarding and soldering cool stuff together.

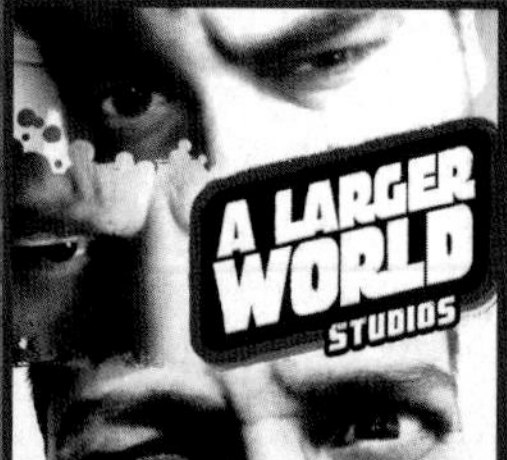
A LARGER WORLD
STUDIOS

Troy Peteri

Troy, Dave Lanphear, and Joshua Cozine are collectively known as A Larger World Studios. They've lettered everything from *The Avengers*, *Iron Man*, *Wolverine*, *Amazing Spider-Man* and *X-Men* to more recent titles such as WITCHBLADE, CYBERFORCE, and *Batman/Wonder Woman: The Brave & The Bold*. They can be reached at studio@alargerworld.com for your lettering and design needs. (Hooray, commerce!)

Thank You!

Writing A MAN AMONG YE has been an incredibly fun adventure. I started writing this story because I have always been influenced and inspired by the action-packed stories of pirates and I wanted to give those stories a new and unique take. I could not have done that without the support from Top Cow. Matt Hawkins, Marc Silvestri, and Elena Salcedo championed this book from its inception and helped to give this story a home. Elena Salcedo has been an incredible editor and gave Craig and I the room to make this story exactly as we wanted it. Henry Barajas worked tirelessly to help us reach retailers and fans to talk about this story and engage their questions, and Vince Valentine designed this book and made the finished product gorgeous.

Of course, I can't thank the creative team – Craig Cermak, John Kalisz, and Troy Peteri – enough for their work on this book. They all made an absolutely gorgeous story. Every single page is engaging and more amazing than I could have ever imagined.

Finally, we want to thank all of the readers and retailers for supporting and reading this book. It turns out, there's a lot of you who enjoy a good pirate adventure just as much as we do. The excitement has really fueled us and I'm glad we had the chance to share this story with you.

Stay tuned for more adventures in 2021!

Stephanie Phillips
December, 2020

The Top Cow essentials checklist:

A Man Among Ye, Volume 1
(ISBN: 978-1-5343-1691-1)

Aphrodite IX: Rebirth, Volume 1
(ISBN: 978-1-60706-828-0)

Blood Stain, Volume 1
(ISBN: 978-1-63215-544-3)

Bonehead, Volume 1
(ISBN: 978-1-5343-0664-6)

Cyber Force: Awakening, Volume 1
(ISBN: 978-1-5343-0980-7)

The Clock, Volume 1
(ISBN: 978-1-5343-1611-9)

The Darkness: Origins, Volume 1
(ISBN: 978-1-60706-097-0)

Death Vigil, Volume 1
(ISBN: 978-1-63215-278-7)

Dissonance, Volume 1
(ISBN: 978-1-5343-0742-1)

Eclipse, Volume 1
(ISBN: 978-1-5343-0038-5)

Eden's Fall, Volume 1
(ISBN: 978-1-5343-0065-1)

The Freeze, OGN
(ISBN: 978-1-5343-1211-1)

God Complex, Volume 1
(ISBN: 978-1-5343-0657-8)

Infinite Dark, Volume 1
(ISBN: 978-1-5343-1056-8)

La Voz de M.A.Y.O.:
Tato Rambo, Volume
(ISBN: 978-1-5343-1363-7

Paradox Girl, Volume
(ISBN: 978-1-5343-1220-3

Port of Earth, Volume
(ISBN: 978-1-5343-0646-2

Postal, Volume 1
(ISBN: 978-1-63215-342-5

Stairway Anthology
(ISBN: 978-1-5343-1702-4

Sugar, Volume 1
(ISBN: 978-1-5343-1641-7

Sunstone, Volume 1
(ISBN: 978-1-63215-212-1

Swing, Volume 1
(ISBN: 978-1-5343-0516-8

Symmetry, Volume 1
(ISBN: 978-1-63215-699-0

The Tithe, Volume 1
(ISBN: 978-1-63215-324-1

Think Tank, Volume 1
(ISBN: 978-1-60706-660-6

Vindication, OGN
(ISBN: 978-1-5343-1237-1

Warframe, Volume 1
(ISBN: 978-1-5343-0512-0

Witchblade 2017, Volum
(ISBN: 978-1-5343-0685-1

For more ISBN and ordering information on our latest collections go to:
www.topcow.com
Ask your retailer about our catalogue of collected editions, digests, and hard cover
or check the listings at: Barnes and Noble, Amazon.com, and other fine retailer

To find your nearest comic shop go to: